The Disappearing of Klaus Wagenmann

It had been three days since Larsen and MacFarlane had transported a handcuffed Wagenmann back to Frankfurt. Private Roberts, visibly relieved that his role in the whole affair was over, had dropped them off at the nearest American military airfield.

From there, the two men took a Curtiss C-46 Commando transport plane from Nuremberg to Frankfurt. Their journey continued with a bumpy ride in the back of a U.S. Army supply truck, driven by an unusually gregarious black serviceman from Mississippi who nonetheless knew better than to ask who the "package" was.

They then rode from an airfield outside Frankfurt and into the still largely ruined central city district where broken glass and scattered debris lined the streets. When the diesel truck squealed to a stop at its final destination, two men in suits and one with a black sack over his head emerged from the back of the truck and promptly disappeared deep within the confines of a medium-sized office building.

From that moment on, the man known as Klaus Wagenmann officially ceased to exist.

Jonathan E. Lewis Bibliography

Editor
Ancient Egyptian Supernatural Tales (2016)
Strange Island Stories (2018)

THE NUREMBERG PAPERS

BY JONATHAN E. LEWIS

Stark House Press • Eureka California

THE NUREMBERG PAPERS

Published by Stark House Press
1315 H Street
Eureka, CA 95501, USA
griffinskye3@sbcglobal.net
www.starkhousepress.com

ISBN: 979-8-88601-115-9

Book design by Mark Shepard, shepgraphics.com
Proofreading by Bill Kelly

First Stark House Press Edition: November 2024

PROLOGUE

Allied-Occupied Germany
Summer 1947

Just as the dark green 1941 Plymouth Special De Luxe began to approach the corner of Dennerstrasse and Fürther Strasse, it stalled, emitting a loud sputtering noise. Small plumes of smoke flowed from the exhaust pipe, helping to pollute the Bavarian city of Nuremberg, a city that already felt dirty. Several years earlier, this ruined shell of a city was host to some of the worst public displays of Hitlerism. The Führer may have offed himself, but the taint nevertheless remained.

The commotion and the smell from the car attracted the attention of an elderly woman on the sidewalk, her hands clasping a paper bag filled with bread and cheese. The two men seated in the back seat of the car, one significantly older than the other, fidgeted slightly. Neither spoke a word.

It was left to Private Roberts, the driver, to state the obvious.

"I told the boys at the shop that they should have put more time and effort into making sure this gal ran smooth. I'm really sorry, sir. I mean, sirs."

A lanky twentysomething, Roberts could just have easily been an American high school student. That is, but for the shrapnel scars lining the creases on his forehead.

Right now, he looked stressed. Fearful that he was about to be reprimanded by his passengers. Frustrated and a bit flustered, Roberts slammed his sweaty palms on the steering wheel.

"How far is the Palace of Justice from here?" asked the older of the two men seated in the back of the sedan.

"Right around the corner, then down the block, sir," answered Private Roberts. He turned off the ignition and promptly restarted it. The Plymouth hummed and purred, as if what happened moments before was a mere fluke, rather than the sign of a systemic problem.

"Looks as if it was nothing after all," replied the older man in the backseat. He was busy playing around with a pair of handcuffs. As if they were merely a toy.

Approaching his sixth decade, Larsen was as physically fit as he was when he was an undergraduate fencer at Princeton. He looked more like a senior insurance company executive from Chicago than a man instructed by the U.S. Government to do what even a cynic such as himself recognized to be morally dubious work. Dressed in a charcoal gray suit and a silk dark blue tie over a white cotton shirt, Larsen's dress and demeanor marked him as a civilian among the military brass back in Frankfurt.

He wiped away perspiration caused by the late July humidity with the contradictory nonchalance of a man too old to care what others thought of him, but with the desire to look as intimidating as possible.

His traveling companion, a bright-eyed young man about thirty years old with sandy hair and penetrating brown eyes that hinted at curiosity rather than cynicism, craned his neck forward.

"That's it there, isn't it?" Jefferson "Skip" MacFarlane adjusted his black-rimmed eyeglasses, pointing an index finger in that direction. He indicated the slanted reddish-brown roof of Nuremberg's courthouse building in the near distance.

"Yes, that's it," replied Larsen.

Private Roberts, having regained his composure, completed the turn onto Fürther Strasse and drove west at moderate speed. The rest of the ride took only two minutes. Soon both Larsen and MacFarlane could see their destination clearly. Built some two decades before the National Socialist German Workers' Party had consolidated their stranglehold over Germany, the Palace of Justice remained largely undamaged from Allied aerial bombardments that had turned a once vibrant urban center into seemingly endless piles of rubble.

It was a large building complex with a sandstone exterior, housing several courthouses and a large prison facility. The latter now held numerous men charged with crimes against humanity for their role in facilitating the Nazis' war of annihilation against Europe's six million Jews.

Klaus Wagenmann, the man Larsen and MacFarlane had traveled from Frankfurt to see, was somewhere inside. He was most likely sitting alone in his cell tucked away in the back of the complex, where the prison was located.

"Park in front," ordered Larsen, his voice taking on an authoritarian tone.

"Yes, sir," answered Roberts.

He maneuvered the car to fit a space only a few yards from the main entrance. Roberts put the car into park, glad that he got his important passengers where they were going despite the momentary delay.

As he prepared to leave the car, MacFarlane turned to Larsen. He noticed his older colleague had returned the handcuffs to his jacket pocket.

"You ready for this?"

"It's an order. We have to follow it. Whether I'm ready for it or not is irrelevant."

"I know, but—"

"But what?"

"But what, indeed," said MacFarlane. His voice wavered. As if he were trying to convince himself that what he was about to do squared with his solid Methodist upbringing.

"You're not going to get all preachy now, are you?"

"Just saying. There could be long term repercussions to what we are about to do here today."

"For each action, there's an equal and opposite reaction. Or something," Larsen said. He coughed and spat on the sidewalk. His mucus was tinged with black soot.

While Private Roberts stayed with the car, Larsen and MacFarlane walked along the pathway leading to a black metal gate—the sole entrance to the building's outer courtyard. Standing at attention on each side of the pillars which buttressed the gate were two stone-faced American MPs from the 793rd Military Police Battalion. Dressed in their trademark drab olive uniforms with white Sam Browne belts and white gloves, the two MPs stood up a little straighter, as if they had been expecting Larsen and MacFarlane.

Earlier that day, their superior, Colonel Davenport, had told them two federals from Frankfurt would be arriving this afternoon. Federals. Men whose loyalty was to a group of old "wise men" back in smoke-filled rooms in Washington D.C. Men who had moved on from the war against the Nazis.

Larsen took the lead.

"Agents Larsen and MacFarlane from Unit 612," he said without any trace of emotion in his voice.

"Yes, sir. We've been expecting you, sir." said the taller of the two MPs, as he glanced at the clipboard he held tightly in his hands.

Larsen reached for his identification card and handed it to the MP. He acknowledged the soldier with a curt nod. MacFarlane followed suit. But, unlike his cynical colleague, he did it with a brief hint of a smile. One that belied a conscience not fully on board with what was about to happen.

□ □ □

It didn't take long for others to realize Colonel Joe Davenport was from the South.

It wasn't his merely his appearance. It was the drawl that gave him away. Although his surname was of Norman origin, his paternal great-grandfather had in actuality hailed from a plantation in Ulster. That was generations ago. In truth, he had known nothing but Appalachia coal country since he was a young boy.

The war had changed all that.

Suddenly, a business degree from West Virginia University meant that he could finally see a different part of the world. It also meant that he wasn't going to be an enlisted man. He was going to be an officer.

By the time he had received his commission, however, the Krauts had unconditionally surrendered. After all the grueling combat training he endured in the mosquito-ridden Louisiana swamps, he had ended up with a desk job, one he wasn't thrilled about at first.

He was tasked with doing the paperwork needed to detain accused Nazi war criminals as they sat in jail awaiting either trial or—far more likely—exoneration.

Davenport had never met a Jew in his life, although he had heard that Benny Goodman was one. He had seen the short films that the Allies had made at Belsen and Dachau. That was enough. Men under his command quickly realized that Davenport hated Nazis to their core. That he was determined to make sure that those Nazis entrusted to his custody were going to pay the penalty for violating every tenet in the Bible. That was going to be his combat. Fought here in the Palace of Justice with papers, rather than on the battlefield with guns and tanks.

Davenport walked down the corridor to the building's interior courtyard. He steeled himself for an unpleasant conversation, one he had hoped to avoid. He had heard through the grapevine that two spooks were going to show up today. That they'd almost certainly show up in fancy suits no one back home in West Virginia could afford. Show up and require he sign a MD-12 authorizing the release of Klaus Wagenmann for national security reasons the spooks weren't at liberty to discuss.

National security.

The wellspring of all excuses. Davenport was the kind of man to know bullshit when he saw it. And he didn't appreciate it. Not in the slightest.

Larsen and MacFarlane made their way to the far side of the front room, their shoes making distinct clicking noises on the stone tiled floor.

They approached Davenport as he walked in toward them.

"Colonel Davenport, I take it?" Larsen asked.

"In the flesh," Davenport replied, deliberately highlighting his drawl.

He looked Larsen up and down. With an officious nod, he acknowledged MacFarlane's presence.

"You know why we're here, I trust?"

"I reckon I do," Davenport snapped.

"It's not as if we're enjoying this—" MacFarlane interjected before realizing that he was speaking out of turn. Shit. There was no need to piss off Larsen now. They'd be working together for the next several days. At least until their "package" was safely delivered back to Washington.

"Look, I'm going to lay it on you boys straight," Davenport said.

"Oh?" Larsen answered.

"I know what you're up to. And I don't like it. In case you can't tell," Davenport said, completely aware that Unit 612 had no permanent authority over him.

"Not one bit," he continued.

He held nothing back.

"In fact, I'm going to be honest with y'all. I made a few phone calls and did my damn best to figure out who in the hell decided that you guys were going to walk into my prison. My prison. And give me the order to release that damn Kraut into your custody."

His face expressionless, Larsen reached inside the breast pocket of his suit. He retrieved a folded piece of paper. He shook it in the air. It crinkled. He handed it to Davenport as MacFarlane stood by silently.

"These here words," Davenport said as he pointed to the release order, "they are going to bite all of us—not only you, but also Uncle Sam square in the ass someday."

"Well, I'll be either senile or dead by then," Larsen said. He pulled a cigarette out of his packet. Lit it.

"I won't," MacFarlane demurred.

Larsen pretended he hadn't heard what his junior colleague had said.

"All right then. Might as well get on with it. But first I want to show you something," Davenport said.

"Fine with me," Larsen answered.

Davenport, still holding the document ordering the prisoner's release, escorted Larsen and MacFarlane through the Palace of Justice and into the complex's eastern wing. He stopped abruptly mere inches in front of a pair of tall wooden doors. Doors that, by their very construction, seemed to exude a solemnity befitting a courthouse.

Davenport temporarily handed the release order back to Larsen. He grabbed the large brass door handle and opened the door, revealing a courtroom with drab carpet, wood paneling, benches and numerous tables. As if they were just waiting to be repositioned for yet another tribunal.

"Do you know what this room is?" Davenport asked.

"Courtroom number 600," MacFarlane answered even before Larsen had a chance to speak.

"Someone's been watching the newsreels," Davenport said.

Much like those civilians back home who had taken an interest in postwar Germany, MacFarlane had watched the black and white footage taken two years ago at the International Military Tribunal. Right here in Courtroom 600, the world's media had gathered in a makeshift press box where the back wall had once stood. In front of a panel of jurists from the United States, the Soviet Union, Great Britain, and France, Nazi Germany's crimes were exposed to the world. Proving once again that sunlight often served as the best disinfectant. That, and of course, the full might of the world's superpowers which had reduced the once mighty Third Reich to rubble. All of which allowed Allied prosecutors to hold leading Nazi figures, men such as Hermann Göring, Rudolf Hess, and the notorious antisemitic publisher Julius Streicher, to account for their role in the worst crimes the modern world had ever witnessed.

Courtroom 600 was also where Klaus Wagenmann was scheduled to face judgment in what the media were calling the "subsequent" Nuremberg trials next week. Trials designed specifically to hold titans of industry and scientists to account for their actions during the war.

But that wasn't going to happen. Not to all of them.

Not now. One of the defendants was going to disappear into thin air, Davenport mused, thanks to the last-minute intervention of amoral functionaries like Larsen and MacFarlane.

"Okay, so this is the courtroom," Larsen said, "so what?"

It was obvious Larsen was annoyed by Davenport's attempts to appeal to his conscience.

"So what indeed," Davenport said dryly.

He was now fully aware that his words would have no effect. Davenport understood that for men like Larsen, orders were orders. And that his pleas for Larsen to reconsider were futile.

So he gave up and led Larsen and MacFarlane down several corridors.

The three men passed a parade of law clerks barely out of university seminars, court translators wearing badges identifying them as such, and numerous MPs carrying boxes filled with miscellaneous documents.

They continued their journey until they found themselves in a part of the complex that had a distinctly different feeling to it.

Even though the late July sunlight beamed through the narrow window—highlighting dust particles as they danced through the air like protons under an electron microscope—the doorway facing them felt dark. Dark and foreboding, as if the entire area beyond it was tainted with evil.

They had arrived at the main passageway to the Palace of Justice's holding area. It was here that various opportunists who joined the Nazi Party for an ephemeral moment of glory were held. Along with the sundry Nazi businessmen who profited from slave labor at Birkenau, chemists and scientists who facilitated industrialized mass murder at Auschwitz, the Nazi extermination camp in Poland where over a million Jews from across Europe were murdered before the complex was liberated by the Soviet Red Army in January 1945.

Among those chemists and scientists was one Klaus Wagenmann.

"Give me the MD-12," Davenport said.

Larsen obliged without any hesitation.

Davenport pulled out a silver pen from his front jacket pocket. He initialed the form and dated it in black ink. JD 07/28/47.

"My fingerprints on this thing make me feel dirty," Davenport said as he ordered two MPs standing guard to open the iron clad door. He handed the MD-12 back to Larsen who promptly put it in his back pocket.

Davenport, without saying a word, led Larsen and MacFarlane to Wagenmann's cell. The Kraut chemist was their problem now.

It was a cramped cell, but it was hundreds of times better than any accommodations the Red Army provided for POWs in the Soviet Zone.

It was not completely unsanitary.

There was a small cot with dirty linens, a barely usable toilet, and a small desk. On top, were three small handmade clay sculptures and two scientific textbooks.

Klaus Heinreich Wagenmann, sitting at the small wooden desk at the far corner of his cell, was deep in thought. He was reading a book, *Newest Methods in Chemical Engineering* by Professor Graham Smith of Columbia University. A work dense both in volume and subject matter.

"You have some new friends, genius," Davenport said. He swung the now unlocked steel door into the small cell. The unmistakable sound of metal hitting against brick wall reverberated down the sporadically lit hallway.

"Gentlemen. Do come in," said Wagenmann.

He spoke in a nearly perfect Oxbridge accent and with the haughty confidence of a man twice his age. For an incarcerated man who was still potentially facing execution, Wagenmann had a surprisingly cheerful demeanor. Sporting a faded tan blazer, white shirt, and neatly pressed beige cotton pants, he didn't present as a man accused of participating in industrialized mass murder—death on a scale unheard of in the annals of mankind; of aiding and abetting the SS with heinous crimes under the blanket of night and fog in the Polish countryside; of consorting with leading Nazi physicians who oversaw the execution of thousands of Jewish men, women, and children.

No. In his demeanor, he comported himself as if he were still a Lecturer in Physical Chemistry at Leipzig University. The very place where he had spent the closing chapters of the war. That is, before he fled the advancing Red Army for the American Zone.

MacFarlane cocked his head back, thrown off guard by how damned ordinary their prisoner appeared. He didn't look like a monster.

Because Wagenmann did look ordinary. Apart from a minor scar on his upper lip, there was nothing about the professor's appearance that would make anyone passing him on the street take another look. Just an ordinary German of medium build and average height with blue eyes. Neither skinny nor fat, neither tall nor short. He was an everyman who could easily disappear into a crowd. The premature greying of his hair could easily have been attributed to environmental, rather than genetic, factors. His fingertips showed signs of recent bleeding, as if he had recently used his hands to claw his way out of a hole. Despite that, he nevertheless looked surprisingly vibrant.

"Get up!" Larsen barked.

Wagenmann complied. He gave no indication he was remotely interested in putting up a fight.

"You surely know why we've come?" MacFarlane asked with genuine curiosity.

"I have some idea," Wagenmann said.

"Did you tell him?" Larsen said, as he looked at Davenport.

"I didn't need to tell him. He's smart enough to figure these things out. It's not as if the prisoners don't talk to each other when they have time in the yard," Davenport answered.

"Right," Larsen said.

He took out the handcuffs he had been playing with just minutes before and locked them on the compliant German's two hands.

Larsen walked over to the desk. He picked up one of the clay sculptures. It was in the shape of a swan.

"This yours?"

"If you're asking if I sculpted it, then yes," Wagenmann said.

"An artist too?"

"I do some sculpting," Wagenmann said. It was a factual statement. No more. No less.

"Is that right?" Larsen sneered. "You're as much as a failure as a sculptor as the Nazis ultimately were in warfare."

Wagenmann glared at Larsen, who walked over to the war criminal and covered his head with a black sack.

Ten minutes later, the two American spies were back in the car. As the bright sun began to dip in the summer sky, rays of sunlight reflected off the Palace of Justice's myriad array of windows. Private Roberts, keen to get going, started the vehicle with surprising ease. He pulled out from the parking space. The green Plymouth started its drive down Fürther Strasse. This time, with an extra passenger.

□ □ □

It had been three days since Larsen and MacFarlane had transported a handcuffed Wagenmann back to Frankfurt. Private Roberts, visibly relieved that his role in the whole affair was over, had dropped them off at the nearest American military airfield.

From there, the two men took a Curtiss C-46 Commando transport plane from Nuremberg to Frankfurt. Their journey continued with a bumpy ride in the back of a U.S. Army supply truck, driven by an unusually gregarious black serviceman from Mississippi who nonetheless knew better than to ask who the "package" was.

They then rode from an airfield outside Frankfurt and into the still largely ruined central city district where broken glass and scattered debris lined the streets. When the diesel truck squealed to a stop at its final destination, two men in suits and one with a black sack over his head emerged from the back of the truck and promptly disappeared deep within the confines of a medium-sized office building.

From that moment on, the man known as Klaus Wagenmann officially ceased to exist.

□ □ □

From the outside, it was a fairly standard office building, the type constructed in many German urban centers during the economic boom of the late 1930s. With rows of translucent glass windows that deflected the early August sunlight, it was one of the few structures that had somehow survived the Allied bombing raids largely unscathed. Such a building proved attractive to Unit 612's Requisitions Department back in Washington. The agents assigned to work there needed a place that wouldn't stand out; one that could be used for office space as well as for holding the various German "guests" for short durations of time.

Guests like Klaus Heinreich Wagenmann.

Wagenmann hadn't spoken much over the last seventy-two hours. Then again, he did not have a reason to speak. Nor was there anyone to speak to. The abrupt change of accommodations in and of itself spoke volumes. No longer confined to a small prison cell in the Palace of Justice, Wagenmann found himself in a comfortable room—locked from the outside to be sure—but with a private bath and a small kitchenette with a pot for coffee, a writing desk with several pads of yellow paper and a clear glass ashtray, a worn but still usable sofa and two wooden sitting chairs. It was more like a modest hotel room for weary traveling salesmen than a prison cell. Someone had been kind enough leave him a stack of books to read. Tucked among them was a copy of Professor Smith's work on chemical engineering. The very same book Davenport had insisted he not be allowed to take from his cell in the Palace of Justice. But clearly someone was trying to curry favor with him here—wherever here was. That much was clear. All he had to do was to play along.

Wagenmann was on the sofa reading when there was a knock at the door. He promptly stood up.

It was Larsen. This time, he came alone. Around his neck, a camera.

He carried with him a brown folder with a metal clasp at the very top and a small yellow decal affixed to the front. Written in red ink on the decal: TOP SECRET ULTRA.

Larsen sat down at the writing desk and pushed the ashtray out of the way. He placed the folder on the table, took the camera from around his neck, and set it down next to the folder. Larsen raised his right hand and motioned for Wagenmann to pull up a chair.

Much as he did in Nuremberg, the German chemist silently acquiesced to what was asked of him. He sat down, ran his palms through his hair, then placed them face down on the desk.

"You Americans, you take your time. The accommodations are bit drab, but a definite improvement from that horrible little place your Army had me holed up in back in Nuremberg."

"The last thing you should be doing right now is talking," Larsen growled.

"Straight to business. Understood," Wagenmann said. He folded his arms across his chest, indicating he knew all too well it wasn't worth taunting his captors too much. After all, they still had the upper hand. By far.

"Your British accent's cute. It's always amusing when a Kraut sounds like he's from London," Larsen said, catching Wagenmann's eye with a stare and refusing to relinquish it.

"Oxford."

"What now?"

"I spent a year at Oxford. Perhaps you've heard of it."

"Is that a technical school? Like where you can learn a trade? Like how to kill innocent people because you don't like the color of their skin?" Larsen asked.

Wagenmann was savvy enough to know enough not to reply.

Larsen opened the brown folder marked TOP SECRET ULTRA. He pulled out a sheet of slightly faded paper, glanced at it, and put it directly in front of Wagenmann so the professor could read it.

"And you, of course, want me to sign this?"

"That's the general idea."

Wagenmann leaned back. Stretched his back. Placed his arms behind his head.

"Someone in Washington really must want me," he said. Again, a factual statement as much as an inquiry.

"Don't push your luck. If it were my call, you'd be lined up against that wall and shot," Larsen replied.

"But it's not your decision. Is it? You follow orders like I did."

"Your side lost, you know," Larsen replied.

Wagenmann had no clever retort.

Just then, there was a knock at the door. It was MacFarlane.

"Sorry I'm late. Was just checking on our other guest," he said, entering the holding room and closing the steel door behind him.

"Ah," Larsen replied knowingly. "You didn't miss much. Just the prima donna here insinuating how damn smart he is," Larsen said.

"I wasn't insinuating." He paused. "I was telling."

"I see what you mean," MacFarlane said, as he walked over to the sofa and sat down.

"Yeah, he's a real piece of shit, this one," Larsen replied, lighting his cigarette with the flick of his lighter.

"Those things are disgusting," Wagenmann said.

"Is that so?" Larsen replied, as he blew smoke into the air.

"My body is a temple."

"A pagan one."

"Now that's not a way to talk to a future ally in the struggle against

Bolshevism, is it?" Wagenmann said.

"Future ally. Makes my skin crawl," murmured MacFarlane from the side of the room.

Wagenmann turned his neck sideways and glared at the younger of the two agents. He quickly returned his attention to Larsen. Then focused his gaze on the form that Larsen had placed in front of him.

He began to read it out loud.

"I, Klaus Heinreich Wagenmann, born 1919 in Riga, Doctorate in Physical Chemistry, have agreed to provide my full assistance to the Government of the United States for a duration of no less than fifteen years in exchange for the expungement of any and all records pertaining to my participation in any and all organizations affiliated with the government that ruled the German lands between 1933 and 1945 ..."

Wagenmann stopped reading. He set the form back down on the desk and took a deep breath. He exhaled slowly.

"So that's how it is," he said, a sly grin on his face.

MacFarlane noticed. He wished he could smack that grin right off of Wagenmann's face.

"That's it. Believe me, I don't like it. As I think I've mentioned to you before. If it were up to me—"

"Yes, yes. You'd have me lined up against a wall and shot."

"Perceptive son of a bitch, ain't he?" Larsen said dryly, turning to MacFarlane.

For some reason, MacFarlane found this funny. He barely suppressed laughter.

"There is one more item we have yet to discuss," Wagenmann said.

"Oh?" Larsen replied. He blew cigarette smoke in Wagenmann's direction, extinguished his cigarette in the glass ashtray. "And what might that be?"

Wagenmann coughed as the plumes of Larsen's cigarette smoke migrated across the table.

"Yes, there's the matter of my brother Hans. Well, he's not actually my brother, you see. The son of my father's best friend. I have a special fondness for him."

"You're close to another actual human being?" Larsen asked.

"Ha! He's actually quite the bastard," Wagenmann said. "Well, not literally."

"What makes you say that?" asked MacFarlane.

"Because despite every opportunity he was given, he never applied himself. Never took his studies seriously. Always drifted toward the useless and futile. Wrote worthless poetry to impress girls. Always with the girls."

"Yeah, sounds like a real loser," Larsen said sarcastically. He shuffled through the papers in the binder. He retrieved a photograph. It was of a young man, no older than sixteen or seventeen years old, dressed in a uniform that wasn't exactly military, but wasn't civilian dress either. Something a member of a fraternal organization would wear on a special occasion.

"You mean Hans Berman?"

Wagenmann grinned.

"Impressive. I see you Americans are more organized than I had imagined. Perhaps it's because your country is run by the Jews. Ah, yes. That explains why I am sitting here as your ward. Yes, we Germans underestimated you and how much fight FDR had in him." Wagenmann paused. "He was a Jew, you know? FDR."

"He was not. And you know it," MacFarlane said.

"Well, someone is sensitive. Perhaps I was mistaken. He did the Jews' bidding as does your Truman."

MacFarlane glared at Wagenmann as he began to get up from the sofa.

With a shift wave of his right hand, Larsen motioned his junior colleague to remain seated.

Wagenmann realized he was skating on thin ice. From the look in his eyes, one could tell he was thinking that it was almost as if MacFarlane had a soft spot for the Jews. Either that, or that he was really clueless about who was running the government he was working for.

Americans.

So naïve about how the world really works.

"Can we get back to Hans?" Wagenmann asked, realizing he shouldn't press his luck with the Jewish question anymore. Not now. First things first. Right now, he needed to focus on one thing and one thing only. His survival. There would be time for him to return to the Jewish question later. It might be months. Years, even. But return to it, he would. That was a promise.

"Your bastard brother," Larsen prompted.

Wagenmann laughed.

"Yes. The bastard. He wasn't really devoted to the glorious cause, you know. Far from it. Merely a hanger-on."

"Right. We know all about his wartime activities. So, what about him?"

"After all, I feel sort of an obligation to the fellow. His parents were killed in that horrible bombing raid, the one your president ordered on Dresden. And well, I would just feel terrible for him if he were to be left behind here in this ruined land."

Larsen bit his lower lip. "You don't strike me as the type of guy who would feel an obligation toward anyone."

Wagenmann laughed. In that instant, he sounded more like a hyena than a man. "You really don't get it, do you? If I am the one who arranges for Hans's departure to the States, then he will always—always—know it was I who provided this second chance to him. He'll always feel an obligation to me. And that is something that is very delicious indeed."

"You're sick," Larsen said.

"Be that as it may, a deal is a deal."

Larsen cocked his head and looked at Wagenmann quizzically. Words failed him. He said nothing.

"Now let's get a move on, shall we? I'm ready for the good life in the United States." Wagenmann grinned as he spoke. It was a menacing, devious grin. Like that of a wolf.

"Who said anything about the good life?" Larsen asked.

"A scientist always works better when his accommodations and lifestyle align with his intellect. But I wouldn't expect someone of your background to understand that."

Larsen looked at MacFarlane. He shook his head in disbelief with a look that said, "Can you believe the crap we have to put up with?"

"Well, Mr. Genius. I have news for you. We already have your precious good for nothing 'brother.' We're not idiots. We know more about you than you know about yourself. And if you sign here, you and he will be out of our hair forever and believe you me, nothing—and I mean nothing— would make me happier. And let me remind you once again, your side fucking lost!"

MacFarlane got up from the sofa, reached for the ink pen that was in his jacket pocket, and handed it to Wagenmann.

Wagenmann took the pen and signed the form.

Larsen took the document, now an official contract, and placed it back in the folder marked TOP SECRET ULTRA. He then picked up the camera and ordered Wagenmann to stand up against the wall.

"Ah, for posterity's sake," Wagenmann said.

"Just shut up. Face me and don't smile," Larsen replied. Larsen ignored Wagenmann's barely suppressed insolence and took several photographs of him. It was standard procedure. The photos were to be developed and included in Wagenmann's file.

Larsen set down the camera and motioned Wagenmann to sit back down. With a glance, he signaled to MacFarlane that it was now time to bring Hans Berman in.

To reunite him with his "older brother."

As MacFarlane walked out of the small holding room, Larsen shuffled through the folder. He took out what appeared to be two passports. They didn't appear to be American.

Wagenmann murmured something under his breath.

Larsen ignored him.

Several minutes later, MacFarlane knocked at the door and then opened it. Accompanying him was a young man who looked to be around about twenty years old. He had warm hazel-colored eyes, blonde hair, and narrow cheekbones. Tall, slim, and fair-skinned with an aura of dissoluteness, Hans Berman was dressed in a white cotton shirt marked with sweat stains under his armpits and ash grey pants one size too big for him. On his feet, a pair of scruffy black shoes with numerous cracks in the leather and a gathering of dust on the tips.

On his left index finger, a prominent medium-sized brass ring with a ruby red stone insert. Although its luster had dimmed over the course of the past several months, it still radiated an unusual warmth.

A close examination of the ring would reveal a message attached to it. Engraved in small lettering around the stone insert was the Latin phrase *Fatum habemus.*

"We have a destiny."

For the first time since he had been taken out of his Nuremberg cell, Wagenmann had showed real, visceral feelings. Like a wave sweeping over the shore at high tide, a strange amalgam of happiness and relief seemed to overtake him. For a brief shining moment, he showed the emotions of an ordinary human being, rather than that of a hubristic scientist who had helped make possible mass murder on an industrial scale. But it soon dissipated and a cold, distant look returned to his eyes.

"Mein Gott. It really is you," Wagenmann said, his gaze fixed steadily on Berman.

"You're alive! You really are. They didn't lie to me!" Berman exclaimed as he rushed to hug Wagenmann.

"No, these fine gentlemen did not lie," Wagenmann said, recoiling slightly as he spoke.

"So, it really is true. We're going to New York together," Berman said, his eyes wide with excitement. As if he were a child going on his first vacation.

"You're going to America together. But that's as far as you go. Genius here is going to Nebraska. You'll be going to New York. Just you," Larsen explained.

"Ah, you're going to house me permanently with the rocket scientists.

Is that it?" Wagenmann asked.

"You have years of service to the American government ahead of you," Larsen said as he picked up the two passports.

"What's this?" Berman asked, as he took the passport from Larsen.

"IRC papers. They'll get you through the first part of your journey. What happens next is not my concern."

"IRC?" Wagenmann asked.

"International Red Cross. They've been particularly helpful in aiding us with our relocation efforts."

"Maybe not so unusually," Wagenmann said, taking the other passport into his hand.

"Oh?" asked Larsen.

"They've always had a soft spot for our cause," Wagenmann said. His tone was vaguely sinister.

"I don't really care about their motivations. I just know that these documents will get you both out of Germany."

"Beck? That's my name?" Wagenmann asked.

"It is now."

"And I'm Hesse?" Berman asked.

"And I'm Gary Cooper. You'll both never be anyone but who you really are. But those are your names now," Larsen replied.

"Should I go get the guards?" MacFarlane asked.

"Yeah, go ahead," Larsen said, before pausing. "Wait, just a moment. What's that you have on your finger?"

"Are you speaking to me?" Berman asked, pointing at his own chest.

"Yes. You," Larsen said curtly.

"What about my finger?"

"That ring of yours. Where'd you get it?"

"Oh, it's just a fraternity ring from my Gymnasium days."

"I don't think you're going to be able to bring that with you," Larsen said dryly.

Berman looked at Larsen, a blank stare on his face.

"What's the harm, really?" Wagenmann interjected. "It's not like it's him you're protecting. No one will care—let alone notice—a fraternity ring."

"It's that important to you, huh?" Larsen said, focusing his sharp gaze on Berman.

"It's all I have left of my teenage years."

"You are one sentimental bastard," Larsen said.

It was up to MacFarlane to play the peacemaker.

"What's the harm? We might as well let him and get on our way. We've already spent too much time on these two. It's not like we're going to be paid any less if this guy wears his ring. No one is ever going to give a shit about him or his ring."

Larsen threw his hands up in disgust.

"Whatever gets me out of this cursed country as soon as possible works for me. I'll never get those films the Brits took at Belsen out of my head."

Several minutes later, two MPs from the 793rd Military Police Battalion escorted two men named Samuel Beck and Peter Hesse out of the room and down a long hallway. From there, they would be processed, given a change of clothes, and put on a flight to Washington D.C. What came after was of little concern to Larsen and MacFarlane.

"Well, I'm going to need a long hot shower now. I feel dirty just being around that arrogant creep," Larsen said, as he lit yet another cigarette.

"No kidding," MacFarlane replied as he paced around the small holding room.

"Like peas in a pod. Those two."

MacFarlane laughed uncomfortably. "You even think they like each other?"

"Who knows? Who cares? It's not our problem anymore."

"Right."

"Which reminds me. Later today, I'm going to need you to box these papers up." He pointed at the binder. "You can get one from Records and they will tuck it away somewhere."

"Will do."

"I mean it. Classify it and move on with your life. Time for me to forget this ever happened. That I was ever a part of this nonsense."

"You got that right," MacFarlane said, pausing slightly before continuing. "I have a question for you."

"Shoot," Larsen said.

"Do you really think he believes all that shit?"

"What shit?"

"About the Jews?"

"Not sure. They told me back in DC that he was just a scientist. But who knows?"

"Yeah," MacFarlane demurred.

"Best forget about it. It's not our concern," Larsen answered.

"I'll do my best," MacFarlane said.

Larsen glared at his younger partner.

"Okay. It is forgotten."

"That's more like it," Larsen said.

MacFarlane nodded.

Larsen didn't say anything, but he could see doubt in MacFarlane's troubled eyes. He could see it so very well, because it was in many ways, a reflection of how he felt. That this may have all been a giant mistake. That they were releasing a committed Nazi into the wild.

CHAPTER 1

New York City, Summer 1985

It was a red brick two-family attached house nestled in the beating heart of the Bay Ridge, Brooklyn. With small bushes and pruned trees lining the cracked cement sidewalk in front, the home radiated tranquil domesticity. Four brick steps, recently swept to the meticulous degree of cleanliness one would expect to see at a Lutheran church, led to a small but welcoming front porch. Attached to the front of the solidly built structure, a prominently displayed Norwegian flag, a blue and white cross on a red backdrop, drooped under the weight of the late summer air.

Inside, a thin woman with a delicate frame was busy in the kitchen. She had blue eyes, soft shoulder length white hair, and a face with wrinkles that hinted at melancholy. Busy preparing a silver tray of refreshments, she took two porcelain cups filled with steaming hot black coffee and placed them on it. She added a serving cup with cream, two small spoons, and a plate filled with an array of cake and cookies.

"I will be right in, Mike," she called.

"Take your time, Aunt Christina. You sure you don't want any help?"

Mike Levinas crossed his arms across his chest, looked down, and noticed goosebumps on his arms.

He looked around the room, wondering why he was a little bit chilly. Then he saw the culprit. It was the wall air conditioner unit, the one he had personally installed a year ago. His great-aunt had put it on full blast. And it was blowing directly on him.

"I need to keep active in my old age. Or so my doctor tells me," Aunt Christina said from the kitchen. "Exercise is good for keeping my blood pressure at a healthy level."

Mike smiled.

His great-aunt was the youngest octogenarian he knew. Not that he socialized with many octogenarians. Or met too many in his line of work. But he was pretty sure that not all of them paid as much attention to their fitness as scrupulously as Aunt Christina did. Between her monthly visits to the doctor and her obsessive devotion to freshly brewed filtered coffee, she was seemingly determined to be active in the world for many years to come.

Mike didn't get out to Bay Ridge often. But when he did, he found the time he spent with his aunt to be a nice escape from reality.

These visits did have the inevitable tendency also to make him brood. This time was no different.

Looking around his great-aunt's small but tidy home, Mike began to ruminate.

What his life would be like when he to be her age? Was he too going to end up single and alone like her?

All that was yet to be determined. And it scared the living hell out of him.

"Here you go," Aunt Christina said, interrupting his reverie.

She entered the living room at a slow, but steady pace, her black sneakers squeaking on the hardwood floor. Pushing aside a copy of the *New York Post*, she placed the silver tray on the wooden coffee table in front of Mike. She wiped her hands on her checkered apron, removed all the items from the tray, and set them on the table.

"Darn it. I forgot the sugar," she said. "I'll be right back."

"I don't need sugar," Mike replied.

"Who drinks coffee without sugar?" she asked, as she headed back to the kitchen.

Mike sat quietly.

He looked around the living room. How very little had changed over the years. His great-aunt still had the same family photos of old Norwegian men and women, many dressed in handknit wool sweaters. The same framed portrait of the Royal Family remained prominently displayed on the wall outside the kitchen.

Mike spotted the photo him with his cousin Erik back when they both played on the same Little League team. So much had changed since then. But somehow this quaint neighborhood nestled in the urban jungle had indelibly shaped them both to be model citizens. Whereas Mike had chosen the life of a prosecutor, his cousin Erik had joined the New Jersey State Police. He shifted his attention to the curtains that were being slightly blown back and forth by the air conditioning unit. Aunt Christina had never changed them. They were the very same curtains Mike remembered being there way back when he was in elementary school.

Just then, Mike noticed something out of the corner of his eye. It looked to be a framed document of some kind. He could have sworn he'd never seen it hanging on the wall before. He got up off the couch and walked over to get a closer look.

It took him a few seconds, but he immediately recognized it. And why he had been drawn to it.

What Mike saw in front of him was a younger version of himself.

More specifically, a handwritten essay that he, as a fifth grader, had written about how it's always important to do the right thing.

Even if—especially if—you stand alone.

Looking at the faded brown paper upon which he had written his thoughts in cursive letters, Mike reflected on how the past few years had all but erased that idealistic child from the world. The one that had always wanted to go to law school and pursue justice. The one who wanted to put the bad guys in jail.

It all overwhelmed him. Gave him the chills.

As he sat back down, Mike reflected on how it was as if time had stood still in this house. As if the tumultuous course of history had passed it by, rendering it as much a sanctuary as a home.

While Aunt Christina was still puttering around in the kitchen, Mike glanced down at the empty silver tray. Recently polished to an obsessive degree, it reflected his image much like a vanity mirror would.

He picked it up and took a good look at himself. To his surprise, he wasn't completely sure he recognized the man staring back at him.

Although he was only in his mid-30s, Mike had the face of a much younger man. Cleanly shaved with a couple nicks here and there it radiated youthful energy. Although he was now a licensed private investigator, he could still just easily pass as a law student, much as he was over a decade ago.

Couldn't he have?

Mike looked closer. His thick brown hair had not thinned much. This was all to the good. And the small scar on his left cheek, a reminder of his ill-fated decision to take up fencing in college, neither added nor detracted from his age.

Then he noticed the crow's feet under his eyes.

Imprints of a forced career change and the remnants of a deep personal loss were now etched in the corners of his eyes.

There was no way getting around it. The past several years had aged him. Restful sleep had been a luxury he could ill afford. And it showed.

The more he stared, the worse he felt about himself.

Maybe he didn't look quite as young as he had thought. Did time move that quickly? That mercilessly? Was it not just yesterday he was the happy-go-lucky elementary school kid?

The sound of Aunt Christina's squeaking sneakers was a punch back to reality.

She walked into the room and put the sugar bowl on the table. It landed with a small clink.

"Here we go," she said, as she poured two cups of coffee. One was for her and the other was for her favorite nephew.

"Where did you get that essay, the one I wrote in fifth grade?" Mike asked, pointing to the framed document on the wall.

"When your mother died, I found it among her things," Aunt Christina said.

"Oh. Wow. She kept it all these years?"

"Indeed. Does that surprise you?"

"No. No, I guess not," Mike said.

"Now you tell me," she said, as she eased herself into the armchair adjacent her dedicated Bible stand.

"Tell you what?" Mike asked.

"How are you doing?"

"How I am doing?" he repeated, picking up his coffee cup.

"Yes. I can't help but worry about you. Ever since Anne—your mother—passed—"

Mike crossed his legs, then immediately uncrossed them. He fidgeted as he reached for a slice of Norwegian almond cake.

"I'm doing fine."

"Are you? Remember, Mikey, you can't fool me," she said.

"Things are okay."

"Well, if you say so. I'll have to take your word for it," she replied.

Aunt Christina took a sip of her coffee.

"And are you still courting that woman?" she asked, setting her coffee cup down on the table.

"Nah. It never was that serious," Mike said.

"Ah. I see."

"Where did you get the almond cake?" Mike asked, attempting to change the subject.

"Why, at Olaf's Bakery on Eighth Avenue, of course."

"I can't believe that little hole in the wall still exists."

"And why would it not?" She sounded genuinely surprised at his flippancy. Almost hurt. "I go there every Saturday."

"Oh. No reason," Mike said, before picking up another cookie from the tray. He looked at his watch. It was now a quarter after four. Still plenty of time for him to get out of Brooklyn and back to his office. Time enough to meet this new client of his, the one who had emphasized she couldn't come in during normal business hours.

"I mean, there are some days that are harder than others," Mike admitted.

"I understand," Aunt Christina said.

"Life is life, you know."

"I always thought it was so unfair how those politicians treated you."

"They weren't really politicians. And what's past is past," Mike said, unable to hide his annoyance.

"Is it really, though?"

"What now?

"Are you sure? Is the past really past?"

Mike sighed. He had all heard this before.

Aunt Christina nodded. She was not about to press the issue any further.

"And how is your new profession going?" she asked.

"Nothing's much changed. Not since the last time I was here to see you."

"When was that again?"

"You know, back in early June. When I took you to your friend's funeral couple of months ago."

"Yes. That is correct," Aunt Christina said.

She hesitated for a moment, then continued speaking. "You're not putting yourself in danger? I worry what your mother would think of you having to be around all those people. All those dangerous and unpleasant people.

"You have to admit," she continued. "That people who come to see you could be involved in some very bad things."

"They're just people who need some help," Mike replied matter-of-factly.

"So why don't they go to the police? That is their job, after all."

"The cops can't handle everything," Mike said.

"Ah. I see."

Mike didn't think she sounded remotely convinced.

Just then, Aunt Christina shifted her gaze away from Mike and back to the *New York Post*. The one she had moved out of the way to make room for the serving tray. As if she had saved it for a reason that she couldn't immediately recall.

Mike noticed that she seemed momentarily distracted.

"What's this about? Any reason you saved this?" he asked, picking up the tabloid.

"Oh, something I thought your Dad might be interested in," Aunt Christina replied.

"What is it?" Mike asked.

Aunt Christina reached across the table and took the *New York Post* from Mike. She turned to Page 3.

"It's this story, here. You see the one I mean?" she asked, pointing to the page.

Aunt Christina had apparently circled a short article in blue ink. The headline read: "Former UN Secretary General Waldheim Seeks Austrian Presidency."

"My Dad would care about this?" Mike asked.

"Go ahead and read it," she said, handing the paper back to him.

Mike squinted and took a closer look.

The story described how the former United Nations Secretary General, a lanky, aristocratic-looking Austrian named Kurt Waldheim was planning to run for the presidency of his native country. Rumors persisted, however, that he hadn't been exactly honest about what he did during the Second World War. Some Jewish organizations claimed he was a Nazi war criminal. That he had blood on his hands.

"You're right," he said, pausing to consider his next words. "My Dad would be interested in this."

"I thought so. I mean it's your people's greatest tragedy," she replied.

Your people's.

Mike never knew what to say when she brought up the subject. Most of the time, he didn't really consider himself to be Jewish. Not in the way his Jewish friends did. It wasn't like he had had a bar mitzvah. Or knew a word of Hebrew aside from *shalom*. He barely even knew what that meant.

It all began when a blonde haired Norwegian-American Lutheran girl of solidly bourgeois family roots in Stavanger, Norway, had married a tough Brooklyn Jew named Irving Levinas. Not just a tough guy. But a guy with a black sheep father, a man rumored to have been a hired gun for a crime syndicate during Prohibition.

Talk about worlds colliding.

Not that Aunt Christina was remotely antisemitic.

Quite the contrary.

She just couldn't get beyond the odd pairing of Anne Johannsen and Irving Aaron Levinas. As much as she doted on Mike since he was a toddler, treating him as if he were the child she never had, she couldn't quite get fully comfortable talking about the obvious. That Mike, as the product of his parents' marriage, was caught between two different worlds. He would never be fully at home in Brooklyn's insular Norwegian community. No matter how much his mother had dressed him up in traditional bunads, the traditional Norwegian folk costumes embroidered with elaborate designs. No matter how many Norwegian sweets he ate, he'd never be fully at home in her world either. He would never quite be her surrogate son.

"And how is your Dad?" she asked.

"He's doing okay, I guess. Complains about the humidity."

"Well what did he expect to find there? It is Florida, after all."

"I'm not exactly sure what he was looking for, to be honest. Spring training baseball?" Mike laughed.

Irving Levinas had spent a lifetime complaining about New York. How he wanted nothing more than to get away from the cold. From the rats in the subway tunnels. From the graffiti-covered subway cars that smelled like urine and degeneracy. Things weren't like that when his father was growing up. People had respect for other people back then. Mike had heard it all. His dad's endless litany of complaints about the city. How Mayor Koch was a good man, but fundamentally incapable of doing what needed to be done to clean up the place. You needed to be tough to do that. Koch was tough. But not that tough. Now, after a year in Florida, Irving Levinas's love affair for the Sunshine State had grown cold. The people were dumb. Couldn't hold a simple conversation about politics. And the humidity there made summer in New York feel like a sojourn in the Arizona desert. Mike knew that his father was always going to find something to complain about. Always.

"You know what," Aunt Christina said. She got up from her armchair and walked across the room to a small writing desk. "I'm going to clip out that article and you can send it to him."

"Oh, you don't need to do that."

"But you yourself said he'd be interested in it," she replied, picking up a pair of scissors with green plastic coating over the small finger holes.

He smiled apologetically.

"You don't need to bother yourself with it."

"You used to care about things."

"I did?"

"Yes."

"I guess," Mike demurred.

"Just take it. And mail it to Irving when you get a chance."

As if mailing his father some clipping was going to be a priority for him. As if he could barely keep up with all of his cases, paying his bills, and trying to eke out a semblance of a social life.

"I really—" Mike said.

"I must insist."

"Yes. I'll do it."

"Smile," she said.

"What?" She had taken him by surprise.

"Nothing. It's just that you used to smile more. I haven't seen you smile in a long time. A real smile. Maybe you should watch Johnny Carson. He's on after the news. He's really funny."

"That's not really my thing," Mike said. He looked at his watch again. 4:30. Time for him to get going.

Aunt Christina noticed his impatience.

"I'm not going to keep you."

"It's not that I don't want to stay—"

"It feels like you just got here."

"I would stay," Mike said, as got up from the couch and hugged his great-aunt, "but I do have to meet a client in the city."

"Okay. Come back soon. Yes?"

"Definitely," he said.

"You still have the spare key?"

"Yes, I do."

"Good. I always wanted you to have an extra key to my house. For whenever you need it."

Mike nodded. More to humor his aunt than anything else. When would he ever come back if she weren't here to greet him?

But it was good that he had both a person and a place to retreat to. Where Mike could, for a fleeting moment, return to the safety that he knew. The Brooklyn of his childhood.

After promising Aunt Christina that he'd visit her again soon, Mike hugged her goodbye. He walked out the front door. Down the steps. Into the sweltering air. He knew the walk to the subway would take ten minutes, but in this weather, it would take only two before his shirt and blazer were drenched.

As Mike made his way to the station, his thoughts once again returned to his childhood. Seeing all the small Norwegian bakeries and gift stores lining Eighth Avenue reminded him once again of his youth. The main difference was that now they were buttressed by Chinese groceries that sold exotic vegetables and cramped hookah cafes filled with Egyptian men arguing politics in Arabic. As much as he hated to see things change, he knew that it was inevitable. Nothing remains the same. Not in New York City, anyway.

Fifteen minutes later, with Mike aboard, the R train pulled out of the Bay Ridge subway station.

Mike reached inside his jacket pocket and pulled out the newspaper clipping that Aunt Christina had given him. He took another look at the headline, imagining how his Dad would react to this.

Who was he kidding?

He didn't need to imagine anything.

He knew exactly what his Dad's reaction would be. It would be the same way his father responded whenever European politicians were mentioned. He could just hear his Dad telling him that deep down, all Europeans are just Nazis.

Mike shook his head. What a pessimistic way to see the world. A world with enemies constantly lurking in the shadows.

Mike put the clipping back in his pocket. It'd be a while until he'd have to change trains to get him to Union Square. Time enough for a mental break before he met his newest client. From the short conversation he'd had with her on the telephone the other day, it sounded as if it were going to be just another missing person case.

Same old story. Nothing new under the sun.

As the train chugged into the dark tunnel ahead, Mike closed his eyes. And no matter how hard he tried to banish the thought, his mind kept returning to that moment when he saw his reflection in the silver tray. Cascading through his mind was a question to which he simply did not have a good answer.

Just who was the man staring back at him?

CHAPTER 2

The R train rattled into Union Square station, jolting Mike wide awake. He rubbed his eyes, glanced down at his watch. It had taken a full hour to get from Bay Ridge to here. It usually didn't take nearly that long. The train must have had some trouble along the way. Either that, or there was a sick passenger who had to be removed from the train. Not that Mike remembered any of it. He apparently had dozed off for quite a while.

Climbing the worn steps that led to street level, Mike couldn't help but think of what Aunt Christina had told him. That he had to find some purpose to his life. That he had to find some way to feel alive again.

Whatever.

That was easy for her to say. She hadn't thrown years away on law school. All to end up working as a gutter-level PI.

Walking briskly down Broadway, Mike noticed he had just passed The Strand, the bookstore where over the years he had spent a ton of money. Back when he had free time to read—and money to spend.

He turned the corner and walked east along 8th Street. As he passed the Astor Place subway station, Mike spotted a small gathering of punk kids.

Mike smiled.

Their bright colored mohawks didn't make them look edgy. It made them look like exotic specimens in an aviary. One of the kids was kicking an empty Pepsi can along the sidewalk, deliberately aiming for the feet of passersby. Mike quickly crossed the street, hoping to get away from the kid and his friends as quickly as possible. Not that he was generally bothered by teenagers.

But because he knew people in groups often behaved in ways they never would as individuals.

As he walked along St. Mark's Place, past vinyl record shops, street cafes, and greasy falafel joints, Mike got to thinking. Was this particular neighborhood really a good fit? When Mike decided to take the plunge and open up his own shop, he knew he needed an office.

What was he going to do? Work out of a trailer like James Garner did on *The Rockford Files*?

It was only because of a personal connection that he had ended up here. As luck would have it, his law school classmate, now friend, Barry Stein, had told him about some office space that his father had for rent on Second Avenue. Barry had asked Mike if he'd mind having an office located above a Ukrainian bakery?

Mind?

For the price, he jumped at the opportunity. An office was an office. And Mike could hardly afford some plush Midtown digs. Not when he was first starting out and most of his cases were either divorces, teenage runaways from Long Island, or missing persons.

Mike opened the front door to the building where he had his office. As he walked into the narrow entrance way, the door banged shut behind him. It rattled a bit. But Mike knew the chance of Stein senior fixing it was next to zero.

The stairway to the second floor was bathed in a buzzing white fluorescent light. It always made Mike feel as if he were in a hospital ward, only one less antiseptic and far mustier.

The floor above the Ukrainian bakery was home to four small offices. There was the sketchy real estate agent, Sean McGuire, who never seemed to have any clients. An aging Yiddish theater manager Irv "The King" Rubenstein who was still hanging onto a dream long stomped out of existence. And the deadbeat accountant, Charles R. Smith, who spent more time at the off-track betting parlor around the corner than in his office.

Mike's office was through the second door on the left.

Whenever he saw the brass placard bearing his name, he could scarcely believe his eyes. If you'd had told him several years ago that he'd be earning his keep by spying on straying husbands, prying into the intimate lives of potential corporate hires and tracking down teenage runaways, he'd have called you a Yiddish word his Dad always used.

Meshuga. Crazy.

Mike tried his best to keep his office as professional looking as possible. Located front and center was a medium-sized desk with several drawers. It was currently overrun with newspapers, ballpoint pens, and stacks of unopened mail. There were the two wooden chairs he had picked up at a discount furniture store down the block. Two half-empty oak bookcases lined with a mix of law books and phone books were positioned on the side wall. Several boxes filled with stuff he had accumulated in law school were tucked away in the corner. Junk that he probably would never look at again. He just didn't have the heart to toss it in the trash.

After all, it was *his* junk.

The district attorney's office couldn't take that away from him. They could take his job as an ADA. Most of his pension. To speak nothing of his pride.

But they didn't dare try to have him disbarred. That would have been a bridge too far. Even for them.

And they certainly couldn't stop him from working as a PI. This was, for better or for worse and a lot of the time he had to admit—it was for the worse—his domain. His ramshackle kingdom.

Mike looked at his watch again. Not quite seven.

He had some time to kill. Why not make the most of it?

The first thing Mike did was empty a glass ashtray filled with cigarette butts into a basket next to his desk. Although he wasn't a smoker, his clients invariably were. Mike picked up one of the chairs and set it back down, facing the opposite side of his desk. He then straightened the stack of unopened mail, uncovering his daily planner in the process.

So that's where it was. Hidden in plain sight. Holding the planner in one hand, Mike walked over to the small window and tried to push it open with the other. Stuck again. He tossed the planner on the desk, made use of both his hands, and gave it another try. With some elbow grease, it creaked open. Mike detected the unmistakable scent of ozone.

Rain was coming.

Just then, there was a knock at the door. It was immediately followed by the sound of a woman's voice.

"Hello?"

Mike glanced down at his watch. This must be his seven o'clock.

He walked to the door and opened it. Standing there in the doorway was a short attractive woman. She had deep brown eyes and a face that hinted at a wild past. Mike noticed how her bright yellow long sleeve blouse accentuated her fiery shoulder length auburn hair. How it gave her the aura of youth. As if calendar years simply did not apply to her.

"Hi. I'm Mike Levinas. Won't you come in?"

"Millie Johnson. We talked on the phone. It's good to put a face with the voice."

She spoke with a slight accent. Mike knew it was Southern. That much was obvious. But he couldn't place exactly where she was from, of course.

Mike shook her hand. It was delicate.

As he guided her into his office, he noticed that the palm of his right hand had been slightly dampened by her touch. Sweat. She must be a bundle of nerves. Probably the first time she's ever hired a private investigator, he thought.

"I'd thought you'd be older," she said.

"Why's that?" Mike asked.

"Based on your voice. From our phone conversation. I thought you'd be older than you really are."

Mike didn't know how to respond. He said nothing.

"Sorry. I didn't mean to offend," Millie said.

"Don't worry about it."

"And again, sorry about having to meet with you so late. My boss doesn't like me taking any time off during the day. Commercial real estate is pretty intense and they like having someone manning the phones all day."

Mike just smiled.

Millie sat down. Mike followed suit and sat down at his chair on the opposite side of the desk.

Millie placed her black leather handbag on the desk in front of her. It looked like one of those knock-offs sold by West African street hustlers in Times Square.

"It does appear like it's going to rain," she said. It was a transparent attempt on her part to restart the conversation.

Mike noticed she was looking through the small window behind him. He turned around and peered out. A dark gray rain cloud hung like a shroud in the evening sky.

"Yeah, I mean, it's really humid," he said.

"Thunderstorms," she said quietly.

"What's that?"

"Could be a storm headed our way."

"Very true. So. Tell me, Mrs. Johnson—"

She interrupted him.

"Ms."

"Ms.?" Mike asked, picking up a pen from his desk, twirling it in his hands.

"Yes. I prefer Ms.," she said.

"Ah, I see," Mike said.

"A lot of women prefer it these days."

"I'm familiar with the practice," Mike said.

"Yeah. I mean, everyone's using Ms. Like my friend Rebecca from Long Island. She ..."

It was Mike's turn to interrupt.

"I'm not here to judge you," he said.

Mike realized that Millie Johnson wasn't going to open up to him on her own, so he thought he'd try a more direct approach. Some clients were like that. They'd be spilling their hearts out over the phone. But once they showed up in person, once they'd crossed that Rubicon, they got cold feet. Somehow the impersonal nature of a telephone call with a stranger allowed them to continue the illusion that whatever troubles plagued them could be worked out without the intervention of someone like Mike.

Now it all hit home.

They were about to pay a man money to do something for them. Something they couldn't, or wouldn't, do for themselves. In that sense, he was like a prostitute. The thought made him laugh inside.

"Tell me a little about your husband," Mike said.

It was a prompt.

An open invitation for her to say whatever was on her mind. He knew that initial consultations with clients had a tendency to be circular in nature. A few significant nuggets of useful information were inevitably followed by some small talk. Followed by some highly valuable information mixed with some irrelevant chatter about the missing individual's favorite movies and baseball players.

Millie Johnson shifted back where she was sitting. It squeaked like older chairs do.

"Well," she paused, as if she were choosing her words with care. Words that held more meaning in her mind than when she spoke them. "He teaches at Nassau Community College out on Long Island. He's well liked. By the students, I mean. He disappeared on me."

Mike nodded.

"Yes, you said as much on our phone call yesterday. That you haven't seen him in five full days."

"Right," she replied, tapping her recently painted nails on the desk.

"So as of today, it's been six days now since you saw your husband last?" Mike asked.

"Yes."

"Okay. He disappeared. And you don't know where or why? But you've gone to the police?"

"They weren't all that helpful," she said. "They were nice enough, I guess," she demurred. "They did take a report. That's good, right?"

It wasn't good.

It was a mere formality. Nothing more. Nothing less.

And it came as no surprise to Mike.

In this era of budget cuts and the Mayor's insistence that the cops at least make a pretense of cleaning up Times Square, missing persons—unless they were from some of the city's tonier neighborhoods—were not of the highest priority. Mike knew from experience that, for the most part, people who went missing in the city were people who often didn't want to be found. The other thing that Mike knew was that clients who came to him after going to the cops always hid some key details that needed to be pried gently out of them. Always. What was it going to be this time?

"It's good that they've shown some interest," Mike said.

Millie leaned forward. She placed her elbows on Mike's desk. "Wait. There's no conflict with you taking a case even though there's a police report? Because I remember what you said on the phone."

As if somehow pulled toward her, Mike instinctively leaned forward. There was now only a foot between them. Close enough to smell her perfume. It smelled like fresh lilacs.

"In general, I don't take missing person cases when there's been a police report filed. That's so. But nowadays it really doesn't matter that all much. It's a good sign that the cops took a report.

"But I'm going to be honest with you," Mike added, trying to find a way to spin this in the best way he could. "The cops can use whatever extra help they can get."

The truth, of course, was that the cops really didn't care one way or the other. Whether an ambitious PI made some extra cash working on an open case didn't much faze them. Worst case scenario was that nothing would come of Mike's efforts. Best case for everyone involved would be that Millie would get her missing husband back, Mike would get paid, and the cops would have one less unsolved case on their hands. Everyone from the Mayor's Office on down would be happy. End of story.

"Okay. Ah, I see," she said.

"Remind me how you found me again," Mike said.

"The Yellow Pages. I—We—live in the area," she said.

"That's right. I remember now," Mike said. "I know we discussed some of this on the phone. But let me get some more information from you," Mike said. He opened the top drawer of the desk and pulled out a yellow legal pad.

"Okay," Millie said, removing her elbows from the desk and crossing her arms across her chest.

"Your husband's name," Mike said, opening his daily planner, "is Peter Hesse. Did I get that correct?"

"Yes."

"Okay. Good," Mike said.

Mike often found that it was sometimes awkward for a client in cases such as these to even speak the name of the person in question. As if uttering the name would bring bad luck. He understood though. His clients were living in a waking nightmare. And once a PI wrote down a name, there was no mistaking the hard reality of the situation. That and the potential outcomes. Such as the missing person might never be found. Or, they might be located, but they might no longer be breathing. And dead men didn't do much to let the world know if and when they were going to be found. It was all very sad. But it was his profession.

"I brought this," Millie said.

She handed him a Polaroid. It was a photograph of her with a man who looked like he was in his sixties. Although his hair was mostly white, some strands of blonde still were visible at the sides of his face. With his gaunt pale face and narrow cheekbones, the man reminded Mike of the punk-looking kid he had seen earlier that night at Astor Place kicking the Pepsi can down the sidewalk. Maybe that's what that kid is going to look like after several decades of hard living. Because in Mike's mind, Peter Hesse didn't look fully alive. He looked more like a living corpse.

"Is this Peter?" Mike asked, trying in vain to hide his surprise that Millie was married to the man captured on film.

"Yes, that's Peter. I also brought a larger photo with me," she said, reaching for her purse.

"That could definitely help," Mike said, trying to keep the interview as upbeat as possible.

Millie opened her purse and pulled out an 8x10 photograph. She handed it to Mike. Slightly folded, so as to fit inside her handbag, it was a glossy color photograph of her and her husband on a sunny beach. In the background were vacationing families, children playing, and a few rascally looking seagulls. The first thing Mike thought was that Peter Hesse looked completely happy here. A far cry from the hollowed-out figure permanently captured on Polaroid. Standing on Millie's right, he had his left arm wrapped around her thin shoulders. Millie looked more than merely content in his embrace. She looked like she was in love.

Mike held the photo up to get a closer look.

"What's that on his left hand?" he asked.

"Oh that? That's some fraternity ring from his teenage years. He refuses to take it off for any reason. It's got some special meaning to him."

"Was he in a fraternity in college?" Mike asked. He knew that fraternity brothers usually remained in touch for decades after they had graduated. Maybe one of them had an inkling of where Peter might be.

"Oh, yes. But the ring isn't from this country. This is from his high school years in Switzerland," Millie said.

"Right. That's what you told me on the phone," Mike said, remembering.

"Yeah. As I told you, he was born in Germany, but he and his parents fled Hitler and ended up in Switzerland before the war started. Then he came here after the war after his parents were killed in a car crash."

"He's a naturalized American citizen then?"

"Yes. Naturalized. That's it."

Mike nodded. Then he looked at the photograph again.

Upon closer inspection, Mike then noticed something rather incongruous. Something that he felt he was going to have to bring up with Millie, no matter how awkward. Although the photograph was almost certainly taken in the summertime, Peter Hesse was wearing a long sleeve Oxford shirt. Based on past experience, Mike had more than of an inkling of what that might indicate.

"Let me ask you," Mike said, fully knowing he was treading on sensitive territory. "Does your husband usually wear long sleeve shirts in the summertime?"

Millie pressed her hands together. She cracked her knuckles but did not say a word.

"It's just that—"

"I was going to tell you," she said hesitantly.

"Tell me what?" Mike asked. Playing slightly dumb occasionally got the job done.

"Well. That he's had some problems."

"Problems?"

"With drugs. With—"

"Heroin?" Mike interjected.

"Yeah, I was going to tell you before I left. Obviously."

"Right."

For the next half hour, Millie explained to Mike that her beloved Peter was really a brilliant man. A kind soul at heart. But that he had his demons. She explained that it was because he was too empathetic for such an indifferent world. And how he found a temporary escape first in occasionally smoking dope. Then by shooting heroin straight into his arms. The hard stuff from Southeast Asia. The kind of junk you can only find above 110th Street. She told Mike how her husband nearly lost everything to his addiction. How his path to a tenured professorship at Columbia University disintegrated before his very eyes. Which was why he was now teaching literature to working-class kids at a community college out on Long Island. They liked him there. But the other faculty didn't. They knew what he was. Not just an addict. But an addict pressing sixty. And the stigma that went along with that made his addiction worse. Again, because he was so sensitive. So very kind.

When Mike asked how she had met Hesse, Millie initially demurred.

But then she admitted a truth that Mike had suspected. Something that had entered his mind ever since he realized that Millie was also wearing a long sleeve shirt. Just like Peter Hesse in the beach photo.

"We met in a rehab clinic. Two years ago."

"Here in Manhattan?"

"Yes. In Chelsea."

"So," Mike said, leaning forward. "I take it you've had your own struggles with addiction as well?"

"Sadly, yes," she said, attempting to avoid direct eye contact with Mike. A nearly impossible task given he was seated right across from her.

"As I said before, I'm not judging you, Ms. Johnson." He paused before continuing. "That's not what you're paying me for."

Millie nodded.

"I have to ask," Mike said. "Do you suspect that he is using again?"

"Yeah. I mean it wouldn't be the first time. But to be gone for six full days. Something's different this time." She paused, before continuing. "Something's definitely different."

"I see," Mike said.

So there it was. What Millie had almost certainly left out of the police report. That her college instructor husband was a junkie. A junkie who was likely using again. That's something the cops were not going to be particularly sympathetic to. Sixty years old? He should know better, they'd say. It all made sense. Why she came to him. He didn't know how to feel about that. On the one hand, it was good to have a new client. On the other, it meant that he'd be operating in a gray area. He'd know something the cops didn't. Although it's not like they were making the search for Peter Hesse a top departmental priority. If they were even bothering searching for him at all.

For the next ten minutes, Millie provided Mike with the additional information he thought could be useful in his quest to find her husband. Mike jotted it all down, all the while reflecting how humiliating it must have been for Peter Hesse to go from rising academic star at Columbia to just another community college instructor. Teaching students who likely didn't share his passion for literature. How his drug habit shattered his life's dreams. How Peter Hesse likely never imagined he'd end up wherever he was right now. Wherever that was. Mike shuddered. He knew that if he didn't have Aunt Christina and his father to keep him on the straight and narrow, no matter their political disagreements, he could just as well have descended into the living hell of addiction himself.

"You said that your husband was liked by the students," Mike said.

"That's right."

"But not so much by the other faculty?"

"Well, not really," she said, with more than a trace of hesitation in her voice.

"Is there someone at the college he's close to?" Mike asked.

"There is, I think," she said, twirling strands of her auburn hair tightly in her hand, then releasing them like a coiled spring.

Mike imagined where this was going.

That Millie would tell him about a younger faculty member of the opposite sex. One that Peter Hesse shared office space with. Or something to that effect. People were all the same. Always predictable.

And sure enough, his instincts proved correct.

Millie told him about Emma Schneidermann, an instructor in German Studies. Emma was also from Central Europe. She and Peter had lunch every once in a while in the faculty café. Since both their mother tongues were German, it made perfect sense. Did it not? Millie assured Mike there was no funny business going on between Emma and her husband. None at all. Their relationship was purely professional. But she hardly sounded convinced.

Mike listened as he jotted down notes to himself for future reference.

"I know this isn't pleasant. But I have to ask you one more thing which might prove to be useful," Mike said.

"Go ahead."

"Is there any place in particular where your husband goes when he's using?"

"I don't know about using. But he likes to go see movies at the Fulton Theater. It's near Times Square, I think."

"It is," Mike said. He was familiar with that theater and its reputation as a hangout for junkies. He scribbled "Fulton" onto his notepad and underlined it twice.

"Blue movies, you mean?" Mike asked.

"Heavens, no. Not stuff like that. Just movies he likes."

"I see."

"I hope you do."

"Out of curiosity, have you gone to the Fulton looking for him?"

"No. I hate that part of town. Too many scary people."

Mike couldn't tell if she was being completely honest about not going to the Fulton to look for her husband. Or the reason why she didn't much care for that part of town. But it really didn't matter.

"Oh," Mike said. "One other question that I should have asked before."

"Yes?"

"Has your husband ever disappeared like this before?"

Millie thought about it for a minute, then answered. "Not really," she said.

"Could you elaborate? It's for your benefit. I mean, to help me help you find your husband," Mike said, realizing how terribly awkward he sounded. Like a stammering junior high school kid asking the popular girl to prom.

"Well, he has," Millie said, choosing her words carefully. "But never like this. Not for this long."

"Ah," Mike said.

"Yes, this is different. I can feel it."

"May I ask what was going on then? The times he disappeared before that is?"

"He was using. Obviously. But I also think he may have—how should I put this—sought out female company."

"No need to be embarrassed."

"I think he's visited whores in the past. It makes me sick even thinking about it."

Mike nodded.

"Another thing I should know," Mike said, "is whether your husband has any family in the New York area."

"Family?" She laughed uncomfortably. "God no. His parents are dead. And he was a single child."

"Got it."

"So that's it?" Millie asked.

"I think I have everything I need," Mike said.

"Good."

Just then, Mike tried to stifle a yawn. Not quite successfully. Embarrassed, he immediately covered his mouth.

"It's okay," Millie said, unable to hold back a smile. A moment of levity in the midst of darkness. "No one in this city gets a decent night's sleep."

Mike smiled back. She was perceptive. And what she said was true. Between the constant drone of cars, buses, and delivery trucks and the tiny, cramped living quarters most New Yorkers found themselves in, a good night's sleep in Manhattan was a luxury. For those persons who had a lot on their minds, thoughts circling in their brain like windstorms on a prairie, falling asleep at night was like a second career. It was a task that had to be worked at, perfected.

"Sorry," Mike said.

"As I said, I get it," she replied.

Mike glanced at his watch. It was pushing nine o'clock. Time to wrap it up. She had told him as much as he needed to know for now. And he had her contact information that he would later put in his address book. He went over his typical fee schedule, giving her his typical spiel. Thirty dollars an hour plus expenses.

"Well, I guess that's it," he said, scribbling his home phone number on a scrap of white paper and handing it to her.

"What's this?"

"My home phone number. Just in case you ever need it."

"All right. It was good to meet you, Mr. Levinas," Millie said, gently pushing loose strands of auburn hair out of her face.

She picked up her purse and got up from the rickety chair.

"Mike. Please. Mr. Levinas lives in Florida," Mike said, as he got up from his desk chair.

"What's that?"

"It was a poor attempt at humor. I always think of my father as Mr. Levinas," Mike explained.

"Got it," she said.

As they shook hands, Mike thought he noticed something in her eyes. He didn't know quite was it was. That she was hiding something? Or that she was just scared? Scared that she may never see her husband again.

"Well, goodbye," Millie said.

"Good night, Ms. Johnson. I'll be in contact with you soon."

She smiled.

After Millie closed the office door behind her, Mike straightened up some papers on his desk. As he glanced again at the two photographs Millie had left, he heard what sounded like the clicking of her high heels growing ever so faint.

Thinking it wouldn't occur to Millie to look up once she got down to the street, Mike walked toward his office window and peered down.

Second Avenue was bathed in a red neon glow. It was wet in the way only New York city streets get when it rains. When oil slicks, exhaust fumes, and dirt mixed with rainwater create a gross, slippery residue.

Looking through the heavy rain, Mike was able to make out his newest client darting across the street. Her hands were waving as she attempted to hail a yellow cab. He wondered whether she would have any luck getting one to stop in the rain. He never did. It was just one of those things for him. When it rained, the chance of him getting a cab those times he was caught outside without an umbrella was next to zero.

Just then, Mike noticed a yellow cab put on its turn signal and pull over toward the curb.

Well, would you look at that?

He remained at the window for a few more seconds and watched the cab transporting Millie pull away from the curb, its red tail lights disappearing into the night.

Mike exhaled. He walked over to the bookshelves, removed the White Pages, and sat back down at his cluttered desk.

He looked at his watch. It wasn't all that late. Still plenty of time to call Emma Schneidermann before he left the office for the night.

Time to get to work.

He had a case to work on after all.

CHAPTER 3

"He told me he was going leave her. But don't all married men say that?"

"I wouldn't know about that," Mike said.

"I guess you wouldn't."

It was then that Mike noticed Emma Schneiderman was looking at his hand, at where a wedding ring would be had he been married.

She smiled. But it wasn't a friendly smile.

Mike did his best. He forced a smile back at her.

It wasn't that Emma Schneiderman was necessarily a mean person. She was just a sullen one. Not exactly what Mike had expected. But not a total surprise, either. However, her physical appearance wasn't all that different from how he had pictured her in his mind on the cab ride over to the college. Thin and attractive with an aura of Continental sophistication.

But with looks that would almost certainly fade in years ahead. It was not her appearance that gave her away though. It was in how she spoke to him. A tenor with an unmistakable bitterness.

It was something with which Mike was all too familiar.

The night before, after Millie had left his office, he had phoned Emma Schneidermann. He had found her home number in the White Pages and had decided to cold call her. It took some persuasion on his part, but she finally relented and, notwithstanding the trepidation in her voice, had agreed to meet him the next day to discuss the matter of the missing Peter Hesse.

Before he left the city, out of sheer curiosity, Mike had made a quick stop at the public library on East 79th Street. Rather than search the card catalogue himself, he had gone directly to the reference desk. There, he had asked the elderly grey-haired librarian if they had any books authored by Emma Schneidermann. The library did indeed have one, she had said. A dense academic tome with a long title: *Representations of Violence in 19th-Century Austrian Prose and Poetry*. The librarian had told Mike that the city's sole copy was not at this branch, but at the main library on Fifth Avenue. She had asked Mike in a hushed tone whether he wanted her to call and reserve the copy for him. When Mike had explained that it wouldn't be necessary, the librarian gave him a look that Mike knew all too well from his interactions with law school librarians. A look that said in no certain terms, "Why are you wasting my time then?" But to Mike, it wasn't remotely a waste of time. For him, it was necessary background research. A chance for him to get to know something about Emma Schneidermann before heading out to Long Island to speak with her in person.

When the cab had arrived at Nassau Community College, dropping Mike off at the main entrance, the tree-lined campus was as empty as a minor league hockey arena. Summer classes were in session, but apparently not that many students chose to spend their August picking up additional credits where they could.

Mike had walked briskly along the campus sidewalks, past a large outdoor fountain and a large patch of grass where a couple of students were throwing a frisbee back and forth. Such a change in atmosphere from Manhattan, Mike had thought. People out here have room to breathe.

After initially walking in the wrong direction on the unfamiliar campus, Mike had finally found Dobbs Hall. Which was where she had told him to find her office.

He had found Emma Schneiderman squirreled away in a room more like a cubbyhole than a real office, a rather bland looking space with aging cardboard boxes stacked against the wall on the scuffed linoleum floor.

Mike's initial impression, from the darting look in her suspicious eyes, was that she was more than a little on the paranoid side. That she was not totally comfortable with authority figures. It took no small amount of cajoling, skills that he had honed while working in the DA's office, to get her to open up to him. He had assured her that anything she told him that could help him locate Peter Hesse would be treated as strictly confidential. He had assured her that she wasn't going to get into trouble with law enforcement.

Mike did not exactly lie when he had told her that. But he didn't have the heart to tell her the hard truth either. Which was that the cops simply didn't give a rat's ass about Peter Hesse. Nor did they care about her. When Mike had phoned Tony Doran, a friend he knew in the NYPD's Missing Persons Bureau earlier that morning, he was told as much. That they had a report on Peter Hesse, but the general sense was that the guy was a washout. An aging white junkie who had gotten himself picked up by the boys in Narcotics every so often before his much younger wife came and bailed him out. To the bureau, Peter was nothing more than a missing addict. And missing addicts weren't worth much time or effort.

That's when Captain Doran had told Mike he had to go and had abruptly ended the call.

"And you're absolutely sure you don't have any idea where he might be?" Mike asked in the gentlest tone he could muster.

"Honestly, I don't. Peter didn't tell me too much about his, uh, extracurricular activities, Mr. Levinas. Although I can tell you, I'm pretty sure he was using dope again," Emma said.

She grabbed a few books off a shelf as she got ready for her upcoming class. Mike noticed they all had German titles, but other than that, he had no idea what kind of books they were.

"You and he were close enough that he felt comfortable confiding in you about his addiction?"

"I don't think Peter ever felt comfortable a day in his life," Emma said dryly.

"What do you mean?" he asked.

"What do I mean by what?" she asked tersely.

"Your last remark. That Peter Hesse never felt comfortable."

"Oh," she laughed nervously, before she steadied herself. "It's just that he never seemed completely comfortable in his own skin. Like he was always on guard. Something was always bugging him. You know?"

"No, not really," he replied, noticing Emma looking up at the clock mounted on the wall.

"I would help you more if I could, but I really have to get going. I have a class in five minutes and I'm going to be late as it is, thanks to you."

"I'm only doing my job," Mike said.

"And I'm only trying to do mine."

As Mike headed out her office and down the fluorescent lit hallway, he heard Emma call after him.

"I really do hope you find Peter. He's really not a bad individual. He's just troubled," she yelled down the hallway.

Not a bad guy. Just troubled.

Mike found the word choice interesting. It was just like what Millie had said about her husband. How Peter Hesse was such a sensitive, kind, loving soul. Mike began to wonder how much of Peter Hesse's persona was natural. And how much was carefully constructed. As if he were a character in a Hollywood movie. Mike was beginning to suspect that under the surface, there was a lot more going on in Peter Hesse's life. A lot more than the fallen professor had ever let on to either his wife or to Emma Schneidermann.

What that was, Mike had no idea.

Back outside in the sunshine, Mike took in the fresh air. It was so much healthier out here on bucolic Long Island than it was back in Manhattan.

It was a reasonably nice day. Not too humid yet. Mike decided to walk to the closest bus stop rather than take a cab back to the city. He knew he could catch the commuter bus and take it directly to the Port Authority Bus Terminal on 8th Avenue. He was heading to Times Square anyway. Hoping he could get a lead on Hesse at the Fulton Theater.

□　□　□

Some forty minutes later, as the cramped bus got off the highway and crossed the Williamsburg Bridge, Mike began to wake up. He must have dozed off. He rubbed his eyes, yawned loudly. Temporarily embarrassed, he immediately covered his mouth. But no one was paying attention to him. Not in the slightest. Neither the two Hasidic Jewish men across the aisle conversing animatedly in what Mike imagined to be Yiddish, nor the older solitary Chinese man reading a newspaper in his native Mandarin. The two loudmouthed black kids in the row behind didn't remotely seem to give a damn, either.

Mike glanced sideways out through the tinted bus window.

Decaying tenement buildings lined the block. And it looked like someone had taken a bazooka to a brick building.

The Lower East Side.

While never known for glitz or wealth, the neighborhood had certainly seen better days and has changed dramatically over the years. Once the center of working-class Jewish life in Manhattan, now nearly every shop had a roll-down metal gate strewn with graffiti. Gang tags. One of the many signs that this neighborhood, like so many others, had changed immensely over the years.

Mike knew exactly what his father would say if he were here. That the city was going down the toilet under Mayor Koch. That first comes the graffiti. Second, the muggings. And finally, they kill you. Kill you and leave you to bleed out on the street like a feral dog.

In his mind, Mike could hear his father's gravelly voice say those very words.

That reminded him.

He still had the clipping. The one Aunt Christina had insisted he take yesterday afternoon. The article about the United Nations guy that she wanted him to send to his father. He supposed she would have felt awkward doing it herself. She could have just sent the article with a short note. Mike supposed her real agenda was slightly different. She wanted Mike to get closer with his father and saw the article as a useful device.

Or maybe he was overthinking it.

Mike reached inside his jacket pocket and as he pulled it out, the Polaroid that Millie gave him fell out onto his lap. He put it back in his jacket, then he unfolded the newspaper article.

The bus was snarled in soul-crushing commuter traffic that was backed all the way up on Delancey Street. He had time to kill before they'd get to the Port Authority. Might as well read the clipping.

As he finished reading the article, Mike got to wondering.

Who was this Waldheim guy really? If what those Jewish groups were saying was true, how the hell did an ex-Nazi get a high-ranking position at the United Nations, of all places?

Mike shrugged. It wasn't that he didn't find the topic interesting; it just wasn't his problem.

He folded the clipping, put it back in his pocket, and peered out the window.

After daydreaming for who knows how long, Mike noticed that the bus had finally pulled up on a concrete incline ramp. It was the one that led to the gargantuan parking terminal at the Port Authority. The driver flicked the bus's interior fluorescent lights on and off, deliberately awakening the groggy passengers. Some growled and complained. They weren't really mad at the driver. He was simply doing his job. It just meant that they were going to have to get back on their feet and face the harsh world again.

Mike made his way down the aisle, down three black rubber steps, and out of the bus.

He walked briskly into the Port Authority Bus Terminal. No matter how many times he had traveled through here, Mike always found it to be an unsettling place. A giant multi-leveled steel labyrinth constructed less like a building and more like a prison.

Mike wondered what first-time visitors to New York City thought when they got off the bus and immediately encountered the building's casual indifference to their very humanity. When they went into the bathrooms and found themselves engulfed in a world filled with homelessness, addiction, and sadness. If he had grown up elsewhere, would he have chosen to live in this city? Looking around the bus station and seeing the quiet desperation all around him, he wasn't so sure.

All of a sudden, Mike felt something brush across his knee and crash into his upper thigh.

He spun around, only to see a family of tourists. From the way they were dressed, Mike assumed they were from the Midwest. One of them, a teenage boy of around sixteen, was carrying a large canvas suitcase and had haphazardly slammed it into Mike's leg.

Mike attempted to make direct eye contact with the kid. But rather than apologize, the teenage boy just yanked down his St. Louis Cardinals hat and just kept on walking. It was as if Mike were invisible to him, a non-entity. He smiled to himself and shook his head. Now here's a kid who has what it takes to make it in this city!

Mike pushed his way past a gaggle of religious cultists, lost souls trying to find their way in a complicated world. He kept on going until he saw the glowing red exit signs.

Rather than try to take the escalator up to street level, Mike opted for the concrete stairs. It was fine. Some exercise would do him good. It would get his blood pumping.

As he walked out onto the street, Mike reflected on how walking out of the Port Authority was like ascending out of Dante's Inferno and into Purgatory. Here, out on the short block of 8th Avenue sandwiched between 40th and 41st Streets, the mid-afternoon summer air stunk of desperation, sweat, and sin. Yellow cabs pulled to the curb at breakneck speed, then sped away, their medallion owning drivers hoping for just another dollar in tips. Mike always got disoriented in this part of town. It didn't matter that he was a native New Yorker. He always ended up walking the wrong way before it dawned on him that he was going in the opposite direction.

This time was no exception. Stopping for a moment at the corner of 8th and 43rd, next to a dingy pizzeria hidden away under layers of scaffolding, Mike realized he should have gone east on 42nd. Not a big deal. He'd just cross over 43rd, then head back down 7th Avenue half a block to the Fulton Theater.

Mike was familiar with the place and knew of its reputation as a place addicts went to score. He had first come across the Fulton while working on a case involving a runaway from an Upper East Side prep school where the boy was on an athletic scholarship. The kid's parents were frantic and the police, per usual, weren't exactly going above and beyond to protect and to serve. It had turned out that the kid—Joey was his name, if Mike was recalling it correctly—had developed an infatuation with Jim Carroll and *The Basketball Diaries*, that late 1970s memoir about heroin and teen rebellion. After getting some leads from a cop he knew working Narcotics, Mike had found the kid strung out at the Fulton watching a rainy afternoon triple feature of blood-soaked celluloid schlock. Mike had looked around the movie theater, observed its particular brand of clientele, and made a mental note of it. That the Fulton was Times Square's premiere destination for those outwardly respectable junkies afraid to head up to Morningside Heights, but not yet quite desperate enough to scrounge around the winding back alleys further downtown.

That had been two years ago. And now Mike was back yet again outside the Fulton. Yet alone this time looking for another person who had gone missing. And this time he knew the guy he was looking for was an addict.

Just then, he heard a man shouting at him.

"Hey, young man. Young man!"

A black dude. Probably around thirty years old. Dressed in a sleeveless white undershirt, red jeans, and Converse high-top sneakers, the guy was handing out paper flyers to passersby. Printed on the bright orange flyers was an advertisement and a discount coupon for "Marvin's Girls," a low-rent topless bar on 40th Street and 10th Avenue.

"Me?" Mike shouted back. "You're calling me young man?"

The guy laughed.

"It's just a phrase, my man. Just a phrase. Here let me give you something special."

The man handed Mike a flier.

Mike took it and promptly folded it, then he tucked it away in his back pocket.

"Thanks, but not for me," he said.

"You never know, man. You might get the urge if you know what I mean. If you go, tell 'em that Jerome sent you. And ask for Candy. She take care of you real good."

Now it was Mike's turn to laugh.

This guy was good. Real good. An authentic street hustler. Would a guy like this have a place on this block if and when the Mayor Koch's neighborhood rehabilitation plan for Times Square came to fruition? Time would tell.

The Fulton had a long history in this very location. Built originally in the 1930s, it had withstood the Depression, provided moviegoers with celluloid escapism during the Second World War, and premiered numerous French New Wave films throughout the 1960s. The building, its white marquee and red lettering, was as intact as ever. But the ownership had changed hands several times over the decades.

Grind house had eclipsed art house. The current moviegoers, with a passion for cinematic sleaze and cheapo horror movies, were an entirely different breed from the bohemian downtown kids who used to spend their Friday nights taking in Michelangelo Antonioni and Federico Fellini films and then discussing them animatedly in the lobby afterward.

The first thing Mike noticed was how utterly dirty the glass doors were. So grimy in fact that he could barely see through them.

Things hardly improved when he walked inside the decaying movie palace and saw how tattered and rancid the carpet was. Even more so than the last time he was here two years ago. It was now covered with cigarette butts, dried up pink chewing gum, and who knows what else. He walked through the lobby to the ticket booth off to the side.

"Tickets are three dollars. You can see whatever movies you want but you have to leave when we close at midnight. I'd recommend the Charles Bronson triple feature in Theater 2. He's a fucking bad ass."

Mike was about to make a sarcastic comment. Something about whether the theater manager looked kindly on his employees eating jumbo pizza slices while on the clock. But he thought better of it. He needed the guy's cooperation for now.

"I'm not here to see a movie," Mike said.

"Then what the hell?" the guy said, wiping greasy fingers on his giant-sized corduroy jeans.

"I need to talk to your boss. Where's his office?"

"What's in it for me?" The guy tilted his head upward, a Cheshire cat grin widening across his face.

Mike reached for his wallet in his back pocket. He took out a pair of dollar bills.

"Is this what you're looking for, friend?"

The guy nodded with approval. His eyes widened, as if he had struck gold.

"Yeah, this could be very helpful," he said.

"I thought as much."

"I'll be right back. Mind the booth for me."

And with that, he was off.

Mike stood in front of the ticket booth. No one came into the Fulton then. Good. It allowed him to avoid an awkward encounter. He wasn't about to sell anyone a ticket.

Several minutes later, the ticket booth guy returned. With him, a creepy looking white guy, over six feet tall, with thick eyeglasses and a misshapen goatee on his chin.

"You wanted to see me?"

"Yeah, I wanted to ask you if you've seen this guy recently?" Mike retrieved the Polaroid from his jacket pocket. He set it down on the counter.

"I might have. I might have, indeed." The manager didn't speak his words, so much as purr them. Another lowlife looking for an extra buck.

Aunt Christina was right. He sure did meet a lot of unsavory characters doing his job.

Mike reached once again for his wallet. This time, he took out a ten-dollar bill. He never felt particularly good about using cash to get things done. But it was the way the world worked. And he would bill Millie for it. It was, after all, a business expense. He held the bill just above the manager's head. A perfectly sliced piece of cheddar; the manager a sniffing mouse yearning for a reward.

"Okay, yeah," the manager said, grabbing the ten-dollar bill from Mike.

"Yeah, what?" Mike said, as he noticed a gaggle of quarrelsome teenagers walking out of one of the theaters and into the lobby.

"I've seen him here many times. But I don't remember when I saw him last. Slipped my mind." He rubbed his filthy goatee as if pondering the wonders of the universe.

Mike reached again for his wallet. He took out a another ten-dollar bill. It was raggedy. Someone had doodled on it with a ballpoint pen.

"That's going to be it for you," Mike said curtly.

"Ha! Okay." The manager's laughter echoed through the lobby. Even though he was paper thin, he had the laugh of a much heftier man.

"He was here yesterday, then he had some business with that fine fellow." The manager tilted his neck to the right, indicating the bustling street outside.

"Who?" Mike asked.

"Take a guess? The black guy handing out flyers. Who else? Be it as it may, I simply have no idea what they might have been discussing. I'm just a businessman trying to make an honest wage. That's all I am."

The manager looked at the ticket booth attendant. He looked right back at his boss. They smiled knowingly.

So that was the deal.

They'd allow junkies in to plop down in their seats for hours at a time, but they wouldn't actually sell the stuff. No. They'd outsource the dirty work to a black guy. Because they knew he wouldn't turn on them if the cops came calling. Mike knew all too well from his time in the DA's office that the arresting officers would always add a few bullshit charges whenever they arrested a colored dealer in Midtown. Just to make sure that even if he wanted to cut a deal, he'd still have to do some time in Rikers.

"Thanks for your time, gentlemen," Mike said.

"Want some popcorn to go?" The ticket booth clerk decided to join in the conversation.

Mike looked over at the concession stand. With liquid butter spilt all over the glass counter and a salt shaker that had been knocked to the floor, it made a fast-food joint at a rest area on the Jersey Turnpike look like a five-star Michelin rated restaurant.

"I'm good. Thanks."

Mike walked through the lobby at a steady clip and headed out the front door.

Had he been deaf and blind, he still would have known he was back out on the street again. The smell alone reminded him.

Just then he felt an unusually cool breeze on his face. The weather had been erratic the past few days. Today was no exception. That was New York City in the summertime for you. One minute, the humidity would saturate your clothing. The next, the rain would soak it like an overflowing washing machine.

Mike looked up, his gaze now squarely focused on the sky above. Several cumulus clouds hung in a darkening sky. It was going to rain, just like it did late last night. But not just yet.

Mike took out the folded orange flyer, the one for Marvin's Girls that the hustler had given him just minutes before. Mike pretended to read it over. Then he walked up next to the guy, who was busy haranguing passersby, hoping to turn complete strangers into clientele.

"Hey man, you need to tell me more about this place." Mike pointed to the flyer.

"Do they have good drink specials?" Mike shouted over the din of a fresh fish delivery truck rattling along the street.

"You been in and out of the movies this quick? Damn."

"What I want is a little different," Mike said, as he leaned in closer to the man who he hoped would lead him to Peter Hesse.

"Oh yeah? Perhaps you don't want Marvin's bitches. They're a little dark for your kind, if you know what I mean? No. You want the white lady? Am I right?"

Mike understood the coded language this dealer was speaking.

"The white lady. That's right," he said, silently reflecting on how much his life had changed since the first day of law school. Here he was, in the middle of Manhattan, pretending that he was in the market for heroin. All to find a missing man who was probably already dead.

"Well, if you got the bread, the white lady can be all yours." The guy didn't seem to be remotely concerned anyone might be eavesdropping. It was as if he was completely used to doing deals in broad daylight. The Fulton probably had the beat cops on their payroll. No wonder that any attempt to clean up this cesspool was futile from the start.

"What if I'm in the market for a white man?" Mike asked. Just then, a balding man carrying a cheap looking briefcase plowed into him on the sidewalk. The guy waddled away without so much as an acknowledgment of their encounter. It was just how people acted in this part of town.

"Son, if you want a white man, that's your own damn business. But I ain't gonna help you. No, sir."

He stomped his foot in disgust.

"Not even if I wanted to find this particular white man?" Mike took the Polaroid out and showed it to the guy. Impatient cabbies stuck in gridlock were honking their horns.

"Ah, you're looking for Mr. Peter," the guy bellowed.

"You know him?" Mike yelled back over the cacophony of traffic, car horns, and now a jackhammer down the street grinding into the asphalt.

"We've done business."

"You know where he is?" Mike asked, noticing a man in a drab grey suit out of the corner of his eye. The guy, of medium build and with a face that looked like it had not been shaved in a day or two, was standing outside one of the XXX theaters that lined the block. Hesitant, as if he were afraid to enter. For some reason, Mike thought the guy might be an undercover vice cop prowling around for someone in particular. Something about his intense posture and his demeanor suggested he didn't belong. But the guy quickly turned around and walked in the opposite direction of the nudie theater and disappeared into the crowd. Probably just another Westchester suburbanite who got cold feet.

"You listening to me, bro?"

"Yeah," Mike said, realizing that for some reason the guy he spotted had distracted him from the task at hand.

"How do I know you're not the fuzz?"

"Do I look like a cop?" Mike asked.

The guy laughed. It was borderline insulting.

"I'm just playing." The guy put his tattooed arm around Mike's shoulder. It smelled like sweat and malt liquor.

"I just need to know where he is," Mike said.

"I have these spells you see. These mental spells. Where I forget things that I should know. Terrible disease."

"Is that so?"

"It is. But you know what always helps?"

"An aspirin?" Mike said sarcastically.

"Haha. My man. No. What helps is taking two Andrew Jacksons and a glass of water. You dig?" The guy scratched at his crotch.

Everyone wanted one thing in this city. Money. It was no different among the denizens on the street than it was among the Hugo Boss-attired executives on Park Avenue just east of them. People's desires, their values, their hopes and their dreams were all tied up with money. Was the Fulton's operation really that different from a boiler room outfit that fleeced investors out of millions? If someone had posed Mike the same question five years ago, he would have of course said they're completely different. No question about it. One is white-collar crime that doesn't immediately impact public safety. The other is street crime that does. Now he wasn't so sure. But then again, that was true about a lot of things these days. Everything was topsy turvy now.

Mike once again reached for his wallet. Another business expense that Millie would have to pick up the tab for. He took out two crisp tens and handed them to the dealer.

"Okay. He's been with this girl who hooks on this block. She's a white girl. I mean, a real white girl. You know what I mean? Looks like she's about twenty or so. And they both shacked up at the Big Apple Hotel in Chelsea."

"How do you know this?" Mike asked.

"Because, my man," the guy said, gripping Mike's shoulder uncomfortably tight, "I did a special delivery to them both earlier this morning. I'm like FedEx."

Five minutes later and over forty dollars poorer, Mike was on the 1 train heading downtown to Chelsea.

Time to find Peter Hesse.

This was proving to be a very easy case. Mike thought that maybe once all this was over and done with, he'd even have time to hit the gym. Pumping iron would do him some good. Maybe even get him out of his current funk.

As the subway train careened under Manhattan, Mike's thoughts returned to Emma Schneiderman. What did she do when she got home from campus? Did she have anyone to talk to—to really talk to? If his time in the DA's office and as a PI had taught him anything, it was that there were millions of Emma Schneidermans in the city. Lonely, unfulfilled people going through the motions of life, but without any life left within them.

All he knew was that he didn't want to end up like that. Not if he could help it.

The train rattled on.

CHAPTER 4

When he knocked on the door to Room 12 at the sleazy Big Apple Hotel, Mike was all but certain what he was going to find.

Deep in his gut, it was more than a feeling.

It was a premonition.

Somehow, he just knew that when the door creaked open, he would find Peter Hesse. But that the man he had been paid to find would no longer be among the living. That the final chapter of the community college professor's life had already been written in a filthy hotel room.

How right he was.

What was done was done and it couldn't be reversed.

There was no sense denying the tragic reality of the situation. Peter Hesse was sprawled dead on the floor, his haggard face caked with blood. A large-handled kitchen knife protruded from his chest, enveloping the entire scene in horror.

Mike immediately noticed there was a third person in the room.

Kneeling on the floor between Hesse and a rickety nightstand was a girl no older than twenty-one. Dressed in a man's undershirt that clung to her skin and polka-dotted boxer shorts which nearly reached her knees. She looked like one of those Upper East Side girls who had had grown up way too fast. Her blanched face was a soggy mixture of cheap drug store mascara and tears. Although dazed and confused, she was—unlike Hesse—very much alive.

She focused a laser-like gaze on Mike. Mike stared back. She shrieked, as if calling up from the depths of hell. It was a cry of despair that could have awakened the dead.

But the dead don't wake up.

Peter Hesse's bloody corpse was just as motionless as it had been seconds before.

The young girl's screaming wasn't without consequence.

It accomplished one thing—alerting the desk manager. Indicating to him that all was not well in his tawdry little kingdom. He surely had already phoned the cops. Mike reckoned they were on their way this very second, lights on and sirens blaring.

He stepped further inside the room, proceeding with caution through the door.

Before he even noticed the chipped paint on the walls and the cheap ramshackle bed, his nose took in the putrid smell that filled the cramped space. It reeked less of sin and more of despair.

Mike inched closer to the body. But not too close. He knew better than to contaminate a crime scene. Let alone actually touch a corpse before the cops arrived. He merely wanted to get a closer look for himself.

He examined the body.

It was Hesse sure enough.

No case of mistaken identity here. Even if he hadn't seen the man's face, there was always the fraternity ring from the photograph to identify him. For on the carpet was Peter Hesse's outstretched left hand. And on one scraped and bloodied finger was a brass ring with a ruby red stone insert. The very same ring. The one that once belonged to a much happier man, his arm wrapped lovingly around his young wife's shoulder.

"What the hell happened here?" Mike asked.

"I didn't do anything," the girl said, her soft voice cracking through a bevy of tears. "I went out for a pack of smokes, got back, and just found him like this. I swear. It wasn't me! It wasn't me!"

"What's your name?" Mike asked.

"What's my name? Why does it matter?"

"It just does."

"Julia," she said, after hesitating for a few more seconds.

"All right Julia. Get your ass off the floor and onto the bed!" Mike barked in an authoritarian tone. He could hardly believe his own voice. That he was capable of such verbal ferocity.

The girl who called herself Julia complied.

After all, what real choice did she have?

Shuffling her petite frame across the cluttered room, she took another look at the body. She gagged and proceeded to vomit all over the small pile of men's clothing strewn on the floor at the end of the bed. Wiping her face, Julia plopped herself down on the bed. It creaked and moaned.

She then buried her head in her trembling hands.

"I'm so fucked," she said, then repeated it as if for emphasis.

Mike looked down at the pile of rumpled clothes, now coated in the girl's vomit.

Yet among the clothes, Mike noticed what appeared to be an empty tan leather wallet. It had to be Peter Hesse's. That was the most logical possibility.

Fighting back his disgust, Mike bent down and got on his knees.

Careful not to touch the wallet lest he add his fingerprints to the crime scene, he took a closer look. It gaped open. It seemed as if someone had ruffled through it, stripping it of its contents. Who knew how much cash Peter Hesse had with him? It could have been a little. It could have been a lot. Whatever the amount, it was long gone now.

Just then, Mike heard a flurry of activity in the hallway outside the dingy room. The unmistakable sound of heavy footsteps echoed in his ears.

"NYPD! Open up!" shouted a gruff voice in the hallway just outside the room.

It was followed the sound of a gloved fist pounding on the door.

"I'm a PI. There's a body in here and a girl. No one is armed," Mike bellowed.

"Open the fucking door! Do it now!"

Carefully, slowly, Mike turned the door handle and opened the door.

Knowing how trigger-happy cops were in this neighborhood, Mike immediately put his hands atop his head, the way police officers liked to see. He didn't need to be shot by some disgruntled street cop, one whose wife nagged him earlier that morning. One who was now just itching now for a legal kill to let out some of his anger.

The first cop to push his way through the door was baby-faced, with deep blue Irish eyes. He had the physique of a college wrestler and sergeant stripes on his uniform.

Mike immediately noticed that the cop's right hand was tightly grasping his service revolver. Thankfully, he just didn't fit the profile of the cop Mike feared most. The one who would shoot first and ask questions later.

"Arms up against the wall," the cop barked.

Without so much as a moment's hesitation, Mike followed the cop's instructions to the letter.

He pressed his sweaty palms against the wall and spread his legs shoulder length apart. He knew the procedure. The blue-eyed cop or one of his partners would soon be patting down Mike to look for any weapons or contraband.

Three more uniformed boys in blue rushed into the room.

"Who's the girl?"

"You ask her," Mike replied. He did not even know which cop even asked the question.

Two of the other uniformed cops yanked the still crying girl off the bed and patted her down. Once they realized she posed no real threat to them, they allowed her to plop back down on the mattress, her small body nearly causing the cheap bedframe to collapse.

"I need to know what the hell is going on here," the cop in command barked. "Because it looks like I've got two prime suspects for murder on my hands."

One of the cops, who Mike took to be Puerto Rican, began his standard pat down.

"He's clean, Sergeant," the cop said, as he turned to the first cop who had come through the door. "But I found this."

He handed Mike's wallet to his superior. In it was his PI license. The piece of plastic he kept right in front of his driver's license. Just in case he ever faced a situation exactly like this.

"Ok," the blue-eyed sergeant said to the Puerto Rican cop. Then he turned his attention to Mike. "I've got a lot of time. But not a lot of patience. And you're going to have to explain to me what this is all about." He pointed to body on the floor and the crying girl on the bed.

Mike took a deep breath and steeled himself for what lay ahead.

It was going to be a long night.

□ □ □

"Hey chief! I thought you might want this."

The door swung open. Detective Tony Doran strolled back into the interrogation room like a panther on the prowl. Tall and muscular with tan skin, his eyes reflected a youthful intensity that hadn't dimmed with time.

Tony moved closer to Mike. He set a white Styrofoam cup filled with black coffee on the table between them.

Mike picked it up and took an eager sip. The liquid felt like heaven in his parched mouth. Not surprising. Given that he had spent the past few hours repeating the same details of the crime scene to a parade of inquisitive homicide detectives. Nothing like talking non-stop to make your mouth as dry as the Arizona desert.

To needle Tony, Mike said, "God, this is vile. My great-aunt would curse you in Norwegian for giving me something as putrid as this. And, being a good Christian, she doesn't even curse." He grinned and set the cup back down on the table in front of him.

"Our very best, but I know it's not as good as what you have at your fancy PI digs, Mike. We're public servants here. Remember?" Doran asked.

Mike remembered all right.

How when he was a young prosecutor fresh out of law school, he had been assigned to work on a closed missing persons case. Closed because the girl had been found, but barely alive. The perp who snatched her, a balding middle-aged fish market worker, had been apprehended and was facing charges of kidnapping and aggravated assault. The supervising ADA had told Mike to work closely with a freshly minted detective from Staten Island named Anthony Doran.

Tony for short.

Mike and Tony had ended up spending hours working the case together, making sure that each and every piece of evidence was properly gathered, accounted for, and prepared for trial.

What the two men bonded over was deeper than law and order.

If Mike thought that his mixed heritage was unusual, Tony's was even less common. The son of an Irish-Italian father from Staten Island and a black mother originally from Jamaica, Tony had never been fully accepted by either side of his family. More than once did he hear his paternal cousins refer to him with racial epithets. And his maternal grandmother never quite understood who he was.

His greatest ambition was following in his father's footsteps by joining the NYPD. At some point, Tony had given up deciding whether he was white or whether he was black.

He had settled on Blue.

When they worked together, Mike and Tony had ended up continuing their work late at night at the Good Eats Restaurant on Chambers Street, just a few blocks from City Hall. Jokes about their late nights together became fodder for interoffice hazing, with Doran's commanding officer mockingly nicknaming them "the lovebirds." At that time, neither Mike nor Tony had minded that much.

Both men knew that they were working in a pressure cooker of an environment. That the hardnosed men who worked these types of jobs had to blow off steam somehow.

They were green, so they were a target.

But all that had changed when they put together so solid a case that the jury had found the accused guilty on all counts within thirty minutes. At that point, both of them had become stars; a future in public service had seemed bright for both of them.

How times had changed.

While Doran had moved up the ranks burying the unpleasant memories of his youth deep inside, Mike had fallen out of favor with the powers that be and had been delivered a stark choice. Either start cutting some corners and upping his plea deal rate or find work elsewhere. And by cutting corners, the newly minted supervising ADA didn't mean slight nips and tucks here and there. He meant wholesale violations of legal ethics. All to please the real estate titans who were demanding that Midtown be cleaned up before they started investing their time and money into big projects that promised the city a plentiful stream of tax revenue.

So, faced with that choice, Mike, no longer the idealistic youthful crusader for justice he had been when he first met Doran, had resigned. And using what he had learned on the job, had started his one-man private investigations firm in a shabby space office that his friend Barry helped him procure.

That was two years ago.

Now he was sitting in an interrogation room at One Police Plaza as a person of interest in the ongoing homicide investigation into the death of a deadbeat and junkie named Peter Hesse.

Doran had never thought for a second that Mike was involved. He had pulled a few strings with Homicide. Those guys were always demanding favors so it was only natural that Doran would eventually call in a couple of chits. It got Mike out of the hothouse custody of the Homicide Division and into that of the Missing Persons Bureau. At least here, he'd be watched out for by Doran. Back in Homicide, they didn't know his backstory. And even if they had, it was entirely doubtful that it would have worked out well for him.

"Can you at least tell me what in the hell time it is?" Mike asked.

Doran shook his head. "You know I am not supposed to do that. We keep clocks out of the interrogation room for a reason."

"Well, fuck me then."

Mike threw his hands up in the air.

"I suppose that's why you took my watch," he said.

"Yeah, but you can get it back when you leave," Tony said.

"It's a new Casio watch I just bought. Hopefully it doesn't accidentally go missing."

Mike noticed Doran was now looking directly at him, a look that told him that he was close to stepping over the line.

Tony relaxed and said, "If you really need to know, it's getting close to 2 AM."

"Is it really? That late?" Mike asked wearily.

"These rooms are like hospitals. You never have an idea of how fast time is passing outside."

"That's fucked up."

Mike buried his head in his hands. His brain ached from the constant buzzing of the cheap fluorescent lights. It was like being in a psych ward.

Just then, the door swung open again.

This time, it was the blue-eyed sergeant from the Big Apple Hotel. The one who had taken Mike into custody as a material witness close to ten hours earlier. The one responsible for the hunger pains in his stomach and the putrid coffee residue on his tongue.

"We found him, detective," the sergeant said.

"And?" Doran asked.

"O.D." The cop spoke in a tone bereft of emotion. Clearly, he had seen drug users croak from their habits before.

Doran nodded. "Ah, that's none too surprising."

Mike, sitting quietly, looked at the cop. Then right back at Doran, who staunchly refused to make any direct eye contact with Mike for the time being.

"Yeah, we found the money too. The cash he took from the body. Logged it in as evidence about twenty minutes ago."

"Homicide is happy?"

The cop snorted laughter. "Yeah, they're downright pissing themselves with joy."

"Got it. Thanks for letting me know."

Nodding, the sergeant left the interrogation room.

Mike, once again alone with Doran, wasn't shy about asking whether this meant that he was free to go.

"Mind explaining to me what the hell is going on?" Mike asked.

Doran smiled. He knew he wasn't supposed to divulge any details of the case to Mike. But he wasn't going to let official rules stop him. Not that anyone would really care. Not in a case like this.

"So, as it turns out, we found a good set of prints on the knife. The one stuck in Hesse. And we were able to trace it to a guy in the system. Some loser vagrant half-wit who saw an opportunity to steal some cash from someone just down and out as he was. You know the type."

Mike wasn't exactly sure what Doran meant by that last remark, but he found himself nodding in agreement anyway. It was always best to play along for the moment and figure things out afterward.

"Well," Doran continued. "We were able to find a temporary address for the guy. He was living in a crappy studio apartment down the block from that rathole you found the body in."

"I see," Mike said.

"Well," Doran laughed. "He wasn't exactly living, if you catch my drift."

"He's the one who overdosed?"

Doran scratched his face. "Heroin. Likely that he stole a few hundred dollars from Hesse and used it to buy a shit-ton of dope. Then he had himself a little party. And well, the rest is history."

Mike leaned forward and picked up the coffee, taking a sip. Cold, it tasted awful. He put it right back down.

"And the girl?"

"She's not in the system as far as we can tell. But her prints weren't on the knife. I think she was telling the truth. She went out for cigarettes and came back and found him like that."

"You're not going to charge her with anything?"

"Me?" Doran asked.

"Whoever has the case."

"Nah. I mean, as you know, someone could easily make a case for prostitution. But who's gonna bother?"

"So, you let her go?" Mike asked.

"That's what I said, wasn't it?" Doran genuinely sounded angry at that moment. As if he and Mike didn't have a history of working together.

"Yeah, I guess it is," Mike said quietly.

"Anyway, tell me about yourself," Doran said, sensing the awkwardness in the room.

Mike looked up. "Me?"

"I assume this is the first case in which your missing person turned up dead. Unless I'm missing something."

Mike realized he hadn't had a moment to process that. That this was his first case that had ended in murder. It wasn't the first time he had seen a body—his work as an ADA got him into more than a few grisly crime scenes—but it was the first time that he was involved in a homicide investigation as a private citizen. It was as if he had crossed an invisible line. One that separated itself from the mundane investigations he had been specializing in for the past two years. He was in uncharted territory now. And with that realization, he had another one. He was going to have to tell Millie Johnson that her husband was no longer among the living. That is, unless the cops had already done so in their typically awkward fashion.

Doran picked up the coffee cup from the table and threw it in the trash. Then he looked at Mike. But without making direct eye contact. "Well, you are free to go. I'm sorry it had to be this way."

Mike opened his mouth to speak, but he didn't have the words. Was Doran speaking about this particular night? Or how Mike's career had taken a giant nosedive since the first time he and Doran had worked a case together?

"No problem, Tony."

"We should catch up for a drink sometime."

"Sure. That would be fine," Mike said, without much emotion in his voice.

"Go home. Get some sleep. You look exhausted."

"Yes, Dad," Mike said sarcastically.

"I mean it," Doran said, "you could use a good night's rest after all this. Take the next day off if you can."

Mike smiled. He knew that even if Doran had seen him on one of his better days, that he'd still have looked tired. It was just like when he had seen the reflection of himself in Aunt Christina's silver tray. Upon first glance, Mike looked normal. But upon closer inspection, he knew that he looked depleted.

"One last thing," Tony said.

"Yeah. What's that?" Mike asked.

"I was surprised anyone gave a damn about your dead guy. Most junkies don't have anyone. This one had a wife. Makes him a little better than the rest, I suppose."

"I suppose," Mike replied.

□ □ □

Ten minutes later, Mike, despite his constantly yawning and feeling as if he might collapse any second, was relishing his newfound status as a free man. Before leaving, he had retrieved his watch and other belongings from the desk sergeant at the station house. Sitting in a red faux-leather booth at the Rhodes Diner in Chelsea, he quickly polished off a plate of scrambled eggs, buttered toast, and pork sausage links.

Mike always found diners in the middle of the night to have a surreal aura to them. They were gathering places for truck drivers, insomniacs, drunks, and lonely drifters alike. All looking for some momentary brightness in the midst of the darkness. Just a lot of people sitting alone wishing they were somewhere else with someone else. All except the punk kids who had decided to stay out way past the time their concerts had ended. They always traveled in packs and made themselves as conspicuous as possible.

Mike looked at the clock on the wall. Just past 3 AM. It was far past time to get some sleep. The way his day had been, who knew what tomorrow would bring? In the meantime, no matter how much he tried, he simply couldn't get the image of Room 12 out of his mind. The body, the crying girl, and the knife. And for some reason, that pile of clothes on the floor. The one a young girl named Julia had emptied the contents of her stomach on.

Mike pushed his breakfast plate toward the other end of the Formica tabletop. His appetite had vanished. He dropped a dollar bill on the table as a tip, got up, and walked into the dewy morning air.

A garbage truck rumbled down the street behind him. The smell of trash was unmistakable.

CHAPTER 5

Located on the corner of 85th and 3rd, the Salonika Diner, with its neon pink sign and chrome interior, was a neighborhood institution.

Everyone in Yorkville, from the bored housewives waiting for their husbands to come home from Wall Street to the local delivery men who occasionally had trysts with said women, knew of it and of its history. How the owner, a gregarious older man from northern Greece had opened it in the 1950s after fleeing the violence of the Greek Civil War. How it had withstood the decades of rapid change in this formerly German immigrant neighborhood by serving both traditional Greek delicacies as well as American comfort food.

Two days after his ordeal at the police station, Mike had decided it would be a good place to catch up with his law school classmate and landlord's son, Barry Stein.

Barry was not exactly overweight. But he was the type of guy who would wake up one day in his fifties, discover old clothes in the attic, and wonder how it was possible that he had ever fit into them. Mediterranean in appearance, with thick curly black hair and bronzed skin, he always seemed to be wearing the same outfit. A light blue collared shirt over a crisp white undershirt.

His sartorial choices tonight were no exception.

Mike had first met Barry when they were assigned to the same section in their first-year law school courses. Be it Contracts, Property, Constitutional Law, or Civil Procedure, Mike found himself in the same classroom with Barry. One day, when Barry had dared to make a snarky comment to an obnoxious professor, the whole class had gasped. After the class had ended, Mike formally introduced himself to Barry. He had told him how much he appreciated someone willing to challenge the old coot. Mike liked him. As the semester progressed, they had bonded over somewhat similar backgrounds. Both had working-class Jewish fathers who had moved up the socio-economic ladder. Mike's father in the garment industry; Barry's in real estate.

Unlike most law school friendships, theirs lasted well past graduation.

Both men shared similar career trajectories. Both had ended their legal careers prematurely. Mike because of the internal politics of the DA's office. Barry because he saw greener pastures elsewhere and had jumped at the opportunity of a lifetime. That is, for a man who wanted nothing more than to see his name in print. Through a connection he had with his now ex-wife, he had gotten to know one of the owners of the *New York Globe*. This owner had promptly taken a liking to him, and had offered him the position as the paper's latest legal affairs correspondent. Which was where he now worked.

Over dinner, Mike had explained to Barry what he had been up to the past several days. He had skirted around his official policy of never revealing a client's personal information by changing the names and some of the details. To protect the innocent. Just like they did in those crime shows back in the 1950s. When Mike had finished his story, right down to his quasi-interrogation at the hands of his former colleague Tony Doran, he took a sip of his now lukewarm coffee and set it down on the table. At first, there was just silence.

Barry, always savvy at reading facial expressions, spoke the obvious.

"That's quite a story."

"I thought you'd be interested," Mike said, as he tapped the last remnants of the glass ketchup bottle onto his French fries.

Barry put down his turkey club. He took a sip of his Tab straight from the can.

"Yeah, I'm definitely interested. On a personal basis, that is. It doesn't sound like it's anything my boss would find particularly compelling. But, yeah, you're like a true to life detective now."

Mike laughed. "Is that what it takes though? Finding a body?"

"Doesn't hurt," Barry smiled. He grabbed several white paper napkins from the stainless-steel napkin dispenser at the far end of the table.

"Also, who said I was trying to pitch you a story?"

"Weren't you?" Barry replied, a sly grin on his face.

Just then, the attractive Greek waitress reappeared.

"Can I get you guys anything else?" she asked.

Mike noticed Barry couldn't keep his eyes off her.

"I think we're good," Mike said.

"You know what?" Barry interrupted. "I think I could use another Tab."

"Ok," she said, smiling. As she walked away, Mike noticed Barry's eyes were still lingering on her.

"So just to be clear. We're chasing after immigrant waitresses, now? Is that how it is?" Mike asked.

Barry grinned.

"It is what it is."

"You really have no shame," Mike said.

"On that note," Barry said with a widening smile on his face. He got up from the table and walked to the rear of the diner where the restrooms were.

Mike could see that Barry was going to be gone for some time. There was a line at the bathroom door. This was more usual than not at the Salonika. The food was terrific, the service was hit or miss, and the restroom situation was a disaster. It was almost a certainty that at least one of the bathrooms would be out of order and that the other one—the good one—would have a faulty sink. It made one wonder how clean the hands of the kitchen staff were. But it was best to push those thoughts to the recesses of one's mind.

Looking around the diner, Mike noticed a copy of today's *New York Times* on the counter. Someone must have left it there. Mike got up from the booth, walked over to retrieve it, and sat back down.

He quickly read the headlines, then he scanned the Sports page (the Mets had won again, thanks to their strong pitching staff). For no particular reason, Mike turned to the Business Section.

The lead story caught his eye.

It was a story about how a reclusive wealthy industrialist named Samuel Bennington had decided to take his chemical company public. All the market analysts were apparently saying that this was an incredibly bold, but risky move. Some contrarian business professor at Fordham, however, was quoted as saying that it could turn out surprisingly well for him. Or it could ruin both his reputation and his finances. The article also quoted a low-level official in the Reagan Administration who said something about how Bennington's bold vision was the type of entrepreneurial capitalism that America was founded upon. And that Bennington's willingness to take risks was not a reckless gamble, but rather something that should be celebrated.

Mike set down the *Times* and shut his eyelids.

He still hadn't caught up from sleep he had lost in the past couple of days. To say that a lot had happened was an understatement. After he had gotten home from his long night at the police station, it had taken him only seconds to fall into a deep sleep. But it did not last long. A few hours later, he was wide awake.

Millie Johnson had been on his mind. He was sure that the cops had told her the tragic news about her husband's death, but he knew it was his professional duty—not to mention an ethical one—to tell his client what he'd witnessed. That her beloved college professor husband had been found dead in a seedy hotel room. Not alone. But with a young prostitute. And his death appeared to be a robbery-homicide committed by one junkie against another. Mike had spoken with bereaved families many times over the years, but this time it just hit differently. Somehow this missing person case felt more tragic than all the others.

Maybe it was because, at some level, he saw a little bit of himself in Peter Hesse.

And that scared him.

Thankfully, the phone call hadn't lasted long. Millie was crying when he called her from home. He told her what she already knew. He told her he'd be in touch in a week or so to go over the necessary paperwork to close out the case. And he told her that he was truly sorry for her loss.

"Well, that took fucking forever."

Barry's voice snapped Mike right out of his reverie.

"What?" Mike asked, as he watched Barry plop back down across from him in the booth.

"I was saying the line took forever. They really have to do something with their bathrooms. This shit is ridiculous."

"Oh, yeah," Mike said, his mind drifting back to the crime scene, back to the orange carpet upon which Hesse lay dead. He worried that he might never rid his mind of the grisly scene. Not just of the images. But of the smell. He hadn't noticed it at the time, not on a conscious level anyway. But the room had stunk of sadness and desperation. And then there was the crying girl. Julia. He couldn't get her out of his mind.

"Mike," Barry said, his tone noticeably more serious, "I'm going to be honest with you. I think you're going to need to find something more fulfilling to do than running all over town looking for deadbeats and junkies."

Mike, once again abruptly dragged out of his daydreaming, scratched his forehead. He ran his index finger over his facial scar.

"How do you mean?"

"It's just that you could do better," Barry said.

"Better? Explain."

Barry leaned across the table, nearly knocking over his Tab can, while positioning himself closer, catlike, to Mike.

"I just think you were meant for bigger things, Mike. That's all."

"That's all?" Mike said, laughing.

"What?"

Mike laughed again. "Bigger things? I'm supposed to save the world? I can't even hold down a job at the Manhattan DA's office."

"Oh, so we're we back to that again?" Barry asked, grabbing a sad looking cold French fry from Mike's plate.

Mike shook his head. It wasn't exactly a look of disgust. So much as much as one that said, "you best stop talking now" and "hands off my food."

"All right, whatever," Barry said, clearly sensing Mike's unwillingness to continue this line of discussion.

"What's that you've found?" he continued, pointing to the Business Section of the *Times*.

"Oh, this?" Mike said. "I was reading this article about some company that's going public soon."

Barry snatched the paper and began reading it, his mouth silently enunciating the words as he read.

"You looking to get rich?" Mike asked sarcastically.

Barry smiled. "It's interesting to me. That's all. Sometimes, I wish I'd taken more corporate law classes back in the day."

"Yeah, so you'd be working like a dog all day and all night. Checking documents for misplaced commas and semi-colons. All so companies and their executives can make even more money."

"Welcome to the 80s," Barry said. "Or haven't you heard?"

"I've heard."

"I wonder how our classmates who got reeled in by the big firms are faring these days," Mike said.

"Say," Barry said, his mind suddenly jumping to the next topic. "Didn't your old nemesis, Lawrence Van Orden, used to work for some big corporate hellhole in Midtown?"

Mike leaned back. "Yeah, I think so. I haven't thought about that guy in years. Remember when you once called him Larry instead of Lawrence? How he threw a fit. Everything had to be so formal with him. Even back then."

"What can I say? He was always a prick. Probably born one too," Barry replied.

"You know I think he's in Washington now. Or so I've heard," Mike said.

"Yeah, he's some sort of power broker, wheeler-dealer sort. That is what I hear. I don't know if he's officially even employed in the Administration, but he definitely has high-level connections. He just does these three martini lunches. Maybe he's a registered lobbyist, but I don't really know," Barry responded.

"I could see him as a lobbyist. A sleazy one to be sure. The type of guy who makes all the young female interns feel jumpy around him," Mike said.

"Life is funny," Barry said. "You catch him for cheating the first year of law school and now he's a power broker with an expense account while schmucks like us eat at a diner."

"What's wrong with this place?" Mike asked.

"Nothing," Barry replied.

"They're all crooks in Washington," Mike said, before he realized he was starting to sound just like his father.

"You could have turned him in to the Dean."

"I did," Mike said.

"You did what?"

"I turned him in. Dean Taylor took an official report, but then buried it. Apparently, his father was a legacy and liked to give money to the school."

"But Taylor filled out a whole report detailing the incident?" Barry asked.

"He did, indeed," Mike said.

"And what became of it?"

"Nothing."

"Really? I think there's likely more to the story than that. You can't bullshit a bullshitter."

Mike grinned. It was a grin Barry knew all too well.

A grin that acknowledged that, even back then, Mike was more than capable of playing hardball when he needed to. If he had to, he could.

"Remember that thin blonde girl who worked in the Dean's office?"

"Remember? I tried to get her to go out to dinner with me!"

"Tried is the operative word here, Barry," Mike said.

Barry threw his hands up in the air. "Well, what about her?"

"Her name is Sally Solberg and I went to elementary school with her in Bay Ridge."

"Ah, yes, I always forget you are Norwegian."

"Half," Mike said.

"So?"

"Well, I convinced Sally to make a Xerox copy of the disciplinary report. The one that Taylor buried. Just for leverage. I wasn't about to let Lawrence beat me out for a summer internship by cheating again."

Barry grinned.

"You sly dog, you," Barry said, wagging his finger in a mock scolding fashion.

Mike stretched his arms out and raised them over his head.

"I never said I was that innocent," he said.

"I never thought you were," Barry replied. "What did you end up doing with the report?"

"You know me," Mike said. "I'm a packrat. I save everything."

"Speaking of, I remember hearing something else through the grapevine about Larry," Barry said.

"What's that?" Mike asked.

"You're not going to believe this, but apparently he's seriously considering a Senate run in our beloved state."

"You got to be shitting me."

Barry smiled mischievously.

"It's what I heard. That his Dad is willing to bankroll his campaign and that he's got a few heavy hitters in DC willing to go to bat for him. How he has integrity. Apparently, he's working to clean up his image and reinvent himself as the paragon of virtue. Run as an honest, family values candidate. The religious right loves him."

"He is such a scumbag. I wonder what they'd think if they knew he cheated his way in law school."

"You really hate his guts."

"I do. I plan to never see or talk to him ever again."

"What if he becomes Senator Van Orden and you need his assistance someday?" Barry prodded.

"Fuck that," Mike replied, before falling quiet.

"Hey, Mike," Barry said. "I gotta ask you. How come you never told me any of this shit before. About Dean Taylor and Sally and all that."

"I dunno. No reason I guess," Mike said. "It just never came up."

"Obviously he's still on your mind," Barry said. "He lives rent free in your head. It's like you've got an extra tenant in your office," Barry laughed.

"Don't be asshole," Mike said.

□ □ □

Ten minutes later, Mike and Barry were on their way to an Irish bar they had both frequented in law school. As they walked up Second Avenue, Barry attempted to regale Mike with his latest romantic conquests. Mike heard the words Barry spoke, but nothing registered.

He was too immersed in his own thoughts.

Even in death, Peter Hesse wouldn't leave Mike alone.

He was all Mike could think about it. How far that man must have fallen. To take your final breath in a cheap hotel room seemed to him to be such an unbearably horrible fate. Just horrible.

Barry playfully nudged him.

They had arrived at their destination.

Sandwiched between a Kosher bakery and a laundry run by a hardened immigrant family from the Chinese interior, The Shamrock had an interior dark in luminescence, yet airy and light in spirit. With wood-paneled booths on one side and a long bar with stools on the other, it was a place where neither solitary day drinkers nor groups of work friends felt unwelcome.

Mike and Barry found empty seats in a back booth, close to a small elevated stage where musical acts performed. Several minutes after they ordered onion rings and beers, a brawny white guy with arms covered in colorful tattoos walked up on the elevated stage.

"Ladies and gentlemen," he said, in an Irish brogue as thick as smoke in the air, "we're pleased to announce that tonight we have a special treat for you. In just a few moments, the Callahan Sisters will be right here on this stage performing for you."

The bar's patrons clapped and whistled.

"I guess these ladies are famous," Mike said.

"They're huge in Cork," Barry said dryly.

"Is that a thing?"

Barry laughed. "How should I know?"

The lights dimmed and the band took the stage. Two women, both probably in their early twenties. They were accompanied by a lanky fiddle player and a heavyset older man with a tin whistle. As the Callahan Sisters started to sing to their musical accompaniment, Mike noticed Barry was looking at a young woman. She was standing alone by the bar.

Typical Barry.

Mike noticed Barry was waving at the woman.

What the hell? Why was he being so obvious?

But then she waved back.

All of a sudden, Mike realized that she might be someone Barry actually knew. Not a complete stranger. Mike looked over. The woman was now walking over to their table.

"A friend?" Mike said, his voice barely audible over the music.

Barry merely nodded.

Less than a minute later, the woman sat down in the booth next to Barry. She planted a soft platonic kiss on his flushed right cheek. Mike couldn't make out what they were saying, but the conversation seemed friendly. Vaguely professional even.

Definitely not romantic.

That was a good thing.

This lady friend of Barry's was one of the more physically attractive women Mike had seen in some time. She would have been stunning, even if she were wearing nothing fancier than a white blouse and a pair of torn blue jeans. Delicately feminine, but with a hardened edge that belied hidden anguish, she radiated a certain type of rebelliousness often found in twentysomething women who chose to make a life for themselves in a dangerous city. Her olive skin, shoulder length curly brunette hair, and chestnut-colored eyes all gave her an exotic look. She could just as easily be taken for Sicilian, Greek perhaps. Or Israeli.

It was in her accent though, that her origins were revealed. For when she spoke, there was no mistaking that she was a Long Island girl.

The band finally stopped playing and left the stage.

It was then that Barry formally introduced his friend to Mike.

"Mike, I want you to meet Katie Rosenfeld. She's a copy editor at my paper."

Katie outstretched her hand across the table.

"Nice to meet you," Mike said. He immediately noticed the silver rings adorning her hand. That and how warm her hand felt.

Katie curled her thin lips upward. "Nice to meet you, Mike."

"So, what do you say? Another round of drinks?" Barry asked.

"Definitely," Mike said, attempting to negotiate just the right amount of eye contact with Katie.

Too little and he'd appear aloof and socially inept; too much and he'd put all his cards on the table far too soon. It didn't help matters that she had a certain intensity in her eyes. One that bespoke a strength and a wildness disproportionate to her petite frame.

Barry raised his palm. He tried to grab the attention of one of the two red-headed waitresses working that evening. It didn't take long for one of them to come over to their booth.

"Another round, guys?" she asked, her hands placed casually on her hips.

"Actually, I'll have a Guinness this time. Three pints. One for each of us," Barry said, pointing to both Katie and Mike.

The waitress turned around. She headed back to the bar.

"So, what do you do, Mike?" Katie asked.

"It's really not that interesting," Mike said.

"Oh, come on!" Katie exclaimed, a curious smile on her face.

"He's a PI. A private detective! Would you believe that?" Barry said, nearly snorting with laughter.

Katie leaned forward.

"He's kidding, right?" Her voice tingled in Mike's ears.

"No," Mike said, glaring at his friend.

"He's not joking. I work as a private investigator. Like Barry, I went to law school, but ended up in a career outside the legal profession."

"He's just like me." Barry said, the whiskey clearing getting to his head.

"Except I'm not Swedish."

"Norwegian," Mike said dryly.

"Really what's the difference?" Barry replied.

"Wait. You're Norwegian?" Katie asked, her emphasis on that word. *Norwegian.* As if it signified something important. That it meant something.

"My Mom is," Mike said, before pausing for a few long seconds. "Was."

"Oh," Katie whispered, a bit embarrassed.

"His Dad is like us, though," Barry said.

"Member of the Tribe?" Katie asked, taking a long drag on her cigarette.

"Indeed," Mike said.

"Where did your family come from?" Katie asked.

"Canarsie."

She laughed. "That's not what I meant."

"Originally?"

"Yeah."

"Latvia," Mike said. "No wait. Lithuania. I think."

"You think?" Katie said, her eyes widening.

"I don't really know, to be honest. I'd have to ask my Dad. I don't really care about all that stuff. Why does it matter? Ya know?"

At that very moment, the waitress returned and set three frothing pints of Guinness down on the table.

"Anyway, that's so totally rad about you being a private detective," Katie said.

"It's not all that exciting, truth be told," Mike said.

"Do you carry a gun?" Katie asked, her eyes widening at the possibility that she was in the presence of potentially dangerous man.

Mike shook his head.

"No. For the type of cases I work on, I don't need to."

Katie nodded.

"Well, you seem like you're tough enough." She smiled.

"He's real tough guy, this one," Barry said. "Even has a scar to prove it."

Katie looked closely at Mike's face.

"I hadn't noticed," she said.

"Just a stupid thing from when I fenced in college."

At that moment, Mike wished for nothing more than for Barry to disappear.

He was a good buddy to be sure, but boy could he be a third wheel. Then again, it was because of Barry that he was here right now.

Here with Katie.

"I have to be tough, to put up with you," Mike said, half in jest, half as a signal to Barry to give him some breathing room.

Just that very second, Katie retrieved a cigarette and placed it in her mouth, slightly biting on it. Then she took a match and lit it against the edge of the table, before putting the hot orange flame to her cigarette.

Barry waved away a plume of Katie's smoke.

"Ugh, you know I hate cigarette smoke," he said, nudging Katie with his elbow. She got up out of her seat so Barry could stretch his legs.

"Since when?" Mike asked.

"Since always."

"Oh really?"

"While I'm gone, you can ask her about her singing," Barry said, focusing his gaze directly on Mike.

"He doesn't hate cigarette smoke," Katie said.

Mike watched Barry walk over to the bar and start talking to two college-aged girls.

"I know," he said.

"He wanted us to be alone," Katie said, taking a sip of her Guinness.

Blunt, this one. She just spoke whatever came to her mind. No censoring for social convention. Not for her.

Mike felt a slight throbbing in his chest. It was his heart beating just a little bit faster than usual. Perhaps it was the second-hand smoke. Perhaps it was effects of the beer. But much more likely was the fact that he hadn't felt this connected to another human being in quite some time. Let alone one who lit her cigarettes in such a devil-may-care manner.

"So, what's this about singing?" Mike asked. His boldness surprised him.

"It's nothing," Katie said, as she started to chew on her fingernails.

"It has to be more than nothing. It has to be something."

"What do you want to know?"

"Well," Mike said, "what type of singing do you do?" He paused. "Not opera, I bet."

She grinned.

"No. Not opera."

"What then?"

"It's new stuff. Sorta punk. I guess," she said.

"Lots of screaming into a microphone?"

"It's just something I do for fun. To let off some steam," Katie said.

Mike nodded.

"Tell me about your latest case," Katie said. It was somewhere between a request and an order.

How to proceed?

He could tell her all about finding Peter Hesse's corpse. About the night spent in an interrogation room. Or he could speak in generalities. How he had been working on a missing persons case, which was typical, but that this particular case had ended so very atypically. At least for him.

"Well," Mike demurred. "My last case was what you might call different."

Katie took a drag on her cigarette.

"How so?"

"This one ended in murder," Mike said in a matter-of-fact tone.

"Wow. That's really kind of cool," Katie said. "Well, not for the dead guy. But you know."

Mike laughed. "Yeah, it wasn't too awesome for him."

"I didn't mean to—"

"It's fine" Mike said, waving his hand.

"So, who was he? The dead guy, that is?"

"A college professor. Community college, that is. Taught literature. Mainly German and European, I think. He was from Switzerland originally."

"Did you say German?" Katie asked, seemingly intrigued.

Mike coughed. "Yeah," he said, trying to clear his throat, "German. I actually went out to Long Island the other day to talk with one of his colleagues at a community college there. She also teaches German literature. Why do you ask?"

"Oh," Katie said, leaning back in the booth. "My Dad's from Germany, too."

Mike shifted uncomfortably in his seat.

"What do you mean?" he asked, all but certain he knew exactly what she meant.

"My Dad was born in Germany," she said, as she took a long drag on her cigarette, before extinguishing it in the clear glass ashtray near the salt and pepper shakers.

"I see," Mike said, giving her space to continue.

"Jewish," she said. "Obviously."

Mike nodded.

"My Dad is as well," he said.

"Is what? Jewish?"

"Yeah," Mike said.

"And your Mom is—was Norwegian for real? I don't think I've ever met a Norwegian." Katie said, her eyes widening.

"Yup."

"I feel like I just took part in this conversation," Mike said.

"What do you mean?"

"Barry and I were talking about the same thing."

Katie laughed.

"Sorry for getting you off track," Mike continued. He didn't know what to say next, so he said the first thing that came to his mind. "Tell me about your Dad."

"Oh," she said, clearing her throat. "He got out before the war. In 1938, he paid off some people to get him fake papers and he was able to get to Havana, where he stayed during the war. It was only after that he came here."

"Got it," Mike said, picking up his Guinness and taking a very small sip.

"His parents and sister were the unlucky ones," Katie added.

"That's awful," Mike said.

"Yeah, it's definitely transformed him into the man he is today."

"I can imagine," Mike replied softly.

Katie quietly nodded.

"You have no idea," she said, lighting yet another cigarette in the same peculiar manner as she did before.

Mike once again didn't know what to say, but this time he said nothing.

"It's okay," Katie said. "My Dad can be pretty intense about those sorts of issues, that's all."

Mike exhaled a bit.

"I get it," he said. "My Dad is kind of the same way. He was born and raised here. Mean streets of Brooklyn."

"Does he still live in the area?" she asked, as she began to slightly pull her curly hair into long strands before releasing them.

"Jew route," Mike said. "Florida."

Katie smiled. "Does he like it down there?"

"Of course not. All he does is complain about the humidity. That and the people," Mike said.

She laughed.

"I understand," she said. Then, upon noticing that the band was gathering again at the foot of the small stage, she reached into her purse and pulled out an ink pen. She reached over to where Barry had been sitting and grabbed one of his unused white paper napkins. Then wrote something on it.

Before he had time to figure out what was going on, Mike looked down and saw the napkin in front of him. On it, she had written her full name in all capital letters as well as her phone number.

"If you ever want to learn more about my family history," she said, slightly biting her lip.

At that very moment, Barry came rushing back and tapped on Katie's shoulder. Interrupting what she was about to say next.

"Scoot over. Band is about to start up again."

Mike shook his head, aware that he and Katie wouldn't be able to hear each other above the music. For once, things seemed to be looking up for him.

"So, what did you guys talk about?" Barry asked, as he munched on a cold onion ring smeared in ketchup.

Mike looked at Katie and Katie looked right back at Mike.

"Nothing special," they both said in near unison.

CHAPTER 6

It was a streamline moderne house nestled high in the Hollywood Hills. Built in the late 1930s during the oil boom that propelled the city's rapid growth into a nascent megalopolis, the Art Deco structure was one of Los Angeles's hidden architectural gems. It was perched a mile or so above the smoggy, neon wasteland of Sunset Boulevard and its dingy pay-by-the-hour motels, pawn shops that offered quick and easy cash to those who needed it (no questions asked), and darkened tattoo parlors who catered to rock stars with oversized dreams and even bigger hair.

With its prominent horizontal lines and a design inspired by the boundless optimism of the aviation industry, the house exuded not just wealth, but also the haughty confidence that Nature could be mastered by the forces of scientific and technological progress. The tall palm trees surrounding the home, much like the koi pond in the backyard, were mere appendages to the steel and glass material which lent the house a timeless quality.

Although it was nearly fifty years old, in many ways, it looked as if it could have been constructed mere days ago.

In the far back of the multi-room house, overlooking the pool, there was a cozy study featuring a wet bar designed for light entertaining. Myriad bookcases were lined with dense scientific tomes. Interspersed among the books, small marble sculptures were prominently displayed. On the wall, a well curated collection of antique swords and firearms, many of them artifacts from the Franco-Prussian War, could be seen. Bright rays of California sunlight streamed through the glass panel windows. They illuminated a large mahogany desk on which sat a rotary dial telephone.

Swishing his way quietly across the beige Persian rug, a man who appeared to be in his sixties or seventies paced back and forth. He was of average height and average build. And although his hair was grey, his healthy, radiant appearance and informal dress gave him an unusually youthful look. One would never guess him to be the head of a major industrial concern. Nor that he was right on the cusp of nearly tripling his already substantial personal wealth through an upcoming public offering on the New York Stock Exchange.

His guest, on the other hand, was a slightly unkempt man. He had a borderline stocky build and looked to be in his early forties. Dressed in the type of bland grey suit a department store manager might wear, he sat quietly and listened attentively to the older man who was speaking rapidly, his mind seemingly racing quicker than his mouth.

"I assure you, sir, it's all been taken care of," said the man in the crumpled suit. He spoke in an accent that sounded far more Staten Island than Southern California.

The older of the two men abruptly halted his pacing. He rubbed both hands over his closed eyelids before opening them again.

"You're quite sure about this, are you, Arthur?" he asked. He spoke with an intonation that marked him as someone for whom English could have easily been his first tongue, but with an educated British accent so posh that he too would never have been mistaken for a California native.

Arthur nodded.

"Yeah."

"Yeah? I pay you a small fortune to do what you do. Something you'd never make on the trifling amount that your government pays you, and all you can say is 'yeah'?"

Arthur, who was seated in a large leather armchair on the side of the large oak desk in the center of the room, fidgeted slightly. He did not immediately respond.

"Please forgive me," Bennington said, suddenly aware how his demeanor might be off-putting to his younger guest. He still needed the man's help. Best be as reasonable sounding as possible for the time being.

Bennington shook his head, thinking to himself.

Out of all the feds in the country, he had to have a drunk on his payroll. Arthur better not screw this up for me, he thought. Not if he knew what was good for him. There was far too much riding on getting Hans out of the way so the public offering could take place as smoothly as possible. He had been waiting too long for this. For his revenge at those who wronged him for so very long.

Arthur, realizing Bennington was mentally somewhere else, hesitated before attempting to restart the conversation.

"It's all kosher," he said.

"The last thing I need to think of right now," Bennington said with more than a hint of annoyance in his voice, "are the Jews."

That was a lie.

All Bennington could think about right now were the Jews. How they had not only destroyed Germany, but also his life. How they had denied him and his country its rightful place in History.

"I know you don't like them," Arthur said, before pausing for a few seconds. "I just found it funny was all."

Bennington, who, apart from a minor scar on his lower lip, had a completely ordinary face, smiled. But he refrained from saying anything for a few seconds.

"Do tell me," he said finally, "how did you get it done?"

"You want the grisly details then?"

Bennington smiled. This time it was genuine. "No one can possibly hear us in here. I've taken care of that."

Arthur nodded, though he wasn't quite sure what Bennington meant.

Perhaps Bennington had installed some sort of sound proofing. Or, more likely, he'd had the room recently scanned for listening devices.

Just then, there was a light knock on the closed study door.

"One moment," Bennington said, clearly annoyed at the interruption.

Arthur cocked his head slightly to the right. But he said nary a word.

"You may enter," Bennington said. His voice was just loud enough to be heard on the other side of the door.

A much younger woman with shoulder length blonde hair and radiant chartreuse eyes, one who looked as if she once had a successful modeling career, entered the room.

"Hey, I was wondering if you like knew where the key to the wine cellar was?" Her voice channeled Marilyn Monroe perfectly.

Bennington gritted his teeth.

"This is what you interrupt me for?"

"Sorry," Jackie said. Her mouth delivered a word of contrition, but her eyes bespoke fiery defiance.

"Ask the fucking maid!"

The woman forced an inauthentic smile, highlighting the expensive orthodontic work her older husband had only recently financed on her behalf. She then looked briefly at Arthur, who was still sitting quietly in his armchair. Then she focused her gaze directly at her visibly older husband.

"Okay. I will do that," she said, her voice a pitch even higher this time.

She closed the door behind her. It banged shut.

Bennington threw his hands up in the air. His face registered an air of disgust, as if he had just opened an old jar of vegetables and realized they had steadily rotted away.

"What an awful pain she is."

Arthur clasped his hands together, shrugged. Uncertain what to say.

"Were you ever married?" Bennington asked, settling down into his beige leather desk chair.

"Me?" Arthur asked with a genuine look of surprise on his face. He pointed at his own chest.

"Who else?"

"No," he demurred.

"And do keep it that way. Women are only after one damn thing," Bennington said, rubbing his fingers together. "Money."

"I'll be sure to keep that in mind."

"Where were we? Oh yes, you were going to tell me how you took care of that unfortunate business back in New York."

"You sure you need to know?" Arthur asked. He pulled out a flask from his jacket pocket, took a quick swig of whiskey, and then tucked it between his knees.

"Good God, man. Get on with it," Bennington said, his frustration obvious.

"Well, I spent a week or so following Hesse—I mean Berman—and let's just say the stars aligned for us this time."

"Oh?" he asked, his curiosity obviously piqued.

"Yeah, just this very week, your friend decided to shoot up again."

"Oh really?"

"Yeah."

Arthur, seemingly oblivious as the shaky ground on which he stood with his employer with his drinking habit, took another long gulp of whiskey.

"Put that bloody thing away," Bennington thundered.

"I'm half Irish. I can hold my liquor."

Bennington glared at Arthur. It was a cold look. The look of a man who was more than capable of murder.

A few awkward seconds passed. Neither man spoke a word. Arthur then decided to put the flask back in his pocket.

"So, yeah, as I was saying," he said, "this week of all weeks Hesse decided to start up his habit once again. I spotted him buying junk from some black dude in front of a movie house near Times Square. Then I tailed him to a flophouse in the Meatpacking District where he was slumming it up with some whore."

"Poor Hans. Never could resist temptation. And what happened next?" Bennington asked, his eyes widening.

"And I got one of my former informants to get rid of him. To make it look like a robbery. Junkie robs junkie. So that no one will care."

"Splendid. And what of your informant?"

"Oh," Arthur said, laughing. "I took care of him later than night. He took a ride to the river in the trunk of my car. He's fish bait."

Bennington nodded. He looked pleased, but not overly so.

"Mind if I have a smoke?" Arthur asked, pulling out a pack of Marlboro Reds and a folded matchbook from his inside jacket pocket. He tapped the pack of cigarettes against his left palm.

"Don't even think about it!" Bennington's voice was raised up a notch.

"Sorry. I forgot you don't like smoke." His voice oozed with sarcasm.

"For someone who was once entrusted with national security secrets, you seem prone to forgetting an amazing amount."

"I won't forget who's paying me," Arthur said dryly.

Bennington laughed. "Touché!"

"You like what I did?" Arthur asked.

"What I would most like," Bennington said, "would be if you could provide me with a match."

"A match?" Arthur asked.

"Yes."

"You can have the whole thing. I have a pocket full of them," he said, taking a matchbook from his pocket and casually tossing it on the desk, "here you go."

Bennington looked at the small match book. It was black with white writing on it. An advertisement for Sully's Pub on 49th Street in Manhattan.

"Your usual hangout?" Bennington said, indicating the name of the establishment printed on the matchbook.

Arthur shrugged.

"So, what comes next?" he asked.

"Hmm," Bennington replied, "that is a good question. A good question, indeed."

Arthur, having put his cigarettes back inside his jacket pocket, sat and chewed his fingernails.

"Follow up with the wife," Bennington said.

"I thought you said you were pretty sure Hesse didn't say anything to her."

"Oh, I'm sure. Hans had too much to lose by revealing to her—to anyone—who he really was. I may not have seen him in decades, but trust me, I know him. He was going to the grave with his secret." Bennington laughed. "And he did."

"So why tail the wife?"

Bennington took a deep breath.

"Just to make sure there are no loose ends. You can never get too careful when it comes to women. The public offering is just a couple weeks after Labor Day, and I can't afford anything getting in my way."

"I can tail her," Arthur said.

"I know you can," Bennington replied.

"For the right price, of course."

"Naturally," Arthur said, knowing that although they were born an ocean apart, he and Bennington spoke the same language.

"Well that just about does it," Bennington said. "Does your supervisor know anything?"

"He doesn't know anything."

"Are you certain?" Bennington asked. "It would be most unfortunate if he found out about your ... extracurricular activities on my behalf?"

Arthur glared at Bennington. "As I said, he's in the dark. And I intend to keep it that way. No need to drag him into this."

Bennington clapped his hands together. "Bravo, my good man. Bravo. A fine theatrical performance. You almost had me believing you were a man with a conscience."

"Are we done here?" Arthur asked, his working-class Staten Island accent more prominent than usual.

"We are. It's always a pleasure to do business with you, Arthur."

"Likewise," Arthur said, as he got up from his chair. He saw himself out of the room, eager to leave. He had a plane back to New York to catch and, Hollywood traffic being what it was, it was going to be an exceptionally stop-and-go taxi ride down the 405 to LAX, so time was of the essence.

Bennington, finally freed from having to humor a man of lesser intelligence and whom he held in contempt, got up from his desk chair and closed the heavy blinds.

The room, now shrouded from outside view, was significantly darker, but light enough for Bennington to see where Arthur had left the book of matches. He picked it up and sat back down in his swivel chair. He opened his desk drawer, pushed aside a loaded Luger pistol he kept for self-defense, and removed a small stack of five crumbled white envelopes, their corners bent from being shoved into the far corner of the drawer. There was no return address on any of them. But each was stamped and postmarked in Long Island, New York. A long way from smoggy Los Angeles.

Although the letters were all different in tone, with the most recent of the bunch the most vociferous in its demands, they all made the same basic point: I know who you are. You owe me. Pay up or else.

It was no mystery who the disgruntled author of the letters happened to be. For they were all signed with the initials HB.

Hans Berman.

The little bastard was blackmailing him.

Bennington knew what had to be done. It was well past time to get rid of any remaining trace of Herr Berman, his fuck-up of a "brother" who had thought it would be a good idea to threaten him with exposure. To pierce the veil that masked Bennington's true identity.

Bennington stood up and, with a slight crack of his back, picked up a ceramic trash can. It was heavier than it looked. He placed the trash can on his desk. He dropped the stack of envelopes into it. They landed with nary a sound.

Bennington flipped open the matchbook, pulled out a flimsy excuse for a match, and flicked it against the coarse striking surface. It emitted a small orange flame, one which temporarily brightened the darkness. But within an instant, Bennington had cast the match down into the bottom of the trash can. To incinerate the entreaties of a desperate fool, of a disloyal brother. Of a man who let his passions for getting high and getting laid get the best of him.

Bennington sat back down in his chair and closed his eyes while the letters burned.

A tsunami of images from the past flooded through his mind, as if he were watching an old black and white newsreel. Although it was close to forty years ago, he could still vividly recall that day in Frankfurt when the two American agents had reunited him with Hans. How he and Hans had survived the war relatively unscathed was miraculous. So many of his fellow countrymen had not been so lucky, least of all those Germans unfortunate enough to live in the path of the Red Army. Yet, somehow, some way, fate had given the two of them a second chance. A golden opportunity for a new life in America. Was it a complete and total surprise that Hans fucked it all up for himself? Not really. What was surprising, or at least somehow unexpected, was that Hans would think that he would be able to screw things up for him as well. So, when the letters started arriving—first once a week and then, twice a week— Bennington knew he was going to have to take decisive action. How dare this dissolute fool think he was going to extort a single dollar from him in exchange for, as the letters said, "keeping your secret safe with me." Bennington walked over to the wet bar and picked up a carafe of cold water.

Bennington doused the remnants of the fire. He reduced what remained of the envelopes and the letters inside to a soggy charcoal grey mash.

Poor Hans. He never stood a chance.

Bennington focused his gaze on the telephone, as if he were pondering whom he should call. And what he should say once the connection was made. But there was no mistaking who he needed to speak to. And why.

He picked up the receiver and rested it on his shoulder. Number by number, those he had memorized in case he one day had to dial from a phone booth, he dialed the one man he knew he could count on.

"TV repair," said a man on the receiving end of the call. There was a cacophony of human voices, light banging, and traffic in the background.

"Bennington," he said.

"Good to hear from you, sir."

"Looks like I will be needing your services once again."

"Whatever my people can do to support the cause."

"Excellent. Good to hear that the upcoming generation hasn't abandoned our people's struggle."

"Our triumph is the natural evolution of things," the man said.

"Good to hear such optimism," Bennington said.

"Because it's true."

"Right," Bennington said, no longer feeling the need to play the game of mutual flattery. "So, listen closely. I am going to need you to keep an eye on Arthur."

"What's that sorry son of a bitch up to now?"

"He's watching someone for me, and I want you to watch him."

"Right. Watch the watcher."

Bennington remained silent for a second or two.

"Hello?"

"I am still here," Bennington said.

"And we're damn glad about that," said the voice on the other end.

Bennington laughed. Flattery would never cease to be effective when dealing with him. And he knew it.

"When the wife breaks another TV in one of her drunken tantrums," Bennington said, "I'll be sure to send some business in your direction."

The man on the other end of the call coughed, then laughed.

"Sending a TV cross country for a repair is pretty fucking expensive," he said.

"Oh, didn't I tell you?" Bennington asked.

"Tell me what?"

"That we'll be staying in my home in Westchester for a month or so."

"When?"

"Starting in a few days and until the company goes public," Bennington replied.

"I understand."

"Payment will be per usual."

"Good. Anything else?"

"No, that's everything." Bennington said, as he ended the call.

Just then, there was a light rapping on the door.

"Come!" he shouted.

It was Jackie.

She had obviously taken his advice to heart, for she had a bottle of Riesling from the wine cellar in one hand and a drinking glass in the other.

"I'm gonna need you to give me one of the credit cards tonight." She slurred her words.

"What the devil? Are you drunk again?"

"Not drunk," she laughed. "Just a little tipsy." She giggled.

Bennington walked over to the bookshelf, picked up one of his less preferred sculptures—this one a minute rendering of a Greek goddess playing a harp—and threw it as hard as he could against the wall where Jackie stood. Fragments of marble flew through the air like pellets from a BB gun. Several of them ricocheted and hit Jackie on the arm.

She dropped the Riesling bottle onto the hardwood floor where it shattered into a heap of broken green glass.

"Now get the hell out of here!" Bennington shouted. It was bad enough that the federal agent he had put on his payroll was turning out to be a filthy drunk. He had neither the time, nor the patience for his wife's drunken bullshit. Least of all now.

Jackie, who was on the floor trying to pick up the broken shards, quickly got to her feet. She darted out of the room as if she were her husband's prey.

But before she did, Bennington got a good look at her eyes. For he saw something in them.

It was fear.

And that made him feel alive. Vital even.

But serenity still alluded him. Arthur's problems troubled him as well. Would he have been better off cutting his losses with Arthur the minute the fool's wife walked out on him? Perhaps. But then he would have had to find someone else to take care of Hans at the very last moment. That would have been too risky, he had reasoned at the time. So that's where things stood. Like it or not, he was stuck with Arthur. At least for now.

CHAPTER 7

The phone rang once. Then twice. Then perhaps as many as fifteen times before Mike was able to wrestle himself from a deep slumber. It took him a few seconds to reach over to pick up the receiver. As he did so, the phone cord nearly knocked over the glass of water perched on his nightstand.

"Hello?" he mumbled, his mouth dry and his voice cracking.

"Mr. Levinas," the woman's voice on the other end said, "I'm sorry to call you at home, but I think I'm in trouble."

Mike rolled over, grabbed his pillow, and used it to prop himself up in bed. He didn't want to wake Katie. She lay sleeping on the other side of the mattress, her hands gently clasping the light blue blanket draped across the bed.

"Who—who's this?" he asked, his hand instinctively grabbing the digital alarm clock on the nightstand. He accidentally knocked the glass on the rug.

It landed with a small thud. Water spilled out onto the floor.

Mike turned the alarm clock toward him, almost dropping it in the process as well. The bright red numbers told him it was nearly 3:30. Dead of night. What a time to be woken up. Especially when he had female companionship, a rarity these days.

"Millie," the voice paused. "This is Millie Johnson."

It had been a little less than a week since he placed that dreaded phone call to her. The one where he had told her the unfortunate news. How he had located her husband in that seedy hotel room. He had apologized that he would have called sooner had he not been stuck in an interrogation room the night before.

Mike rubbed the dust from his eyes and the warm sweat from his brow. Although still groggy, he was slightly less disoriented than he was a few seconds ago.

"Millie?" he asked quietly. "Something wrong?"

"I really didn't want to wake you, Mr. Levinas—"

"Mike," he said, looking down at the small puddle of water on his rug. "Call me Mike."

For several seconds, apart from the crackle of the telephone line, there was near complete silence.

"Hello?" Mike said, unsure whether the line had been disconnected.

"I'm still here, Mike," Millie said.

"How did you get this number?" he asked, still half asleep.

"You gave it to me in your office. In case I ever needed it. Remember?"

"Right," Mike said. He remembered now. So much so that he could visualize the very moment he had scribbled it on a scrap of paper for her.

"I think," she stammered, "I think I'm being followed. And I think it has something to do with Peter's death."

"What's going on?" This time it was Katie. Although Mike had tried to keep his voice down, it had obviously not been good enough.

"It's okay," Mike said while looking directly at Katie, "You should go back to sleep."

Katie rolled over again, her back to him.

"Who are you talking to?" Millie asked.

"A lady friend," Mike said.

"Ah," Millie said. There was an embarrassed recognition in her voice. "Sorry."

"Not a problem," Mike said. "Tell me more. You think you're being followed? Is that right?"

"Yes," Millie said. "I was going to wait until morning to call, but I couldn't fall asleep and it's just that I think something's really wrong with all of this. If it's money you're worried about, I have more than enough to keep paying you. I have a trust fund from my aunt in Little Rock that I never told Peter about."

Mike took in her words. Then he sat quietly. Thinking.

"Maybe we shouldn't be talking on the phone," Mike said.

"Do what now?" Millie asked.

Mike looked at the alarm clock again. As much as he wanted to go back to sleep, he knew that was not going to happen.

"There's a diner in my neighborhood that's open all night long. The Salonika. Do you know it?"

"The one in Yorkville?"

"Yes. Exactly."

"I do know it," she replied.

"Can we meet there in about an hour or so? Maybe ninety minutes."

"Sure," Millie said. "Thank you. Thank you so very much. You're a darling."

Mike untangled the phone cord and set the receiver down on the base. Then he picked up the phone again and listened for a dial tone. Now he was the one who was paranoid.

"I have to go meet a client," Mike said to Katie.

"What the hell, Mike? At this hour? We didn't get home from my gig until almost two."

"Yeah. I know. I know," Mike said.

"Whatever," Katie said, her grogginess fully evident in the tone of her voice. "I guess I'll see myself out this morning."

"I'll be back before—"

"Mike," she said, "I'm a big girl. Don't worry about it. Seriously."

Mike got out of bed and trudged across the creaky hardwood floor. As he grabbed a white polo shirt, a pair of tan khaki pants and boxer shorts, his mind returned to the night before. To Katie's concert—her gig, as she had called it—at the Pink Flamingo, an East Village dive bar that squeezed in as many patrons as the fire code would allow. And then some. Her band, whose name he already had forgotten, took the stage around nine o'clock. Loud, brash, and punk, they sounded to him like a mix between Led Zeppelin and a chainsaw tearing through an overgrown tree. Katie's vocals weren't exactly what he'd call singing. More like screeching really. But he could see she was enjoying herself up on the stage. A suburban girl letting loose and finding herself in the bowels of a decaying neighborhood. She was just playing pretend like everyone else in this city. Only everyone else didn't have black mascara plastered under their eyes when they went out at night.

Realizing he should get going, he headed into the small bathroom at the far end of his one-bedroom apartment. Still dazed from being awakened in the middle of the night, he turned the shower faucet all the way to the left. The water was freezing. Typical. It took nearly three agonizingly long minutes before he was able to get the water warm enough so he could get a move on. Careful not to stumble on the uneven bathroom floor tiles, he got into his cruddy excuse for a shower stall, grabbed the dried out, half-used green Lava soap bar, and lathered himself up as quickly as he could.

With his eyes closed and steam rising all around him, Mike began to wonder just what the hell he had gotten himself into.

This all seemed potentially risky. Dangerous even.

Mike took a deep breath.

Then he smiled. Life was not really that bad. He had a case. He had a girl. And that was a lot more than many people in this lonely concrete jungle could say for themselves.

Manhattan that early morning, with the low hanging white clouds obscuring the approaching dawn, was a surreal place. It reminded Mike of his time in law school when he used to get up early and go to the gym.

It was a time when storefronts were still shuttered closed and the street traffic was eerily calm, as if civilization had temporarily been put on hold. When the only sounds that could be heard were those of delivery trucks pulling up to curbs, their weary drivers delivering cardboard boxes filled to the brim with fruit and vegetables to corner bodegas. Quiet and still, an unsettling calm before the bustle of the morning commute took over. The darkness made Mike Levinas feel very alone in the world. Both in law school and now.

Briskly walking along 86th Street toward Lexington, Mike stopped and grabbed a copy of the *New York Times* from the brightly lit 24-hour news kiosk on the corner with 2nd Avenue. Might as well have something to read if Millie was delayed in making her way uptown. Although by the harried tone in her voice on the phone, it sounded as if she were already fully dressed and made up and ready to head out the door.

The ten-minute walk to the Salonika gave Mike time to think.

Time to ponder who might be following Millie and whether or not be believed anyone actually was doing so. Did it have something to do with Peter's death. But what? Peter Hesse was a nobody. He didn't have the heart to tell Millie that, of course. But it's not like she didn't know it, anyway. He was a loser, a semi-employed community college instructor who, even in his sixties, couldn't abandon his seemingly insatiable desire for pleasure. It was a wonder that he had survived as long as he had. To be a junkie in your fifties is a rarity. To be one in your 60s, a newly married one no less, is a statistical anomaly. Maybe Tony Doran had been in touch with Vice and they put a tail on Millie just to make sure she wasn't mixed up in the heroin business. No. That didn't make sense. Was the hooker who called herself Julia the one having Millie watched? That made even less sense. What could it possibly be? Maybe it was all in her overtired mind. Maybe she was using heroin again?

Mike walked into the Salonika. It was exactly as he thought it'd be. Nearly deserted. Some deliverymen having early egg and sausage breakfasts before another backbreaking morning and late-night partiers trying desperately to sober up from their latest hangovers. And a small cornucopia of metropolitan weirdos mumbling to themselves. But it was a relief to be inside air conditioning and out of the already suffocating August humidity.

Mike walked directly to the last booth, the one furthest from the entrance. He sat facing the front. That way Millie would see him as soon as she entered. That way he could see everyone who came in after her.

Just to make sure that whomever she thought was spying on her didn't come in to eavesdrop on their conversation.

He checked his watch. It was now 4:45. No sign of Millie. He unfolded the *Times* and scanned the front page. Yet another story about palace intrigue at the United Nations. Something about fighting between Israel and some Lebanese militias. And a story about how a few real estate moguls were pressuring Mayor Koch to clean up Times Square even more so that they could start marketing it as a family vacationland. Mike laughed. Like that was ever going to happen.

Just then, the front door swung open and a woman dressed in a headscarf and sunglasses walked in. Strewn across her right shoulder was a large black handbag, the type women far older than Millie usually carry.

Mike looked up from reading the paper. Was this Millie? He couldn't tell. As she got closer, he realized that it almost certainly was.

Had she completely lost her marbles?

Maybe the only thing following her was her own personal demons.

The woman who sat down across from Mike looked like a cross between an Italian movie starlet from the 1960s and an aging Ukrainian grandmother from the East Village. Removing her headscarf and glasses, Millie revealed herself to be nothing more than a terrified woman looking for some support.

"Hello, Mike," she said. Her voice cracked. Her hands were trembling like leaves in the wind. There wasn't a hint of flirtation in her voice.

"Millie," he said, reaching over the table to lightly clasp her hands, "I am so sorry about what happened to Peter."

She tensed at the touch. It was as if he had delivered an electric shock.

"As sad as it is to say, I kind of expected it would end that way for him. What I can't wrap my head around is why anyone would be following me."

Mike thought that if Millie didn't take a deep breath, she was going to collapse. He sensed her thoughts were racing. And from the look of her flushed face and sweaty forehead, he assumed her heart was as well.

"You ready?" A voice seemingly out of nowhere.

Mike looked up. Standing over him was the young waitress, the very same one Barry tried to flirt with a week ago. She must work irregular shifts, Mike surmised.

"Um," Mike paused, "two coffees." He made eye contact with Millie. She nodded in approval.

"Any food?" The waitress was seemingly oblivious to how distressed Millie was. That, or she simply didn't care.

"Not right now. Maybe in a bit," Mike said curtly. Knowing full well he and Millie weren't going to be having breakfast together.

"Oh. Okay," the young waitress said, heading back to the kitchen.

"So," Mike said, "tell me what's happening. You said someone is following you. Did I understand that correctly?"

"I don't know what the hell is going on," she said, before proceeding to explain to Mike in unexpectedly lucid detail what she had experienced over the past several days. How starting three days after she learned of her husband's murder, she noticed a white guy—he looked to be in his forties—following her at the supermarket. She thought nothing of it at the time, but then she saw him again on the street when she left the Korean nail salon on 4th Street.

Two times in one day.

She initially chalked it up to coincidence. Nothing more, nothing less. Then two days after that, she spotted the same guy again. This time he was sitting alone in a parked car. She didn't remember the make and model, although it could have been an Impala. A dark grey one with tinted windows. As she approached the car, she noticed that the driver— the same guy—made quick eye contact with her, quickly cranked the ignition, and drove away.

Mike listened intently and let Millie speak. Although he dared not say anything, his initial impression was that Millie was just completely exhausted—understandably so—and was likely seeing things that weren't there. That or making connections in her own mind that didn't exist. After all, if the car she alleged she saw had tinted windows like she said they did, how could she have seen the driver so clearly?

"What do you think?" Millie asked, when she finished recounting her harrowing past week.

"Let me be honest …" Mike said.

Just then, the waitress returned with a large black tray in her hands. She removed two cups of coffee in dark brown mugs and placed them on the table, and walked away. She pretended not to hear what the two of them were discussing.

"Please," Millie said, her Southern twang amplifying her politeness.

"Don't take this the wrong way, but it may very well just be possible that you're not in as much danger as you think."

Millie crossed her arms, sat back in the booth. She pressed her body against the foam orange cushioning.

"Weren't you listening? Didn't you hear what I just said?" she asked.

Mike took a gulp of his coffee, then put it down on the table. A small amount spilled.

"I did, Millie. It's just that stress can do funny things to people's minds. God knows it has happened to me more times that I would like to admit."

"You don't find it at all suspicious?"

"It may just all be one big coincidence."

"Well, would you at least consider this somewhat suspicious?" she asked, opening the zipper of her black handbag and pulling out an envelope, its original white color faded by the passage of time. Examining it closely, Mike saw it had been postmarked in Arlington, Virginia. It appeared to have been sent to Peter Hesse way back in 1951.

"What is this?" Mike asked. His curiosity now genuine.

"Take a good look," Millie said. She cracked her knuckles, stood up, and walked to the back of the restaurant to go to the ladies' room.

Mike delicately opened the envelope, slowly pulling out a typewritten letter. Folded into thirds, the parchment was very brittle, as if it would crumble into dust if not handled properly. The letter was addressed to "Herr Hesse" and looked to be sent from a guy by the name of Larsen. No first name. Just Larsen. That wasn't the intriguing part, however. What was intriguing was both what was included and what was missing in the body of the letter. First, there was the matter of the redaction. Someone—perhaps a government censor from the looks of it—had used a thick black marker to obscure large segments of text.

Why would someone be censoring a letter to Hesse?

But there it was.

Both names, fragments of text and complete sentences were obliterated. Yet the gist of the correspondence remained. This Larsen guy had written to Peter Hesse informing him that he was to have absolutely no future direct contact with his brother and that any correspondence had to go directly through him. Brother? Millie had never mentioned anything about Peter having siblings. In fact, he could have sworn that she had made some offhand remark back in his office the first time they met about how he was not only a war orphan, but an only child.

Mike took one of the sugar packets from the container at the far end of the table, ripped it open, and poured it into his coffee. He stirred it with his spoon. It clanged. He took a long sip and then set his mug back down.

As Mike slid the letter back into the envelope, he noticed that Millie was walking back to the table from the ladies' room.

"Where did you find this?" Mike asked her as she sat back down across from him.

"My husband has—had—a safety deposit box at the Manufacturer's Bank on 39th Street. He didn't know I knew about it. But I did."

"Ah," Mike said, taking a brief sip of his now sweetened coffee.

"So. Tell me."

"Tell you what?"

"What you think it all means," Millie said.

"I don't know what it means," Mike replied, "but it sure looks as if your Peter may not have been totally honest about his past."

"Well, that's obvious," Millie snapped back.

"Sorry," Mike said softly. Just then, he noticed that what looked like track marks on her left arm. Was she using again? Not that it was any of his business. But he couldn't help but wonder. Maybe the stress of everything that had happened to her sent her back to the needle. He looked again. They didn't look fresh. Good. The last thing he needed was an addict for a client. If she was still his client. It was a good question.

Both of them stared down at the table. Neither spoke a word.

"I guess I'd have to know who this Larsen guy is in order to make sense of it all. But whoever he was, I'm sure this letter had nothing to do with Peter's murder."

"Are you?" she asked.

Millie had a point. He didn't know that. He didn't know anything about Peter Hesse. All he knew was what she had told him. And what he witnessed in that fleabag hotel room.

And now this cryptic letter that cast more far more shadow than light.

"I don't know what to think," Mike said, taking another sip of coffee before putting it down again. It was now only lukewarm at best.

"And then there's this," Millie said, reaching into her handbag and pulling out what appeared to be a small piece of jewelry. It took Mike only a few seconds to recognize it. The ring. The one Peter Hesse always wore. The one from the photograph. The one he had on his hand when he took his final breath on the floor of that wretched hotel room.

"Where'd you get that?" Mike asked, immediately embarrassed by how loud his voice was.

"The police," Millie replied.

"They gave it to you?"

"Yeah, they said that the case was closed and that I might like to have it."

Mike nodded. Everything had happened so damn quickly that night. Finding the body. Dealing with Julia. Time spent cooped up in the interrogation room. It had never occurred to him that Peter Hesse's killer had left a piece of jewelry behind. One that probably had some value. Wouldn't a junkie have taken everything he could have gotten his hands on? As he seemed to recall, all that was taken was cash from Hesse's wallet.

"Can I take a closer look at this?" Mike asked.

"Here you go," Millie said, as she dropped the ring into Mike's outstretched palm.

Mike held the ring up to his face, squinted his eyes.

"There's something written here."

"Yeah, I think it's in Latin."

"*Fatem habemus*," Mike said, slowly enunciating the words engraved on the ring.

"What does it mean?"

Mike laughed.

"Wish I knew," he said. "I dropped Latin after two weeks into the semester my first year at Princeton."

"Wait," she said. "You went to Princeton and you're doing *this* for a living?"

She immediately blushed, embarrassed how harsh her words must have sounded to Mike.

"Yeah. It was fine. I learned how to fence while I was there, so it wasn't a total waste."

Millie nodded, uncertain whether Mike was being sarcastic, droll, or just plain cranky.

"I was thinking," she said, after a few awkward seconds passed between them, "that the ring may have something to do with the letter."

"With this?" Mike asked skeptically, indicating the envelope into which he had returned the folded letter.

"Yes."

"How so?" Mike asked, unsure of what could possibly connect a letter from 1951 with a ring that Peter Hesse wore up until his death barely a week ago.

"If Peter wore this ring basically his entire life, that would mean he was wearing it when he read this letter in 1951."

Mike scratched his chin. It didn't make sense. If Peter Hesse's entire life were a fabrication, a masquerade, why would he have chosen the life of a literature professor? It didn't make a whole lot of sense.

"Okay …"

"Don't you see?" Millie asked, her Southern accent growing more pronounced as she became more excited.

"No, Millie," Mike sighed. "I don't."

"Peter told me that the ring was from his high school years in Switzerland. If we find out where exactly he went to school, maybe we can find out who this brother of his was."

Mike listened intently and didn't interrupt.

"And," Millie continued excitedly, "it's not like there aren't a bunch of jewelry experts and pawn shops in this city. There has to be someone who can tell us what we need to know."

Mike leaned back in the booth. His face grew brighter, thinking how Millie wasn't quite as hopeless as she portrayed herself to be. People didn't often surprise him. But she was different somehow. It had never really occurred to him to think that something from so very long ago could have a bearing on the present. This was the type of stuff that interested his father, not him. But right now, it was his case. Not his father's.

"I think that you might be on to something," he said, making the first direct eye contact with Millie since she sat back down at the table.

"Yeah? You do?" she asked, delicately biting her lower lip.

"Yes, I do indeed."

"What comes next?" Millie asked.

"Well," Mike said, clearing his throat. "If it's all right by you, I'll hold on to the ring and letter for safekeeping. And I will try to find someone who might help us shed some light on all of this."

"You have someone in mind?" she asked.

"Yes, I do," Mike said. He knew he was lying. But he told Millie what he thought she wanted to hear.

"And what about the guy who is following me? That's still my main concern, even though you don't seem to be fully buying my story."

"I think that if you see him again, you should go to the police. File a report at the local precinct."

"That's it?"

"Did this guy threaten you at all?"

"Well," Millie said. She paused to ponder the question more carefully. "No. I can't say that he has."

"Then I wouldn't worry too much about it," Mike said. This time he was being honest and not just telling her what he thought she needed to hear.

"Oh, maybe you're right. Maybe it's just stress. But that doesn't change how very odd this letter is."

"Well, let me take care of that. You should go home and get some sleep."

Millie nodded in agreement.

"I feel bad I wasted my coffee. I didn't even take a tiny sip." Millie looked down at her cup of coffee. She stuck her pinky finger into it.

"See? It's ice cold."

Mike stared at her. "In the grand scheme of things, I don't think that matters too much," Mike said.

"Very true, Mike. Very true."

Mike picked up the envelope containing the cryptic letter and Peter

Hesse's ring. He shoved them in his pants pocket. Then he reached for his wallet, grabbed two singles, and left them on the table.

"I should get going," he said.

"That's a mighty big tip," Millie said, noticing the amount of money Mike had left for the waitress.

"I come here often enough."

From the look in Millie's eyes, she understood. "I should be on my way too," she said. For the first time since she phoned him earlier this morning, she didn't sound completely frantic.

Outside the Salonika, the pulse of the city had picked up. It was nearly dawn. The morning sun climbed steadily over the East River. Street pigeons now jostled for space with people.

Mike checked his pockets to make sure he had both the letter and the ring. He did. Just as he was about to say goodbye to Millie, she did something completely unexpected.

She reached her arms around his shoulders and kissed him.

Not an overtly romantic or a passionate kiss. But a kiss, nevertheless.

Before Mike could say anything, Millie nuzzled her face against his freshly shaved cheek and whispered softly into his ear.

"Don't look now, but that's the man. The man who's been following me. He's across the street in front of the bagel store. In a white shirt and blue tie."

Mike felt his heart drop.

As she removed her arms from his body, Mike looked directly at her and nodded. But instinct took over. And before he knew what he was doing, he slightly shifted his gaze and looked diagonally across Third Avenue.

Standing under the maroon awning in front of Goldberg's Bagel was a middle-aged man attired exactly as Millie had described him. Taking a long drag on a cigarette, the man threw it on the ground, looked down, and stamped it out with his foot. From Mike's vantage point the guy looked to be slightly on the heavier side. But that wasn't what was on Mike's mind at the moment. What was on his mind was the notion that he had seen this guy somewhere before. Recently. He just couldn't place where he had seen him. For several seconds, that gnawed at him more than the fact that Millie might be in danger from this person.

Despite his intention to be as discreet as possible, Mike had no such luck. For before he knew what was happening, before his mind could process it all, the stranger under the awning focused his attention back upon Millie. And then his gaze shifted to Mike.

Although it seemed to last for an eternity, it was only for a second or two that Mike and the stranger had locked eye contact. Two seconds isn't very long. But it was long enough. Long enough for the white-shirted man to turn his back to Millie and Mike and begin a brisk stride north toward 86th Street. Out of all the things that Mike was never prepared for when he decided to become a PI was the fact that it wasn't just a desk job. Sometimes it required more. Legwork was called that for a reason. Because sometimes, it meant following people. Sometimes dangerous people.

And right now, it meant Mike had less than ten seconds to make a choice.

Stay and comfort Millie or do what he was hired to do and find out who the hell was tailing his client?

Taking a deep breath didn't do much to slow his pounding heart rate. Nor did it steady his hands. Adrenaline pumped through his body much in the way that heroin had flowed through Hesse's. He rubbed his sweaty palms against his pants, leaving a damp residue.

"Stay here," he said to Millie. "I'm going to find out what the hell this guy wants with you." His mouth was dry. Like he had cotton balls stuck in his mouth.

"Okay," Millie said.

"Hey! Hey you!" Mike yelled across Third Avenue. His gaze was laser-focused on the man who was now nearly on the corner with 86th Street. He wasn't about to let him out of his sight.

Perhaps stunned, the man in the white shirt and blue tie stopped for a brief second. He quickly looked over his left shoulder, making momentary eye contact once again with Mike. Then, without hesitation, he darted down 86th Street. He ran past an electronics store, a fabric supply store, and a discount mattress store. All were still shuttered. None had yet opened for the day.

Shit. It hit him in the intestines like a bag of rocks. Mike knew where the man was likely headed. The subway station. On 86th Street.

If the man happened to get himself on a train, there'd be no way for Mike to ever find out who the hell this guy was and, more importantly, what was up to. Why he had been spying on Millie.

That he was running away told Mike two things. One, this guy was definitely up to no good. And two, he couldn't possibly be law enforcement. If he were a cop, a narc who had been tailing Millie, he wouldn't be bolting like this. Like some fucking mugger when things went wrong.

The man in the blue tie increased his pace. Mike did the same. It had been a while since Mike ran like this, but it wasn't as if he were completely out of shape. He went to the 92nd Street Y gym as often as he could.

One foot in front of the other, Mike kept right on after the man.

His heart pounded, providing blood to his legs. His lungs took in the polluted dewy morning air. He coughed, then spit onto the sidewalk, nearly hitting a pigeon minding its own business. Mike cleared his throat. It was still cotton candy dry.

Before he knew it, Mike was sprinting. Sweat poured down his face.

Mike's mind spun in circles. Too fast. Like a record playing at the wrong speed. What if he did catch up with the man? What then? What was he going to do? Demand he tell all? Beat it out of him like in the movies? No. That wouldn't work. Hadn't be already been in a police station once this week? But what could he really do? He had to be quick. Decisive. Make up your mind, he told himself. Have a fucking plan.

Shit. What if the guy had a gun?

Within seconds, though, his once racing thoughts evaporated into the early morning air. Instinct took over. He was now a cheetah chasing its prey. His body almost didn't exist anymore. It felt as though he were outside his body.

Floating. Ethereal.

For a brief second, an unusually vivid image flashed before his eyes. It was as if he were an actor watching a character on TV. Running. Chasing. A real PI. Not a failed prosecutor who had to find something else to do to pay his bills.

More ground covered. His body ached.

Mike kept the man in his field of vision. There he was! Almost on the corner of Lexington.

Shit. Too late. Mike saw his prey as clear as day. Just yards in front of him. Right in front of the green and white painted entrance sign to the 86th and Lex subway station.

For a brief second, it looked like the mysterious white-shirted man had turned around. Turned around and looked straight at him.

But Mike wasn't sure.

How could you when things were moving so fast?

Time to make a go for it.

Time to bolt as fucking fast as he could without falling down the subway steps and breaking his neck. All for a measly payment from Millie.

Blood pulsed through his veins. Sweat soaked through his shirt. It attached itself to his wet skin like Saran Wrap to a sandwich. Had he had time to consider the situation, Mike would have realized how fucking uncomfortable that cheap shirt of his was.

But he didn't have time to ponder such matters.

The white-shirted man bolted down the concrete subway steps, pushing aside a young black girl in denim overalls and Converse sneakers who nearly tripped and lost her balance.

"What the fuck, mister?" she shouted.

No one cared.

Mike darted right past her and headed down into the station. The smell of exhaust fumes, urine and body odor was as strong as ever.

There, yards in front of him, he saw the man. The guy was shoving his way through a throng of commuters, backing an elderly woman into a turnstile. Then he hopped over the adjacent turnstile, landing on the other side, where the train platform was. An object went flying out of the man's pocket and landed on the ground.

Mike, very quickly, saw there was no one at the token booth. He followed. He leaped over the turnstile. He slightly banged his right ankle in the process. Mike gritted his teeth. But he kept on going.

Without slowing his speed, Mike bent down and scooped the object that had fallen from the man's pocket. Put it in his pocket. Whatever it was. It was his now. He was running on instinct. No time to look. No time to think. Keep going forward.

There he was!

He now had his target directly in his sights.

The man was running to the far end of the platform, darting and weaving. Not many people on the platform. Just a few Hispanic women and a young white guy in blue jeans and a black shirt. He was seemingly absorbed in reading a newspaper.

That's when Mike heard it.

The chut-chut, squeal, and throttle of an approaching subway train. The fizzle and hum of the electrified tracks.

Mike looked straight at the white-shirted man. The guy was now on the very far north end of the platform.

You got nowhere to run, buddy boy.

The train was now almost in the station.

But it wouldn't arrive before Mike caught up with the white-shirted stranger.

You're trapped, fucker.

Gone was the worry that the man might have a gun. Gone was any fear of danger. Mike was running on something more primitive than reason. Pure drive. Pursue the threat. Protect the woman.

And that's when it happened. With no warning.

Out of nowhere, the guy on the platform. The one in the blue jeans. He dropped his newspaper, lunged and grabbed Mike by the collar of his soaked shirt, and threw him with almost acrobatic grace onto the subway tracks below.

What. The. Fuck.

Mike's body landed with a thud and a crack. But he wasn't injured. Or if he was, he didn't know it. He just knew he was alive.

For now.

He heard shrieks. Women. The Hispanic women on the platform above. And lots of chatter. All in Spanish. Then a few screams. And an "Oh, My God".

Belly down on the wood, Mike looked up and saw the bright circular light approaching.

Get up. Those two words. Nothing more.

Was he thinking them or was someone speaking to him?

It didn't matter.

Quickly, operating on sheer instinct, he stood up and careful not to touch the electrified third rail, he leaped up and over to the other side of the tracks. No train coming from that direction.

"I got you, chief. I got you."

A hand reached out to him. Pulled him up.

It was a cop. He was with a woman. She looked familiar. Who was it? Millie. Yes, it was Millie. She hadn't paid attention. Hadn't followed his orders. She evidently got hold of a cop and went down into the station on the opposite side of the street.

The train was now in the station. A graffiti strewn metallic snake. The doors rattled open, then slammed shut. And with that, was on its way again.

The platform where the white-shirted man had been standing mere seconds ago was now empty. He had disappeared like a phantom.

"Mike! You're bleeding," Millie said.

"Am I? Where?"

"Your face!"

Mike reached to his face, rubbed his hand against it, and took a look.

It was as scarlet as cheap drugstore lipstick.

Mike tried to stand up. He couldn't do it. His legs wobbled. His arms trembled. He had no balance.

He felt something in his stomach. Pain. No. A gurgle.

A mixture of saliva and coffee jetted upward through his esophagus, before flowing like a geyser right back down onto the platform. His vomit missed the cop's black shoes by an inch.

The last thing that flashed before his eyes before complete darkness enveloped him were the red tail lights of a subway train disappearing into a dark tunnel.

Although Mike didn't hear it, right before he lost consciousness, Millie had asked him something.

It wasn't meant to be sarcastic. And it wasn't meant to be cruel. It was meant to be sincere.

"You believe me now?"

CHAPTER 8

Westchester, NY

"Why did you run?" Bennington thundered, his fingers tracing the edges of the P08 Luger pistol that he had placed on the table a few minutes earlier. He knew the answer all too well. His hired gun was a filthy drunk. One who could no longer be depended upon.

"I fucked up. That's all I can say."

"That's all you have to say?"

"As I said, I fucked up," Arthur said, as he looked down at the Luger, wondering if its presence here on the table was something he should be concerned about.

"I should say so, Arthur. I should say so." Bennington's subdued voice was ominous. More so than if he had been shouting.

"As you know, I like conducting business as much as possible face to face. And the wife is in the city spending my money. That's why I asked you here today. Just let it be known that you should thank your lucky stars things aren't the way they used to be," he said coldly.

"You don't meet with Donny face to face," emphasizing the name with borderline contempt.

"Donny and I have a particular arrangement that doesn't apply to you."

"I see," Arthur said quietly.

"I hope you do. For your sake." Bennington let the words reverberate in the room as a chilling warning.

Arthur received the message loud and clear. At that moment, he deeply regretted mentioning Donny's name at all.

"What's our next move?" he asked in an unusually meek tone, his hands shaking ever so slightly. He fidgeted in his chair. Small beads of perspiration inched down his forehead.

Bennington took a large gulp of his mineral water, before setting his glass back down on a coaster on the dining room table. He inhaled, trying to control his rising anger. He didn't want his fury to get the best of him. Not now. Not with so much on the line.

"*Our* next move?" he said. "There is no 'our' anymore. If there ever was. What you are going to do is to do nothing. Nothing. You sit on your hands, don't make a peep, and allow me to clean up the mess you made.

Then, and only then, will there be a chance—a chance, not a guarantee—that you can redeem yourself."

Bennington set the Luger down and clasped his hands together. His knuckles whitened. Never on the charter plane ride from Santa Monica Airport did he imagine that he'd be spending his first evening back on his Westchester estate containing a mess of Arthur's own making. When he had learned of what had happened at the subway station, Bennington hit the roof. All he had asked was for Arthur to keep an eye on Millie. Not for him to give himself away. Not to make things worse. Thankfully, Donny had been on the scene. Had been doing what had been asked of him. And he had done it well. If Donny hadn't followed Arthur to the station, who knows what might have happened? It was just unfortunate that the train didn't run over that bloody PI. But that wasn't Donny's fault. It was one of timing. Donny thought quickly. He had acted without hesitation when he shoved that PI down onto the track. Maybe it was because Donny believed in more than just money. He believes in the cause.

Unlike Arthur. A degenerate whose seemingly only concern was the almighty dollar.

It wasn't particularly easy to find feds who'd work for him on the side anymore, so Bennington had ended up with the runt of the proverbial litter. A very inebriated runt. One whose colossal fuck-up on 86th Street had the potential to derail his plan for good.

"It's time for you to leave," Bennington said, without the slightest hint of emotion in his voice.

Arthur, his knees buckling ever so slightly, rephrased Bennington's statement as a question.

"You want me to go?"

Bennington said nothing, but merely glared at Arthur. He didn't need to say anything further. The cold steely look in his eyes spoke volumes.

"Okay, then."

Arthur got up from the wooden chair. He straightened his tie, walked out of the dining room and into the main entrance. He headed out the front door and walked toward his car parked in Bennington's cobblestone driveway.

Bennington, taking another sip of his mineral water, looked straight into the adjacent drawing room. The one he used for entertaining guests. With a dark yellow Persian rug as its centerpiece, the meticulously designed room had hosted numerous cocktail parties and black-tie affairs over the years before he had decided to take a step back from all that. Social affairs where the *crème de la crème* of Manhattan society had gathered in tuxedos and gowns for banter, flattery, and business dealing. It was where Bennington had housed some of his favorite sculptures, both those he had purchased and those he had crafted with his own hands.

"You can come down now!" Bennington called out at the top of his lungs, seemingly to no one in particular.

Silence.

A few seconds later, Bennington heard the creak of a door opening and closing upstairs. Then he heard nothing at all.

"Donny!"

"On my way down, sir." Donny's voice echoed loudly. He began the descent down the carpeted spiral staircase leading from the second floor to the drawing room below.

Bennington stood up and stretched his tender back. He walked into the drawing room, his beige moccasins lightly brushing against the ornate rug.

The man once known as Wagenmann, then as Samuel Beck, crossed the threshold from the dining room to the parlor. As he did so, the painting he had purchased at auction last year caught his eye. It was an original work from one of the lesser-known painters of the Dutch Golden Age, an artistic rendering of what appeared to be two armies positioned strategically on opposite sides of large field of wheat. It was the type of painting tourists would see at the Metropolitan Museum of Art, casually acknowledge with a slight indifference, and then walk on to admire better known and more accessible works of art.

But what did they know?

To him, it was visually intoxicating.

It held special meaning for him. Plus, he had always admired the Dutch. They too were an industrious, educated people with a rich cultural heritage. Even if their language sounded ridiculous to his ear. He had hoped that they would have been more accommodating to the Germans during the war. But their populace had willingly collaborated with the Nazis on the Jewish problem. And that was something that he had appreciated very much.

Just then, Bennington noticed Donny standing a short distance away. He shifted his gaze away from the painting and toward his visitor, immediately noticing how the dark blue tracksuit Donny wore only served to heighten his toned physique.

"I trust you heard everything upstairs through the intercom," Bennington said, making direct eye contact with his hired gun.

"Yup," Donny said, as he adjusted his speech to be slightly more formal tone. "Yes, sir. I did."

With his short haircut, narrow brown eyes, and chiseled facial features, it occurred to Bennington that Donny looked as if he could have been a Hollywood stunt man. Either that or a motorcycle cop. But he was neither. He had taken a far different path in life. One of ideological commitment.

"Arthur is absolutely terrified of me," Bennington said.

"I can tell."

"As you know, with you—and unlike with Arthur—I prefer to keep our interactions over the phone. But I wanted to speak with you in person today for a reason. I think we're going to have to scale up our precautionary activities. Just for a while until things settle down. You understand me?"

"Yes. Makes sense."

"My primary concern right now is making sure this PI that Hans's wife hired doesn't somehow get in our way. This public offering is too essential to what I aim to accomplish," Bennington said.

"What you want me to do? All you gotta do is just say the word. You know me. I'll do whatever."

Bennington rubbed his chin, then wrapped his right arm delicately over Donny's shoulder.

"You see this painting?" Bennington asked, pointing directly at the one he had recently been admiring.

"Yeah. It's right in front of me," Donny said.

Bennington knew Donny wasn't trying to be sarcastic. It was just the way he spoke.

"Do you see what the artist depicted here?" Bennington asked, pointing directly at the painting with his free hand.

"It's pretty dark."

"Dark?"

"Yeah, I mean, you can't see that much. The colors, you know. It's definitely a battle scene, though."

"Right you are. But it's the subtext that matters."

"Subtext?" Donny asked.

"Yes."

"What does that mean?"

Bennington's face lit up in anticipation. It was the type of look a professor gets when his students show an eagerness to learn. Perhaps finally he had found someone who would come to appreciate his favorite showpiece as much as he did.

"It would be my pleasure," Bennington said with pride. "The first thing you need to know is that the Dutch rarely painted battlefield scenes.

Naval battles, yes. But land armies. Not so much."

Donny nodded. He was taking it all in, absorbing it.

"So, this one is unique from the artist's point of view. You see, Donny, it takes a certain indifference to current trends to see things differently from everyone else. So many people just accept the dictates of their society and go about their lives unquestioning. Unthinking. Just mindless drones going about their days, thinking of how to stuff their bellies with junk food. It's all so tedious. So very tedious."

"You're right."

Bennington wasn't blind to Donny's flattery. He liked it.

"But that's not all. Look at the far left of the painting," Bennington said.

In an attempt to get a better look, Donny walked closer to the wall. He was careful not to get too close.

"I see it. The guy in the black hat with the red sash draped across his chest. He's like a general or something?"

"Not exactly a general. But he certainly was their leader."

"I never understood art very well," Donny admitted.

"You're doing fine, Donny," Bennington said. "Just fine."

"So, what's the …" He thought of the word he was looking for. "Subtext. What's the subtext?"

Bennington smiled.

"The subtext is us."

"Yeah? How so?" Donny asked.

"You see, the man you indicated is a leader. You can see it in his eyes. And although his army is clearly outnumbered, he still has determination." Bennington paused. "You can see it in his eyes, can you not?"

Donny craned his neck forward. He squinted, his face now mere inches from the painted canvas.

"Yes, I see it."

"Well, that's us. We may be outnumbered. We may be out of step. But we're on the right side of history."

"The war is ours to win," Donny said in a matter-of-fact tone. One which indicated that, while he may not have had a formal education, he wasn't at all stupid. No, Bennington thought to himself. Donny was a shrewd character, that was for certain.

"Exactly! But we may need to sacrifice some of our brave soldiers along the way."

Donny thought it over.

"But we're gonna fight," Donny stated, knowing full well that was what

Bennington wanted to hear.

"Of course. Nothing comes without effort and dedication. Which is why I need you in top form now. I think we're going to have to dispose of Arthur pretty soon. He's becoming a liability. And I don't like liabilities."

From the cold look in Donny's eyes, it was clear he understood. It was the look of a soldier ready for battle.

"You got Arthur's home address?" he asked.

"He's sure that I don't. But then again, he has been mistakenly sure about a lot of things lately," Bennington said.

"Ha!" Donny exclaimed.

"Just a minute," Bennington said, as he walked back into the dining room. He pulled open the main drawer of the hutch. The one where he kept his most expensive china.

"This should help," he called into the other room.

"What's that?" Donny asked.

"Here," Bennington said, placing an empty matchbook into Donny's open palm.

Donny looked down at the object now in his hands.

"Sully's Pub?"

"Arthur left it with me back in LA."

"So that's where that sorry son of a bitch holes up."

"That appears to be the case. I'm pretty sure he's there almost every night. He has no woman in his life now, but he has the bottle."

"Good to know," Donny said. "This is gonna help a lot. Yeah, it sure is."

"As I said, we simply cannot let anything foul up the public offering. Once I have the money on hand, I will be able to transfer some of it to you and then you can provide some additional funds to your European associates."

"We all got the same goal in mind," Donny said.

"That's very true," Bennington said, as he focused his gaze directly at Donny once again. "I recall when we first were introduced. I remember it vividly. How you had impressed my friend Franz back in Frankfurt so very much that he thought you and I would work well together."

Donny nodded.

"Yeah," he said, "It's so fucking funny how life works out."

Bennington fell silent for a moment. Pondering. If only Hans could have been as diligent and committed to *the* cause—or any cause—as Donny, he thought. How different it all would have turned out. For both of them. But especially for Hans.

"You remember the first operation we financed?" Donny said.

"That was four years ago now, but of course I remember," Bennington said thoughtfully. "I very much remember. I was very impressed by what your network was able to accomplish in Rome."

"The kosher restaurant job? Those Jews never knew what hit them," Donny asked. For some reason he thought Vienna had been the movement's first project.

"Indeed. It sent a most necessary message," Bennington answered without skipping a beat.

"I remember seeing a clip about the bombing on the nightly news back in my apartment when it all went down. It's funny 'cause my sister Teresa was over for pasta that night and she wouldn't stop yapping while I was trying to watch," Donny said, quickly realizing that Bennington wasn't remotely interested in his family problems.

"It made all the American newspapers," Bennington said unable to keep the rising excitement out of his voice. "The international Jewish lobby did its best to make it look like they were the real victims. But so many people learned the right lesson from that. That at the end of the day, no matter how friendly the politicians are to the Jews, they aren't going to do much to stop future operations. Even in the heart of Europe."

"Funny how that works out," Donny snorted.

"You know, Donny, what I like about your associates in Paris is that they understand that they need not be in the limelight all the time. They're more than happy to let our Arab friends take full and total credit for operations against Jewish targets in Europe."

"You're right, but we have got a common enemy. I mean, it makes sense we'd pool resources," Donny said.

Bennington smiled. He was impressed. This kid was going to go places in the movement. Hell, he'd be a leader someday. It was good to know that people like Donny existed, Bennington thought. There needed to be people around to continue the struggle when he was gone.

"Absolutely," Bennington said. "I think the police ended up concluding that some fringe revolutionary Arab student group was solely responsible for the bombing. Not that they bothered to dig very deep to find out who financed it."

"They would have come up with a dead end anyway," Donny said. "The people I know are very good at shuffling money around. They've done it for heroin, so why not for this?"

Bennington's face lit up. There was something undeniably charming about the way Donny spoke. About the people he knew. He spoke with confidence, as if he were the ringleader in all this. But Bennington didn't mind. He liked it. It showed how deeply Donny was committed to the cause. That wasn't something to be mocked. It was something to be appreciated.

"Ya got anything else for me to do?" Donny asked.

"No. Not right now. We'll talk about getting the diamonds later."

"Definitely," Donny said, before repeating himself so Bennington would feel reassured. "Definitely."

Bennington smiled.

"Okay, then. I should get back to the city before rush hour. Have a few more sets to fix before I can call it quits for the day," Donny said.

"Oh," Bennington said, something quickly springing to mind. "One last thing. I will need you to follow up with that PI. I looked into his background. He doesn't seem to be a concern. He's simply not in our league, but ..."

"Not in our league?"

"Not in the slightest."

"Good to know," Donny said.

"I will give you his office mailing address right now before you leave. You can send him a note or something," Bennington said.

Donny nodded. He understood.

The two conspirators shook hands.

A blood pact was sealed.

CHAPTER 9

"It's way too hot."

"It's supposed to be hot."

"Not this hot," Mike said. He placed the spoonful of chicken soup back in the white ceramic mug just in front of him.

"Chicken noodle soup is supposed to be hot. Have you ever had cold chicken soup? It's fucking disgusting," Katie said, scrunching up her nose, mimicking a look of disgust.

If anyone had told Mike forty-eight hours ago that he'd be sitting across from Katie at his kitchen table arguing about the merits of lukewarm soup, he would have thought them absolutely crazy. Two days ago, he was a in Lenox Hill hospital bed, with crabby nurses and harried doctors poking and prying him, trying to make sure he didn't have a concussion as a result of the unfortunate incident on the subway platform. That's what the cops were calling it. An incident. Best not to put it down in the crime blotter as an act of attempted murder. Why do that and scare the locals? After all, what purpose would it serve other than to diminish real estate values in a rapidly gentrifying neighborhood?

For someone who was nearly killed, Mike had a surprisingly calm and lucid recollection how that morning had started off. Being awakened by a phone call. Meeting Millie at the Salonika. Chasing the man in the grey suit. Being pushed by another man onto the tracks. But what transpired between that and when he had woken up in the emergency room was still a blur. He knew he had blacked out, but he couldn't remember exactly when. Millie must have lied, told the paramedics that she was a relative. Because they had allowed her to ride along in the ambulance and to stay by his bedside for the first few hours he was in the ER.

Another thing he remembered very clearly was talking to a revolving door of uniformed police officers and plainclothes detectives, each pretending to give a damn about him. They scribbled down notes on small pads. Material for their obligatory reports. And went on their merry way. At first, Mike had tried to explain to them that the guy he was chasing was likely a danger to one of his clients, but by the time the third cop came into his room, he had decided that he didn't feel like sharing anymore. They weren't going to do anything about it. So why bother? He might as well play this close to the vest. Take care of it in his own way on his own time.

Plus, he had his own lead as to the identity of the man he had been chasing. One that the cops—even if they cared—didn't have.

Once he had been fully settled in his hospital room—they wanted him to stay overnight for observation so that the doctor could do a second MRI—one of the orderlies had brought him a large clear plastic bag. Enclosed in it were all his personal belongings. He hadn't lost anything important during the whole affair. Amazing. He still had his watch, wallet, and apartment keys. The ring and the letter had survived the ordeal as well. That in itself was unusual. Perhaps it was a sign. Not that Mike believed in signs.

But there had been something else in the bag as well. Something that he didn't recognize at first.

It was a black matchbook. Across the back in gold lettering was printed the name of a commercial establishment. Sully's Pub. Mike first thought that the hospital must have put in with his belongings by mistake. Then Mike remembered. That must have been the object that went flying when the man in the grey suit had leaped over the turnstile. It had to be.

Merely thinking about it jolted his memory, got his synapses firing.

That was it. Mike was now sure he was remembering things as clear as day. He had scooped up what he thought was a piece of cardboard from the platform and had jammed it into his pants pocket. That was mere seconds before he had been given a shove onto the tracks by that asshole in blue jeans.

Mike had no idea who the hell that guy was. Was he an associate of the man in the grey suit? Or just some random crazy person that haunted the underground tunnels? Questions he didn't have answers to yet. But he was determined to find out.

The day after he was released from the hospital, Mike had phoned Katie to apologize and to explain what had happened. To his surprise, she wasn't mad. Not in the slightest. That, or she was terrific at masking her emotions. He told her all about the chase, the subway incident, and the hospital stay and had invited her to come over.

She did. And she had brought chicken soup from Eli's Deli around the corner from his apartment building with her.

"So, how do you feel about the whole thing?" Katie asked. They had moved to the couch, where she was now cuddling up closer to Mike. Her tight black shirt pressed softly against his skin.

"Truthfully?" Mike asked, now sipping a Canada Dry ginger ale through a bent plastic straw. His jaw still ached from the fall onto the train tracks.

"No," she laughed. "Lie to me."

"I can't believe I'm saying this but—"

"But what?" Katie asked, her eyes widening.

"I kind of liked it," he admitted.

"Liked what? Nearly getting killed?"

"No," he said. "Not that part. It's just that, life has been so boring for me for so long that a little excitement kind of did me some good. You know?"

"No, I don't know," she said. Her voice was strained. "Damn it! You sound exactly like my father. Excited to be putting himself in danger."

"Wait a minute. I thought you said that your dad owns a discount electronics store near Union Square?"

"He does," Katie said, twirling her curly brunette hair with her slim narrow fingers.

"So how does that put him in danger? He has to pay protection money? Something like that?" Mike laughed. He was aware that he may be misreading her. After all, in many ways they still barely knew one other.

"It's really not fucking funny, Mike," she said. Her eyes had the same fire—the same intensity—that night they first met at the Limerick.

Mike focused his attention squarely on Katie. Despite her tough exterior, she looked almost as if she were genuinely perturbed. This surprised him. Usually nothing seemed to faze her. Which was definitely one reason why they had gotten on so well.

"Ok, so what is it then?" he asked.

"Remember what I told you about my dad the night we met?"

"Sort of. I had a few too many pints of Guinness that night, to be perfectly honest with you."

Mike tried as best he could to read the expression on Katie's face. To him, it failed to register any emotion.

"Well, I think I said something about how he used to be an activist."

"Honestly," Mike said quietly. "I don't remember. But you can tell me all about it now." He reached over and attempted to put his hand on her shoulders.

She tensed.

"So, when it comes to issues close to his heart, my Dad can get pretty passionate. He's not religious. Not at all. But I think he feels guilty that he got out of Germany early and most of his childhood friends did not make it."

She fell silent for a moment, then made direct eye contact with Mike.

It was a look that spoke volumes. A look that said, "If you know what's good for you, you better be listening to me now."

"What?" Mike asked, realizing his mind had trailed off elsewhere for a few seconds. He rubbed his aching jaw, hoping that the painkiller the doctor at the hospital gave him would soon kick in.

"My Dad. I was saying that he can be have tunnel vision when it comes to Nazi bullshit."

"I see," Mike said.

"Do you?"

"What is it you want me to say?" Mike asked.

"You don't get it, do you? The way you were talking earlier. About the thrill you got out of what happened to you at the subway station. That's exactly how it started for my Dad. When he first got involved with all this stuff, he used to get death threats in the mail. And it terrified my Mom and she was already battling breast cancer. She literally pleaded with my Dad to stop. And he told her he would. But he couldn't. It became an addiction. And pretty soon, he used to get a little thrill out of receiving death threats from neo-Nazi scum. The absolutely most vile garbage, you wouldn't believe it. It didn't take long until he almost started enjoying getting the threats. Like it excited him. Made him feel alive. He's pretty much stopped all that, but boy, did he ever fucking love getting under their skin."

"Who is they?"

"Huh?"

"Whose skin is he getting under?"

"Oh," she laughed. "Some neo-Nazi groups in the area that he worked to expose years ago. Bunch of fucking losers. He loved poking them in the eye."

"I see," Mike said.

"This kind of stuff doesn't really interest you, though, does it?" Katie said, getting up from the couch and walking into the small kitchen. She opened the refrigerator and put away the rest of the chicken soup.

"What makes you say that?" Mike asked, still seated on the couch.

Katie walked back to the living room and opened the window curtains. She peered down to the street below.

"Do kids who dress up in Norwegian folk costumes grow up to be adults who care about Nazis?" she said, turning around and walking back to the couch.

"Wow," Mike said. "That's not really fair." He made direct eye contact with her.

For the first time since he had met her, it seemed to Mike that Katie looked genuinely embarrassed. Contrite even. As if she immediately realized what she intended to be sarcasm instead came out as just plain hurtful.

"Sorry," she said softly, turning around and walking back to take a seat next to Mike on the couch.

"It's okay. You're not half wrong."

"How do you mean?"

"Hmm," Mike said. "You know, it's not as if I really think of myself as being part of any community. I don't really belong anywhere."

"It's not good for a man to be all alone," Katie said. Her tone wasn't remotely flirtatious. Nor was it didactic. It was as if she were reciting words. Pronouncing a statement of fact, a truism which couldn't possibly be contested.

"I guess," Mike mumbled.

"Anyway," Katie said, "tell me more about the guy you were chasing. You think you can find him?"

Mike picked up the black matchbook from the coffee table and gently placed it in the palm of Katie's hand.

She looked at it closely, as if she were a forensic scientist examining a clue.

"Sully's? Never heard of it," she said.

"It's in Hell's Kitchen."

"Oh? That's a pretty rough area."

"Tell me about it."

"So where did you get this again?"

"It fell out of the guy's pocket on the subway platform when I was chasing him. I assume that he has some connection to the place."

"Could be," Katie said.

"It's my only lead."

"And you still have no idea whether that asshole who pushed you on the tracks was connected to this guy?"

"None. But I assume so. Unless the guy was just a total loon. Which is very possible."

"I guess," Katie demurred.

"Yeah," Mike said quietly.

"Enough about the guy you were chasing. Tell me more about the case itself."

"I shouldn't involve you in this," Mike said.

"You already have."

"Have I?"

"Pretty much yeah," she said.

Mike quietly thought it over. In a way, she was totally right. He already was disclosing a ton to her. As if she were his therapist as well as his lover. Whether that turned out in the long run to be a good idea was yet to be determined. He had already let her in. No purpose in shutting the door in her face now.

"I told you about the ring, right?"

"Ring?" Katie asked, cocking her head slightly to the left. "I don't remember you telling me about a ring."

Mike got up from the couch, walked across the living room and into his bedroom. He opened the drawer to the nightstand next to his bed. He had placed the ring there for safekeeping. He picked it up and walked back to the living room. Katie had gotten up, gone to the fridge, and gotten herself a beer.

"This," he said, setting the ring down on the coffee table, "used to be belong to a dead man."

"That's a pretty fucking weird way of putting it," Katie said, as she walked back into the living room and sat down on the couch.

Mike shrugged his shoulders.

"What's this here?" Katie asked, holding the ring up at eye level. "Looks like something is written here."

"It's in Latin. I have no idea what it means, though."

"You know who would?" Katie blurted out.

"Who?"

"It's nothing. Forget I said anything."

"Come on. You can't say something like that and just pull back."

"My Dad. All right. My Dad knows Latin."

"He knows Latin?"

Katie looked directly at Mike.

"Yeah. Why?" she said. "Is that so weird?"

Mike hesitated for a moment, choosing his next words carefully. "I just didn't expect it," he confessed.

Katie laughed. "Oh, I assure you. My Dad is full of surprises. He loves learning languages. He loves to learn."

Mike smiled. He understood not just the plain meaning of her words, but their subtext. He imagined that, deep down, Katie was deeply proud of her father. A man, who by her own account, sounded like an autodidact and a polymath. The type of man Mike had aspired to be when he first arrived as a bright-eyed college freshman on Princeton's campus some fifteen odd years ago.

"You know I just had the craziest idea!" Katie cried.

"What's that?" Mike asked.

"Oh, it's really stupid," Katie said quietly, seemingly backing off from the enthusiasm she exhibited mere seconds ago.

"You can't do that," Mike said. "Just throw a fishing line out there like that and then pull it back. You have to reel me in."

"So, you're a fish now?" Katie asked, a sly grin on her face.

"I'm a tuna," Mike said. "Tuna salad with little dill pickles in it."

"That's frighteningly specific."

Katie laughed.

"Okay," she said, taking a deep breath. "I thought, well, maybe my Dad could translate the Latin for you and that way you'd get to meet him."

She let the words hang in the air for a moment.

"Uh," Mike said. "That certainly would prove to be interesting."

"I'd say so," Katie said, once again twirling her hair between her fingers.

"Anyway, what are your plans for the rest of the day?" Mike asked.

"Dunno really. I have to do some errands. Need to take the crosstown bus to pick up some stuff at Zabar's. Plus a shit ton of laundry. It's been piling up. Stuff like that. You?"

"I need to rest. Tomorrow, I am going to head down to this Sully's Pub and see if I can locate that son of a bitch."

"You can't be serious," Katie said.

"What makes you say that?"

"Because the last time, that guy nearly got you killed!"

"Look, it's my job. I have to do this. I don't have a choice."

"Sure you do."

"What? To chicken out and tell my client I got cold feet. That I'm not up to the job?"

"You could always tell the cops about the matchbook. Maybe they can snoop around Sully's and look for the guy if you give them a good description," Katie said.

"Not going to happen," Mike said.

Katie was about to say something, but instead bit her lip.

"Ok, then," she said. "At least hear me. I have an idea."

"Shoot."

Katie smiled. "Funny you should say that."

"Say what?" Mike asked.

"Shoot. Because I think what you really need to do is to get yourself some form of protection. Like a—"

"Gun," Mike said, finishing her sentence for her. "Like a gun. Is that it? You want me to get a gun?"

"You know how to use one, right?"

"Yeah, actually I do," Mike said. "When I was in law school, I did this program with the NYPD where they taught those of us who wanted to be prosecutors all about firearms and lethal force."

"There you go," Katie said.

"But how am I going to get myself a gun so quickly? I'm going to need a permit."

"You have your PI license, though?"

"Of course," Mike said.

Katie got up from the couch and walked into the small kitchen.

"What are you looking for?" Mike shouted.

"A pen," she yelled back.

"Look in the counter drawer. The one under the toaster."

"Got it," she said, walking back into the living room. "Now, I am going to need something to write on."

"There's some legal pads over there, I think," Mike said, pointing to the small bookshelf adjacent to the television stand.

"You still use those?"

"Habits are hard to break."

"Ah," she said, grabbing a yellow legal pad. She walked back to the couch, a bounce in her step.

"What's so important that you have to write down?" Mike asked, his curiosity piqued.

"This," she said, scribbling something quickly onto the top sheet of paper. She tore it off at its perforated mark, held it out for Mike to take.

"Who the hell is Josh Skolnick?"

"My cousin," she said, a slightly mischievous grin on her face.

"And he is?" Mike said, letting the last word of his question trail off.

"He works at City Hall."

"Doing what exactly?"

"He works in the Personal Firearms Permit Department. Tell him you know me and I'm sure he won't have a problem, uh, expediting the process for you."

"You've got to be shitting me," Mike said.

"Not at all. He'd do it. He's a cool guy."

"I don't think that's happening."

"Suit yourself," she said. "Don't say I didn't warn you."

"Are you disappointed?"

"Nah," she said. "I assume you know what you're doing. What you could be getting yourself into if you show up at that bar in that neighborhood. But hey, it's your life."

"I'll be careful. I promise."

"You better," she said, leaning forward and kissing him gently. Mike could taste cold beer on her soft lips.

"I'll see you later then?" Mike asked.

"Sure. Just call me tomorrow or the day after. Cool?"

"I can do that."

Katie got up from the couch, grabbed the black purse she had left on the kitchen table, and headed out the door.

She really was a whirlwind.

A slightly dangerous and unstable one perhaps. But she had an effect on him that was undeniable. She made him feel alive. In a way he had not felt in years. And right now, that's all that really mattered. Wasn't it?

Mike was now alone in his apartment. Time to decompress. He enjoyed Katie's company, but she took a lot out of him. He sipped his Canada Dry through a white plastic straw.

Damn it.

His jaw still ached. He leaned back on the couch and wondered when it would no longer hurt like a son of a bitch.

But that wasn't the most important thing on his mind right now.

The most important thing was finding out who that man was. The one tailing Millie. The one who nearly got him killed. That fucker was going to pay.

Mike picked up the matchbox and flipped it over.

He'd made up his mind. Tomorrow evening, he'd go down to Sully's Pub and see if he could find the man there.

That's all he had to go on, but it was worth a shot.

What did he have to lose?

CHAPTER 10

Mike walked up the concrete steps from the 50th Street subway station and stepped out into the fading sunlight. He jostled his way through the throngs of people, nearly colliding with a delivery boy. The kid was riding his bicycle far too close to the curb.

"Hey jackass, watch where you're going!" Mike shouted.

"You look out yourself," the Chinese bicyclist shouted back, his middle finger prominently raised in an offensive salute. One that needed no translation.

Mike wished he had a quick comeback.

But he didn't.

Within seconds, the delivery boy had already peddled his way down Tenth Avenue, weaving through a congested maze of honking yellow cabs backed up at a red light. And what would he have said anyway? What good would it have done? Nothing good ever came from escalating no-win situations.

Mike had to keep his mind on his mission. On what brought him here. To locate the man in the grey suit and to find out, one way or the other, what the hell he had been doing spying on his client.

Turning the corner onto 49th Street, Mike caught the distinctive smell of grilled meat. The odor hung in the late summer air. Instinctively, he looked around to see where the smell was coming from. And with that, he inadvertently made eye contact with a portly Hispanic man hawking Sabrett hot dogs from a small pushcart, one that had clearly seen better days.

Shit. Too late.

"Hey boss, I give you two dogs for one dollar. What you say? You look hungry. Good deal," the guy called out. He was obviously thinking he had a hungry would-be customer on his hands.

"Not today," Mike said, waving his right hand in the air as if it would make the guy vanish. Like in one of those ridiculous magic acts that street performers did for tourists' money in Central Park.

"What you no like hot dogs? You not real New Yorker then?" the man asked in a nearly unintelligible accent.

"Trust me, I'm a real fucking New Yorker," Mike retorted. He immediately averted eye contact and quickened his step.

The further he got away from the subway stop, the more things seemed to calm down.

Looking down the block, Mike was struck by the sheer volume of dilapidated apartment buildings lining both sides of the street. From the look of them, they were almost certainly constructed in the early 1920s but had steadily decayed over the decades. Being in this part of town reminded Mike of the old timers he'd worked with in the DA's office. Tough, unforgiving guys who had regaled him with sordid tales from this once crime-infested part of town. They had told him of a time when Irish and Puerto Rican street gangs ruled the streets. When a switchblade knife could make you both master and king. But it wasn't just storytelling for its own sake. It was their way of establishing a pecking order, of letting Mike know that it was because of men like them that the neighborhood was no longer a complete no-go zone.

As Mike picked up his pace, small beads of nervous perspiration trickled down his forehead. They fell onto his already soaked black polo shirt. He was getting closer to Sully's Pub. That's what his gut was telling him.

Mike rubbed his jaw. He looked around the area, his eyes scanning the immediate vicinity for signs of danger. He wasn't about to let himself get ambushed again.

All he saw was a motley crew of locals.

Old grizzled white guys, their lives all but over, sitting on stoops likely telling each other the same jokes they had told the previous week and the week before that. Puerto Rican street kids chasing each other and yelling in Spanish, a language Mike never studied and didn't care to understand.

And a small brood of tall women, made up in brightly colored dresses, high heels, and plastered on makeup. Gossiping on a street corner and sounding like birds recently flown home to nest. They actually seemed content. One of them caught Mike's eye. She smiled at him. For a second, Mike could have sworn that the she was really a he.

A white dude in a wig.

You never really knew in this part of town.

Not that it really bothered him. People should be able to able to do whatever they wanted as long as they didn't harm others. And he was hardly in the position to tell other people how to live their lives.

Then he saw it.

Sully's Pub.

Just west of 49th and 10th, the local Irish bar that had been there through it all. Both the bad times and worse ones.

Standing just outside the entrance, Mike couldn't help but notice the pub's neon yellow sign. Brightening the sidewalk in the twilight, it buzzed and crackled with luminous energy.

But the sign really wasn't what most captured his attention the moment.

No. It was his heart.

What had started as a slight jumpy palpitation had morphed into an unsteady thump. An increasingly heavy and rapid pounding that made him jittery. Jittery and exhilarated.

As unsafe as going to Sully's might be, it was a hell of a lot more exciting than all of the other things he'd done as a PI. Digging through people's trash to look for signs of marital infidelity, for instance. Something he had done far too many times for far too many clients, all of whom were far from saints themselves. Or sitting in a cold rental car in February, engine off, and peeing in a plastic soda bottle. All to watch who was coming and going in and out of an Upper West Side brownstone.

Mike looked down at his hands. They were doing something that they hadn't done since the night his mother had died at Sloan Kettering. They were shaking.

Mike took a deep breath.

Who was to say that the guy would even be here tonight?

All he had to do is go inside, order a drink, and then talk with the bartender a bit. See if he might know the guy Mike was looking for. Something he had done in one fashion or another many times before. Don't chicken out now, he told himself. You've come too far to turn back.

Mike looked up at the darkening sky. He saw the last remnants of a bright day, the sun fading fast in the twilight. He steeled himself, his busy mind weaving possibilities of what might happen next.

Sully's Pub was nothing like The Limerick.

The Upper East Side bar where he had met Katie for the first time had a major kitsch factor. It may have been dark inside. But its spirit was bright.

Not so with Sully's.

There were no radiant yuppies here. There was very little *joie de vivre*. No. Sully's was a sad little place filled with sad little people. What he saw were working-class guys who drank not to celebrate, but to forget. To forget that their lives did not live up to the promise that their schoolteachers assured them was just within their reach. If they only applied themselves. They drank to forget that with each passing day, their chances at turning their lives around, of finding happiness, seemed to diminish exponentially.

Not that he came here to take in the ambiance.

Mike sat down on a rickety wood stool facing the bar.

"Name your poison," the man behind the counter said. He sounded tired.

"Jack and Coke," Mike said, briefly making eye contact with the ruddy-faced bartender. He imagined that this fellow must have spent the better part of the last three decades behind this bar.

"You got it, boss."

Less than a minute later, Mike had his drink in front of him. He didn't usually drink hard liquor. But this was not an ordinary situation. His hands were not shaking anymore. He still needed something to calm his nerves. And his pounding heart.

After nursing his drink for what seemed like an eternity, Mike steeled up the nerve to ask the bartender if he knew a slightly overweight middle-aged man who usually wore grey suits. A smoker as well.

The bartender laughed.

"Not many people come in here wearing suits," he said. "But there is one guy who always does. Always."

Jackpot.

"Can you tell me more about him?" Mike asked, immediately realizing he sounded way too eager. Suspiciously so.

"Why don't you ask him yourself," the bartender said, pointing over Mike's shoulder, toward the back of the bar.

Mike spun around on his stool.

There he was. The man in the grey suit. The man he had come to find.

Wiping his hands on his trousers, the man in the grey suit was stumbling out of the bathroom. He looked up and made unmistakable direct eye contact with the bartender. Then he focused his gaze squarely on Mike.

Mike's hands began to shake again.

Shit. It was now or never.

Mike stood up. He rushed across the room, nearly toppling a small empty table in the process. And before he knew it, before he had a chance to reflect on his actions, Mike had grabbed the guy in the grey suit by his collar.

"Who the fuck *are* you?" Mike bellowed. Saliva flew out of his mouth. Mike couldn't believe the ferocity in his voice.

"You're making a big mistake, buddy. A huge mistake," the man said, slurring his words. He was plastered. Drunk as a skunk.

"Really?" Mike asked, increasingly conscious that many of the bar's patrons were now staring right at him. "And why is that?"

"Because, you dumb bastard, I'm a goddamn federal agent."

"Bullshit." Mike didn't say the word so much as enunciate it. He patted down the guy's chest on both sides. He didn't feel a gun.

"I'm giving you two seconds to get your goddamn hands off me," the man snarled.

Out of all the scenarios that had raced through Mike's mind mere seconds ago, the notion that this guy was a fed had never occurred to him.

What if this had all been a giant mistake?

No. It wasn't. It couldn't be. Mike wouldn't let it be a mistake. He had a client who was paying him. This was his job.

"Well," Mike said, "if you're a fed, where's your fucking badge?"

"Back pocket."

"What? I've known more than a few cops in my day and none of them carried their badges in their back pockets," Mike said tersely.

Just then, man in the grey suit tried to take a hard swing at Mike.

He missed.

His coordination was lacking. A good thing too. If Arthur weren't completely inebriated, he could have done some serious damage.

Mike instinctively shoved the man against the bathroom door. He was tempted to slap the guy back and forth across his face. Just like Humphrey Bogart did in the movies.

But Mike wasn't about to do anything that stupid. He was fully aware that he had only a small window of time before one of the bar's patrons got up and intervened. Whose side they would choose, if they even chose a side, was anyone's guess.

His right forearm was pressed up against the guy's neck.

With his left hand, Mike reached deep into the man's back pocket. He felt something. A wallet? No. It was smaller than a standard size wallet. Mike grabbed the object and pulled it out. His first thought was that it was a money clip wallet.

Mike flipped it open. What he saw unnerved him. On one side was a badge. On the other was a laminated identification card.

Arthur Zeffirelli.

Either this was one of the most skillfully produced fake IDs Mike had ever seen, or shitfaced Arthur here was speaking true: He was a fed!

It didn't make a whole lot of sense.

Why would a federal agent have been so eager to get away from Mike on 86th Street? And why wasn't he carrying a weapon?

Something was off.

Mike didn't know what to say, so he merely mouthed the first words that entered his mind.

"Is this for real?" he asked, holding up the laminated ID card.

Arthur—if that was really his name—coughed. Spittle landed on his own face.

"Tell me!" Mike cried out.

"It's my name and you're in a giant heap of shit, my friend. Assaulting a federal agent. And that's for starters."

Mike removed his arm from Arthur's throat.

"Why were you following Millie Johnson? And who the hell was that guy who pushed me onto the tracks? He a fed too?"

"That's confidential," Arthur managed to force out, his knees buckling. He nearly stumbled to the floor.

What the hell was going on, Mike wondered. This drunken slob was a fed? This guy who looked as if he had one foot in the grave?

Fuck it. Time to get some answers. Once and for all.

Mike grabbed Arthur by his lapel.

"Tell me what is going on! I nearly got killed the other day, and I need some answers."

Mike couldn't believe the words coming from his mouth. Never in his life had he talked to another person like this.

Not until today.

"You really don't want to know. You really don't. If you know what's good for you. I'm warning you. Let it go," Arthur said.

For a drunk, Arthur's words were abnormally lucid.

Mike's head spun. Thoughts cascaded in his mind. What if he had overstepped? What was preventing him from, as Arthur had put it, letting it go? Was Millie Johnson really that important? He could just sever the relationship. Cut ties and move on with his life. What was stopping him?

"Why should I let it go?"

"As I said," Arthur repeated, "if you know what's good for you. I'm willing to forget any of this even happened."

Stunned, Mike removed his hands from Arthur's lapel.

Make up your mind, Mike told himself. Make a decision. He wondered why he was always like this. Always overthinking. Especially when he was confronted with the possibility of getting himself in deep shit.

It was too late.

Arthur had already made his move. Seemingly imbued with a newfound energy, Arthur shoved Mike out of his path and bolted for the exit.

Mike couldn't believe his eyes. It was as if he were frozen. Paralyzed. It was all happening again.

After everything he had put himself through, was he really going to just let it go?

No.

He steeled himself. One way or the other, he was going to get some answers. Even if he had to beat it out of a federal agent.

Mike walked briskly through the bar and headed for the door.

He was fully aware just how many eyes were on him. Lucky for him no one had intervened when he grabbed Arthur. He supposed these poor slobs in here just didn't see it as their concern. Still, he was amazed at their sheer passivity.

Back on the street, Mike took a deep breath and looked in both directions.

That's when he heard the scream.

CHAPTER 11

Attempting to locate the source of that blood-curdling cry, Mike quickly looked first to his left. Then to his right. He saw nothing out of the ordinary.

Then he heard it again.

A cry for help.

It sounded like it was coming from behind Sully's.

The alleyway.

The scream had morphed into a shriek. The type that pierced your eardrums. It was like a feverish baby screaming its lungs out in the middle of the night.

Mike ran toward where he thought the scream was coming from. At some level, he was aware that he might be running into danger. Into a trap. But he didn't care. He turned the corner and peered down the alleyway.

A shadowy figure was running in the opposite direction. Away from Mike. Disappearing into the night like an assassin.

Although the alley was dark, he could make out two distinct silhouettes. He saw what looked like a tall woman in a dress. She was looking down at a person curled up on the ground. A middle-aged man.

Arthur.

It was his screams that Mike had heard. Had to be.

Mike approached the darkened figures with caution.

"Hey, what's going on?" he shouted, wondering if Arthur had fallen and hurt himself in a drunken stupor.

"Get back! This is a police matter." It was a woman in a dress who spoke, but her voice was that of a man. She flashed a badge.

What the hell, Mike thought.

That very second, it all just clicked. The woman in the dress was the hooker he had seen earlier. He had been right. The she was indeed a he. An undercover cop no doubt. Probably from the vice squad. Had to be. They did a lot of work in this neighborhood. It only made sense. Still, Mike wondered how the cop got here so quickly.

"I'm a PI," Mike yelled back. As if the cop would give a damn. He wasn't sure if the undercover even heard him.

"This is a police matter."

"It's also part of my case," Mike replied stubbornly.

"Turn the fuck around and get the hell out of here," the cop yelled back. Harsh words from what looked like a broad.

Mike chose not to heed the command. He proceeded as if the cop wasn't even there. He inched forward.

It was then that Mike realized what had happened. Exactly why Arthur had screamed for his life.

It wasn't because he had fallen down in a drunken stupor. It was far more serious than that.

There, on the pavement, lay Arthur in a pool of his own blood. Protruding from his stomach, a large kitchen knife.

He was crying, squirming on the ground.

The cop, who had now taken off his wig, was trying to apply pressure to the gaping holes in Arthur's abdomen.

But it was seemingly of little use. Blood was spurting out of Arthur, soaking his white shirt.

Arthur whimpered. Gentler than shrieks, his sobs echoed primordial terror. They were the entreaties of a man not yet ready to meet his maker.

Mike heard something. A gurgling sound. The likes of which he had never heard before. Something that made his stomach churn.

It was Arthur again. He was choking on his own blood. He was gasping for air.

"Hold on, boss. I called in a bus," said the undercover cop. He was holding a small walkie-talkie that he had retrieved from his purse in his hands.

Arthur cleared his throat, spit out blood.

"I ..." he said.

"Don't try to talk. Just keep still," the undercover commanded.

"No," Arthur managed to say.

"No what?" the cop asked.

"I need ..." Arthur said, pointing squarely at Mike.

"Need? Need what?" the cop asked again.

"He wants to talk to me! Don't you see?" Mike roared.

The situation was one of pandemonium. Too much was happening too fast. But Mike was certain of one thing. Arthur had something he wanted to say. Something he wanted to get off his chest.

Mike positioned himself closer to both Arthur and the cop. He slowly bent down. He kneeled on the pavement.

It appeared as if the cop was no longer was bothered by his presence.

"What? What is it?" he asked Arthur, doing his best to speak in a somewhat gentle tone. As if that alone would save Arthur from his all but certain fate.

Mike couldn't help but notice the sadness in Arthur's eyes. Eyes which looked more like those of a puppy dog than those of a man.

Blood dripping down his chin, Arthur focused his gaze directly at Mike. He held eye contact for as long as he could manage.

"Bennington is Wagenmann. Nuremberg Papers," he whispered directly in Mike's ear so that the cop couldn't possibly hear. Arthur was using all his remaining strength to get the words out.

"Who is Bennington?" Mike shouted, getting even closer to Arthur.

The cop was distracted on his walkie-talkie, giving directions to the ambulance on the way. Telling them where the alleyway was.

"What are the Nuremberg Papers?" Mike asked. He knew Arthur's end was near.

It was too late.

Arthur took his final breath as the ambulance pulled up.

"He's dead. He's fucking dead. I don't believe it," Mike sighed.

"Just who are you and what are you doing here?" the cop barked, as he finished his conversation with the ambulance driver.

"I'm a PI. And this guy is apparently a federal agent."

Mike flashed his PI license, still shocked that a cop let him get so close to a dying man.

"What the hell?" the cop said.

"Yeah. I don't know. I had nothing to do with this," Mike said, pointing to Arthur's body.

"I know that. I saw the guy who did it. Couldn't make out his face. He likely thought I was just some hooker and didn't try to hide himself very much. He and this fellow here got into it in the alley, then the guy stabbed him and ran away. Down there."

He pointed to the opposite far end of the alley. Where it opened up again onto 50th Street.

"I'm going to need you to stay here with me. You're going to need to come with me to the precinct for a few questions and a report. You hear me, chief?"

"I hear you," Mike answered. He looked down at his shirt and noticed spots of crimson. It was blood. Arthur's. He had gotten too close.

"What did he say to you?" the cop demanded.

"Say to me?" Mike asked.

"Yeah, when I was on the call, I saw him trying to tell you something. What did he say?" the cop asked.

Think fast, Mike told himself. Have a believable answer.

"He said that he wanted a Catholic funeral," Mike said.

"Is that right?" the cop snarled.

Mike didn't know whether the cop believed a word he said. What he did know was that this was the second time in how many days that Mike had found himself in the presence of a dead man. And not just a dead man. A dead man with a knife stuck in his chest.

Just who were these men that Arthur mentioned? The name Bennington seemed oddly familiar, but he couldn't quite place where he'd heard it before. He sure as hell never heard of anyone called Wagenmann before. But it sounded like a German last name. Just like Scheidermann.

Just like Hesse.

This can't all be one giant coincidence, Mike thought. This has to mean something.

CHAPTER 12

There was a thunderstorm later that evening. It seemingly came out of nowhere. Steady downpours with winds up to forty miles per hour and gusts so forceful that they took down telephone wires and more than a few tree branches. So torrential that the Yankees had their home game against the Tigers called in the second inning. There was hardly a yellow cab available for hire in all of Manhattan that night. Those unlucky enough not to have had an umbrella with them either had to wait out the storm somewhere or get completely drenched.

Mike had been able to wait out the storm. But not in a place he had wanted to be. Once again, he had spent his night inside a police station. Unlike the Peter Hesse situation, he was never considered a suspect in the murder of Arthur Zeffirelli. But the cops sure as hell wanted to know what Mike had been discussing with Zeffirelli at Sully's just prior to his brutal murder in the alley just outside.

Mike had done his best to explain the basics. And did so as truthfully as possible in a language the cops would understand. How he had been hired by Millie Johnson. How he had found Peter Hesse on the floor at the Big Apple Motel. And how Arthur had been tailing Millie. How he had run away from him that morning on the Upper East Side. How he was pushed onto the subway tracks. The cops took their report and told Mike to remain available.

Mike had asked whether he was a suspect. They had said no. That he wasn't. But they would likely be following up with him in a few days.

They seemed to have trusted him. He had been honest. But he didn't tell the cops everything, least of all what Arthur had whispered in his ear. That was between him and a man no longer of this earth.

There were too many aspects of this case that raised far more questions than answers. And the NYPD was the last group of people who wewre going to be helpful. He didn't feel any obligation to tell them of this apparent German connection. Given that a federal agent was somehow involved in all this, he didn't quite know who he was able to trust either.

No.

He wasn't about to tell a bunch of uniformed patrolmen things they weren't going to understand. Things that they'd probably mock anyway. Just like they always did with things they did not understand. Plus, if

Arthur truly was who he claimed to have been, the feds would surely be doing their own investigation into the matter. If they wanted to speak with Mike, they weren't going to have a hard time. He wasn't a difficult man to find.

Throughout his ordeal at the police station, Mike told himself that he'd find a way to figure this all out. To make sense of everything piling up all around him. The death of Peter Hesse. The mysterious letter. The ring. The murder of Arthur. His final words. About a man named Bennington and something he called the Nuremberg Papers.

Mike made up his mind. He would figure this puzzle out on own terms. This was his case and he was going to see it through to the very end.

One way or the other.

□ □ □

It was nearly seven o'clock in the morning when Mike finally emerged from the police station on 26th Street. He looked up at the breaking dawn. It was going to be a cloudy day. He glanced down at the sidewalk and saw the small puddles. He smiled to himself. Maybe he should go back inside and thank the cops for giving him a place to wait out the storm with donuts and coffee. As if that would go over well with those hyenas.

Mike walked down the block, his senses on high alert for the next available cab. There weren't all that many people out this early. Just a few workmen here and there. As he made his way toward Fifth Avenue, his mind kept returning to those two names. The ones that Arthur had whispered to him just before he died.

Bennington and Wagenmann.

Mike wondered just who these men were and what exactly they had to do with this madness.

The first name in particular haunted him. It sounded so damn familiar, but he couldn't quite place it. He was sure that he had heard it before. Or read it.

That's when it came to him. Like a punch to the gut.

That night in the Salonika when he had waited for Barry to get back from the bathroom.

He hadn't heard the name, after all. He had read it.

Bennington was the same name as the guy in that *New York Times* article he had been reading. The one about a wealthy industrialist about to take his company public.

But it couldn't possibly be the same guy. Could it? Bennington was a common enough name. It sounded English. Protestant. Mike was even pretty sure there was a college in New Hampshire with that name. No. Vermont. It was in Vermont.

Just then, Mike saw a yellow cab turn the corner and quickly make its way along 27th Street.

He ran toward it, furiously waving his right hand so that the driver would notice him. He promised himself that if this cab stopped for him, he'd go straight to his office and get cracking. Last time he'd talked to Millie, she assured him she was still his client. And that he'd still be paid for his services. So at least that part was taken care of.

Now all he had to do is make sense of all these different bits of information. To see if he could put together small piece of jigsaw puzzle so it all added up to make a coherent picture.

The cabbie slammed on his breaks, bringing his vehicle to a complete stop.

Mike opened the door and got inside. "East Village. Second and Ninth," he said.

"You got it, boss."

The cab sped away, its rubber tires splashing puddle water onto the adjacent sidewalk.

Mike, sitting in the back seat, looked past the driver and through the front windshield, dirt caked on the glass. He noticed the sun was starting to peak through the clouds. It provided the early morning with a little brightness.

It wouldn't last, he told himself. The clouds will be back soon enough.

Mike closed his eyes and took a series of short deep breaths.

So much to figure out. So much to try to understand.

Just then, Mike opened his eyes and caught a glimpse of himself in the cab's rearview mirror.

His first impression was that he looked tired. Just like he did when he was at Aunt Christina's last week. That now seemed so long ago.

But it was his second thought that really struck him. For Mike thought that he saw something in his eyes that he hadn't seen for a long time. Not since he was working in the DA's office.

What he saw was determination.

The same look he used to have when he was about to go into the courtroom.

He closed his eyes, plopped back in the seat, and immediately dozed off.

The cab continued its journey.

CHAPTER 13

It was now a full week since Mike had last set foot in his office. Since that humid night he had met Millie Johnson for the first time, when he had taken her on as a client.

How long ago it all seemed.

So much had changed in such a short time. Not only had he witnessed two murders, but he had almost been killed himself. And he had a new woman in his life. Someone with whom he actually clicked.

Or at least he did for the time being.

Mike yawned loudly as he sat down at his desk. As he sorted through the stack of mail that had accumulated during his absence, he ruminated upon Arthur's final words. A message from beyond the grave.

The Nuremberg Papers, as Arthur had called them.

What did Nuremberg have to do with any of this?

Wasn't that the city in Germany where the victorious Allies had their war crimes tribunal for Nazis? Mike remembered watching the newsreels from the trial in his course in international humanitarian law he had taken his third year in law school.

It didn't make a whole lot of sense. But clearly something was going on. Something that went well beyond New York. Something out of the past that was haunting the present.

Mike noticed another small pile of junk mail that the cleaning woman must have left on his desk. He picked it up and tossed it into the trash. He did the same for a few unopened envelopes. Clearly junk as well.

Seeing all those envelopes reminded him of that cryptic letter— the one that Millie had brought with her to the Salonika Diner. The one that was now safely ensconced in his desk at home. If he was remembering correctly—and he was pretty sure he was despite his current exhaustion— the letter was dated 1951.

That wasn't so long after the Nuremberg Trials.

What was the connection?

That Hesse was some sort of secret Nazi? Patently and completely absurd. The guy was a hardly a criminal mastermind. He could barely run his own life, let alone have been part of vast and evil conspiracy. What type of aging Nazi gets himself doped up in a shabby hotel room with a young hooker?

Mike grabbed a small blank legal pad and reached for a ballpoint pen. He wanted to write down the names Arthur mentioned last night. Words spoken by a man who only had seconds left to live. On the paper, in cursive handwriting, Mike wrote the names. He knew he had spelled Bennington correctly. He spelled the other name Wagonman; it looked funny, but …

Immediately after tearing off the piece of paper and sticking it in his pocket, Mike looked down into the wastebasket and spotted a large plain manila folder sealed with a gold clasp and clear tape.

It had been tucked in with the junk mail, but somehow Mike had missed it. He retrieved it from the basket. Written on the front in black marker were his full name and office address. It was meant for him all right. But there was no stamp or return address. No way to know who sent it.

Well, that's odd.

His curiosity getting the best of him, Mike slowly pried it open. He reached inside and removed the contents.

What he saw nearly made him collapse.

He vigorously rubbed his eyes, making sure that the lack of sleep wasn't causing him he to imagine things.

He was not.

Someone, deliberately anonymous, had mailed Mike a series of glossy black and white photographs. Aunt Christina coming out of her house, walking around her neighborhood, and shopping at Olaf's Bakery in Bay Ridge. And not just photographs.

There was a note enclosed as well.

Mike picked it up and read it. His lips silently mouthed the words scrawled in black marker.

"If you know what's good for you, kike, you will let it go."

Mike slammed his closed fist on his desk, jettisoning several pens every which way and sending a bunch of loose paperclips onto the floor.

This does it. *This fucking does it.* Someone is playing a deadly game with him.

All right, then, he told himself. If someone wants to play a game and bring Aunt Christina into this, he would reciprocate in kind.

Time to play his own game.

Mike looked at his watch, noticing how the crystal was cracked as result of the subway incident. It told him that it was now around seven in the morning. His cousin Erik would likely be up by now.

If Aunt Christina would be safe with anyone, it would be with his cousin Erik. The grandson of Christina's cousin, Karen, he had a lumberjack build. A New Jersey State Trooper for nearly two decades, he was the type of guy you wanted to have in your corner when shit went down. He didn't fuck around.

Mike picked up the phone and dialed his cousin. The phone rang once. Twice.

"Hello?"

It was a child's voice. A girl. Erik's daughter, Sophie.

"Hey there. Is your Dad home?" Mike asked.

"Yup."

"Can you get him for me?"

"Who is this?"

"This is his cousin Mike."

Silence.

Then a child shouting.

"Daaaaaad! Your cousin Mike is on the phone!"

Mike shook his head. This was taking too long. Time was of the essence here. Aunt Christina could be in real danger.

A shuffling of footsteps. Then a voice.

"Hey Michael. Is something wrong?"

"Hi Erik. Sorry to call you so early, but I am going to need your help."

"Talk to me," Erik said.

Ten minutes later, right after he finished the call with Erik, he dialed Aunt Christina to tell her that he and Erik would be paying her a surprise visit this morning. She typically got up at the break of dawn and by this time, had already finished her coffee and morning crossword puzzle.

The phone rang once. Then twice.

Pick up. Please pick up, he pleaded silently.

The phone rang a third time. Then a fourth. Still no answer.

Beads of sweat formed on Mike's upper lip.

Mike covered his mouth, gulped. His tongue felt like a piece of gauze stuck in his throat.

Fifth ring.

Where was she? She couldn't still be sleeping at this time.

Sixth ring.

Still no answer.

Mike put down the receiver and took a deep breath. He looked down at his hands. Although his heart was pounding just like it did when he was about to go into Sully's, this time his hands weren't shaking. Not at all. He held them both in the air at eye level. He looked again. Closer this time. They were completely steady.

That's right. You better toughen up.

His thoughts immediately returned to his aunt.

Maybe she's in the bathroom, he thought. She's old. It takes her a while to get places.

That would explain it.

Who was he kidding? Aunt Christina moved pretty fast, especially when she had her sneakers on.

He'd just try again in a few minutes. There had to be a good explanation.

Mike picked up the receiver again. No time to waste. He dialed Katie. She was probably still asleep. But he didn't care. What he had on his mind was too important to wait. She'd understand.

The phone rang once. Twice. Katie answered just after the second full ring. Her grogginess came through loud and clear.

"Hello. Who's this?" she groaned.

"It's Mike."

"What can I do for you, Mike?"

"Sorry to do this to you, but do you remember when you gave me your cousin's number the other day?" Mike asked.

"Sure. It was my idea after all."

"Can you give it to me again?"

"Right now? What time is it anyway?"

Mike heard what sounded like Katie knocking her alarm clock on the floor.

Mike quickly glanced down at his watch again.

"Around seven."

"Okay, I had my alarm set for 7:30 anyway."

"Can I have the number?" Mike asked breathlessly, totally oblivious to his tone.

Once again, Katie gave Mike the phone number of Josh Skolnick, her cousin down at City Hall. The one who could expedite the processing of a firearms permit for Mike. That's what she had claimed that night in Mike's apartment anyway.

"Thanks babe. I owe you one. I will see you later," Mike said, as he hung up the phone and looked down at the scrap of paper on which he had written the phone number. This time, he was much more enthusiastic about it. This time, he was absolutely sure he was going to use it. As if his life depended on it.

Because from all indications, it seemed as though it might.

Just then, Mike realized it was not as if Josh Skolnick was going to be in his office this early. Which meant that he needn't have woken Katie up so early after all.

Damn.

He put the paper with the number in his pocket. He would just call Josh after he was at Aunt Christina's.

Which reminded him. It was time to try Aunt Christina again.

Mike exhaled as he dialed. His heart skipped a beat. Then two.

Success. She picked up on the third ring.

"Hello?" she asked, clearly wondering who might be phoning her so early in the morning.

They didn't talk long. Just long enough for Mike to tell her that he and Erik would be stopping by to visit within the hour. He wanted to tell her more. Both about this case and about the threat. But he realized he would scare her half to death if he did it over the phone. In person would be better. Not good. But better.

As to where she had been when he'd called before, the answer was not very complicated. She had been outside chatting with Sara Andersen, a friend who she happened to see when she had gone outside to get the morning paper. They had ended up talking about the upcoming autumn festival at the First Evangelical Lutheran Church. Sara was on the planning committee and had wondered if Christina had any time to volunteer that weekend in October.

After he ended the call, Mike took a deep breath and exhaled slowly.

Then it hit him.

He should get back in touch with Millie to make sure she was still on board with everything. Especially now that someone had threatened Aunt Christina. She was his client after all. He had a feeling that she'd be awake.

Mike picked up the receiver and started to dial.

A split second later, he put the phone down.

In many ways, it really didn't matter anymore. Even if she didn't want to continue to pay for his services any longer. Even if she said to drop the case, he still was going to get to the bottom of things.

Things had changed.

□ □ □

Two hours later, after having taken the train to Bay Ridge and seen Aunt Christina off with Erik safely, Mike was finally back in his apartment in Yorkville. Glad he no longer had to worry about his aunt, he decided that he best get at least some rest. A warm shower. A fresh change of clothes.

Mike slept for several hours and awoke with a violent start. He didn't ease his way out of a deep slumber, so much as leap out of it. Temporarily bewildered, he looked at his watch to check the time. 1:15 PM. Time enough to get to the bank and then head directly downtown for a firearm permit.

After showering and getting dressed, Mike went through his apartment. He gathered up everything having to do with the Peter Hesse case. The ring with the ruby red insert. The letter from 1951. And the threatening letter and the unsettling photographs of Aunt Christina which he was undoubtedly sure was connected to it.

While going through his desk, he came upon the clipping about Waldheim, the one that Aunt Christina had wanted him to mail to his father in Florida. Mike picked the clipping up. He held it in his hands.

For some reason, one he couldn't quite put his finger on, he felt as if it were no mere coincidence that Aunt Christina had given him this article. No. As much as he disbelieved in the supernatural, he felt as if, somehow, in some way, the universe was speaking to him through this *New York Post* story. Absurd. It sounded ridiculous on the face of it.

And yet.

What were the chances that the very same night after his aunt had insisted that he take the article with him that he would meet a client and take on a case that had a German connection? Things like this happened for a reason.

Didn't they?

The individual threads were all there. Mike knew it. Thin strands of information that didn't make any sense on their own. It was as if they were just waiting for him to stitch them together into a recognizable pattern. Deep in his gut, he wasn't even sure he was up to the task. That he might not be the person who would be able to weave together a coherent explanation for everything that he had experienced this past insane week.

But he had an inkling of who might.

Mike yawned loudly as he set the article down on the kitchen table next to the ring and the envelope. He took out a manila envelope from his desk drawer. Mike put the clipping, the ring, the envelope with the letter from 1951, and the paper upon which he had written the two names a dying man had spoken with his last breath, inside. He sealed the envelope and with a blue ink pen, he wrote on it, "Hesse."

Mike glanced at his watch again. Still plenty of time for him to call Josh Skolnick and get to the bank to lock this stuff securely away in his safety deposit box.

Mike picked up the phone again and dialed the number Katie had twice provided him with. As he listened to the phone ringing, Mike wondered how much, if anything, Katie had told Josh about him.

"Hello?"

"Hi. This is Mike Levinas. I'm a friend of Katie Rosenfeld's. I was looking to speak to Josh Skolnick."

"You've found him."

"I was hoping it would be you."

"What can I do for you, Mike?"

"Well, here's the situation. I—"

Josh cut him off.

"I'm just playing with you. Katie told me all about the situation."

"She did?" Mike asked.

"Yes. And it's fine. Why don't you come in around four this afternoon?"

"Are you sure it's okay?" Mike asked, immediately regretting how needy he must have sounded.

"I'll take care of everything," Josh replied.

"Thanks."

"Just bring cash. I'll see you then," Josh said.

"How much?" Mike asked.

"A hundred," Josh replied, then ended the call.

Mike took a deep breath.

Well, that went as well as it could have. Didn't it?

Was he doing the right thing? He could still walk away from all this.

But Mike knew he couldn't just walk away. And he knew that if his aunt found out that he had done so on her account, she would be furious with him.

After all, wasn't it she who said that he had to find a purpose in life again? Maybe this was it.

Mike ran his hands through his hair and adjusted his shirt. He opened the door and walked into the hallway, putting the key in the keyhole and locking the door behind him. Before heading down the stairs, he double checked, then triple checked that it was fully locked.

He looked down at the manila envelope that he had in his hand. Time to get to the bank and tuck this away where no one besides him would be able to access it. He'd have to make a withdrawal there as well. Enough cash to take care of whatever bureaucratic hoops Josh was going to have to go through. For all Mike knew, Josh was going to pocket some of it. Not that he cared.

At least then he could finally get on with arming himself for whatever challenges lay ahead.

CHAPTER 14

By the time the yellow cab dropped Mike off on Broadway across from City Hall Park, the sun had reappeared from behind a bevy of puffy cumulus clouds. With no time to lose, Mike walked briskly through the crowded park, past City Hall, up Centre Street, and toward the Manhattan Municipal Building.

No matter how many times he saw that city office building, he couldn't help but be impressed by the sheer audacity of its original architects. Where else in the world but here in Manhattan could you find such a tall, eclectically designed local government building? And it wasn't merely a building. It was also a monument. A reminder that New York had its own history. Both a glorious past and a future yet to be written. And that this city was more powerful, more influential than most of the countries in the world. That was the true message of the Municipal Building. That what happened in New York City mattered to the rest of the world as well.

Mike walked under the arched columns in front of the Municipal Building and went inside. The first thing Mike noticed upon entering the Municipal Building's lobby was how relatively empty it was this afternoon. Usually it was a madhouse, filled with harried city employees and irate citizens alike. Odd. At least this was going to make it easy for him to get on the first available elevator and head directly up to the 15th Floor.

Mike stood in the empty UP elevator. Lights illuminated each floor number as it ascended.

Mike took a deep breath. He glanced down at his hands. They were completely steady.

You've toughened up, old boy.

As the elevator doors slid open, Mike tucked in his shirt and walked into the florescent-lit hallway. After initially heading in the wrong direction, he turned around and made his way to the far end of the corridor.

Walking along the beige carpeted floor, Mike thought about how much had transpired over the past week. How when he was at Aunt Christina's for coffee, he never could possibly have imagined that she would now be holed up with Erik in New Jersey. And that he would be on his way to get his first-ever firearm permit from the city.

Maybe it's time to stop reflecting, Mike thought. Maybe it'll be better that way. This was no time for wool gathering.

Things were different now. It was time for action.

Then he saw it. A closed wooden door with a gold name plate on it.

Joshua Skolnick.

Mike lightly rapped on the heavy door.

"Come," bellowed a loud voice from the other side.

Mike opened the door slowly, careful not to swing it too far open, so as to bang into the coatrack and shelving units on the other side.

"Hi Josh. I'm Mike," he said.

A heavyset man with short dark hair and thick plastic eyeglasses stood up from his cluttered desk and sauntered over, one foot dragging in front of the other. He had thick fingers and a face begging for a fresh shave.

"Hey, Mike. Glad to help you out. Why don't you take a seat?" Josh said, indicating a chair on the opposite side of his desk.

As Mike sat down, he couldn't help but notice how many empty soda cans Josh had accumulated in this relatively small space. Coke cans. Dr. Brown's Cream Soda cans. Generic ginger ale and root beer cans from Gristides. On the desk and atop filing cabinets. It was as if he were curating a small personal collection.

"I have these forms all filled out for you," Josh said. He shuffled some papers around, nearly toppling over a stack of off-track betting forms.

"Oh?" Mike replied.

"All I need from you is your John Hancock and a hundred bucks."

"You're sure that's all?" Mike asked, slightly snorting through his nose as he spoke. He was astonished at the price Josh had just quoted him. But Mike understood everything when he saw the pile of betting forms fall to the floor. Katie's cousin evidently liked to play the ponies and might be a little desperate and afraid to risk asking for more money and end up with nothing.

"Yeah, that's all," Josh replied. He grinned deviously.

Mike had seen that same smile on the faces of different men. Too many times to count.

"Bureaucracy. You know how it is," Josh continued. He spoke in a knowing manner. It wasn't what his words said. It was what they implied.

"I know how it is," Mike agreed.

Mike reached inside his wallet and removed five twenties. He was lucky he had withdrawn more than enough cash to smooth things along. If Josh wanted more than the standard gun permit fee, it was likely that any gun store owner would want a surcharge as well.

Just to expedite the transaction, of course.

Mike handed the twenties to Josh, who eagerly took them and put them in a manila envelope.

"What comes next?" Mike asked.

"This. This is what comes next," Josh said, opening his desk drawer. He pulled out what looked to be a square laminated identification card of some sort. From where Mike what sitting, it appeared slightly larger than a driver's license, but smaller than a passport.

Josh tossed the item onto the desk. "This is what you came here for, right?"

"So, this is it. It's all set?" Mike asked, picking up his expedited firearm permit.

"You're good to go. I had it made an hour ago. You can buy a gun in the city tonight, if that's what you want to do."

That was exactly what Mike wanted to do. No question about it.

"Thanks for everything," Mike said. He smiled.

"No," Josh said, indicating the manila envelope sitting on his desk. "Thank you."

"All right then," Mike said, getting up from the chair, nearly knocking over a crumpled McDonald's paper bag that had been teetering on the edge of Josh's desk. "I best get going."

Mike turned around and headed toward the door. As he began to close it behind him, he heard Josh shout out after him.

"Just don't do anything stupid," he bellowed.

"I know what I'm doing!" Mike shouted back. It wasn't exactly a lie. But it was hardly the full truth, either.

Through the door, Mike heard Josh cracking open a soda can.

□   □   □

It was a small nondescript storefront nestled between a Chinese take-out restaurant and a beauty parlor owned by three Korean sisters. Ike's Army and Navy Surplus on Bleeker Street, which he had found in the Yellow Pages, was exactly where Mike needed to be right now. They had what he needed, what the visit to Josh's office now made possible. A little something to maybe ensure that he wasn't going to end up bleeding to death in an alley like pitiful Arthur.

Maybe something to help even the score with the son of a bitch who sent those photographs of Aunt Christina to his office.

Not that he had any idea who that was. Or where he could find him. Not yet, anyway. But he was determined that he would solve that particular mystery in due course.

Mike opened the door to Ike's, causing a loud chime to ring. He walked inside.

"Are you looking for anything in particular?"

Mike quickly turned to see an elderly white man standing behind the back counter. Dressed in a worn black cotton T-shirt and camouflage pants adorned with multiple pockets on all sides, the thin balding man was likely in his late sixties. Directly in front of him was a glass case filled with what looked to be military memorabilia. Among the myriad objects displayed, Mike saw what looked to be some World War II artifacts from Nazi Germany.

Just seeing them made Mike feel dirty.

Why would people collect this shit?

Mike looked the man over, wondering what his politics might be. Everything about him seemed to be out of place here in the West Village. But just because he sold some old Nazi trinkets didn't mean that he endorsed the ideology. After all, there was plenty of American and British memorabilia for sale as well.

Not that Mike could afford to care too much about it right now. He wasn't here to make a new friend.

He was here to do one thing and one thing only.

"I'm actually looking to purchase a handgun tonight," Mike said confidently.

"You're cutting it pretty late," the man said, pointing to the clock on the wall. It was nearly 6:30. "But I think I can help you out. I'm the owner here. The name's Ike, like on the sign outside."

He grinned, revealing teeth that were badly in need of repair.

Mike smiled back.

"Thanks, Ike."

"What is this for? No. Let me guess," Ike said. "Home protection for you and the missus?"

Mike frowned at Ike.

"Not that it's any of my business," Ike quickly interjected, seemingly aware that he still had a deal to close.

He's right, Mike thought. It's not any of his damn business.

"I'm actually a private detective. I need it for a case," Mike said in a matter-of-fact tone that surprised even him. Mike took out the permit he had been granted by the city only an hour before.

Ike looked it over. He nodded.

"What kind of piece are you thinking of taking home with you?" he then asked.

"What do you recommend?" Mike replied.

"Personally—and now this is just ol' Ike talking now—but I like the classics. You can't go wrong with a M1911. It's reliable and ideal for concealed carry. But if you want some fun, why not go with a .38 Special. It's accurate as hell and has a manageable recoil. It'll be great under your jacket. You'll feel like one of those PIs they show you on the TV."

For the next thirty minutes or so, Ike showed Mike a series of models. He had Mike handle all of them.

Mike finally settled on a .38 Special. He liked the look of it. The feel. Plus, he couldn't get out of his mind what Ike had said about how it would make him look like a real PI. It was admittedly a silly thing to think about at a time like this. But that didn't stop his mind from operating on its own trajectory.

Why not look the part? If he was going to be putting himself in potential danger, why not at least look cool doing so? Mike smiled to himself. He actually could see his Dad smiling along approvingly.

"So how are you going to carry it?" Ike asked, immediately after Mike finished putting his signature on several forms.

"Carry?" Mike asked, repeating the word. He had forgotten all about the need for a holster.

Ike shook his head like a disappointed kindergarten teacher.

Mike immediately realized what he had been asked. It was not as if he was going to be able to just stick the gun in his back pocket next to his wallet.

"I'm going to need a holster, I guess," he said.

"Right. You're going to need a holster."

Mike couldn't tell if Ike were deliberately mocking him or whether that was just the way he talked to all first-time gun purchasers. But what did it matter? In a few minutes, he'd be well out of here with his gun, holster, and some ammunition. Ike and his little store would be nothing but a distant memory.

For the next fifteen minutes, Ike showed Mike a series of holsters, explaining in excruciating detail the differences between each and every one.

Finally cognizant of how much time had elapsed, Mike suggested that Ike just pick one and Mike could gladly buy it regardless of the cost.

That was music to Ike's ears. He had just made a big sale.

□　□　□

By the time Mike had finished filling out all the necessary paperwork at Ike's, twilight was settling in. The West Village always had an electricity in the air at this time of day. When the workday had ended. When the night had just begun. A transitional time when the last commuters of the night had departed on the PATH train to New Jersey and the nightcrawlers were emerging from their deep slumbers, ready to party until dawn.

Mike walked down Bleeker Street a few short blocks, passing a record store, a bookstore specializing in mysticism, and a sushi place. As he passed people on the street, Mike couldn't help but wonder if any of them could have guessed that he was carrying a weapon. Almost certainly not. Why would they? Most people were so singularly focused on their own lives that they didn't have a second to spare thinking about what other people might be doing, let alone what might be happening in the wider world.

It was funny.

Just over a week ago, Mike himself was like that. Focused entirely on the daily grind of living in this city. On finishing his previous case and getting on to the next one.

Now he was walking around with a holster under his jacket and a firearms permit in his jacket pocket.

Life takes its own course.

At that very moment, Mike spotted what he had been looking for out of the corner of his eye.

A phone booth.

One somewhat out of the way of traffic where it would be quiet enough to have a real conversation. For Mike had one last phone call to make today. And it was an important one. To Katie. One that he thought might help him piece together this puzzle.

The phone booth's glass walls were covered in blue spray-painted graffiti. Mike couldn't make out any words or what the hooligan who did this intended to convey. To him, it was just a total mess, a sign of the times. Someone had ripped out the white pages, leaving an empty binder hanging from a cord in its wake.

Mike reached inside his pants pocket, pulled out a dime, and slid it into the phone.

After three rings, Katie picked up.

"Hello?"

"Hi Katie, this is Mike again."

"Hey, Mike. Did you get to see my cousin?"

"Yeah. He took care of everything just as you said he would. I can't thank you enough."

"You don't have to be so fawning."

Mike didn't know exactly how to reply to that. So he remained quiet.

"What can I do for you now?" she asked.

"How did you know I was going to ask you for another favor?"

"I had a feeling. Don't worry about it. Tell me what you need."

"I was wondering …" Mike said, clearing his throat.

"Get on with it."

"I was wondering if I could talk to your father about this German connection. The one in my case."

Silence.

"Mike, I don't know."

"I wouldn't ask if it weren't really important."

"I know, but—"

"Look, I know how awkward this must be."

Just then, Mike heard the sound of banging on the phone booth. He quickly turned and saw a group of teenagers on the street. One of them, a kid in a leather biker jacket with pink mohawk on his shaved head, was standing just inches from him.

"Hey man. We need to make a call!" the punk yelled.

"Just a minute!" Mike furiously shouted back.

"Who was that? What's going on, Mike?" Katie asked through the wire.

"Some kid. Don't worry about it. What do you say?"

Again silence.

"Okay," Katie said. "I'll do it. Meet me tomorrow at noon in front of the arch at Washington Square Park and we'll walk over to my Dad's store in Union Square."

"Thank you so much. I promise I'll make it up to you somehow."

"Mike, you don't need to be like this. You're friends with Barry. Barry is kind of my boss, so I would help you regardless of whatever it is that exists between us. I'll see you tomorrow."

A click.

After being brutally honest with him, she had hung up the phone.

Mike looked through the glass phone booth, making direct unavoidable eye contact with the punk kid. He looked like a giant asshole.

As he opened the door to the phone booth, Mike spoke to him softly.

"It's all yours, freak show."

Mike walked past the gaggle of teenagers and toward the subway. While he was more than happy that Katie had agreed to introduce him to her father, he began to wonder.

Was he going to lose her in the process?

CHAPTER 15

"You're going to listen to me, you ungrateful bitch, you! You're bloody well going to listen to what I have to say!"

Bennington could barely contain his fury.

Directing his aim far away from his prized sculptures, he hurled his glass against the drawing room wall. It smashed and broke into myriad fragments near the Bergdorf Goodman Fifth Avenue shopping bags that Jackie had just set down.

Jackie stopped in her tracks. She turned around. Looked straight into Bennington's eyes. They were angry.

For a moment, Bennington thought his wife was about to apologize. After all, she invariably did when faced with his wrath. Times when she knew that what she needed to do was to get back in his good graces, lest she find herself at the receiving end of his wrath.

But rather than retreat deep inside herself and suppress her anger, Jackie surprised him and stood her ground. She put her hands on her hips and glared at her much older husband. A frigidity enveloped the room like a cold front making its way through the night sky.

"Don't you ever do that to me again," she said. Her voice was eerily calm. But her striking green eyes bespoke a level of bold disobedience. One that he had never witnessed in her before.

"Do what exactly?" Bennington asked. "Treat you like the profligate useless cunt you are?"

"I mean it, Samuel. This is your last warning. Just because you make the money around here does not give you the right to speak to me that way."

Bennington saw her lips moving and heard the words coming from her mouth. But he still couldn't believe who was speaking them, let alone to him. All he could do was laugh.

"I see," he said. "You have been watching those women's shows on television. Where they try to teach you to stand up for yourself. Well, bravo! Bravo! An Academy Award for your performance, my dear!"

Bennington slowly clapped.

"You know, just because you have this—what do you call it—IPO coming up doesn't mean you have the right to treat me like shit. You don't want to have your little party here all alone, do you? Wouldn't it be strange for your guests if I happened not to be there? If I happened to, say, visit my sister in the city that night? Wouldn't that be like totally awkward for you, Samuel? Having to explain to all your precious friends you've barely seen for years that your trophy wife had run out on you?"

Trophy wife. Her words. Not his.

What the hell has gotten into her, he wondered.

She noticed her husband was staring at her. She smiled, biting her lower lip. It was done with a delicateness that hinted less at seduction and more at defiance.

Bennington couldn't quite put his finger on it, but there was something new going on here. Something etched in her face that demonstrated that the days of her being completely submissive were over.

It irritated him.

"You wouldn't dare!" he shouted.

"Wouldn't I? And what's stopping me?"

"Credit cards. That's what. You can't live without my money. And you know it. You want to go back and live with your pathetic parents in godforsaken Northridge? Is that what you really want?"

"I have options," she said quietly.

"Oh, you have *options*," he laughed angrily. It was almost as though he were about to lose control.

"Yes, Samuel, as a matter of fact, I do."

"Well go on, then! Exercise your options. We'll see how long you last with your options."

Bennington glared at her. His sweaty face was growing more crimson by the second.

Jackie removed her hands from her thin hips. Without saying a word, she steadied herself and picked up the three shopping bags. Quickly turning around, she marched straight through the front hallway and up the stairs to her bedroom.

Bennington, still stunned by her display of defiance, heard the sound of a door slamming upstairs.

"Dumb fucking broad. Maybe I'll have Donny take care of her too," Bennington muttered under his breath as he bent down and carefully picked up shards of broken glass.

Just then, he was reminded that Donny was taking a few hours off from work and driving up from the city to see him. He was set to report back about Arthur and this annoying private investigator.

Maybe the gods were smiling upon him after all. Jackie was almost certainly going to take her pills and go to bed for the night. She'd be out of his way. He certainly didn't need Donny to know anything about his home life. What good would that possibly accomplish?

They had a higher calling than what the female sex could provide.

Bennington walked through to the drawing room to the main hallway and opened the door. He walked outside. Standing for a moment on his front doorstep, he focused his gaze intently up to the night sky. Here, out in Westchester, he could actually see the stars clearly at night. Unlike in California, where the light pollution made it all but impossible to take in their majesty.

Bennington thought of Jackie. Of how she defied him. It made his blood boil. But he had more important things to tend to right now. He'd deal with her later. He took a deep breath and headed back inside.

Some thirty minutes later, after he had tucked his plane ticket to Argentina back in a desk drawer, Bennington heard a light rapping on the front door. He looked up like a cat awakened from a nap. He walked briskly through the drawing room and into the main entranceway. He peered through the peephole like a submariner looking through a periscope.

It was Donny. Punctual as always. Bennington appreciated that.

He opened the door and invited his underling inside. As he guided Donny to the dining room table where he had left a fruit plate, Bennington lightly draped his arm around Donny's shoulder.

"Tell me all about it," he said, as they took their seats at the table.

"Did Arthur cry like a feverish baby? Because, to be perfectly frank, I could see him doing that. It was in his nature."

"I didn't stick around long enough to see whatever the fuck he did," Donny said, as he grabbed a slice of cantaloupe.

"Ah," Bennington said. "That makes sense. Why would you? I, of course, wouldn't want you to get caught. I rely on you too much."

"You know I'm as good as my word," Donny said, quietly chewing the melon.

"But he is indeed dead?"

"He'll be six feet under soon if he ain't already," Donny said, flatly.

"Excellent. How'd you get it done?"

"Standard kitchen knife. I borrowed it from a restaurant kitchen. No one will ever trace it."

"That was very wise."

Bennington yawned, then he smiled. He'd really lucked out when he found Donny. Here was a young, virile man who could just have easily wasted his energy on drinking, drugs, and chasing women. But he didn't. He chose a different path, a noble one. He may have worked an ordinary job as a television repairman during the day, but it was at night that he made his mark on the world. He was now a link in a great chain of men who had come before, men who sacrificed much to combat the international Jewish menace whose tentacles threatened to strangle the world.

"And what about that PI? What's his name again?" Bennington asked, rubbing his chin aware that he didn't usually forget things like that. Too many things going on right now to keep track of them all.

"Mike Levinas."

"Levinas? Is that what you said?" Bennington asked, his ears perking up at the mention of Mike's last name.

"Yeah. That's his name. Why?" Donny queried, as he took a sip of the cold mineral water Bennington had poured for him.

"It's a very Litvak name."

"The fuck is a Litvak?" Donny sneered.

"Donny. Those of us from the Baltic states know the term all too well. Litvak Jews are the Jews from Lithuania and Latvia. They're a particularly awful bunch. Thinking they are smarter than everyone else because they study all day. Their supposed book smarts didn't save them forty years ago. That's for sure."

Donny laughed.

"I suppose not," he said.

"Did you take care of this Litvak detective then?"

"I didn't kill him, if that's what you mean. He's a weakling. A bookish type. Used to be a prosecutor."

"You just threatened him, is that it? Did he get the message?"

"Yeah, he got it. Sent him some photos of his aunt. Told him if he wanted to see her alive again, he'd drop this," Donny answered. "More or less that's what I said, anyways. Hope he reads between the lines."

"You *hope* so?" Bennington said, running his finger in a circular motion around the top of his glass.

For the very first time, Bennington was genuinely taken aback by Donny's seemingly lackadaisical approach.

"Sorry. Been working my ass off at the shop lately. Just tell me what you need me to do."

"Just get him out of the way. I don't need any more hassles in the days ahead," Bennington said, his mind once again returning to his fight with his profligate wife.

"Permanently?"

"Permanently," Bennington answered, pausing to collect his thoughts. "You know what? As long as you're at it, go for broke. Take care of everything that you think needs taking care of. Bring some muscle if you need to. You know a few other people in my network. No loose ends. You hear me?"

"No loose ends. Understood. I'll do it myself. Not a problem," Donny said.

"You don't have to give me any details. In fact, I'd prefer you did not burden me with them. Just get it done. I need to focus on the IPO."

"You can count on me."

That was more like it, Bennington thought. That's the Donny he admired. Admired and depended on.

"Have some more fruit. It's good for you."

"Nah. I'm fine," Donny said.

"You sure?"

"Yes."

"Suit yourself."

It was now just before midnight. The two men, each well aware that they had run out of anything to discuss with each other, sat quietly at the large dining room table. Both knew that if their plan went through, they were right on the cusp of accomplishing something big. Something that would be able to finance many operations against the Jews in European cities, both big and small, for years to come. Topping the spectacle of the Kristallnacht was within their reach.

In the near distance, a howling pierced the suburban silence.

"The hell was that?" Donny asked excitedly.

"Relax. Just a neighbor's black dog in the nighttime," Bennington said.

CHAPTER 16

Mike woke up with a violent start.

He had been in a deep slumber for who knows how long, and then in the blink of an eye, was wide awake and attuned to his surroundings. Sunlight filtered in through the partially closed window blinds. It projected a luminescent display upon his forehead. From what he could tell, it looked to be the first purely sunny day in a while. There had been many grey clouds, many storms, over the past week. A clear bright afternoon would be a welcome relief.

After he made himself a quick breakfast and showered, Mike began to get dressed. This time, however, he was going to wear an additional item on his body. Before putting on his lightweight sport coat, he strapped the leather holster he had purchased last night across his chest. He snuggly positioned his new .38 Special into it, gently tugging on the holster to be sure it was securely fastened. The very last thing he needed was to have the holster, let alone the gun, fall off while he was on the subway. Who knows what kind of panic that might cause? That made him wonder. Why should he take the subway at all? He might as well just hail a cab and make sure he got to Washington Square Park in one piece.

After phoning Erik to make sure that Aunt Christina was doing fine, Mike glanced at his watch. It was just before ten. He still had plenty of time to get to the bank and retrieve the items he had placed in the safety deposit box the day before. Then, he'd head on down to the Village to meet up with Katie before the two of them walked over to her dad's electronics store in Union Square.

As he tidied up in the small kitchen, throwing an expired carton of milk into the trash can, Mike began to wonder what Katie's father was going to look like. In his mind, Mike couldn't help but picture a stern, older man with a permanently serious expression on his face and a long white beard covering his chin. Like one of those super pious Jews in the Diamond District on West 47th Street, the ones with black suits and skullcaps. But, as he thought it over, Mike realized that didn't make much sense. Katie was about as non-religious as could be and it was doubtful that the apple fell too far from the tree.

Mike surveyed his living room, then headed directly into his bedroom. It was in his walk-in closet that he found what he had been looking for.

The small red backpack he used to carry books back in law school. It would be perfect now. He could stash everything from the safety deposit box into it and then fasten the straps tightly across his back. That way he could be sure that everything would be secure until he got to meet with Mr. Rosenfeld.

As he walked out of the bedroom, Mike smiled. For some reason, that sounded absolutely hilarious to him. Mr. Rosenfeld. It was as if he were an awkward sixteen-year-old again and about to meet the father of the girl he was taking to the prom.

Mike grabbed his PI license and his concealed carry permit and put them in his jacket pocket. He looked around his living room. He wanted to be absolutely certain he had everything he needed for the day. Once he was satisfied that he did, he grabbed his keys, walked out the front door, and closed it tight behind him. This time, he checked not just once, but twice, that he had securely locked his apartment door. Better safe than sorry.

□ □ □

Under the Arch was a good place to meet.

Aside from the museums and famous office buildings, there was no place in Manhattan as instantly recognizable as the Washington Square Arch.

Located at the lower terminus of Fifth Avenue, the white marble Roman triumphal arch was constructed in 1892 to commemorate the inauguration of George Washington a century earlier. Most locals probably didn't know anything about the history behind it and few would have cared, even if they did. It was just spectacular to look at, a reminder that lower Manhattan wasn't always the decaying wasteland that it often appeared to be today.

After the yellow cab dropped Mike off on West 8th Street in front of a small bakery, he walked down the tree-lined block of Fifth Avenue. He passed the apartment buildings, crossed the street, and went into Washington Square Park. Scanning the immediate area for any potential threats, Mike noticed that nothing seemed out of the ordinary. For that neighborhood anyway. Just your normal array of shaggy NYU students, old men playing chess, and delinquent teenagers with long hair and too much time on their hands smoking pot and who knows what else.

Mike glanced at his watch.

It was almost noon. Katie should be here any minute now. He had timed his trip downtown perfectly. He had been in and out of the bank in no time flat, in large part because it was the same girl working the safety deposit box area who had assisted him yesterday. She was polite, friendly, but probably wondering a bit why he had made such a quick turnaround. Not that it mattered to him. He had more important things on his mind than what a bank employee might have been thinking.

Mike looked around the bustling park, his eyes once again taking in his surroundings. As he looked at the diverse group of people who were hanging around, Mike couldn't help but think that most of these people probably had no idea he was armed. Why would they? They had no reason to suspect. Still, it made him feel both powerful and apprehensive, exhilarated that he could now defend himself with legal force and fearful that he just might have to.

"Hey!"

Mike quickly turned around.

It was Katie. She was walking toward him. Dressed in a white blouse, ripped jeans, and a light blue denim jacket, she exuded an unmistakably downtown aesthetic, making him wonder once again what exactly they had in common aside from their need for human contact. This part of New York wasn't really his scene. That was an understatement.

"Hey, you," Mike said. He embraced her and planted a soft kiss on her right cheek.

"What's in the bag?" Katie asked, pointing to the red backpack.

"I stopped at the bank. I have some things I want to show your father. To see if he could made heads or tails out of them."

"I see," she said, as she gently tossed long strands of hair that had fallen in her eyes.

"So how have you been?" Mike asked, quietly wondering if he was making things even more awkward than they already were. It wasn't as if any of this was remotely normal.

"Fine," she said.

"Good," he replied.

"Wanna get going?"

"Sure. Might as well."

After waiting for several cars to pass, Mike and Katie crossed Washington Square North and headed up Fifth Avenue. They walked side by side, neither saying too much. At the next intersection, Katie stopped, took out a pack of cigarettes and a lighter from her purse. She grabbed a Marlboro, placed it in her mouth, and lit it.

"I need this," she said, turning to look directly into Mike's eyes. She exhaled, blowing puffs of smoke into the humid air.

"Are we a tad bit nervous?" Mike queried jokingly.

Katie laughed uncomfortably.

"You'll see. My Dad can be …" she said, stopping mid-sentence to consider her next words. "Pretty intense."

Mike once again tried to picture what her father looked like. Unlike when he was back in his apartment, his mind's eye didn't conjure up an image of a stern-looking religious Jewish scholar. No. This time he pictured someone who looked more like John Garfield, but older. What the late actor who often portrayed tough guys in films might have looked had he lived into his sixties.

Just then, Mike stopped dead in his tracks. He had noticed a man on the opposite side of the street standing next to a large white van. Dressed in Navy blue slacks with a matching shirt, the man was unquestionably staring at both him and Katie. Of that, Mike was certain.

"Hang back," Mike said, as he gently nudged Katie further away from the curb. "I need to check something out."

"What's going on?" Katie asked, as she retreated, almost instinctively, under the yellow canopy of a luxury apartment building.

"I need to see something, that's all," Mike said, as he reached inside his coat and checked to make sure he had his weapon.

After looking both ways for traffic, Mike darted across the street. Not once did he take his eyes off the man dressed in blue.

"Hey! What's going on?" Mike yelled. He was about to pull out his gun. That's when he noticed that the man was wearing an exterminator's uniform.

"Take it easy, man, I didn't mean to stare. Your girl is pretty fine, that's all," he said.

An exterminator and his white van. Shit. This guy wasn't dangerous to anyone but cockroaches.

Mike felt his muscles relaxing again, adrenaline depleting from his bloodstream as quickly as it entered it seconds before. This could have turned really ugly, Mike mused. Really quickly. He sighed with relief, thankful that it hadn't.

He made his way back across the street, waving to Katie as if to say everything is cool. Everything is fine.

"What the hell was that all about?" she demanded.

"Sorry," Mike said quietly.

"Sorry? You nearly scared me half to death. By the way, and I can't believe I forgot to ask you this, but do you have a gun on you?"

"I do," Mike said.

"So everything worked out with Josh then? I just can't believe I forgot to ask you about that. Fuck."

"A lot's been going on," Mike replied.

"I know. But still. It was my idea after all. In case you don't remember."

"I remember," Mike said in a distant, matter-of-fact tone.

"What did that guy over there want anyway?" she asked.

"Nothing. He just thought you were attractive."

"Well, aren't I?" Katie asked, biting her lower lip.

Mike smiled.

The two of them continued walking, both in near silence, up Fifth Avenue, past the restaurants and the Strand bookstore. Their destination: City Discount Electronics, owned by one Izzy Rosenfeld.

No turning back now, Mike thought. No indeed.

CHAPTER 17

"I just wanted to remind you that my father can be a bit ..." Katie said, pausing to consider her next word. "Much. He can be a bit much."

Katie tossed a half-smoked cigarette onto the concrete sidewalk. Grinding down the remnants of a flame with her designer black shoes.

"You've said that before," Mike said, once again reaching under his jacket to make sure his holster was securely fastened. And that his gun was easy to reach if he needed to.

Mike and Katie were now only a half-block away from City Discount Electronics, the store that Izzy Rosenfeld had owned and operated for some two decades now. From the outside, the store wasn't much to look at. Over the years it had weathered vast demographic and economic changes and come out on top despite it all. Through the crime waves, the street gangs and the recessions, it had kept its doors open, six days a week.

"Let's do this," Katie said, her hand outstretched like an usher eager to get theater patrons to their seats.

"After you," Mike said.

They walked inside the local mecca for audiophiles, collectors of laserdiscs and VHS tapes, and senior citizens looking for small, portable radios to keep them company. City Discount Electronics looked to have it all.

"Hi, Katie. What brings you here today?" asked a short, stocky man with a Spanish accent as he hurried over to greet them. He had sprung into action the very moment he saw his boss's beloved daughter set foot upon the premises.

"Hey Alfonso. I'm supposed to meet my Dad here. He knows we're coming," Katie said.

Mike stood quietly next to her, his arms crossed across his chest. Looking on. Saying nothing.

"Okay, then, sure, go on back. Your Dad's in his office doing some paperwork," Alfonso said.

"Cooking the books again?" she grinned.

"Could be," Alfonso replied with a mischievous smile. It highlighted his noticeably crooked lower teeth. He did a quick about face, walked away, and began to tend to an elderly man who had a most pressing question about which turntable would make the best present for his grandson.

Mike wasn't exactly sure whether Katie and Alfonso had been joking about her dad cooking the books. Not that it was any of his business.

"Ready?" Mike asked.

"Yup," Katie said. She led Mike to the far back of City Discount Electronics. As he followed, Mike looked around and took in the ambiance of the store.

FAO Schwartz this was not.

It seemed like nearly every shelf was filled with all sorts of stereos, telephones, and televisions, both display items and those boxed up ready to take home. Customers of nearly every ethnicity imaginable squeezed through the narrow aisles, many with the latest model boom boxes in their hands. Young kids, screeching with excitement, were running through the store with the boundless energy adults rarely have. Parents, with weary looks on their faces that belied too many sleepless nights, struggled to maintain order, all the while simultaneously chasing down deep discounts.

Mike moved carefully, doing his best to ensure that his red backpack, the one in which he had the ring and the letter, didn't accidentally knock any products onto the scuffed linoleum floor.

The two of them came to a door. On it, a sign. It read: Private. Staff Only.

"This is my Dad's lair," Katie said wryly.

"What is he? A bear?" Mike asked, wiping sweat off his forehead.

Katie smiled.

"Oh, you'll see."

She made a slight fist with her right hand and knocked on the door. Once. Twice. Three times.

Nothing.

After what seemed like an eternity (but was in actuality only thirty seconds), the door opened.

Standing in the entryway was an older man who looked nothing like any of the possibilities Mike had pictured in his mind's eye.

Izzy Rosenfeld didn't look anything like a Midtown diamond merchant.

Let alone like a devout religious scholar. Mike's first thought was that he looked like Martin Balsam, the Hollywood actor who starred in that movie about a heist on the subway. He was the kind of guy baseball fans would find sitting next to them in those bright orange seats at Shea Stadium, loudly chewing a Hebrew National hot dog, and loudly rooting for professional baseball's perpetual underdogs. Dressed in a short-sleeve white dress shirt with a pocket stuffed with pens, he seemed like a factory foreman. His grey slacks were the type that could have easily been purchased at any Alexander's or similar downscale department store. But more than anything, Mike thought that Izzy exuded the bold confidence of a pigeon who wasn't going to move out of anyone's way on the sidewalk. This, after all, was his store. His domain.

"So, let me guess, you're the one who's now running around with my daughter?" he asked in a gruff tone. He cocked his head slightly to the right.

Izzy reached out and shook Mike's hand. He shook with a deliberate firmness. The sign of a man who has made a lot of deals in his lifetime. Izzy then placed his other hand on Mike's right shoulder.

Mike, feeling Izzy's gold wrist bracelet dangle onto his shoulder, understood what was going on. It was unmistakably a power move. A macho thing. One that Mike knew all too well from his time working with street cops, each of them anxious to demonstrate their dominance in any given encounter.

"Well, I—" Mike began, before cutting himself off mid-sentence, his throat exceedingly dry.

In the blink of an eye, the expression on Izzy's face turned from stone cold to affable. It was warm. But not what anyone would call fuzzy.

"I'm just having some fun with you," he said as a devious grin slowly took root on his bronzed face.

"Come on in!" he boomed.

Mike looked around the small back office. He immediately noticed a few old tourist posters and what looked to be an Israeli flag hanging on the wall. He smiled politely, before quickly turning to his left. He looked at Katie for some sort of reaction to how her father began the encounter. Although she spoke no words, the message that Mike read on her face was as clear as a bright summer day.

See what I have to put up with?

Mike unloosened the straps and gently set his backpack on the worktable. He pulled out a wooden chair and took a seat. Katie and her father followed in turn, with Izzy aggressively pushing aside a pile of invoice receipts, folders and flyers, a partially used jar of decaffeinated instant coffee and a few unwashed porcelain mugs.

"What was your name again?" Izzy asked. He spoke in nearly perfect English with only a slight trace of an accent.

Was Izzy was once again having some fun with him or did he not actually remember? Mike wasn't sure. Maybe Katie simply never bothered to tell him his name. How weird would that be?

"Mike."

"Mike what?"

"What?"

"What? What? Are we playing a game? What is your last name?" Izzy growled.

"Levinas."

Izzy's attention perked up immediately, as if he had just received a jolt of espresso.

"Levinas? Is that what you said?"

"Yeah," Mike said quietly, his tone somewhere between a statement and a question.

"Ah. You're a Litvak. Not a Yekke like me," Izzy said, pointing to his pronounced upper chest.

That's when Mike noticed it. Izzy Rosenfeld *was* kind of like a bear.

Mike ran his hands through his hair, noticing that it was slightly wet. No surprise, there. The room was overheated.

"I don't know what those terms mean. Sorry," he said quietly.

Izzy, rather than responding directly to Mike, looked at Katie. She shrugged. But she didn't say anything.

"What's this all about?" Mike asked, wondering what he was missing.

"You don't know about Yekkes and Litvaks."

"No. Sorry. You'll have to tell me."

"German Jews like myself are known as Yekkes. The stereotype is that we are stern, punctual."

"Dad," Katie interrupted, "it's not like your family lived in Germany forever. You even told me yourself that Zayde was born in Hungary."

Izzy pretended not to hear. He kept going with the determination of a man who wants to have his voice heard.

"Yekkes," he explained breathlessly, "are like the Germans themselves. And Litvaks are from the Baltics. Lithuania mainly. Vilna in particular. Studious types. Is your family originally from Vilna?"

"Poland, I think," Mike answered.

"You think?" Izzy glared at Mike.

"Believe it or not, I just don't know. I remember my father saying something about Poland."

"You should learn about your heritage. Be proud of who you are!" His tone was somewhere between encouraging and scolding.

"I mean, I'm not even really Jewish. My mom is—was—Norwegian."

"I see," Izzy said. His tone wasn't particular judgmental.

"You should come out to Brooklyn and meet my aunt. She loves sharing her Norwegian culture with people."

"Perhaps one day," he said with feigned interest.

"She's pretty involved."

"I should imagine."

"Yeah," Mike said quietly.

"You must be hot in that jacket. Why don't you hang it up over there?" Izzy said, pointing to a coat rack in the far corner.

"I think I'd rather not," Mike responded.

"Suit yourself," Izzy said. He sat quietly for what seemed to Mike to be an eternity, his mind temporarily elsewhere. Then, indicating that the time for small talk was now over, he moved without any additional hesitation into the very topic Mike had come to discuss.

"Katie tells me you want to learn something about Germany. That your current case as a PI has some sort of German connection," Izzy began. He placed his hands palms down on the table. Like a fidgety toddler, he lightly rapped on the tabletop with his thick fingers. The sound they made had an oddly soothing rhythmic quality.

"Indeed," Mike said, glad that he no longer was getting the third degree. It was almost as if he were back in law school and ready to learn.

"Well, go on then—" Izzy said, his loud voice drowning out the sounds generated by a floor fan operating at full speed.

Mike cut him off. Then with one hand, he held up his index finger and with the other hand, reached inside his backpack and removed the large manila envelope that he had taken from his safety deposit box.

He opened it, set the items he brought for Izzy to look at on the table. The letter sent to Peter Hesse in 1951. The medium-sized ring with the ruby red stone insert. The paper upon which he had scrawled two names. He left the photograph someone had taken of Aunt Christina inside the large envelope.

"What's all this?" Izzy asked.

"Well, the first one is—"

Izzy held up his hand. "I should really get my reading glasses. I'm blind as a bat without them," Izzy said, clearly irritated that his eyesight was not like it once was.

"Okay," Mike said quietly, noticing that Katie was rolling her eyes, still bemused by the whole situation.

Izzy got up, walked across the room, and opened a desk drawer. He pulled out a hard-shell eyeglass case and took out a pair of standard black reading glasses, the kind easily found at any pharmacy.

"This should work," Izzy said gruffly, as he put on his glasses and walked back to the table. This time, he sat directly next to Mike and once again placed his hand on his shoulder.

Within a matter of seconds, the casual annoyance on Izzy's face quickly dissipated. His new expression was something that Mike interpreted as shock. Perhaps even fear.

"What is it?" Mike asked, noticing Izzy staring down at the medium sized brass ring, his eyes focused on the object in front of him as if he were in a trance.

"Where did you get this?" Izzy thundered. He grabbed the ring. He held it up in front of him and squinted.

"It belonged to the guy I was hired to find," Mike said. His tone was bereft of emotion.

"Who was this man, this man you had to find?" Izzy asked.

"Dad," Katie interjected, clearly sensing something. "What's wrong?"

"Nothing is wrong!"

Katie started to get up from her chair. Izzy waved his hand, indicating for her to sit right back down.

She complied.

"Well, a woman had asked me to find her husband. He is—was—a community college professor. He taught literature. To make a long story short, I did find him. But he had been murdered. This ring—the one I have here—belonged to him. He was wearing it when he died."

"And what was his name?" Izzy asked.

"I don't know if I should—"

"Spit it out. If he's dead, he won't mind."

"His name was Hesse. Peter Hesse."

"He was a German? Yes?"

"That's what I am trying to figure out. His wife said something about him being born in Germany, but that he had moved to Switzerland when he was very young," Mike said, as he noticed Izzy trying to decipher the writing engraved on the ring.

"I've seen this ring. Or at least one exactly like it before. This one says in Latin: 'We have a destiny.'"

"Where? When?" Katie asked, as she sat back down in her chair.

"Back home in Germany. In the 1930s."

"The thirties?" Mike asked, leaning closer to Izzy.

"Isn't that what I just said?" Izzy said.

"Tell me about it, please," Mike said.

Izzy did not respond. Not immediately anyway. Instead, he focused his gaze down at the floor for a moment, his mind once again elsewhere. He sighed. Looked up again. Turned to Katie.

"What is it, Dad?" Katie asked.

"Back in Germany, when I was a much younger man, there was this student fraternity. And before you ask, it wasn't like your stupid college fraternities here with their Greek letters and keg parties. No. This was a different thing. These were like small brotherhoods. Not secret societies, exactly. But close. They were usually upper-class kids, but not always. And usually Lutheran. But not always. Sometimes they were Catholics. What you should be getting from this is that they definitely didn't want people like me in them, if you know what I mean. Anyway, well before Hitler came to power, quite a few of these brotherhoods started becoming not just off limits toward Jews, but hostile. Hostile and violent. I remember one night. It must have been in 1930. Maybe 1931. I was walking home late, coming from a Jewish youth group meeting. They must have been following me. Looking for someone to push around. Because I didn't make it more than two blocks from the meeting before a group of boys cornered me, knocked me down to the ground, and kicked me."

"Dad!" Katie gasped.

Izzy turned and looked squarely at his daughter. Mike couldn't see the expression on Izzy's face, but he sensed what it might be. Katie immediately grew quiet. She let her father continue telling his story.

"I've done my best to forget what happened that night. But what I'll never forget, what I'll never get out of my mind, was what they had on their hands. They had rings. Rings exactly just like this one."

"Holy shit. Are you fucking serious?" Mike blurted out.

"Deadly serious."

"What does this mean, then?" Mike asked.

"It means, there's a very good chance that your dead man was something of an antisemite."

"A Nazi? He was a Nazi?"

"Who the hell knows? Not every antisemite became a Nazi and not everyone who joined the Nazi Party was an antisemite. Some were just opportunists. But there's a strong connection," he said wryly.

"To be honest with you, I still don't know if I'm following all this," Mike said.

Katie sighed.

"What this means," Izzy began, lifting an index finger in the air for emphasis, "is that maybe your case has something to do with this dead guy's past."

"Yes. I understand that part. Which reminds me," Mike said, "I have this letter that was sent to Hesse—that's the dead guy's name—back in 1951. I was wondering if you could make any sense of it."

"Give it to me, then," Izzy said brusquely.

Mike handed it to him.

Izzy opened the envelope quickly, seemingly indifferent to how brittle a letter from three decades ago might be. He unfolded the letter and held it up close to his face.

"Hmm," he said.

"What is it?" Katie asked, apparently trying to make sure her presence in the room was known.

"I think I know what this is," Izzy said, in a manner of fact tone.

"You do?" Mike exclaimed.

Izzy looked up at the clock on the wall. It was nearly two o'clock.

"How much time do you have?" he asked.

"I've got all day," Mike replied.

"Well, then, it looks like I'm not going to get any work done today after all."

Izzy got up from his chair, walked across the small office, and opened the door.

"Alfonso!" he shouted.

"Yes, Mr. Rosenfeld. What is it?" Alfonso came running toward the back of the store.

"I'm not to be disturbed. Not for anything," Izzy instructed.

"Si. I understand."

"Good."

Izzy closed the door and sat back down at the table.

"Have either of you ever heard of something called the Nuremberg Papers?" he said, turning first to Mike and then to his daughter.

"Recently," Mike said, remembering Arthur's final words. It was coming together. Somewhat.

"Not at all," Katie said.

"All right then. I suppose I'll have to start at the beginning."

CHAPTER 18

"The first thing you need to understand," Izzy began, as he forcefully put his palm down on the table, "is that just because World War II ended, Nazism went kaput as well. Or that antisemitism went away. Never to be seen or heard from again."

Izzy coughed. Cleared his throat. Looked directly at Mike.

"Nothing could be further from the truth!" he exclaimed, as if Mike had somehow disagreed with him. He pounded on the table. His fist landed with a heavy thud. Listen up, it said.

"Could you elaborate?" Mike asked, leaning in closer. But not too close.

"You really know nothing about this?" Izzy asked. His echoed more disappointment than it did anger.

"I really don't. What can I say?"

"People live under their fantasyland assumptions that, just because Hitler died in his bunker, that Hitler's hatred died with him. This is not true. This is not how it is," Izzy said. He wagged his finger. A schoolmaster lecturing his intimidated pupils.

"How is it then, Dad?" Katie asked.

Mike realized what Katie was doing. Trying to get her father to be less emotional. More acutely focused. She had probably done it hundreds, if not thousands, of times before.

"You know better than he does," Izzy snapped at Katie, while pointing his finger at Mike.

"All right. Go on. Explain it to him then," Katie said abruptly.

"Well," Izzy began, "my point is that so many people—Americans especially—live in a Peter Pan fantasy world. A world with Hollywood endings and pop music. It's all about falling in and out love and ice cream sundaes. This may be the way of America, but it is most certainly not the way of the world. This is simply not how it is. Too much of this country's entertainment makes the Nazis out to be comic book villains—cartoonish bad men rather than ordinary men who committed unspeakable crimes."

Izzy's vocalized his stream-of-consciousness, making an abrupt segue from the past to the recent present.

"Antisemitism exists still. Why do you think the Russians are arming that son of a bitch Arafat and his thugs? Because they like hanging out with him. Him and his stupid uniform!"

Mike, listening intently, nodded but did not interrupt.

Then, without consciously doing so, he shifted his gaze to Katie.

That's when he noticed a somewhat odd expression on her face. He couldn't quite decipher it. Was it embarrassment? Concern? It was difficult for him to tell exactly what she might have been thinking. Perhaps she was beginning to regret her decision to introduce him to her father.

No. That couldn't be it. It was her idea to bring him to the store in the first place. Then his thoughts grew more cynical. I bet she did it on an impulse, he thought. That's why she's regretting it now.

"I will start at the beginning," Izzy said. His tone was clear. This was going to be important. You had better listen.

Mike focused his gaze back on Izzy, making deliberate eye contact with him.

"Immediately after the war ended, the Americans and the British— but the Americans primarily—wanted to bring the Nazis to justice for what they had done. But they wanted to do it in a way that didn't overemphasize the Jewish aspect. To get around that they called what the Nazis did a crime against humanity. As if humanity in general was the primary victim at Auschwitz!

"They had an international tribunal at Nuremberg. That's what they called it. Tribunal. To make it sound fancy. But at the same time, other branches of the American government had their own plans for the Nazis."

Izzy cleared this throat.

"The Soviets, you see, were growing in power and aggressiveness. And it was beginning to dawn on the Americans that the Russians were going to be their next adversary. Americans always need an enemy, you see. A bunch of pencil pushers in Washington decided it would be a good idea to hire a bunch of former Nazis and German officers to help them prepare for a future war against the Russians. Scientists mainly. Rocket scientists in particular. You know all about Wernher von Braun, of course! But others too. Engineers. Physicists. Chemists. Some biologists probably as well, although I'm not sure. People who could work on weapons programs. People who had insight into the Soviet mindset. People who knew how the Soviet Union operated. Who cared if they had Jewish blood on their hands, even if indirectly? Not the Americans. Not by 1947 anyway. Not the following summer when they had to airlift supplies into West Berlin. Remember, this was more or less at the same time that those antisemites at the State Department were doing everything to prevent Israel from becoming an independent state. And it's not as if Roosevelt bombed Auschwitz when he had the chance."

None of this registered emotionally with Mike, but he nodded anyway.

He could tell how passionate Izzy was about this. Anyone could have. From the way he spoke. From the deep sadness and subterranean anger in his eyes.

Just then, Mike noticed that Izzy was looking up at the Israeli flag he had draped on the wall.

"You see that?" Izzy asked, pointing to the slightly drooping flag, with its white backdrop, two parallel blue lines, and Star of David in the center.

"Yes. I saw it when I walked in," Mike replied. He had no particular feelings toward Israel one way or the other. He had no intention to visit, either. Didn't interest him in the slightest.

"That's the Jewish people's main protection against antisemitism. Not that violent antisemitism is coming from the Nazis anymore. Now it's the goddamn Russians."

"You mentioned that before, Dad," Katie sighed.

Mike again nodded, eked out a forced smile.

"What are the Nuremberg Papers? The ones you mentioned," Mike asked, attempting to steer the conversation back to the past. He wiped beads of sweat that had been steadily accumulating on his forehead.

"I was just getting to that," Izzy replied brusquely.

"Sorry," Mike said quietly.

Izzy pretended as if he didn't hear Mike's apology. He now turned to Katie and continued speaking.

"I don't know if you know this, but years ago when your mother was still alive, I was kind of an activist. Just with a bunch of guys I knew from around," he said cryptically.

"Of course, I knew," Katie said, "What do you think? That I lived under a rock?"

Mike noticed her sarcastic tone, wondering what exactly lay beneath it. He could only imagine what it must have been like for her to grow up under the same roof as this hardheaded man. What must her high school years have been like? No wonder she liked to blow off steam in a weirdo punk rock band.

Izzy turned to his daughter and shrugged his shoulders. As if to say, how would I know what you knew or not.

"Anyway, some of these guys—the Jewish activists I used to be friends with—were survivors and they had shared stories with me. They were pretty sure that there was a secret government program that existed in 1947 and 1948. One that sprung lower-level Nazis from jail in Nuremberg and brought many of them—scientists mainly, you understand what I'm saying—to the United States for new lives. They were given new identities and a new start. In exchange, they had to work for the American government for two decades. Then they could disappear and do whatever the hell they wanted. The documents from this particular government program are called the Nuremberg Papers."

Mike leaned forward. He finally got where Izzy was going. This what he came here for. It was all beginning to make sense.

Somehow Peter Hesse was connected to all of this. Mike wasn't exactly sure how, but he knew it. He felt it in his gut. But Hesse, from what Millie had told him at least, didn't seem as if he was ever an engineer, let alone a rocket scientist or anything like that.

At that very moment, Mike remembered he had the piece of paper on which he had written those two names. The names that Arthur had blurted out as he lay dying in that back alley.

"Just a second," Mike said, as he reached for his backpack.

"What is it?" Izzy asked, removing a white handkerchief from his pants pocket and wiping perspiration from his face.

Mike opened up the backpack and took out the sheet of legal paper and unfolded it.

"Here. Look at these names," Mike said, pointing to his own handwriting with his index finger.

Izzy adjusted his eyeglasses. He looked down on at the paper.

"I don't know the first name. But the name Bennington seems vaguely familiar."

"I remember reading in the *Times* about a guy named Bennington who was a corporate type. He's about to take his industrial concern public," Mike said.

"What's the connection with the other name?"

"There was this federal agent who was killed. He was somehow mixed up in all of this German stuff," Mike continued, "and when he died, he spoke to me. I mean, when he was dying. He mentioned two names. Bennington and Wagonman. But he didn't say them in separation. He said—and I quote—Bennington is Wagonman."

Mike paused for a moment. He turned and looked at Izzy.

"Does this mean anything to you?" Mike asked.

"This," he said, pointing to paper, "is not a German name."

Mike looked down at the paper, noticing that Izzy's had positioned an index finger right under where the name Wagonman was written.

"No?" Mike asked.

"No," Izzy said bluntly, as he yanked out a ballpoint pen from his shirt pocket.

"What is it then?"

"Nonsense," he said, as he clicked the ballpoint pen and drew two diagonal lines through the misspelled name. He proceeded to write a new name in its place: Wagenmann.

"What are you doing?" Mike asked, immediately realizing the answer to his own question.

Izzy didn't bother to answer his question. He just kept on talking.

"I mean," he said, "it's entirely possible that this Wagenmann was one of the individuals that the Americans brought over after World War II. And that he now goes by the name Bennington. It would make sense."

"So, what is you're telling me is it's not totally impossible?" Mike couldn't hide the excitement in his voice. "I have a gut feeling he could be the same guy."

"Well, it may be. But you're going to need more than feeling in your stomach to do anything about it."

"What do you mean?"

"This fellow is having a public offering for his company. He expects to get a lot of cash quickly. You follow me? What do you expect the first thing he is going to do once he gets his money if he was one of these Nazi scientists brought here after the war?"

Mike thought it over for a moment, uncertain what answer Izzy was expecting from him.

"I don't know," he said quietly, instinctively reaching for his forehead. It was drenched with perspiration.

"Use your *kopf*," Izzy replied, using the Yiddish term for head.

"I guess he could put it in a Swiss bank account or something," Mike said, uncertainly.

"True," Izzy said.

"Is that what you were thinking?"

"I was thinking of where he might go."

"Go?"

"Yes."

"As in leave the country?" Mike asked.

"Now you understand," Izzy said.

"I do?" Mike asked incredulously.

"Yes, if—and this is premised on the notion that this Bennington is a former Nazi, would you not think that when his company goes public and he cashes out, the first thing he'd likely do is hop on a plane to South America?"

"What makes you say that?"

"Because—"

Izzy had abruptly stopped, noticing that the fan had stopped.

"That damn thing!" he bellowed, as he got up from his chair, walked over to where the floor was positioned on the floor, and violently unplugged it.

"Sometimes, you need to unplug it, wait a few seconds, and plug it in again to get it to work," Izzy said, his mind having made a seamless transition away from Nazis to appliances.

Although he remained stone-faced, Mike smiled inside. How droll was it that the owner of an electronics store didn't even have a fully operable fan, much less an air conditioner, in his office?

"Now," Izzy said, as he walked back to the table and sat back down, "where was I?"

"You were talking about Argentina," Mike reminded him.

"I never said anything about Argentina. I said South America. He could just as easily be going to Paraguay, Chile, or Brazil," Izzy said.

"You think—theoretically—that if this guy was a Nazi in a past life, but reinvented himself here in America, he would leave the country and start over elsewhere?"

"Absolutely."

"What makes you think that?"

"Because," Izzy said, as he looked Mike straight in the eye, "I know these sorts. I know how they think. They're criminals at heart."

"How do you mean?"

"What do you think I mean?" Izzy snapped back.

"That they have a criminal mentality," Mike said. Again, it was as if he were once again a law student, but now with Izzy Rosenfeld as his professor.

"Not all of them do. But more than a few do. So many fiction writers think that all these Nazis want to establish a Fourth Reich or something. Ludicrous on the face of it. Most of them are old men who want nothing more than to live out their remaining years in freedom, with money under their mattresses and younger women by their side. Sure, they don't like Jews and probably they're behind this recent wave of attacks on synagogues in Europe. But what else is new?"

Katie, who was looking on and saying very little, forced herself back into the conversation.

"So," she asked in a tone noticeably louder than the last time she spoke, "how would Mike find out if this guy Wagenmann is really Bennington and whether or not he was involved in the case he is working on?"

Izzy turned to look at Mike.

"Do you know anyone in Washington?" he asked.

"Washington? No. I don't," Mike answered quickly.

"That is then, as they say, tough shit," Izzy said.

"Why do you ask?"

"Because, in answer to my daughter's question, in order to find out who Wagenmann is now, you'd have to get your hands on these Nuremberg Papers."

"And how would I do that? I bet they're top secret."

"No."

"No?"

"No. It is highly unlikely. What, do you think your government has any real use for these ex-Nazis anymore? Sure, Syria is still providing haven to some hardcore bastards. And more than a few have reinvented themselves as so-called humanitarians and peace activists. But overall things have changed. The days of German engineers going to Egypt to build their rocket program are long over. Even Reagan seems to want to reduce nuclear weapons. Now, in this country, they are a liability. I tell you what I know. Some people in the government have even been leaking stuff to the press. To tell the story about how some people in the past worked with the National Socialists. Nazis are an embarrassment now. This is true."

"So where would the Nuremberg Papers be then?" Mike asked, overwhelmed by Izzy's myriad historical and political references.

Izzy shrugged.

"How should I know?" he asked almost rhetorically.

Just then, an idea came to Mike.

An idea that seemed to be ludicrous on its face. He pondered for it for a moment and was ready to dismiss it completely, when his mouth seemingly began acting independently of his brain.

"I know someone in Washington," Mike blurted out.

"Well, why didn't you say so before?" Izzy asked.

"It just came to me," Mike admitted.

"It just came to you," Izzy repeated, his tone indicating good natured mockery rather than scorn.

"It did. I swear," Mike said defensively.

"Well, don't just sit there. Tell us who you know!"

"It's someone from law school," Mike began, "someone I haven't seen for years. But someone who supposedly has contacts in high places."

"Someone you and Barry were friends with?" Katie asked.

"No. I wouldn't call him a friend. He wasn't Barry's friend either."

"Then what was he then?" Katie asked.

"More like a rival."

"Then why would he help you?" she snapped.

"He wouldn't."

"*Nu?*" Izzy asked.

Mike looked puzzled.

"It's a Yiddish expression. Surely, you've heard it before."

"Ah, yes," Mike replied.

"I'm asking you, why is this important? If he is not your friend, then it is as if you do not know anyone, is it not?"

"I think I might find a way to get him to help us," Mike said.

Not me. Us.

"Well. What is your plan?"

"I think," Mike said quietly, as if under surveillance, "that I might have some leverage on him."

"Do tell," Katie said, her eyes narrowing in a manner Mike found extraordinarily seductive.

"Well, this guy from law school—his name is Lawrence—he's kind of what you would call a fixer in DC. Someone who is not exactly a lobbyist, but who acts like one. There are a lot of guys like that. They sort of make their money with one scheme after another, putting different people together and taking a fee. I know it's not the easiest thing to explain

"But this guy is supposedly thinking about running for the Senate. And well, let's just say that I know something about his past that would definitely hurt his chances."

"What is that?" Izzy asked.

"He's a cheat, that's what he is. He cheated all the way through law school," Mike replied. "And I have the proof."

"Proof?" Katie asked.

"Yeah, I have documentation."

"This one here, Kathryn," Izzy said, looking at Katie but pointing to Mike, "is a rascal. This idea, I like it."

"So, where do you go from here?" Katie asked.

"I'm going to have to think that over," Mike admitted. "I want to make sure I am doing this right."

"You think, you use your *kopf* like I told you," Izzy said, tapping Mike on the head.

"Yeah, I will. I am going to see what I can do with all this. I think there's more than a slight chance that this Bennington fellow from the newspaper is somehow mixed up in all of this."

"But hunches are just that. Hunches," Katie said, bringing Mike back down to earth.

"I know that," Mike said abruptly, immediately regretting his tone.

"I am glad I was able to help," Izzy said, defusing the tension.

"You did. Believe me, you did. I can't thank you enough," Mike said.

"Anything else before I get back to work? I'm not here on vacation. I have a store to run."

"Well," Mike thought it over, "I'd be curious to learn about this Kurt Waldheim guy. The Austrian diplomat. I brought an article about it. It's still in the manila envelope here, I think –"

Mike reached for the envelope.

As he began to pull out the clipping that Aunt Christina had given him a week ago, he realized he should have mailed it to his father by now. Eventually he would. But that would have to wait.

Izzy laughed.

But even Mike could tell it was from a happy laugh. It was a laugh borne of deep emotional trauma.

"That," he said, his voice gravelly, "will have to be a story for another time."

Mike nodded, then turned to Katie.

He saw it again. The look on her face. Similar to the one she had earlier when Izzy first began telling them about the Nazis. This time, however, he couldn't deny the emotions he clearly saw reflected in her face. He saw it in her eyes, in the way she scrunched up her nose. It was a look of deep regret. Almost embarrassment that she had allowed Mike access to her true self. She wasn't just Katie Rosenfeld, singer and copy editor.

She was Katie Rosenfeld. Daughter of Izzy.

CHAPTER 19

It was mid-afternoon when Izzy had put an end to the conversation. When he had sent Mike and Katie away from his store and back into the glare of the mid-afternoon sun. That time of day when it's too late for a proper lunch and too early for dinner.

Not that it mattered.

After spending close to two hours in that hot back office—with a broken fan no less—Mike wasn't particularly hungry. Katie didn't seem to have much of an appetite either. Not that she had told him outright. No. Once they left her father's store and began their walk back down Broadway in the direction of New York University, she had barely spoken a word.

Was Katie was annoyed at him? At her father? Or at them both?

Mike couldn't tell.

Was she thinking that she had made a big mistake in introducing him to her father? Or whether she felt as though her contributions to the discussion, her input, hadn't really been appreciated?

But who was he to have guided how the conversation had gone? He himself was beyond thankful that her father had agreed to speak to him at all. Not only had it given him much to think about, but it had also provided him with a clear path forward.

After what seemed an eternity, Katie slowly warmed up to him again.

"Tell me. What did you think of my father?" she asked. "Be honest."

"Honestly," Mike said, "I thought you had described him to me pretty well."

"Really?"

"Yes, he was not all that different from how I had pictured him."

"Funny how that works," Katie replied with a smile.

"Say," Mike asked, "is it always hot as hell in his office? For a moment there, I thought I was going to black out."

Katie laughed. "Today was a cool day in there," she said.

"Can I ask you something?"

"Sure, sounds serious. What is it?"

"Are you regretting that you introduced me to your dad?" he asked.

Katie sighed.

"It's complicated, Mike," she said.

"How so?"

"Well it's just that—"

It was right then, as they began to cross East 8th Street that Mike spotted the black Dodge Charger.

He saw it out of the corner of his eye as it turned the corner.

It was like a machine possessed, its front metallic grill a weapon, as it accelerated and raced down the street. Like a crazed demon, it was heading directly at them, clearly intending to run them down.

Mike acted on pure adrenaline. Unlike when he had been chasing Arthur down 86th Street, this time he operated with pure instinctive impulse, like a primitive man running from a saber-toothed tiger. The end result of thousands of years of evolution.

With no time to think, he grabbed Katie's waist with both hands. With his arms wrapped around her, he shoved her to the other side of the street, onto the sidewalk, and covered her body with his own.

Without fully realizing what had just happened, they found themselves in front of a small fruit stand. Next to them was standing a diminutive Sicilian man wearing a felt hat. Just prior to the chaos, Mike had seen him hawking bananas and plantains to people on the street. Now, he was shouting and frantically waving his hands in the air, screaming loud in heavily accented English.

"That maniac, he could've killed you bot'!" the man shouted.

That's when Mike realized he had not only saved Katie's life, but his own as well.

"Holy shit, Mike," Katie said, "that driver was fucking crazy! Even for this city," she shouted over the din of honking cabs and aggravated truck drivers.

"He wasn't nuts. That was goddamn deliberate," Mike gasped, as wheezed through breaths.

"What are you talking about?" Katie asked, as she shifted out of the way of an elderly couple leaving the fruit stand.

"I mean," Mike shouted, "that whoever was driving that fucking car was trying to kill us."

"Oh my god," Katie said. "I didn't even think—"

"They know how close we are," Mike said.

"Close to what?"

"Exposing them," Mike said.

"Who?"

"Bennington. He's behind this. He has to be."

"You're scaring me," she said quietly.

"I don't mean to," he replied, as a gaggle of Japanese tourists, armed to the teeth with cameras, brushed past them. They were talking animatedly among themselves. Although Mike couldn't understand a word they were saying, he knew they were talking excitedly about the car that had nearly crashed into them as well. Their first New York City experience, he thought wryly. Something they could tell their friends back home about. How they had almost gotten killed in Fun City.

Katie opened her mouth to speak, but immediately fell silent.

"What is it?" Mike asked.

"Maybe it wasn't deliberate. Have you considered that?"

Mike could feel his blood boiling. How could she be so blind?

"What do you mean?" he asked, doing his absolute best to keep his voice steady.

"I mean, you're the one who thought that creepy exterminator was some sort of hired assassin out to kill you. The one you confronted earlier."

She was only half right. He had misread the situation then. But that didn't mean he was misreading it now. Totally different situations. The exterminator standing outside his white van was merely staring. Whoever was driving that car had aimed to kill.

"Well, you're just plain wrong!" Mike bellowed.

Just then, someone yelled, "Shouldn't someone call the cops!"

Katie just stared back at Mike. Stunned he would speak to her like that. In such a hostile manner.

For a moment, Mike couldn't help but wonder whether he had been too aggressive. No, he had decided. He had not. This was life and death stuff. And the fact that she seemed to viscerally understand that one minute and not the very next irritated the hell out of him.

What planet was she living on?

How could she not see that the driver of the car deliberately tried to murder them? Was she that blind?

For a brief second, his mind played devil's advocate.

He entertained the thought that maybe—just maybe—he was getting a little paranoid. That the driver was some reckless teenager, not a hired assassin. But he quickly dismissed it. Because it simply couldn't be true. That would have been too big a coincidence. That the one time—the very one time—in his life in which he was nearly run over had to be immediately after he had met a refugee from Hitler's Germany to discuss the very distinct possibility that one of the country's leading industrialists was a Nazi.

No. It wasn't a fucking coincidence.

"You know, I think I'm just going to head home and clean up," Katie said, seemingly out of nowhere.

"You sure you don't want to stop for a coffee or something?"

"No. Not really."

"Okay, then," Mike said, "I'll call you later."

"Sounds good."

Mike sighed.

"You know, I'm just trying to wrap my head around all of this. That there are Nazis—or at least one Nazi—still active here in America. It's all a bit much."

Although Katie didn't say anything, Mike was sure that deep down she understood what he was trying to say. He sure hoped so.

Mike leaned in, intending to kiss Katie gently, but affectionately, on her lips. To tell her, without using words, that everything would be okay. That this madness would soon be over. And they could be just like any other ordinary couple trying to make it despite the odds.

But the kiss didn't land on its intended target.

Katie had quickly turned her head sideways, so that Mike was only able to kiss her cheek.

"I'll see you later, Mike," Katie said, as she turned and began to quickly walk away from him.

As he watched her disappear into the crowd, Mike really began to wonder. When this was all over, when he had finally figured out who or what connected Peter Hesse with a man named Bennington, would there be anything left for the two of them to even talk about? Would there be any reason for their relationship to continue?

Mike stood motionless on the sidewalk for a minute, wondering whether he could really get his hands on the Nuremberg Papers from Lawrence Van Orden. Such a crazy idea. Absurd. Not possible.

And yet, it was an opening. A possibility that he had to explore. It wasn't as if he knew anyone else in Washington D.C. besides Lawrence. No. Not at all. He had no reason to.

Mike thought about it some more, yet his mind was busy drifting elsewhere. As he stood nearly motionless on the crowded sidewalk, his thoughts about Washington dissipated and, in its place, he merely pictured himself as he must have looked like from on high. A singular figure surrounded by throngs of people, all of whom had no idea who he was and what he was thinking.

One man among many. A man confused and bewildered. A man who felt distinctly and utterly alone.

□ □ □

He could hear it from his apartment building's stairwell. The phone kept ringing. Whoever was calling was persistent. That was a fact. It rang a few more times. Then stopped.

Mike reached for his keys and pulled them out of his pocket. He fumbled a bit as he attempted to slide his apartment key into the lock. Despite his shaking hands, he managed to unlock the door. He pushed it open with his foot and ran inside, nearly tripping over the rug as he lunged for the receiver.

"Hello?" he said.

"Mike, it's Tony."

"Hey, Tony, I just got back in. What's up?"

"There's been a development in the Hesse case. There's something I think we ought to talk about."

"What is it?" Mike asked.

"I think," Tony began, "that this is something best discussed in person."

Mike knew Tony well enough to read through the lines. Tony was almost certainly in his office. And this information he had was something he wasn't willing to discuss over the phone. It would have been too risky. Let alone probably illegal.

"Okay," Mike said, "I just got home, but give me an hour or so, and I should be ready."

"Let's meet at our old spot. You know the one," Tony said.

Mike could hear the ruffling of papers and, in the background, a cacophony of voices. Men and women alike speaking over one another. Tony was obviously in his office at the police station. Which meant he could hardly speak freely.

"The old hangout, it is," Mike said, knowing full well where Tony meant for them to meet.

The Good Eats Restaurant downtown. The same place they went for burgers and beers when they worked cases together years ago.

Mike hung up the phone and, despite his exhaustion and all his worries, managed to smile in a way he hadn't for days now. Tony. Good Eats.

Life, he thought, really does come full circle.

Then it goes on.

□ □ □

By the time Mike got to the Good Eats Restaurant, Tony had already gotten a small table in the back. He had also taken the liberty of ordering himself a bacon cheeseburger with a side of French fries and a small pathetic excuse for a salad.

"You're welcome to have some," he said, pointing to the plate of fries.

"No thanks," Mike replied. "I'll just order something for myself in a bit."

"Do what you gotta do," Tony said, as he took three crispy fries, dipping them in ketchup, and stuck them into his mouth.

"So, tell me what's going on," Mike said, as he took a long look around the restaurant, the very same one where they had spent many long evenings years ago. His first impression was that it hadn't changed a bit in all these years. Still the same faux Americana décor, the same vintage New York Rangers memorabilia hung on the wall. And the young, pretty waitresses who did their absolute best to pretend they weren't bored out of their minds. Just waiting for the moment their agents got back to them with the role of a lifetime. One that would mean they wouldn't have to, with fake smiles plastered on their faces, flirt with a predominantly male, middle-class clientele.

Tony smiled.

"So, I see you want to get right down to business. No time for pleasantries, eh?" he said, lighting nudging Mike's rib with his elbow.

"Sorry. It's just been a crazy past few days," Mike said, exhaustion clearly audible in his voice.

"Hey. No problem. Fire away."

Just then, Mike noticed Tony's gaze was fixed where his holster sat. He was pretty sure he knew what Tony saw or at least what he suspected was there.

"You got yourself a piece," Tony said quietly.

Mike nodded cautiously.

"Yeah, things have changed a bit. I can't go into all of it. But yeah. I'm carrying."

"Good thing you took gun courses when you were in the DA's office."

"Yeah. Good thing," Mike said stoically.

Just then, the waitress came by and set a frosty mug of beer in front of Tony.

"You want to order anything?" she asked, looking at Mike.

"Yeah, a club sandwich with potato salad would be great."

"Something to drink?"

Mike thought about it a minute.

"A ginger ale would be fine," he said.

"You got it," she said, not even bothering to write his order down.

As he watched the waitress walk away, Tony took a large bite of his bacon cheeseburger. He set it back down on his plate and proceeded to wash it down with a large gulp of beer.

"Okay," he said. "I can tell you're not in the mood for any bullshit. So, I am going to lay it on you straight."

"Hit me," Mike said, as if Tony were a card dealer in a high-stakes game of poker and he an eager player ready to test his luck against the house.

"Remember when you were in the interrogation room the other night and—"

"How could I forget? You served me the most wretched coffee I've ever had."

"Well," Tony continued, "there was that moment when the sergeant came in and told me that they had found the guy responsible for sticking the knife—literally—into your guy, Peter Hesse."

"My guy?" Mike laughed, reacting to how strange that phrase sounded to him. "Yeah, I remember."

"Well, you probably also remember that the cops found him dead floating in the East River. Coroner's report says it was from a heroin overdose. He was a junkie."

"Vaguely," Mike said, unsure whether he remembered that detail or not. So much had happened over the past week that it all felt like a whirlwind.

"Anyways, the guy's name was George Black and he had been living in a flophouse in Chelsea not far from the Big Apple Hotel."

"Is his name supposed to ring a bell?" Mike asked, wondering whether he was missing something. It didn't seem remotely familiar. Not in the least.

"Nah. You've probably never heard the name before. And to be perfectly honest, there's no reason that you would've."

"Ok, so what's the point?"

"The point is that this George Black was known in the neighborhood for a couple of things—his ongoing heroin use and his willingness to cozy up to law enforcement to feed his habit. You get what I am saying?"

Mike warily looked around the restaurant to see if anyone was eavesdropping on their conversation. All he saw was a table filled with overweight guys in poorly fitted suits and discount neckties—insurance salesmen or something like that—aggressively chowing down on chicken wings and animatedly discussing whether their waitress would ever make it as a model.

"Relax," Tony said, well aware what Mike was doing. "I've already been scanning the room. We're all good."

"Sorry," Mike said, "it's just that—"

Now it was Tony's turn to interrupt. "I get it, man. I get it," he said in a reassuring tone.

"So, this George Black. You're telling me that he was a fucking stool pigeon?"

"Yep," Tony said, as he took another sip of his beer.

"With NYPD? No wait. DEA task force, right?" Mike asked.

"Neither."

"Who then?"

"Feds—the Bureau."

"Wait, what? The FBI?" Mike asked.

"Yep. And you're not going to believe who his handler was."

It hit Mike like a bolt of lightning. But it made perfect sense. It had to be. It just had to. Why else would Tony bring him here?

"You've got to be fucking kidding me," Mike said, looking straight into Tony's eyes.

"It was your buddy, Arthur."

"Holy shit. How in the hell did you find this out?" Mike asked, immediately realizing he was almost shouting.

"Mike. It's me. I get things done," Tony said. His tone could have been smug. But it wasn't. It was more of a plain factual statement.

"Well," Tony went on, "not every day does one of your former colleagues in the DA's office—that's you, buddy—end up at the scene of two murders in one week. So, I snooped around a bit, called in some chits. You know how it is. Got some people to speak to me about things they will have already forgotten they even talked to me about, if you catch my drift."

"Understood," Mike demurred, knowing full well how confidential information was shared among cops and prosecutors. Each pretending the conversation in question had never taken place.

"And here's something else you should know," Tony said.

"What's that?"

"After the connection between Arthur and George Black was made, the medical examiner went back and took another look at Black's body. And guess what he found?"

"It has to be something with the needle tracks on his arm. I'm right, aren't I?" Mike asked enthusiastically.

"You are. They took another look and the way the tracks are in his arm—the newest ones, the last ones in his arm before he died—were almost certainly put there by someone else. The angles of the needles going into his arm and all that."

"I understand," Mike said, simultaneously listening intently and thinking to himself.

"You know what this means, right?" Tony asked, knocking Mike out of his temporary reverie.

Mike nodded.

"It means that not only are the murders of that dirtbag Hesse and federal agent Zeffirelli connected, but that Zeffirelli probably had Black kill Hesse. And then subsequently faked his CI's death to make it look like a heroin overdose," Tony explained.

It was convoluted, but Mike understood the chain of events. The how. But not the why.

"But why?" Mike asked, suddenly realizing he already knew the most likely answer to his question.

Because Hesse needed to be shut up.

Because Hesse knew something that could have hurt Arthur.

No, not Arthur.

Someone Arthur had to have been working for. That had to be the only explanation. And Arthur? He had to be taken out for the very same reason. Either he knew too much or he was no longer useful. Perhaps both.

Mike took a deep breath.

He realized he should probably tell Millie about some of this. Not too much. Not anything that could potentially come back and bite Tony in the ass. But something. He owed her that much. She was his client and her husband had died after all. It wasn't as if he were doing all this purely for his own interests.

"What's on your mind?" Tony asked, clearly noticing that Mike was lost in his own thoughts.

"Nothing much. Just thinking some things over."

"I could see the wheels were turning."

"I think we're going to need to have a conversation that you're going to have to ever forget we had," Mike said.

"Oh?" Tony said, as he took another swig of his beer.

"Yeah," Mike replied. "I learned a few other things earlier this afternoon that give some context as to who Peter Hesse might have been."

"You mean he wasn't who he appeared to be?"

"Not completely. But what I do know—"

"Here you go." It was a female voice. The waitress had returned with Mike's club sandwich, potato salad, and ginger ale.

"Thanks," Mike said, smiling at the waitress.

"Holler if you need anything else," she said, trying her best to force a smile back.

"So?" Tony asked, after she had left.

"Let me eat," Mike said. "I'm starving. Once I've gotten some food in my belly, I'll tell you what I know so far."

His stomach growled in agreement.

CHAPTER 20

After he finished his club sandwich, Mike told Tony everything he knew.

Well, not quite everything.

But enough to paint his former colleague a fairly accurate picture of the situation as he understood it. Unanswered questions included.

Not only was there was a direct chain linking Peter Hesse's death to FBI Special Agent Arthur Zeffirelli and George Black, but that the departed Peter Hesse was likely living under an assumed name. That he had likely been a Nazi—or at least Nazi-adjacent—during World War II. The final kicker, as Mike had put it, was that a wealthy industrialist by the name of Samuel Bennington was probably the one behind it all. And that he too had almost certainly been a Nazi during the Second World War.

Only later did Mike reckon with the fact that everything he told Tony had been conjecture at that point.

How, in his excitement, he had all but forgotten Izzy's admonition that a gut feeling was not enough?

He needed something concrete.

But as to how Mike had come to learn all this, he had a good answer for Tony. A good one and a decidedly honest one.

Izzy Rosenfeld.

And just who the hell was he, Tony had wanted to know. Some eccentric Jewish guy who runs a discount electronic goods store on 14th Street? Hardly. Mike explained how, reading through the lines, it was clear that Rosenfeld had, in the past, been somewhat involved in underground Jewish activism.

Who knows exactly what schemes *they* had come up with?

Still it was more than clear to Mike that when Izzy had mentioned how he knew "some guys," or whatever the exact phrasing of it was, that he was talking about people who didn't exactly want their identities or activities revealed. After all, Katie had vaguely referred to something of that effect. How her dad had tried to out a bunch of neo-Nazis, perhaps on the assumption that sunlight was the best disinfectant.

Without realizing it at the time, Mike had spoken breathlessly for a good fifteen, twenty minutes. Tony had not even tried to get a word in.

Not that Mike would have let him. Rather, Tony had just listened quietly and took it all in. Which, as Mike knew all too well, was an uncharacteristic thing for Tony to do.

Finally, when Mike had finished talking, Tony took a sip of his beer, now lukewarm. He had asked Mike if he thought his client knew anything of this spy shit, as he had put it.

"Millie Johnson? No. I don't think she does," Mike had answered.

As he spoke, two things had occurred to Mike.

First, that he had never thought too hard about that question. And second, that it was well past time to speak with her in person again. See her and fill her in on all that had transpired. On all that he had learned.

Tony had posed a question. One that Mike implicitly understood to be a message: if shit got really bad, Tony had his back.

"What is it you need from me, Mike?" he had asked. With that, Tony had given Mike the boost he very much needed to push on. Through all the exhaustion. The confusion. The delirium of it all.

"I need you to forget we ever had this conversation," Mike said.

"What conversation?" Tony asked.

Mike laughed.

"Exactly."

"I have something else to ask you, man," Tony said, his index fingers tracing a circular motion atop his beer glass.

"Go for it," Mike replied.

"Why do you care so much?" Tony asked, clasping his palms together.

The question took Mike aback.

It wasn't something he was expecting to hear. Let alone prepared to answer. It shook him.

Why did he care so much? What was in it for him? Had he even once stopped to even consider the question? He didn't think so. He had felt fear, terror, excitement. Yes.

But what motivated him?

Why did he care?

Mike shrugged.

"I just do," he replied softly.

"That's not a good answer. Not when you might get yourself killed," Tony said.

"I'm not going to get myself killed."

"You better not."

"Anything else to ask me, detective?" Mike said jokingly.

Tony indeed did have one final thing to get off his chest before they had called it quits for the night.

"Do me a favor, would you, Mike, if you would. Just tell me you'll be careful with that thing," Tony had said, pointing to Mike's chest. To his holster and the gun resting in it.

"I will."

"And if you decide to leave town—and I'm not advising you to leave town—but if you do, leave the piece here."

Mike nodded.

"Understood."

After leaving the restaurant, so tired he could barely think straight, Mike walked a bit to clear his mind.

The night air was unusually cool for August. A cool breeze helped invigorate him.

He stopped at the first pay phone he could find. It was a dingy booth on West Broadway, close to the Chambers Street subway station. Tagged in blood red graffiti that assuredly held meaning for whomever painted it, the booth gave off a pungent odor of something horribly rotten.

Mike entered the booth. He closed the door behind him. Just then, he felt his foot accidentally kick something. He looked down. It was a rotting banana. So that's where that smell was coming from. Figures. That was the thing with phone booths. You never knew what you were going to find inside. He smiled. That rotten banana seemed an apt metaphor for his past week. By taking the Hesse case, all he ended up doing was opening a door to a whole lot of rot.

Mike pulled out his address book from his jacket pocket. He leafed through the pages, until he came across Millie's home number. He inserted a dime into the slot at the top and dialed her.

The phone rang once. Twice. Three times. Nothing.

Then, after the fourth ring, a response from the other end.

"Hello?" It was a woman's voice, but it didn't sound exactly like Millie. Too raspy. Without that distinct melodic drawl. The one that had echoed in Mike's mind for hours after she had left his office on that rainy night.

"Is this Millie?" Mike asked.

"Yes?" came the cautious reply.

"Millie," he said, pausing for a moment before continuing. "It's Mike Levinas. I just wanted to check in with you."

"Hey Mike. What's—what's going on?" From her voice alone, Mike instinctively knew she was groggy. Subdued.

But it was Millie all right.

"I was wondering if we could meet. I have some things I'd like to discuss with you," Mike said, pausing before continuing. "Things pertaining to your case."

"Uh, okay," she said. She still sounded exhausted. But this time it sounded as if her twang had returned.

"Do you want to—" Mike began to ask.

Millie interrupted him.

"Why don't you just come over? It really would be so much easier that way," she said.

"That'll work," Mike said. He imagined a cramped, small apartment. One with clothes strewn on the floor and dirty dishes piling up in the sink.

Holding the receiver with one hand, Mike leafed through his address book with the other. There it was. Millie's address.

"Okay, so come on over when you can. I ain't going nowhere," she said, slurring through her words.

"Will do," Mike said, trying hard to keep his tone as professional as possible. She was, after all, his client. Not his friend. If she were his friend, he wouldn't have held back the question at the forefront of his mind: was she using heroin again? Because it sure sounded like that was possible.

Hell, after this past week, anything was possible.

□ □ □

It was a small, nondescript apartment building nestled in a sleepy part of the West Village. Located just down the block from an all-night pizzeria and a bank, it was no different from thousands of other similar structures. On the surface, there was nothing unusual about the neighborhood that night. A few pedestrians here and there walked briskly past the building, some of them in couples, both opposite and same sex. An occasional bicyclist could be seen zooming down the quiet street. And every once and a while a yellow cab would slowly roll down the street, pull up curbside, and let a passenger out onto the sidewalk.

What was unusual this particular night was that, inside a phone booth less than a block away from the apartment building, stood a man whose thoughts were as dark as the street when there were no cabs or cars to brighten it.

A man dressed in a dark blue shirt, black jeans, and low-rise combat boots. A man dressed for battle.

Donny.

He put a dime into the pay phone and dialed.

The phone on the other end rang once. Twice. Three times.

Then a voice.

"Yes," Bennington said.

"It's me," Donny said, as his eyes scanned the area around him.

"Where are you?"

"I'm here."

"Good," Bennington said.

The two of them had it down pat. Donny thought Bennington had always been on the paranoid side. But lately he had taken it to a whole new level. If anyone had been tapping his calls, Bennington wanted to make sure they didn't get anything incriminating. Not a word more than absolutely necessary was to be spoken.

"I'm waiting until I can get in," Donny said, immediately regretting that he might have said too much. That was the thing with Wagenmann. He wanted to know stuff. But he also didn't.

"You get in when you can," Bennington replied tersely.

Just then, Donny noticed a man walking down the street. A solitary figure. It looked as if he were lost. As if he were not quite sure where he was headed. Donny clenched his fists instinctively.

"I see someone," Donny said emphatically. But not loud enough to draw attention to himself.

"Who's that?"

"The Jew. Levinas," Donny said, contempt in his voice.

"Is that so?"

"Yeah," Donny said, never once taking his eyes off Mike as he crossed the street, double-backed, and headed straight toward the apartment building.

A temporary silence. Donny wondered what his employer was thinking.

"See to them both," Bennington finally said.

"Understood," Donny said, in a businesslike matter-of-fact tone. The tone of a man paid to kill.

A click. The phone went dead. Just like that, Bennington had ended the call. But he had not stopped thinking about Donny. He loved the guy, but couldn't shake the thought that he'd fuck things up.

Donny hung up the receiver on his end. He reached inside his jacket. It was there. His gun. The one he would use to put an end to both Millie Johnson and Mike Levinas.

With the money he had earned from this job, he could hightail it out of the country too. Just like Bennington planned to fly to South America, he would lie low in Mexico for a while. Sit on the beach and down some ice-cold beers with some senoritas. That was the plan.

All he had to do was pump a few bullets into the wife and the Jew.

□ □ □

Mike, oblivious to the fact that he was being surveilled by a gun for hire, stopped on the sidewalk in front of the apartment building.

He checked to make sure he had the right address. He looked. He did.

As he made his way to the front door, he imagined the building's residents to be an odd mix of avant-garde artists; students living away from home from the first time; and lonely pensioners scraping by on meager savings and federal assistance.

And, of course, Millie.

Millie, who was now all alone in her apartment.

An apartment originally inhabited by two. Once lived in by Millie and a man Mike never had even spoken to and had seen only once. A man, who Mike had never even spoken to, was keeping far more nefarious secrets from the world than merely his heroin use and his frequenting of low-rent prostitutes.

The outer door was unlocked. Mike pushed it open and entered the dimly lit foyer and tried the inner door. Maybe that was going to be unsecured as well.

No such luck.

It was locked shut.

Mike scanned the names of the building's residents. Then pressed the buzzer next to the name "Hesse."

The sound of an electronic crackle ripped Mike from his reverie. It was Millie replying from her unit. The foyer door clicked loudly open. Mike made his way through the lobby and walked up the stairs, stopping only to knock gently on the door to Apartment 5B.

"Mike, is that you?" Millie called from inside the apartment.

"It is indeed," Mike replied.

Mike heard a noise. Then the distinct sound of a hand sliding a bold chain off its latch. Then the unbolting of a lock. The door slowly creaked open.

"Come in quickly," Millie whispered, as she checked to see who was at her door.

It was as if she didn't want any of her neighbors to know she had a male visitor. Either that, or she was frightened, paranoid perhaps. But she did seem distinctly more alert than she had on the phone. That was a positive sign. Was it not?

The first thing Mike noticed was how her sleeveless pink nightgown clung to her skin, coating it like morning dew on blades of grass. Mike also saw the bags under her eyes. How could he not? They were dark semi-circles of despair that looked as if they were painted on by an incompetent makeup artist. But what he saw next saddened him. But it didn't shock him. He saw them clearly.

The track marks on her bare arms.

Unlike the last time he saw her in person, this time there was no doubt in his mind that the tracks were fresh.

She was using again, all right.

"How are you holding up?" Mike asked, knowing all too well the answer to the question.

"Fine. I'm fine," she said, beads of cold sweat gathering on her face like stars clustering in the night sky. It probably wasn't a lie. She probably was fine. Given how bad she could have been, she wasn't doing all that badly. Mike thought how misery was all very relative. She wasn't passed out on her bed and was still coherent. She wasn't too far gone. It wasn't like she was about to drop dead in his arms.

"You know," Mike said, realizing that a jolt of caffeine might do her some good. "I was thinking. Maybe it would be best if we went out for a coffee."

"Sure, but after you tell me what you came here to tell me. That's only fair, Mike."

She paused, then repeated that last phrase as if she were a teaching a lesson in morality. "That's only fair."

Walking into the cramped space that passed for a living room, Mike pondered exactly what—and how much—he should tell her. Millie was hardly in an ideal emotional state to learn that her oddball professor husband was some sort of Nazi living in America under an assumed identity. Then again, she certainly had to be prepared for getting some sort of bizarre news like that. After all, she was the one who had phoned him soon after Peter Hesse's death to let him know she was being followed. She clearly suspected that her husband's death was hardly random. She was the one who handed him the cryptic letter at the Salonika Diner.

Just then, Mike focused his gaze down at the glass and steel coffee table. The half-used bags of potato chips, McDonald's cheeseburger wrappers, empty Coke cans, and a pile of stockings didn't exactly inspire confidence in her ability to cope either. But he had to say something. Otherwise, she would get even more suspicious. And given how topsy-turvy everything seemed to him right now, a distrustful and paranoid client was the last thing he needed.

"Why don't you get dressed and I'll tell you all about it?"

"That—that sounds like a plan."

"So," Mike said, as he watched Millie walk into her bedroom and partially close the door behind her, "as it turns out, the police have a better sense of who Peter's killer was."

"I thought you said he was some junkie looking for money?" she called through the door.

Some junkie. Her voice dripped with contempt. As if she wasn't an addict herself. Did she not even remember their conversation at the Salonika when she had brought that cryptic letter for Mike to look at? Mike wasn't sure where her mind was at. Maybe she didn't know either.

"He was a junkie. But I'm talking about what was behind it all. It looks like someone hired him to kill Peter," Mike said.

Mike looked around the living room. While he did so, he almost regretted using the word "junkie" to describe George Black. FBI stoolie would have been a more apt description. Unwitting hired assassin would have served just as well.

"Hired?"

"Yeah."

"Honestly, Mike," Millie said, her drawl even stronger this time, "I don't even remember what I knew and when I knew it."

She laughed like it was all one big cosmic joke.

"Isn't that how it always is with people like me?" she asked.

Mike didn't know how to answer that. But he knew that she pleading for help. That she knew she needed intervention. And right away. But who was he to do anything about it? He wasn't a social worker.

"I think we really should get going," Mike said. He delicately placed his arm on Millie's shoulder. Although it was warm to the touch, it radiated an Arctic chill.

"Fair is fair," she said indifferently, as if her mind was once again a million miles away.

That word was like a dog whistle.

Fair.

As in, life just isn't fair.

Maybe that's what was really on her mind that night. Maybe that's why she began shooting up junk again.

Could he truly blame her for feeling that way?

Her white knight, her partner in recovery, not only ended up dead on the floor of a seedy hotel room, but he had forced her to live a lie. Lies. Mike was pretty sure Millie was able to handle the prostitutes. But the Nazi connection? That would have to wait for another day, he decided.

Now that would be fair.

They walked together out of the apartment. Millie closed and locked her apartment door behind her. Mike let Millie go in front of him, but stayed close to her. He watched Millie walk down the stairs, making sure that she didn't trip and crack her skull. Relief came when he saw she was fully able to navigate one step at a time, if tentatively. In her blue jeans and white blouse, he thought she radiated a youthful glow that belied her age and heroin use. Maybe she has a future after all, Mike thought. Maybe when this was all finished, she could get yet another fresh start.

When she got to the bottom of the stairwell, she looked up and saw Mike above her, his hands gripping a guardrail like gargoyle warding off evil spirits.

"Well, you coming or not?" she asked, her twang as potent as ever.

"I'll be right down," Mike said, as he began to descend the stairs.

When he got down to foyer, he noticed that Millie, to his astonishment, looked distinctly more vital than she did twenty minutes ago when she opened her door.

□　□　□

They walked two or three blocks. By a closed Thai restaurant, a small newsstand, a bank.

Then all hell broke loose.

At first, Mike thought it was the sound of a car backfiring.

What was going on?

There was not a single moving car on the block. But that's sure as hell what it sounded like. One distinct loud pop. The type he'd heard a hundred times or more. The city was filled with clunky automobiles, late for their date with the junkyard, that spewed all sorts of toxic fumes into the air and made noises like that.

It only took less than two seconds for him to realize that no car made that pop.

It was the sound of someone firing a gun.

Not just once this time. But three more times in rapid succession. Pop. Pop. Pop.

Mike turned quickly, attempting to shield Millie with his body. His thoughts cascaded in rapid succession. He realized he had been wrong earlier when he told himself she wasn't his friend. If she wasn't a friend, who was? Barry? He had to have more than one friend in the world. That settled it. Yes. She was a friend. And people should do what they need to do to protect their friends, especially when their backs are pressed up against the wall.

But thoughts alone don't save the world.

When Mike saw Millie hit the sidewalk, he stared in disbelief.

Just ten seconds ago, she had been actually laughing.

Laughing!

Laughing for the first time in who knows how long. He had told her one of Barry's favorite off-color jokes. One that would have made a sailor blush. One that had just made her smile.

"Millie!" a voice shouted. It was his voice.

She looked up at him.

Alive.

She was alive!

But had she been shot? Fuck. He couldn't tell. It looked as if she were clasping her chest. But how could he be certain? He didn't have time to think.

Everything that transpired did so in the blink of an eye.

In seconds or even far less.

For that was all the time Mike had to act. To figure out where the shooting was coming from. To avoid getting a bullet himself.

After it was all over, Mike remembered seeing blood pour from Millie's chest in short, but powerful gushes. He remembered the sound of her crying, of her pleading for her very life. He remembered the cold, blank stare in her irises, as they focused intently on the night sky, then her eyes closing shut permanently under the weight of heavy eyelids.

But most of all he remembered aiming his gun and squeezing the trigger like a gunslinger. Taking three rapid forward steps in succession, fear leaving in the rearview mirror, and pointing his gun squarely at the chest of Millie's assailant—the same fucking guy who pushed him on the subway tracks—and then blasting him straight to hell.

Mike also remembered the disorienting flashes of blue and red, punctuated by bright yellow headlights. How the cacophony of sirens never seemed to end. The harried voices of cops, angry and loud, as New York's finest arrived upon the scene. Arrived in their patrol cars to find two still warm bodies cluttering the street like castaway objects that nobody wanted.

Street cops who found Mike Levinas very much alive. Alive and kicking, but completely out of his depth. A man bewildered and exhausted, but still alert. A man with a PI license and a heart fueled by seemingly never-ending reserves of adrenaline.

A man who had watched his friend Millie die.

□ □ □

The precinct captain had ruddy cheeks, thinning blonde hair that was on the cusp of turning white, and a waistline that showed an appreciation for pastries.

He set down his Styrofoam cup of coffee and dryly noted that whenever Mike was around, bodies had a strange tendency to pile up. Why exactly was that, he wondered aloud. No, he wasn't blaming Mike for anything. And he assured Mike that he wasn't technically a suspect and that it was pretty clear he had acted in self-defense.

But it was strange, was it not?

How many had it been? Two? Three? In nearly a week's time? That wasn't typical, except for maybe people who work in the coroner's office. It had all begun with Peter Hesse in the Big Apple Hotel, of course. Then continued with an FBI Agent bleeding out from a knife wound in a dark alley. Now there were two more bodies to tally. Millie Johnson and a man identified as Donny O'Leary of Jersey City, New Jersey. Making a grand total of four. Three Mike had either come upon or witnessed. And one who had died by his hand.

So how to account for all this, the precinct captain had wondered aloud. Again, stating for the record that no, Mike was not a suspect and that he was technically free to go at any time as long as he didn't skip town. Apparently numerous locals had witnessed it all and they had all said the same thing. Mike had pulled his gun and had fired only after the other guy had shot the woman.

It was self-defense. It helped immensely that Mike had his firearm permit and, as a very preliminary measure, ballistics had matched up the crime scene with his story.

But that didn't stop the precinct captain from trying to figure out what the hell Mike had been up to lately. And Mike felt like he was still on the hook. He nevertheless kept his cool. He asked only for one thing. A very reasonable request.

To phone Detective Tony Doran so he could let him know what had happened.

That request, to his everlasting surprise, was granted.

Furthermore, the cops had a record that Donny O'Leary had been known for some time as a hired gun. But they didn't know for whom. Either that or they knew all too well and were keeping mum for their own reasons.

Tony Doran had also put in a good word for Mike.

But as the precinct captain had reminded him in a tone that was more than a little on the hostile side, just because he wasn't a suspect in a crime didn't mean that the cops were remotely satisfied. Nor did it mean that the police would be pretending as if nothing had happened. No. They'd be keeping an eye on him. That was for sure. They wanted Mike to get that message first and foremost.

And he did.

For as he walked out of the station into the early morning light, Mike knew that unless he took care of things himself—in his own way—more bodies were going to pile up. And that would only lead to more unwanted late evening visits to one of New York City's myriad police stations.

No. He could do better.

And he would.

First thing he would have to do would be to get the image of Millie collapsing and hitting the pavement out of his mind.

That wasn't going to be easy.

With a splitting headache and an indescribable ache in his gut, Mike walked to the nearest subway station and waited for the next train to come through the tunnel.

He had a destination in mind. A place where he could gather his thoughts. A place where he could put together a plan. His own fortress of solitude. Like Superman had in the comics.

Still shocked that the cops let him go without more of a fuss, he headed back to Brooklyn.

CHAPTER 21

It was when Mike stepped into the foyer that he realized he could barely remember anything he had seen or heard on his subway ride to Brooklyn.

Let alone on his walk from the subway station to Aunt Christina's house. He had been too caught up in his own thoughts, in his own mind. It was as if he had been in a trance. Hypnotized. Everything that he had seen, felt, done in the past week stormed through his mind, a gale pounding its way through a dark cloudy North Atlantic sky.

It had all been too much.

So much that every movement he had made—from dropping a token into the subway turnstile, to boarding a rackety graffiti-covered train car, to trudging through the grimy subway station and back on the street—had been done on autopilot. His mind was too busy sorting everything out to deal with mundane tasks such as these.

But when he entered the sanctity of Aunt Christina's home, all that stopped.

Now, finally, he could exhale. Unwind. And let all the emotions that he had bottled up wash over him.

But it was still too much all at once.

Mike expected that he would be able to push himself through it. Just like he'd pushed himself through everything else that had happened in his life.

That he would just walk on over to the couch, the very one where he sat less than two weeks ago when his aunt had served him coffee and sweets. Walk on over and sit quietly for a short while.

Such luxuries were not in the cards. This was different.

For he had just killed a man. And watched a woman die.

Making matters worse, the house felt like an inferno. The rackety air-conditioner was turned off. Mike figured Aunt Christina must have turned it off when she left for New Jersey with Erik. And, with no windows open, the temperature inside the house must have been close to ninety.

Mike took another few short steps before he lost his balance.

His strength gave way as he slowly collapsed onto the floor. He hit the carpet, curled up into a ball. There, he remained motionless for a time.

How long he did not know. Although his eyes were closed shut, he could still see Millie in his mind's eye. Could see her dying on the street.

Nausea overtook him. Dread enveloped him. Such dark images cascaded through his mind for what seemed to be an eternity.

It had been only a few minutes. Five at most.

But it was enough to initiate a change. One that had been a long time coming.

He knew he simply couldn't go on as he had been. That something inside him—something he couldn't quite put into words—had been stolen from him over the past several days. Something he now knew he wouldn't ever get back. No matter how hard he ached for it.

That's when he looked up.

It wasn't the cracked ceiling that caught his eye. Nor was it the photo of the Norwegian royal family, the one Aunt Christina always made sure to dust and to polish with the dedication of a loyal subject.

No. What caught his eye, what forced a long overdue introspection was that handwritten essay of his on the wall. The one he had written back when he was a mere fifth grader. The one his mother had kept with her until her dying day.

The first thought that registered in his weary mind was how far away it all seemed. How time had slipped away from him. The second was how achingly juvenile the essay now seemed in light of the fact that Mike had taken a life. Sure, it had been self-defense. But that didn't change the fact that Mike now had blood on his hands. He had crossed a threshold and he knew it. There was no turning back.

Mike slowly picked himself off the ground. He wiped perspiration from his brow. Took a closer look at what he had written. What he had written years ago in the perfect cursive handwriting his mother and Aunt Christina had been so proud of.

His essay about doing the right thing when a problem arose.

A question occurred to him. Was the mindset that he had back then really all that different from where his thoughts were now? Namely on doing something to put an end to this intrigue and bloodshed once and for all.

Didn't he right now, this very moment, want to—as simple as it sounded—do the right thing?

Or, at the very least, take the most moral course of action?

And more saliently, wasn't he very much standing alone in the face of a faceless invisible enemy? A man who called himself Samuel Bennington?

Katie and Izzy could only help so much; Izzy was an old man, after all. And he wasn't even sure how Katie felt about him anymore, given the awkwardness evident when they had parted the other day.

Tony Doran would help to a reasonable degree, but Mike knew he wasn't going to risk his career at the NYPD, let alone his pension, over this giant mess that Mike had gotten himself into. Nor should he be expected to.

And Millie.

She was no longer alive to support what was turning out to be a much bigger project than merely finding her junkie husband.

He stood alone, that was for sure.

There was no one who could help him.

Mike closed his eyes. Focus, he told himself. Focus like you've never focused before.

All of a sudden, it hit him like a punch to the gut.

Maybe he did have someone to help him after all.

Someone who would have his own incentive to get involved. Someone interested in, above all else, telling a story. And what a story it was! How an ex-Nazi somehow had infiltrated the ranks of corporate America to manipulate it to his own ends.

Yes. Mike definitely knew someone who would be interested in telling that particular story.

And it just happened to be someone who also knew a little something about law and politics.

Barry Stein.

As he sat down on the couch to gather his thoughts, Mike realized how it all made perfect sense.

Yes. That was it. He would get Barry to help him take down this Bennington character, if he indeed was the man behind all the pain, violence, and suffering Mike had witnessed the past two weeks.

It was still a big if. Izzy had been right. He needed something real. Something tangible.

Which was why, in his mind, he was already planning his train trip to Washington. A trip to see Lawrence Van Orden.

But Mike knew he was right about one thing. Barry was someone he could trust. Someone whom he knew and who'd have his back when the inevitable shit hit the inevitable fan.

And most importantly, someone who had more than a merely altruistic incentive to help Mike accomplish his goal of uprooting the rot all around him and getting justice for his deceased client.

Still sitting on the couch and now looking at the coffee table, Mike's mind returned to that day when Aunt Christina had given him the *New York Post* article about Kurt Waldheim. Something she had said now registered in his mind differently than it had at the time.

Your people's greatest tragedy.

Your people.

That phrase. It echoed silently in his ear. The very phrase his aunt had used when discussing the Holocaust, about why his father specifically would be interested in that particular article.

Words directed at him.

Were the Jews his people? Were Kate and Izzy his people?

If he had been asked that question even a few days ago, he would have answered in the negative. He would have said his father was Jewish. And his Mom Norwegian. Just like he did with Katie when he first met her at the bar.

Now, he wasn't so sure.

Maybe the Jews were, despite his youth in the Norwegian Cultural Society, his people after all. Maybe all of this had happened for a reason.

Maybe that was the answer to the question Tony had asked him at the restaurant.

Why do you care so much?

He cared because that's who he was. Even if he wasn't fully comfortable with it. Even if it meant that he was always going to feel somewhat like an outsider.

Mike got up from the couch and walked into the kitchen. He opened the refrigerator door, peering inside to see if there were any cold drinks inside.

Just his luck.

There was one can of ginger ale. Generic brand. Something his aunt surely had picked up at the corner market.

Mike reached and grabbed it. The can was cold to the touch. He cracked it open, took giant gulp. It was like putting a fire out.

It was only then that he realized how awfully dry his throat had been.

It was only then that he realized his hands weren't shaking. Now that he thought about it, Mike realized that neither during the encounter with Donny, nor after his interrogation by the cops, had his hands trembled.

He was getting stronger, bolder, more capable.

As if his negative ruminations had been steadily replaced with something else. Something far more constructive.

Steely determination.

□　□　□

Mike walked over the telephone, picked it up, and dialed.

In a small apartment on West End Avenue, a phone rang.

"Hello?"

"Barry, this is Mike."

"What's up, Mike?" Barry asked, as he peered out the window of his eighteen-floor apartment. He looked down. The teenagers who got shitfaced in the park were back at it again.

"I know I haven't been the best in staying in touch lately, but this case I'm working on has taken an unusual turn."

Mike paced back and forth in Aunt Christina's living room, stretching the telephone cord as far as it could go.

"Yeah, your girl told me as much."

That's when it hit Mike. Barry probably knew quite a bit. He had almost forgotten that Katie and Barry worked together at the newspaper.

"How much did she tell you?" Mike asked. He immediately worried that his tone was too harsh. Too accusatory.

"Enough to know you're getting yourself in some deep shit."

"Funny you should mention that," Mike said.

"Why is that?"

"Because I'm inviting you to join me."

"In the shit?"

"Yes. In the shit."

"What's in it for me?" Barry asked.

"A great story. Your big break."

Barry laughed. "I understand now," he said.

"I thought you would," Mike replied. He proceeded to fill Barry in on all of the necessary details and how he would be mailing him a large envelope of material that he was free to use in a story.

Mike continued speaking until he heard the sound of banging on the other end.

Barry interrupted him.

"Dude, I got to go. There's a girl knocking on my door," Barry said.

"Gotcha. Just do keep an eye out for the package I'm going to be sending you."

"I won't miss it. Promise. I am a professional after all."

Before he hung up the phone on his end, Barry had one final thing to say.

"Look at you. My buddy's a regular fucking Mike Hammer."

"More like Robert Redford in *Three Days of the Condor*."

"You're not nearly as handsome, Mike. Not nearly."

And with that, the call between the two men was ended.

Mike knew it was time to strategize, to organize.

To make a list of exactly what he needed to do to accomplish his goal. If not in writing, at least in his own mind.

First things first.

He needed to make sure he had everything he needed for his upcoming train trip to Washington DC. And to be sure that he left in his office everything that he didn't need.

That meant going to his apartment, the safety deposit box at the bank, and his office in the East Village.

Although his former law school classmate didn't know it yet, Mike was about to blackmail the would-be Senator into getting him what a dying federal agent had called The Nuremberg Papers.

CHAPTER 22

Taking up nearly an entire city block on Connecticut Avenue, the Garfield Hotel had seen more than its fair share of scandal, political intrigue, and adultery over the decades. Built in the 1920s in the neoclassical style of architecture omnipresent in Washington DC, the hotel had served as a home away from home for tourists and diplomats alike. Numerous high-level conferences had been held in its opulent ballroom over the decades. Decisions that impacted the lives and livelihoods of millions were hashed out by lobbyists and lawmakers over breakfast in the tearoom just a short walk from the gilded lobby. It also happened to have a few rooms available at the very last minute. And by the time Mike had checked in, he was beyond exhausted.

Amtrak had a way of doing that to him. Nearly every time he had been on a train ride, he ended up feeling unusually groggy. As if a vampire had sucked life straight out of him. He thought it must have something to do with the lack of fresh air. The lack of fully functioning air conditioning and the constant inflow of exhaust made it difficult to breathe properly. No wonder that his father had hightailed it for Florida. All you needed there was a car. No subways. No buses. No trains. Mike had to admit it sounded more appealing by the day. Maybe he'd have to go down and visit one of these days.

The journey to DC itself had been uneventful. There was the typical array of passengers one would expect to see on the New York-Washington DC corridor. Bland-looking and balding men in even blander suits, nearly all of them thirty to forty pounds overweight. Harried suburban parents with young kids in tow, almost certainly on their final family vacation of the summer before school started again after Labor Day. All overly eager to see the monuments and museums, blissfully ignorant of the decadence and drunkenness that permeated nearly every aspect of daily life in Reagan's capital.

Mike, still keyed up from all that had transpired, had carefully scanned the faces of passengers as they boarded in Newark, Philadelphia, and Wilmington.

Strange faces. Aggrieved faces. Tired faces.

Were any of these people watching him? Were they out to kill him? Were they looking too closely at his briefcase? The one in which he kept his papers? How could he even tell?

They all looked so normal.

Although Mike was confident that he'd be able to see this through to the very end, his constant hyper-alertness was beginning to take a definite psychic toll. Now that the adrenaline high had worn off, he felt nothing but exhaustion. Yet he had to keep his wits about him.

What choice did he have?

How was he to know if another would-be assassin was waiting in the wings? It wasn't as though anyone was there to protect him. He didn't have his gun with him. That he left back in his office.

He realized he probably should have locked it up as he was legally required to do. He worried he was getting sloppy. What did it even matter? It was too late now. Whether it was locked away in a safe or not did not change the fact that, as of this moment, he only had himself to rely upon. He wasn't a cop. He had no partner to come to his aid. He had no backup to call upon.

The cavalry wasn't coming to the rescue.

As he checked into his hotel suite—a nondescript but clean room on the fifth floor—Mike reminded himself that he had come to this city for one reason and one reason only. To blackmail his former classmate, Lawrence—Larry—Van Orden, into allowing him access to what Arthur had called, in his final moments, the Nuremberg Papers.

Documents that should shed some much-needed light on who Samuel Bennington really was; what he had done during the war; and how in the hell he became such a financially successful industrialist. The papers, Mike figured, wouldn't be top secret. Not anymore. They were more likely just forgotten, reminders of (depending on who you asked) a shameful past tucked away somewhere in a Southeast DC storage unit or in a large wooden crate in a warehouse somewhere in rural Virginia. It wasn't like covering up for geriatric Nazis was a top governmental priority right now; whoever gave the orders to shield war criminals from prosecution was probably very old or dead at this point. The documents couldn't bring down the Reagan Administration. Hardly.

But they could bring down Samuel Bennington—or whatever his real name was. And that's all Mike cared about.

Mike placed his overnight bag and his briefcase onto the bed. While the former had enough fresh clothes to last for a day or two, the latter had what it would take to break Larry; namely, copies of those law school papers that showed that golden boy Van Orden was a cheat. It all seemed rather serendipitous. That somehow he had had that conversation with Barry at the Salonika Diner where "The Larry Van Orden Affair," as

Mike called it, had been discussed.

Ten minutes later, after a warm refreshing shower, he put on a pair of comfortable cotton pajamas and was soon fast asleep. Tomorrow was going to be a pivotal day. The first thing he was going to do after breakfast was to phone Van Orden.

□   □   □

Clemington's Bar and Grill was the type of place Mike imagined attracted the Van Ordens of the world. Dimly lit, with wood panel walls upon which framed equestrian prints had been hung and displayed, it exuded a genteel conservatism. Men in expensive suits, many smoking cigars, huddled together in booths, their loud voices making reference to this or that "son of a bitch" in Congress who was getting in the way of their agenda. What an entirely different feel from the gritty East Village, Mike thought to himself. How could two cities, not all that far apart geographically, be so completely different in their atmosphere? Were there even any cool or hip places in the nation's capital? Mike didn't know and wasn't going to be around long enough to find out. Still, from what little he had seen in his cab ride from the hotel to Clemington's the evening after his arrival, the most likely answer was a resounding no. Compared to Manhattan, Washington felt downright provincial; hardly the global metropolis that its more fanatical rival purported to be. No. It was less a global city and more like an oversized country club suburb. A sort of Fairfield, Connecticut on steroids.

Obtaining Van Orden's private phone number hadn't proved particularly difficult, Mike thought, as he sat down at the bar in the front of the restaurant. He was a PI, after all. Perhaps Van Orden wanted to be accessible. All it had taken for Van Orden to agree to meet him tonight was a couple of cryptic messages that Mike had left on his law school nemesis's answering machine. Something about how Mike had really important information to share with him, but it had to be in person. A few choice words about how Mike knew something which could potentially sink his Senate campaign before it even got off the ground. Vaguely intimidating, but polite enough to pique Larry's interest and make sure that he phoned Mike's hotel suite.

Which he did.

Utterly predictable, Mike thought. The guy cares about one thing; his ceaseless ambition and his grandiose aspirations. In that regard, he hadn't changed one iota since law school. And he was a total prick back then.

"What'll it be?" the ruddy faced bartender asked Mike, who set his briefcase on the wooden bar.

"Just give me a ginger ale for now," Mike said, noticing a group of younger women entering the restaurant. Must be interns or something

"That gonna be it?" the bartender asked, over increasing chatter from numerous other people who had gathered around the bar.

"For now," Mike said tersely, looking at his watch. He was thirty minutes early; they had agreed on the phone earlier that afternoon that they'd meet at six sharp; it was now only 5:30. He unlocked the briefcase and shuffled through the papers he had retrieved from his office, the xerox copies of Dean Taylor's report detailing Van Orden's less than ethical conduct in law school. Mike knew Van Orden might try to make a similar play now as in the past. But this time it was different. Van Orden's father wasn't going to be able to throw cash around and get him out of this particular situation. There was simply no amount Mike would take to lay off Larry. Either Mike was going to gain access to the Nuremberg Papers or Larry's law school indiscretions would be the talk of the town, and that would sink his Senate seat ambitions for good. No one wanted to back a known cheat.

Mike had more than a gut feeling that Larry was going to see things his way. Van Orden may have been a lot of things, but he wasn't stupid. He had far more to lose by being revealed as a cheat than as someone who helped leak confidential documents that brought down a Nazi war criminal. On the contrary, there might even be some Jewish groups and Members of Congress who would turn him into an overnight hero.

Lawrence Van Orden: Champion for Justice.

The thought nearly made Mike retch.

Just then, Mike felt a hand press down on his shoulder.

"How goes it, old buddy?" A voice in a mockingly amiable tone.

It was Lawrence—Larry—Van Orden. In the flesh. Dressed in a blue sport coat, white shirt, and red tie, Van Orden looked the part he was playing; namely, a fixer in Ronald Reagan's Washington. Mike noticed that the passage of time hadn't much changed him. He still had sandy hair and a youthful good old boy glow about him. The one thing that did look different were his teeth. Van Orden must have paid for orthodontic work to fix what Mike remembered as crooked lower teeth. Right now, they were straight and white. A perfect smile for the perfect faux aristocrat from upstate New York.

"Hey Larry," Mike said, a smug grin on his face.

Van Orden clapped his hands playfully.

"I don't mind that nickname anymore, Michael. It's folksy. Don't you know? It's going to be great on the campaign trail. Larry is one of the people, don't you know?"

Mike remembered that Van Orden had the annoying habit of repeating phrases for effect. Another reason he didn't care for him.

"Why don't you have a seat?" Mike said, pulling back a wooden bar chair. He took his briefcase and placed it on the floor between his legs.

"Gin and tonic, right here!" Van Orden called at the bartender.

The bartender, seemingly inured to such boorish behavior, nodded and proceeded to fix the drink.

"So let's cut to the chase here. What are you doing in Washington and what is so fucking important that you need to see me in person? It's not like we were friends, so cut the bullshit and give it to me straight. Just man up for once, Mike."

"So that's how it's going to be, eh?" Mike asked, knowing full well that for once he held all the cards.

"Just spill it, Mike," Van Orden said, as the bartender placed a small white napkin and a gin and tonic on the bar.

"Well," Mike said, reaching for his briefcase, "I'm going need your help to get my hands on some government documents dealing with the end of World War II."

"That's why you dragged me here?" Van Orden didn't bother to keep his voice down. He was rattled. Still had a temper, he did.

"It's more complicated than that."

"How so?"

"Well, I'm working as a PI now—I don't know if you knew that. How would you?—and I need to learn the real identity of a prominent American businessman. Name's Samuel Bennington. Perhaps you've heard of him?"

"Of course, I've heard of him. What the hell does he have to do with World War II?" Van Orden asked, taking a long sip of his gin and tonic.

"A lot, actually. Turns out that Bennington is almost certainly a Nazi war criminal living under an assumed identity. His German name would have been Wagenmann. I need you to find any documents and files that have his name on them."

"Is that all?" Van Orden said sarcastically.

"Pretty much," Mike replied.

"You're fucking nuts."

"Maybe. Maybe not," Mike replied, "But I need certain documents to prove it one way or the other. They're part of the Nuremberg Papers, so it seems. Have you heard of them?"

Van Orden took another drink, this time a larger sip. More of a gulp.

"Yeah, I know a couple of archivists and such. As far as I know, they're papers dealing with how the United States brought over Nazi scientists after the war. Mainly to work on the rocket program. Others to help with biological and chemical weapons," he said, then paused. "You're telling me that Samuel Bennington is one of them? That's nonsense. Total absolute nonsense. And I'm not going to be part of anything that ruins that guy's reputation. He's practically the poster child for the American success story. In case you haven't heard, Mike, this is the era of capitalism. And Bennington is well respected in the business community."

"I'm afraid I thought you'd say something like that," Mike said.

"Oh yeah? What the hell is that supposed to mean?"

"It means," Mike said as he retrieved the facsimile copies of Dean Taylor's report, "that I am going to have to ask you differently."

"What are you talking about?" Van Orden asked, his tone increasingly hostile.

"This, my friend," Mike said mockingly, "is your law school legacy. One of cheating, cutting corners, and in general, being an all-around asshole."

Van Orden looked at the papers Mike had placed on the bar between them, then lunged like a tiger, ready to tear them into pieces.

"Not so fast," Mike said, pressing his hand down hard on Van Orden's. "Either you get me access to the Nuremberg Papers or these babies going to end up at the *New York Times*."

"You're a real son of a bitch. What the fuck did I ever do to you?"

Mike shrugged.

"You know I could take you right here, shred these, and that'd be the end of it," Van Orden said.

"What do you think, that I'm stupid? I have copies of these copies waiting for me back in New York."

That was a lie. In all the hustle and bustle of the past few days, it had totally slipped Mike's mind that he should make extra copies of these. Perhaps Van Orden would buy his bluff; after all, he was doing a pretty convincing job so far in pressuring a once somewhat intimidating figure from his past into doing something illegal. Illegal but morally justified.

After what felt like minutes but were, in fact, mere seconds, Lawrence Van Orden finally demurred. He sank back on his bar stool.

"Okay. It's not like anyone really gives two shits about these papers. I'll make a few calls and get you copies of them in a week—maybe a few days—if I can figure out where they might be. Happy now?"

"Very," Mike said. That wasn't a lie.

"Fuck you and your Nazis," Van Orden said deep disgust in his voice. Then he turned to the bartender. "Another drink. And don't take so fucking long this time."

"I'll get your drink, but don't talk to me like that. I'm not impressed. Whoever you are," the bartender replied.

Surprisingly bold, Mike thought. Not taking any shit. He was starting to like this bartender. A lot.

"See you tomorrow. Same place?" Mike said, reflecting on the irony; the family values candidate had quite the mouth on him. If only the more conservative voters upstate knew what Lawrence Van Orden was really like. How phony he was.

"Yeah, same place," Van Orden replied, taking a huge gulp of his second drink.

Mike got up from his bar chair and walked out of Clemington's into the humid evening air. This place really is a swamp, Mike thought. In more ways than one.

CHAPTER 23

Three days later, still in his hotel suite, Mike wondered if and when he would hear from Van Orden. Was the guy calling his bluff, even though Mike wasn't bluffing? Or was he doing what he said he was going to be do; namely, getting copies of any secret files that mentioned a Nazi war criminal by the name of Wagenmann. As comfortable as the Garfield was, it was getting tedious staying in a hotel room, especially with the on and off heavy summer rain. He had used the time to do some eating out, light reading, and making a few phone calls. Tony Doran, on one call, had informed him that the NYPD's investigation into who had hired Donny had stalled. On another call, Katie told Mike she missed him and wanted to see him. But something wasn't quite right in her voice.

It was not until around ten o'clock, on his fourth morning in the hotel, that he heard from Van Orden. He was finishing an English muffin, orange juice, and a surprisingly potent cup of black coffee. The phone rang.

"Yeah?" Mike answered, still sleep groggy.

"It's Lawrence. I have what you asked for. Happy now?"

"Very," Mike said plainly. He realized that being as nasty as Van Orden was in his tone wasn't going to get him anywhere. All he wanted was the documents.

"Well," Van Orden continued, "where do you want to meet?"

Mike thought about it for a moment, then came up with the most obvious choice.

"How about the tea room in my hotel? The Garfield."

"That'll work."

"Tell me," Mike continued, "I'm curious, just how did you get the papers so quickly?"

"Honestly, the less you know, the better," Van Orden replied curtly.

Mike understood that was how it was going to be. Each of them playing a spy game.

"I'll see you at noon?" Mike asked.

"That works. I'll be there."

With that Van Orden hung up.

□ □ □

Several hours later, having endured a few choice insults from Van Orden in the tea room, Mike had a stack of documents in front of him. He had seen a lot of crime documentation at the DA's Office. And he had just recently seen people die violent deaths in the street. But nothing prepared him psychologically for what he discovered in the stack of xeroxed documents that Van Orden passed along to him that afternoon in the Garfield. Not unexpectedly, Van Orden had wanted to know how he could be sure that Mike wouldn't still leak the law school report to the *Times*; Mike had told the would-be Senator from New York that he'd just have to trust him. And that was that.

Although he was back in his room and seated at his hotel room desk, Mike's mind was elsewhere, wondering if first Arthur, and then Izzy, had led him in the right direction, or whether this was all a giant wild goose chase. What if this were a giant waste of time? Perhaps Samuel Bennington had nothing to do with Nazis. These doubting thoughts reverberated in his mind.

As it turned out, the copies of the documents that Van Orden had somehow obtained from a secret government storage facility had come from a treasure trove of information pertaining to the relocation of myriad Nazi-affiliated criminals after the war. While the papers didn't include some of the highest-ranking Nazis or the most sensitive projects, it did include enough for Mike to realize that he had made the right call in coming down to Washington.

When it came to Wagenmann, Van Orden had done what Mike had asked of him. To find any relevant documents with that particular name on it. What Mike learned from the files Van Orden had pulled from the Nuremberg Papers dispelled all his doubts. It confirmed his suspicions; namely, that Samuel Bennington, leading American industrialist and billionaire was, in fact, Klaus Wagenmann aka Samuel Beck. A Nazi war criminal hiding in plain sight.

And the way in which Wagenmann became Bennington disheartened Mike; he was no idealist, not anymore at least. But he shuddered at the amoral cynicism that it must have taken to free Wagenmann from a Nuremberg prison cell and to give him a new life in America.

The initial document Mike looked at was merely a cable from Washington DC to Frankfurt. It didn't shed much light, but it definitely piqued his interest.

TOP SECRET
From: Unit 612, Washington DC
Dated: July 21, 1947
To: L and M
Re: Pick up package in Nuremberg. Klaus Heinreich
Wagenmann. Prepare package for delivery back to Frankfurt for
further transport to USA. Package must be handled with care.

So there it was, a clear reference to Wagenmann, the very name uttered by Arthur as he lay dying in the alley. But who exactly were L and M, Mike wondered. Were they code names for agents working for Unit 612, whatever the hell that was?

A copy of a reply sent from Frankfurt back to Washington DC shed some light.

TOP SECRET
From: Larsen and MacFarlane
To: Unit 612, Requisitions Department
Dated: July 23, 1947
Re: Will arrive in Nuremberg in 2-4 days. Preparing MD-12 for
KHW release to our custody. Understood valuable nature of
package. Will proceed as planned.

So L and M almost certainly stood for Larsen and MacFarlane. Apparently, they were the agents working for this Unit 612's Requisitions Department in Germany at the time; the ones responsible for bringing "packages" like Wagenmann back to the States. Just who were they, Mike wondered. What would motivate someone to work for an agency that freed Nazi war criminals? A false sense of patriotism, a deep-rooted in fear or hatred of communism? Or were they just amoral bureaucrats, doing what they were told and collecting a paycheck at the end of the day? Mike didn't have the answers; all he knew was that he never could have participated in such a program.

As Mike read through the documents further, he learned more of what Unit 612 actually was. Rather than a standalone agency, it was more an interagency task force made up of members from different government agencies. It had one sole purpose, however: to free Nazi war criminals from US Army custody—those with useful skill sets for the emerging Cold War between the United States and Soviet Union—and to transfer them to Unit 612. The task force's agents, drawn from various federal law enforcement and intelligence agencies, would then interrogate the former prisoners, provide them with new identities, and prepare them for transatlantic transport back to Washington.

It was clear from the documents that Klaus Wagenmann was one of the individuals in the custody of Unit 612. But why? What did he have to offer? And more importantly, just exactly who was he? Mike found out more than enough in a brief biographical profile of Wagenmann that Unit 612 had prepared for and cabled to Larsen and MacFarlane. More than enough to know that this Wagenmann, whether or not he was now Samuel Bennington, was a war criminal. The next cable provided Wagenmann's biography.

TOP SECRET ULTRA
July 24, 1947
Klaus Heinreich Wagenmann, born 1919 in Riga, Latvia to middle class ethnic German parents. Is a prime candidate for Unit 612's relocation program designed to provide beneficial relocation for TOP SECRET national security reasons related to defensive chemical weapons program in face of Soviet threat. KHW holds Ph.D. in chemistry and was lecturer in physical chemistry at Leipzig University, 1943-45 prior to Red Army invasion. KHW participated in Nazi Germany's war of extermination against Jewish people and worked at numerous camps between 1942 and 1943. Auschwitz possible, but cannot be confirmed due to lack of cooperation from Moscow. Likely participant in what could be considered war crimes and crimes against humanity. Known as an antisemite, but not fanatical like others. Could likely work alongside American Jews without complaint, given adequate financial compensation. Fluency in English makes ideal candidate. Could provide vital information on Germany's chemical weapons program that could be of IMMEDIATE national security benefit. No known wife or immediate family. Unsure if subject has homosexual tendencies but given status in Nazi Party unlikely. Note: Wagenmann has what he refers to as a younger brother by the name of Hans Berman; not familial relation, but part of relocation agreement, however. Only known close contact. Lack of ties to Germany would also make him an ideal candidate for relocation program. Approved for MD-12. Approved for immediate removal from US Army in Nuremberg. Hobbies and interests include sculpture, European art, vegetarianism and physical fitness. Note minor scar on upper lip for identification purposes.

At that very moment, Mike's heart skipped a beat. This was solid evidence that members of US intelligence and law enforcement agencies worked diligently to bring suspected Nazi war criminals—people who had the blood of millions on their hands—to the United States. Just as Izzy had told him. As he continued to read, Mike noticed that his palms were getting sweaty. He got up for a moment, walked into the bathroom, and splashed some cold water on his face. Then he wiped both his palms and his face with a fresh white linen hand towel, took a deep breath, and went back to his desk.

Upon first glance, the next document that caught Mike's eye seemed to be a written report detailing Wagenmann's release into Unit 612's custody. And written by the same Larsen referenced in the other cables.

> Wagenmann now fully in Unit 612 custody. Uneventful flight from Nuremberg to Frankfurt. Full briefing will follow. MacFarlane assisting me per instructions. Have noted existence of Hans Berman and will proceed with that information for relocation purposes. Will inform.

Not much in this one, Mike thought. But he was intrigued by the reference to Hans Berman. Obviously, he was someone that both Wagenmann and the agent Larsen felt was fundamental to Wagenmann's relocation to the United States.

But why?

It was in the next series of documents that Mike learned the truth. How Unit 612, with the assistance of the International Red Cross, created new identities for both Wagenmann and Berman—American identities. Whereas Wagenmann became Samuel Beck, his pseudo-brother Berman became Peter Hesse.

Mike felt like he was back in the DA's Office, putting pieces of evidence together for a prosecutorial case. It wasn't a linear process; it was more of a haphazard one, finding strands of information here and there and then organizing them logically and sequentially in his mind. After shuffling through some documents that initially had seemed irrelevant, Mike found a memorandum dated June 1947, written in Washington DC that gave a very brief biographical sketch of Hans Berman.

> Born 1924 in Dresden to working-class, but educated; parents. Artistic and shy, known for interests in literature and poetry. Member of fraternal organization during his teenage years. Seems directionless in terms of goals. Bohemian type. Suggested name for relocation is Peter Hesse. Proceed as planned.

There it was! Hans Berman, the working-class boy from Dresden, became Peter Hesse. Millie's missing husband. The college professor. The junkie. The man whose body Mike found on the floor of a fleabag hotel room. He was Klaus Wagenmann's closest contact, the younger brother referenced in that earlier cable.

It was all starting to make sense. Somewhat. At least within the confines of the conspiracy that Mike was starting to unravel. It was never all going to fit together like a completed jigsaw puzzle; but a clearer picture was emerging. Berman ended up as Peter Hesse, a college professor in New York. And Wagenmann? His new identity was that of one Samuel Beck. A bland name, if there ever were one.

But exactly who was Samuel Beck? Something was missing. Mike shuffled through more of the papers, quickly glancing at some, while pushing them aside. It was within a matter of minutes, however, that he found exactly what he was looking for.

The first item was a copy of the very same letter from 1951 that Millie had shown to Mike in the Salonika Diner, the one in which Larsen ordered Hesse not to have any further contact with Wagenmann. The second was a 1952 telegram from Samuel Beck to Unit 612 requesting a name change. It read as follows:

Mr. Larsen. Given my brother's behavior and my desire for a full life in this great country of yours, I am hereby requesting a formal name change. I shall keep my first name. Samuel is fine. But I believe Bennington suits me far better than does Beck. Please consider - SB

Samuel Beck. Samuel Bennington. SB. The same initials—another piece of the puzzle.

Mike deduced that Hesse must have done something that put Wagenmann's new identity in jeopardy; either that, or Hesse was somehow pestering Wagenmann/Beck—maybe asking him for personal favors? Mike then considered the whole situation in its entirety. Two faux brothers, one on his way to becoming a wealthy industrialist; the other on his way to becoming a washout. Surely that could provoke jealousy? But it was nearly thirty years between the time of these letters and now. What could have changed in all these years? That's something that Mike needed to know, but the documents before him didn't seem to give him much in the way of solid answers.

Then he saw another document, one that he had skipped over somehow. It was a surprisingly informal report by MacFarlane, Larsen's partner in Unit 612. Dated August 1947 and wired to Washington, the memorandum read as follows:

TOP SECRET

Package is enroute to Washington DC for relocation purposes. Continue to have serious doubts as to long-term viability of Wagenmann and the relationship with Berman. Tension between men is palpable. Wagenmann refers to Berman as a "bastard" and seems to have contempt for him. Understand that Wagenmann would not cooperate without Berman given new life in US. Note: against normal protocol, Berman will be wearing a ring with no political import that has sentimental value. Mission completed, though personally have concerns about Wagenmann's national security value.

There it was. In black and white. That had to be the fraternity ring with the Latin phrase engraved on it. The one that Hesse wore. That solidified things further. Although there was a lot of missing information and a lot of years undocumented, it was increasingly clear that somewhere along the line, the two "brothers" had a falling out and that the younger one, Hesse, developed a strong sense of resentment toward his older, more established benefactor. And that eventually the pressure cooker of Hesse's life forced him into doing something sloppy; namely, almost certainly blackmailing Wagenmann into giving him money in exchange for safeguarding his identity. But that, of course, would potentially put his life at risk. But he wasn't likely something to attempt blackmail in the 1960s or 1970s. No. It was the act of an older, desperate man. A man like the one who married Millie Johnson. A man on his last legs and addicted to heroin.

Mike gathered the papers on his hotel room desk, put them in his briefcase, and walked over to an all-night copy shop in Dupont Circle, not far from the Garfield. He made copies of the relevant documents. Then he stuffed the copies in an envelope, sealed it, and addressed it to Barry's newspaper office. If Mike knew Barry—and he thought he did— he knew that his friend would see enough there to put out a story. Thank you, Barry.

Mike, his pulse racing, imagined how the headlines might read:

PROMINENT AMERICAN BUSINESSMAN OUTED AS NAZI

AMERICAN CAPITALIST OR NAZI WAR CRIMINAL?

Surely that would rattle Bennington's gilded cage.

Mike knew what he needed to do next.

He needed an eyewitness. He needed to hear it straight from Larsen or MacFarlane. Preferably the latter, given his candid thoughts on the matter way back in 1947.

But how?

CHAPTER 24

It was good to be out the swampy city that was Washington, DC in the summer and back in his Manhattan apartment. Although it was the nation's capital, it had still given him the creeps. It was definitely not his type of city. He felt like a fish out of water with all those uptight grey-suited bureaucrats, lobbyists, and anonymous officials. And seeing Van Orden twice was hardly a pleasant experience. It was just a necessary step.

Before he had left for New York, Mike had phoned Barry, informing him in a half-hour phone call about everything that had transpired. How he had been investigating Samuel Bennington, and that an envelope with documents confirming the man's true identity was on its way to his office. Barry, as Mike anticipated, was eager and willing to go along.

Here was Mike's golden opportunity to strike a retaliatory blow against the man in the shadows, the one who provided the key link between Peter Hesse, Arthur, and most of all, Donny, the hired gun who murdered Millie and whom Mike had just buried.

Mike gave his friend credit. Barry was pretty fearless, willing to put his career on the line to help a friend. And himself. Outing a well-known businessman as a Nazi was going to make headlines. It was a major scoop, no doubt about it. One that could further Barry's well-known ambitions in investigative journalism. All Mike had asked was that Barry hold off on publishing the piece. He wanted the chance to meet MacFarlane, whom he was able to track down easily, and also the opportunity to confront Bennington face to face.

As it turned out, Jefferson "Skip" MacFarlane was living in a small town in Connecticut, not too far from the New York state line. Mike had drawn upon his investigative skills and learned a bit about MacFarlane. Now retired and in his seventies, he had authored several paperback mysteries, often drawing upon his own government experience. Although they didn't sell particularly well, they were well regarded by critics and by the mystery fiction community. Not a bad gig, Mike thought. Maybe that's something he could follow up on his own someday.

He had cold-called MacFarlane early that morning, hoping that the old man wouldn't just hang up on him. To his surprise, MacFarlane was extremely open. Not only did he confirm that he was indeed the Jefferson

MacFarlane who worked for Unit 612, he also invited Mike to visit him that very same afternoon at his house outside of Danbury. Even after Mike had explained the nature of his business—just to make sure there was no misunderstanding—MacFarlane remained undaunted.

He seemed downright eager, Mike thought. MacFarlane was finally able to find someone to talk about the past with.

Perhaps he saw Mike's investigation as a vindication of what he had thought well back in the late 1940s: that bringing Wagenmann/Beck and Berman/Hesse back to the United States was a risky gamble. Whatever the reason for MacFarlane's openness, Mike was pleased that he had already ingratiated himself with the guy.

Mike was looking forward to, as his father would have put it, a trip to the country.

After he had finished his conversation with MacFarlane and hung up the receiver, Mike stretched and walked over to the television set and turned it on. He often liked to have background noise when he showered and got dressed for the day. It made living in a small city apartment less lonely somehow. He clicked through numerous stations, ultimately settling on a local news program.

That's when he saw it.

A news report about an electronics store downtown that was firebombed overnight.

Holy shit.

Could it be?

Mike listened more intently to the newscaster. It was.

It fucking was.

Izzy's store in Union Square.

Mike's thoughts raced.

He felt two things at that very moment. Concern. And unbridled hatred.

Concern for Izzy.

And, by extension, Katie.

Were the two of them okay?

And hatred for the perpetrators of this cowardly arson attack. It simply had to be connected with Wagenmann and Mike's investigation. He then remembered how Katie had mention that Izzy had liked to provoke neo-Nazis in the past; to stir up hornets' nests.

But the timing here was very suspicious.

Why now?

No, it was not a mere coincidence. Mike had to go with his gut here; somehow people either working for Bennington or who were strongly sympathetic to the latter's cause were behind this. That, of course, begged the question: how deep did this Nazi network run? How many sympathizers and would-be assassins were out there in the world, ready to be activated at a moment's notice to do harm to Jews and those who stood for democratic values? It made Mike shudder.

The only good news in all of this was that apparently Izzy wasn't injured in any way. According to the reporter on scene, there was no one in the store at the time. Still, the firebombing was an act of hate and who knows how much damage it had done to the store. Mike didn't know too much about arson, but he knew enough to realize that just smoke alone can cause tremendous damage.

And that was what really pissed him off. It was a pure intimidation tactic. But it wasn't going to work.

No. He was getting close to the end. One way or the other, he was going to bring Samuel Bennington down for good.

He knew he should call Katie to make sure that Izzy was indeed okay. But as he looked at the clock on the wall, he realized there simply was no time. She might be angry at him for not getting in touch, but he couldn't control her reaction. He had to shower, get dressed, and then catch a bus to Danbury, Connecticut. From there, he'd catch a cab to MacFarlane's house.

Time to get moving.

Mike went into his closet and picked clothes to wear. Even though it was hot out, somewhere in the high nineties, he decided to wear a blazer.

After all, he needed something to cover the holster he was going to be wearing.

□ □ □

Rural Connecticut was only a short distance away from New York City, but to Mike it felt like a totally different world. It reminded Mike of Long Island. Instead of the concrete and steel of downtown Manhattan, there were trees, lush vegetation, and ample space to breathe. It also didn't feel quite as hot as it was in the city that morning. It was breezy and pleasant, with a clear blue sky.

As the yellow cab pulled up to Jefferson MacFarlane's large white Colonial-style house, Mike noticed a group of teenage boys riding dirt bikes along the sidewalk. They were happily shouting at each other, having fun. How mercifully oblivious they were to all of the shit he'd been dealing with. Nazis. Politics. Drug Addiction. Murder. Everything that he had dealt with over the past two weeks existed in a completely different realm from what these kids dealt with on a daily basis. Maybe their parents had issues—rural New England surely had its own set of problems. But the kids? Mike hoped they were living in their own dreamworld of girls, dirt bikes, and obnoxiously loud music. For a moment, he was envious of them. Wishing that he could repeat his childhood, this time in Connecticut rather than in Brooklyn.

But that was just a fantasy. He had responsibilities. He was an adult. And he had a mission. There was no turning back now.

"This the house?" the cabbie asked in a thick Jamaican accent.

"What's that?" Mike said, his mind still elsewhere.

"Where you're getting out, this is it, mon?"

The cab had pulled into a driveway. On either side was a well-tended front lawn. Green and bright, the late summer sun giving it a healthy glow.

Mike squinted and looked at the numbers on the house.

1678.

That was it.

MacFarlane had given him his address and Mike had scribbled it on the back of a telephone bill which he had stuffed into his pocket before leaving his apartment. 1678 Poplar Drive.

"Yes, this is it," Mike said, reaching for his billfold. "How much do I owe you?"

The cabbie pointed to the meter: $18.

Mike took out a crisp twenty-dollar bill and handed it to the cabbie.

"Keep the change," he said.

"Thanks, mon," the cabbie said.

As he got out of the backseat of the cab, Mike reflected on how odd it was. The cab ride from the Danbury bus station had cost more than the bus fare from the Port Authority to Danbury.

That thought didn't last long.

All of a sudden, it hit him. He swallowed and caught his breath. He was standing on the driveway of the guy who would be able to put all the documents from the Nuremberg Papers into their proper context. MacFarlane wasn't just a name or a voice on the phone; he was a living person who was behind the house's red front door.

Mike walked up the driveway, noticing a small squirrel running past him. It stopped briefly and looked at him quizzically. He waited for the squirrel to pass, walked up the front steps, and rang the doorbell.

Five seconds. Ten. Twenty. Thirty.

Then the door swung open.

Standing in the doorway was a thin man dressed in a yellow polo shirt, blue jeans, and beige loafers. Although now in his mid-seventies,

MacFarlane had maintained a toned physique and, on better days, could easily have passed for a man twenty years his junior. Mike reflected that although time had passed, it had seemingly failed to wear him down physically. Nevertheless, there was something old about him as well. Mike couldn't quite put his finger on it; then he realized what it was. MacFarlane was older statesman-like. Like Gregory Peck or Cary Grant.

"Jefferson MacFarlane?" Mike asked, reaching out to shake his hand.

"Call me Skip," MacFarlane answered, shaking Mike's hand. It was a noticeably firm grip. The type of handshake you'd expect from a man who worked as an agent in the intelligence services.

"Okay, Skip," Mike said.

"Well don't just stand there like a vampire. Come on in."

A vampire? Mike didn't get it. Had the old man lost his marbles? Then he realized MacFarlane was almost certainly referring to the old movie gag in which vampires won't enter a house unless explicitly invited. The old man sure had an odd sense of humor. That was for sure.

As MacFarlane guided the two of them through the house and back to his study, Mike took in the interior. It was well maintained. The furniture was polished and the wood floors had been swept clean. Either MacFarlane had a maid or he was meticulous about keeping his place pristine. That pleased Mike. For in his mind, it meant MacFarlane was hardly one of those retired government officials who turn into dysfunctional cranks. What would have been far worse than the house's somewhat staid quality would have been a home filled with overstuffed boxes, piles of unread mail, and dusty broken furniture. That would not have been a good sign. Thankfully that wasn't the case at all.

It was what Mike didn't notice that stuck in his mind. No photographs. While Mike didn't expect everyone in their seventies to have numerous framed photographs of relatives like Aunt Christina did, he did assume that most people kept portraits of loved ones prominently on display. There were no such items here.

"Have a seat," MacFarlane said, as they arrived in his study. He pointed to a comfortable-looking chair opposite a large wooden desk.

"Sure," Mike said. As he sat down, he noticed the myriad paperback books that MacFarlane had collected over the years. Besides the books MacFarlane had written himself, on the bookshelves were some authors that Mike knew: Jack Higgins, Frederick Forsyth, and Ian Fleming. And some that he didn't.

"Now," MacFarlane said, drawing Mike's attention back to him, "I understand you want to know the innermost secrets of my time at Unit 612?"

Innermost secrets. That struck Mike as an odd way of putting things. But MacFarlane had certainly earned the right to tell the story in his own way.

"As I said on the phone, I need to know about Klaus Wagenmann. I need to know for sure that he's now living under the name Samuel Bennington."

"For sure?"

"Yes," Mike said emphatically.

"Well, you've come to the right place. Yes, you're absolutely right. It's a complicated story. Wagenmann was once Beck. That's the name we gave him back in 1946. But he's been Bennington for a few decades now. That son of a bitch benefited from a government program that should never have existed. But, alas, it did."

MacFarlane threw his hands up in the air. A what-do-you-expect-me-to-do-about-it expression if there ever were one.

"Tell me about the program," Mike said.

"Ah, yes. The program. After the war, some supposedly very sharp minds in DC decided that it would be a good idea to bring over Nazi war criminals who could be of assistance to the United States to help this country prepare for conflict with the Russians. These guys—let me be blunt—these bastards—didn't give a single fuck how much blood these Krauts had on their hands. They just didn't. So all morality went out the window in service of a greater ideal.

"So Unit 612, of which I was a part, was tasked with finding, freeing, and retrieving Nazi scientists and bringing them back to the States. We gave them all new identities and such. It would have raised a ruckus with American Jewish groups if they knew about it, but they didn't. And they had their hands full with displaced persons and the uprising against the British in what was then Palestine. Anyway, what could they have done about it? Not much."

"So Wagenmann was one of your projects?"

"Projects. Packages. Whatever. Yes, yes he was."

"What was his background? What did he have to offer?"

"He was a chemist. And we needed chemists. So that was that."

"And what about Peter Hesse—I mean, Hans Berman."

"What about him? You want to know about him, too?" MacFarlane asked, raising an eyebrow.

"Why bring him over?"

"Because Wagenmann wanted him. That was the deal for his cooperation. We couldn't turn him into a slave, you know. That was all there was to it. So yeah, Berman. His would-be younger brother. A

Bohemian type. Yes, that's right. He was a Bohemian type. And Wagenmann didn't like it. Thought Berman was very dissolute, but was someone who would always be indebted to him. Sick. But yes, to answer your question, Unit 612 brought over Berman too. I thought it was a stupid fucking idea at the time. I even told my superiors so."

"I know," Mike said.

"You know what I thought about that?" MacFarlane asked. He sounded surprised.

"I read through some documents. Saw a cable you sent—I think it was a cable—expressing your unhappiness—"

MacFarlane interrupted him.

"It was more than that. I was thoroughly disgusted. But how could I say what I truly believed? I was hardly in the position to—"

It was now Mike's turn to interrupt.

"I'm not blaming you. It was what it was," Mike said in a neutral tone. He needed to keep MacFarlane on his side. As much as Mike liked MacFarlane, he couldn't help but think there was something more going on, a secret preying on his mind. One that he was paying for years later. Why else would he be so open about the past?

Guilt. Contrition. Something between the two?

"There is no one to blame. Except the intelligence agencies that put together Unit 612. They are the ones who are guilty," MacFarlane said, his voice rising in anger.

"I see," Mike said quietly.

"Do you?"

"I'm trying to."

"What you don't see is that after all of this shit, after I put all my ethics aside to bring Wagenmann back to the States for a new life, I get forced out of government work because a few bigots couldn't appreciate that I didn't necessarily enjoy the company of ladies as they did."

For a brief moment, Mike had no idea what MacFarlane was talking about. The company of ladies? What did that even mean?

Then it hit him.

MacFarlane was almost certainly a homosexual. That had to be it. Forced out of the intelligence services because of his personal life. That would explain a lot, actually. Why he was so willing to divulge everything about Unit 612's work. Why he felt absolutely no loyalty to his former superiors.

"I'm sorry," Mike said. Not knowing what exactly to say. He remembered hearing about the purge of gay men from government service back in the 1950s. Something to do with Senator McCarthy. Was MacFarlane one of them?

"Nothing for you to be sorry about. There was nothing I could do about it. It was who I was. Am."

Mike nodded.

"So what's next for you? What's the game plan?"

MacFarlane's questions took Mike by surprise. They shouldn't have, but they did.

"I guess now that I have your confirmation, I should call my friend and have him run the story."

"I think that's an eminently wise course of action. It's about time that son of a bitch paid."

Mike stood up.

"Is there a phone I could use?"

"In the kitchen, next to the sink."

Mike walked out of the study, through a narrow hallway and into the kitchen. He noticed a basket of fresh fruit sitting on the small dining table across from the sink. Then he spotted the phone.

Mike leafed through his address book, finding Barry's work number within seconds.

He dialed.

It took about twenty seconds for a voice on the other end.

"Barry Stein."

"Barry, it's Mike."

"What's up, Mike? You got what you needed?"

"And then some."

"So?"

"Run the fucking story, Barry. We're gonna break this guy."

"Roger that, buddy. Roger that."

Barry hung up the phone.

Mike walked back to the study. He found MacFarlane there, seemingly lost deep in thought and smoking a pipe.

"One last thing," Mike said.

"And what would that be?" MacFarlane asked.

"Do you know where Wagenmann lives?"

MacFarlane smiled.

"I thought you'd never ask. I've been waiting for this day for a long, long time. He lives on an estate in Westchester. Not too far from here. I'll even let you borrow my car. If you end up speaking with him face to face, I want you to promise me one thing."

"Sure. What might that be?" Mike asked.

"Tell him, Skip MacFarlane sent you."

MacFarlane smiled. He had a satisfied look on his face.

CHAPTER 25

It was near dark by the time Mike, driving MacFarlane's light blue Chevy, arrived at the gate outside Bennington's house. The first thing Mike noticed were the news vans parked on the street. Three white vans, all from local news affiliates, were parked outside the secluded Westchester estate. Careful not to be on the property itself, the vans—with their satellite dishes on top—made their presence known nevertheless. The buzzing sound of reporters, cameramen, and drivers shooting the shit while waiting for a glimpse of Bennington filled the night air.

Fucking Barry!

He couldn't keep his mouth shut, could he? Who else knew Wagenmann's secret?

There went the element of surprise. Barry, or someone else on his staff, must have leaked it to other news organizations.

Wagenmann had to know something was happening.

How could he not?

The thing was, did he know exactly what was up; namely, that his masquerade as Samuel Bennington was surely on its last legs? That he could no longer remain a respectable part of the American business community?

His identity.

His life.

His career.

His public offering.

All in jeopardy now.

The mask was slipping and there wasn't a thing he could do about it.

Even if things weren't going exactly according to Mike's plan, that Nazi bastard was surely sweating it out with the unwanted attention outside his front door. Mike didn't know the man, but knew enough about him to know that the last thing someone like "Samuel Bennington" wanted was a gaggle of news vans parked mere yards from the end of his driveway.

Knowing Wagenmann was likely under considerable strain allowed Mike, for a brief moment, to smile. Just a little.

But he had to get inside the house.

To confront Wagenmann. To see him face to face. To know what the man lurking in the shadows looked like. To witness how he carried himself in the face of adversity.

Most importantly, to see the look on his face when Mike told him that all the newspapers in America were soon going to be running a story from which he'd never recover. The media would surely condemn him for his corrupt Nazi ideology and mock him for his American corporate hero posturing. And to tell him that sooner or later, the NYPD would trace the murderous Donny back to him.

One thought dominated Mike's mind: he had to get inside the house without being seen.

But how?

There were news vans everywhere and the property was gated like a small fortress.

Mike took a deep breath, steeled himself.

Ninja-like, he zigzagged past the news vans, forcing his body through the oversized bushes which lined Bennington's driveway. He removed his blazer and threw it up in the air. As he had hoped, it landed on top of the fence that aimed to protect Bennington's property from intruders. The blazer would provide a layer of protection for him as he scaled the fence like a Marine in basic training.

Adrenaline flowing, he gritted his teeth and scaled the fence. He could hardly believe he was capable of this level of physical agility. But he was.

After landing on the other side of the fence with a slight thud on the ground, Mike darted up the freshly cut grass until he reached the house itself. He took off his shirt and wrapped his hands in it. Then he proceeded to smash a bottom floor window with his fist. He put the shirt back on and curled his body. He entered the house through the broken window in the cellar.

It smelled musty down there. Although it was dark, Mike found the wooden staircase leading up. He walked up a flight of stairs and found himself in a large room with paintings on the wall. Old paintings. European. Things Mike didn't care about whatsoever.

What he cared about was getting to Wagenmann.

His heart was pounding, his hands sweaty.

But he had no choice.

This was the moment he had been waiting for.

He walked through the large house, old wooden floorboards occasionally creaking under his feet, then turned and saw a light underneath a door.

This must be it, he thought.

He found Wagenmann in his study, his head in his hands. Passive. Oblivious. In furious contemplation.

Was this the posture of a defeated villain?

Mike immediately noticed the Luger pistol on the desk. Was Wagenmann going to follow the path of Hitler and commit suicide? Was he ultimately a coward too, afraid to face the consequences for the violence that he had unleashed on the world?

"You're all washed up, Wagenmann. Every news outlet in this country is going to make sure the American public knows exactly who and what you are," Mike said as he positioned himself in the study's threshold, his gun firmly in hand.

Wagenmann looked up. He looked to be in a daze. The look of a man who realized that his entire life's work was falling apart.

That he was on a downward spiral.

And that there was nobody left to throw him a rope to pull him back up.

"Who the hell are you?" Wagenmann asked. He looked half-dazed, surprised that someone got into his house so easily. But he also looked like he didn't care.

"The name's Levinas," Mike said. "I think you've heard of me."

"Oh. You're that PI Jew. You've been a nuisance for a long time. Tell me: am I 'washed up'?" Wagenmann asked contemptuously.

"You're through. It's over. The world is soon going to learn everything. Who you really are."

Mike realized that he was repeating himself.

"And who might I be?" Wagenmann asked, his fingers inching toward the Luger.

"I wouldn't do that if I were you," Mike said, waving his gun directly at Wagenmann's chest.

Wagenmann backed off.

"You're Klaus Wagenmann, a lowlife Nazi war criminal. That's who you are. By the way, Skip MacFarlane sends his regards."

"Who?"

"MacFarlane. Unit 612."

A look of recognition washed over Wagenmann's face.

Mike could tell he knew. He remembered. Time to apply even more pressure.

"So why have Berman killed? What did he do that pissed you off so much?"

"The little bastard was blackmailing me. Surely you've figured that out."

"I assumed as much," Mike said. "I knew it had to be something like that."

"Oh, did you?"

"Junkies can become really desperate."

"Junkies," Wagenmann repeated. "My, you've really been thorough. So what's next? You're not going to kill me. You don't have it in you. So why not fuck off and get the hell out of here!" Wagenmann yelled.

This was it.

The moment Mike had been waiting for.

The façade of the calm, calculating businessman was cracking right in front of him.

At that very moment, though, it struck Mike that he had no idea what his next move was going to be. He had been so determined to get inside the house, to confront Wagenmann, that he had completely forgotten to come up with an ending.

Then it hit him.

A possible way to resolve this once and for all.

Mike, without blinking even for a second, allowed images to flicker past his mind's eye.

First, Arthur stabbed and dying in the alley. Then the vehicle that nearly ran over Katie and him. Then Millie being murdered. And finally, the news report of Izzy's store being firebombed.

The images served a valuable purpose. They allowed Mike to say what he wanted to say.

"You're total shit, Wagenmann. You probably weren't even a good chemist. You're nothing but a murderer plain and simple," Mike said. There was perceptible anger in his voice. Controlled anger, but anger nevertheless.

Wagenmann looked up, surprised at Mike's defiant tone.

Yes, this is what Mike wanted. To get a reaction.

He continued.

"MacFarlane said that he thought you weren't even worth bothering with—a mediocrity. He would have greatly preferred if you had gone to the gallows."

The first statement was a lie; the second was true. But that didn't matter.

What mattered was making Wagenmann enraged. Making him lose his composure.

Making him reach for his Luger.

So far, Mike's taunts weren't enough for Wagenmann to take the bait.

He had to dial things up a notch or two.

"What did you even hope to accomplish? Just make some money and leave for South America?"

"You're thinking way too small. What do you think I do with my money?"

"And what would that be?" Mike asked.

"It's because of people just like me that your people's synagogues in Europe are being turned into fortresses. It's because of me. And many others! You hear me? Don't think for one moment this will end with me, either. No. There are many willing to take my place. You see, I'm not afraid to die for the cause. No. I've never been afraid. You fucking bastard, you hear what I'm saying?"

"I hear you, but honestly, you're boring the shit out of me," Mike said.

That did it.

"I've had just about a enough of you, you fucking Je—"

Mike was ready to shoot Wagenmann right then and there.

That's when it happened.

Out of the blue, a wild-eyed woman appeared in the study, her hand unsteady, but clenching a small gun.

It didn't take long.

"You bastard!" she screamed at Wagenmann, as she pumped three bullets into his chest. "You've ruined us. You've ruined me."

What in the world had just happened, Mike wondered. His thoughts raced.

"Put the fucking gun down! Now!" Mike shouted instinctively.

She complied.

"Now kick it over to me!"

Without a moment's hesitation, she did as she was asked.

Who was this madwoman now crying hysterically with black mascara running down her face?

Mike noticed Wagenmann was slumped back in his chair.

"And just who the hell are you?" Mike roared.

The woman collapsed to the floor in a sea of tears. She smelled of booze and cigarettes.

"Jackie. I'm his wife. His fucking wife. And he's ruined me forever."

Wife? Wagenmann had a wife? Why hadn't MacFarlane told him about her? It seemed like pertinent information.

"Just stay where you are. I need to think," Mike said.

She curled up into a fetal position, then threw up.

Mike walked over to Wagenmann, who was gurgling blood and barely breathing. Mike put two fingers on the man's neck. His pulse barely registered.

So that was it, then?

The irony of it all.

The great Nazi chemist. The supposed financier of terrorism.

Taken down by his drunken and hysterical trophy wife.

Somehow, in a totally fucked up way, it all made sense.

Mike looked down at the weeping woman and wasn't sure whether or not to thank her.

"Now what do you want me to do?" Jackie asked.

"Sit still. Now we wait," Mike responded.

"Wait? Wait for what?" Jackie asked, her mascara now even more a puddle.

"For the cops I'm about to call," Mike said, walking over to Wagenmann's desk. Careful not to touch Wagenmann in any way, Mike picked up the telephone receiver and dialed 911.

"What's your emergency?" the dispatcher on the other line asked.

"I'd like to report a murder," Mike said.

Although it seemed like longer, within minutes, Mike heard the sirens.

Loud and jolting to his ears, they sounded like a thousand cop cars and emergency vehicles rushing to the scene. A cavalcade of state power ready to assert itself, to serve and protect. One more encounter with the police was nothing to get worked up about. He'd had enough experience with this over the past couple weeks. Enough to last a lifetime. And anyway, he hadn't actually been the one to pull the trigger. Not this time anyway.

Moments later, eight uniformed policemen stormed into the house, up the stairs, and into the study.

"Hands in the air!" one of the cops, the highest ranking among them, shouted as loud as could be.

Two cops, one Black and one Hispanic, rushed directly to where Wagenmann sat, slumped over in his chair.

"This one's gone," another uniformed cop said.

"You two, both of ya," another cop bellowed at Mike and Jackie, "hands where I can see them. Hands! Now!"

Both Mike and Jackie complied.

"Who shot him? Which of you shot him?" the lead cop demanded.

"I did. I fucking did it. And he deserved it too," Jackie said between sobs.

"What about him?" the cop asked Jackie, pointing to Mike.

"He didn't do nothing. He didn't do nothing," she said.

"Well?" Mike said, his hands still raised in the air.

"Well, what, wiseass? Your going to get cuffed too, until we can figure out exactly what the hell happened here."

A few minutes later, the cops led Jackie out of the house. She was handcuffed and covered in a white blanket. They tucked her head down and helped her into the backseat of a patrol car. Its siren was turned off, but the flashing blue and red lights remained.

Mike was also led out of the house and into the front yard.

That's when two men, both dressed in cheap suits commensurate with their salaries, walked up to him. They identified themselves as homicide detectives.

"I hear that wherever you go, bodies start showing up," the younger of the two men said.

Mike, still cuffed, shrugged his shoulders.

Just then, Mike turned. He saw paramedics wheeling out a body on a stretcher. It was zipped up in plastic.

That was it, then. Wagenmann, the man the world had known as high-powered industrialist Samuel Bennington, was dead.

Millie's case was closed. The man responsible for her husband's death lay motionless no more than a few yards from him.

But many questions remained.

Was Wagenmann really financing terrorist attacks against Jews like he boasted? Or was that all bullshit meant to rattle Mike's cage?

The wife had made sure that he wasn't going to get an answer straight from the horse's mouth.

But then again he had been ready to plug the Nazi bastard himself.

Crazy how it all worked out, Mike reflected.

A split second earlier and he would have been the one who put Wagenmann six feet under.

And by murdering Wagenmann his wife had unknowingly dispensed justice to the murderer of the missing husband he had been hired to find by a distraught wife. Neither woman knowing of the relationship between the two men. The two brothers.

"Can you uncuff me now, at least?" Mike asked.

One of the detectives came closer, holding a small key in his hand.

"We may be uncuffing you. But we're far from done with you. Far from done."

His hands now free, Mike wiped perspiration off his face.

At least for now, he was somewhat free.

"Don't leave—" one of the detective said.

"I know, I know. Don't leave town. You can find me in the city whenever you want," Mike replied. "The wife admitted she did it."

"We could nab you for breaking and entering, ya know. What the fuck were you even doing in his house anyhow?"

"I was invited," Mike said, his tone sarcastic.

"You know, Levinas, I don't believe a fucking word you've said yet," the detective said, folding up a small notepad. "But that's for another day."

"Wait. You know who I am?"

"At this point, every police department between New Jersey and Connecticut knows who you are."

EPILOGUE

"Do you want any cake?" Mike called from the kitchen, as he finished pouring two cups of black coffee for his aunt and his cousin.

"No that's quite all right. Nothing for me," replied Aunt Christina who was sitting comfortably on her living room couch next to Erik. Still dressed in his New Jersey State Police uniform except for his signature trooper hat, he looked as physically exhausted as Mike felt.

"Erik! What do you want?"

"Got any cold beer?" Erik shouted back.

Mike laughed. He and his cousin both knew Aunt Christina didn't drink. It felt good for him to laugh. It'd been a while.

Dinner for the three of them had worked out just fine. Mike had insisted that, with after everything she had gone through, his aunt was to leave the cooking to him. What it really amounted to was making a phone call to Luigi's, a nearby Italian pizza place that had been in the neighborhood for as long as he could remember, and having them deliver a steaming hot, greasy large pepperoni and cheese pizza and Mike putting individual slices on paper plates. Aunt Christina couldn't help but tease Mike about his less than polished culinary skills. Mike didn't mind; he was just happy that no harm had come to her. Every once in a while it really hit him. Things could have ended up so very differently. It could have been his aunt rather than Millie who ended up in the city morgue. The thought left him cold.

All of a sudden, the telephone rang.

Mike, who was bringing the cake into the living room, jumped. Nerves. They were going to remain on high alert for some time to come, he realized.

Aunt Christina picked up the receiver.

"Hello," she said. Then she went silent. Just listening.

"Okay, I'll put him on," she said finally, turning to Mike. "It's for you. It's your father."

"My father? Why is he calling here?" he whispered.

Muzzling the speaker portion of the phone with her right hand, Aunt Christina whispered back.

"I told him you'd be here. Now go on and speak with your father," she said. Then she smiled. For she realized Mike wasn't a little kid anymore.

And that she need not speak to him like that ever again.

"I got it," Mike said, taking the receiver from her hand.

"Hi Dad, what's going on?" he asked.

"I'll tell you what's going on. This morning I saw a lizard in front of my door. A lizard, I tell you! A small Godzilla. Can you believe it?"

"I hear they're pretty common in Florida, Dad," Mike replied, twirling the yellow telephone cord with his other hand.

"I'll tell you what's pretty common. The humidity. It's been non-stop for weeks now. Makes me want to move to Phoenix. At least there, they say it's a dry heat."

Mike sighed. He had heard it all before.

"Okay, okay, what's up? Why'd you call, Dad?" A sense of exasperation in his voice.

Irving Levinas cleared his throat.

"I wanted to tell you I got that *New York Post* clipping you sent me. About the Austrian. The war criminal."

"Well, yeah, it's never been proven he's a war criminal, but go on. He probably is, though," Mike said.

"It's just funny you know. Christina has been keeping me informed about everything you've been working on. All the stuff you've been through. How you were involved in exposing this industrialist as an antisemite. How his own wife shot him! It's impressive. My son, the private detective!"

Irving laughed. "You really do belong in the family."

There it was. The reference to the Levinas name. Memorable as the second-rate crime outfit that Mike's great-grandfather and grandfather ran. Shaking down grocers and newsstands; providing protection for first-generation immigrant storeowners. Outlaws with brass knuckles living their own warped version of the American Dream.

"Well, it's done," Mike said. "It's over."

"And to think, the timing was coincidental, was it not? How you were carrying around this Waldheim article all the while you were chasing another Nazi bastard? I tell you—I tell you this, Mikey—there are no coincidences like this in the world. This all happened for a reason. You have to believe that, Mikey."

"And what reason would that be?" Mike asked, his voice drained of energy.

"You're going to have to figure that out for yourself."

"What exactly is that supposed to mean?" Mike asked, an edge in his voice.

"It's just that you've been moping around doing not much of anything since the DA's Office did you dirty," Irving said.

Mike was about to lash out in anger. How dare his father throw that in his face. But then it occurred to him. His father was right on this score. In a matter of seconds, numerous thoughts came crashing through his mind.

He had been moping around for months before Millie Johnson walked through his door.

Feeling sorry for himself.

It was all so clear to him now. He was able, at last, to be objective about the situation.

And this whole ordeal, including his killing one man and being prepared to kill a second, may have all been for some yet to be determined reason. Maybe he was going to get more involved with Jewish life; and yet, despite the newfound interest in his paternal Jewish heritage, he wasn't sure. He was still very much a Norwegian-American. He was very his mother's son, the one she dressed in bunads as a child.

Maybe he was going to have to focus more on serious cases. No more small-scale runaway shit. Time to play in the big leagues. International intrigue? Corporate espionage? He smiled. Maybe.

All he knew was that, for the first time in ages, he didn't give a shit about the DA's Office.

It felt liberating. Like a weight had been lifted from his shoulders. No longer was he Mike Levinas, formerly of the DA's Office; he was now Mike Levinas, Private Investigator.

And that fucking meant something.

He was finally free.

"That's in the past—the DA's Office, I mean—Dad. I don't really think about that anymore," Mike said at last.

"That's good to hear. That's the way it should be," Irving replied.

Mike lingered for a while longer at Aunt Christina's, telling jokes while she tidied up and did the dishes. Only when he was out the door and on the train heading to the East Village did he realize he hadn't once looked at that childhood essay of his, the one that had served as such an inspiration a mere two weeks ago. It simply hadn't registered. Funny how that worked. His mind was focused on Katie. On their future—if indeed they had a future.

It wasn't like she was his girlfriend or anything; still, they had spent an enormous amount of time together over the past few weeks.

That surely meant something.

Didn't it?

□ □ □

Tonight, Katie's new band, The Yellows, were playing at a small music venue on Avenue A called The Lair. Mike decided he would catch her show, then surprise her backstage and take her to dinner afterward. She certainly wouldn't expect him to attend one of her concerts. The whole idea seemed downright romantic to him; juvenile in a way, perhaps. But romantic nevertheless.

The Lair lived up to its name. Sandwiched between a biker bar and an all-night laundromat, it was derelict, grimy, and dark as midnight inside. Mike's first thought was that if vampire bats somehow found out about the place, they'd set up shop and establish a colony here. They'd definitely fit in with the overall aesthetic. The bathroom was even more jarring. Vulgar graffiti covered the walls and the toilet stalls. For the first time in what seemed like ages, Mike felt unusually old again. He simply was not of their world. He didn't have a clue.

The Yellows weren't exactly the type of band Mike would have chosen to listen to, if he had any say in the matter. Loud, brash, and vulgar, they sounded like a cross between The Animals and a broken chainsaw. As the guitarist swayed his hips with a knowing mischievousness, his instrument provided so much feedback that it nearly shook the speakers off the stage. Katie, dressed all in black with matching black mascara around her eyes, sang—if you could call it singing—about horror movies, space rays, and cold-blooded murder. It all seemed so incongruous with what had transpired over the past weeks. The two of them were nearly run down by a hired assassin; her dad's electronics store had been firebombed; and Mike had watched people die. And here she was, singing about plunging ice picks into men's eyes, without a care in the world. For a brief second, Mike found the whole display borderline sacrilegious.

But then he realized it wasn't Katie's burden to carry. It was his. She was, for all practical purposes, a bystander to the whole ordeal. It was he who saw Arthur and Millie die. It was he who killed Donny O'Leary and almost killed Samuel Bennington/Samuel Beck/Klaus Wagenmann. Whatever the hell that sick son of a bitch called himself.

And good riddance too.

The presence of Wagenmann in the world by any name didn't benefit anyone. Still, he couldn't shake the feeling that something seemed off. His standing here among young would-be punks and miscreants, watching them happily bang their heads and sway their bodies to what was effectively a murder ballad.

No matter how justified he was in taking down Donny, he still had taken human life.

But what done was done. And it wasn't worth reflecting too much on anymore. He would be better off living in the moment. In the here and now.

And that meant with Katie.

Mike stood in a corner, nursing a bottle of lukewarm beer, as The Yellows continued on their non-stop musical rampage. After what seemed like an eternity, they finally stopped playing; a hot and sweaty Katie ending the set, hugging the guitar player, with a loud—and distinctly non-feminine—guttural roar in the microphone.

Mike found his way backstage; bribing a tall, white, and balding security guard with a ten-dollar bill to let him pass. Real efficient operation, they had, Mike thought to himself. All you had to do was throw cash around and all rules were off. Just like when he needed to get information on Hesse's whereabouts.

"Hey you," Mike said, calling down the cramped backstage corridor. Thinking that Katie might hear his voice.

If he were being honest, he wasn't sure what he expected by coming here.

He might have expected a cool welcome. Or a half-assed one.

What he didn't expect was to find Katie passionately kissing her guitar player.

That wasn't what he expected at all.

"Mike," Katie said, sopping wet black mascara running down her face. "I didn't think you'd be here."

"Obviously not," Mike replied tersely. What *was* he doing here really? She was too young and wild for him. Now with everything wrapped up and Izzy back on his feet, what was the point?

"Sorry. I meant to tell you," she said, as the guitarist slinked away into the dimly lit corridor.

For a moment, Mike was genuinely perturbed. Not by the prospect of losing her; he never really had her. No. It was more that she seemed to have fallen for someone new who was all flash and no real substance. Wasn't it he who took down a Nazi? Not some dumbass dime-a-dozen guitar player like this dude.

"Tell me what? That I'm not good enough for you? Not young and hip enough?"

"Mike," Katie whispered. "Don't—" She hesitated. "Don't be like that."

In his heart, he knew she was right. The prospect of them as a real, genuine couple was ludicrous on the face of it.

"How's your Dad?" Mike asked, abruptly changing the subject.

"He's okay. Better. The firebombing shook him up more than he'd like to admit. It wasn't a heart attack that knocked him out. Just stress. It could have been so much worse."

She paused.

"So, so much worse. He's put on a real stone-cold face of late. You know. Like it didn't affect him at all. But it did. He's getting too old for this shit. Deep down, he knows it too. He has to. Right?"

Mike wasn't sure if she had asked him a real question or a rhetorical one.

"Well, I'm glad he's fine. That he's okay. I kind of liked him," he said.

"Really?" Katie laughed.

"Well, maybe, not so much," Mike laughed. "Not my personality type. But I appreciated his help. I feel like, in a way, he and I made a good team."

"Probably a better team than you and I could ever be," Katie said quietly.

Just then, a stage hand—a kid no older than fifteen, Mike thought— came up from behind her and whispered something in her ear.

"Mike, looks like the crowd loved us. We're going on for another set in five minutes."

She moved in closely to him, squeezed his left arm, and gave him a soft, innocent peck on the cheek. Then she turned around, called out for someone to find her some new black mascara.

"We got some," bellowed her female bass player from down the hallway. Mike thought the woman looked like a cheetah in human form.

Katie smiled at Mike. Then she turned and walked away.

Just like that, she was gone.

And Mike was alone.

He knew he shouldn't have cared. At all. But he did.

□　□　□

Instead of lingering around in the East Village where he clearly didn't belong, Mike decided he would take the subway uptown to Times Square, knowing full well that it would be an absolute zoo on a Saturday night. A kaleidoscope of humanity on its last legs. After the scene with Katie had played out, it was a place Mike felt like he needed to be right now. Just a speck in the swirling phantasmagoric crowd. There he'd be able to find at least one legitimate movie to watch to pass the hours before he could fall asleep.

Near The Fulton, so pivotal to his case, was another old movie house: The Egyptian. This one showed decent prints of old Hollywood features. Unlike The Fulton and other movie palaces nearby, The Egyptian was actually clean inside. Clean and air-conditioned. A huge plus. And tonight, they just happened to be doing to a repertory screening one of Mike's favorite old movies, a comfort favorite he had watched as a teen numerous times late night on Channel 11: *Casablanca*, starring Humphrey Bogart.

That was the plan then.

A movie would be good for him. It would take his mind off everything. Not just Katie and Millie. But his Dad too. One conversation with Irving Levinas a month was more than enough. Even though his Dad was right for once, he didn't need to think about that any longer. It would be too much to bear.

It happened quickly.

When Mike walked out of the 42nd Street-Times Square subway station and onto the cracked sidewalk, he heard what he thought was a murmur, words buried by the din of the urban jungle. It was as if someone in the crowd was saying his name.

All of a sudden, an old man, thin but well-proportioned, dressed in a blue pinstripe suit—odd attire for a humid New York night—planted his walking cane on Mike's right foot. Hard enough so that it actually hurt. The first thing Mike thought was that it must have been an accident.

He was wrong.

"Mr. Levinas," the man in the pinstripe suit said. He spoke in what sounded like a German accent. He glared at Mike. Eyes, deep blue and icy cold.

That's when all hell broke loose.

"What the fuck?"

"Herr Levinas, if you allow me to introduce myself," the old man with the limp said while slightly gripping Mike's right arm.

"I don't need to know anything more than I already do," Mike said tersely, his left hand making a fist. He had the urge to swing. Knock the guy's teeth right out.

"But you do, Mike Levinas. You do. You need to know that there's more of us out there. That this isn't over. Far from it. You best believe that as you go forward. Just because Wagenmann isn't around to fund our operations in Europe, doesn't mean there aren't others willing and able to take his place."

Mike looked at the man, placing his age around seventy or so.

It then all transpired within seconds, unfolding like a violent dream.

Things had reached a boiling point. Had Bennington been telling the truth, after all? That he really was only one part of a much larger conspiracy?

Mike gritted his teeth, his body filling with a deep rage. One that had lingered under the surface these past weeks.

He lunged. Grabbed the old man by the throat.

And began to squeeze.

Hard. Very hard. As if he were not Mike Levinas, PI. But Mike Levinas of the Levinas crime family.

Without anything or anyone holding him back, he could do as he pleased.

After all, he had already been willing to rid the planet of one Nazi; what was one more? He was Teflon to the police. They couldn't touch him.

That's when the Puerto Rican teenagers hanging out on the corner saw Mike and how he, at his very moment, appeared to be just another raging lunatic running amok on the New York streets. A disturbed individual in the process of choking the life out of what appeared to be an innocent bystander. The victim: an old man with a cane, no less.

"What the hell you doing, man?" one of them, muscular and heavily tattooed, shouted. "He's just an old man. What are you? Completely loco?"

"Stop him, Javier!" shouted one of the girls.

That's when another man arrived on the scene. This guy was dressed in a grey suit, another sartorial oddity in Times Square.

"Easy there, you don't want to do anything stupid, especially in front of hundreds of witnesses," the man said, placing a hand on Mike's shoulder. It was a firm grip.

"What?" Who are you?" Mike spun around. Confusion reigned.

It was enough of a distraction to allow the old man with the cane to elude Mike's grasp and scuttle away.

Mike suddenly realized that grey suit's intervention was intentional.

"Who the fuck are you?" Mike shouted.

"I'm a friend. Right now, at least I am," the man said, flashing a badge and an identification card.

Yet another fed.

"You really almost did something really stupid there, fella," the agent said.

"Yeah? What's it to you?" Mike said, wiping his palms on his pants.

"You've been exceptionally disciplined over the past weeks. Don't think we haven't noticed. That was good work you did. Outing Wagenmann."

"So you've been watching me? Is that it?"

"We like to keep tabs on what's going on," the man said, as a gaggle of Midwestern tourists—awed and bewildered—brushed past them.

"You know, we could use someone like you. Giving us a hand from time to time. You know how it is," the agent said, putting out his hand.

Mike laughed. He knew exactly how it was. And he wasn't going to be a stoolie for the feds.

"It's not going to happen, man. I'm done," Mike said, shaking his head in exasperation and refusing to shake the agent's hand. He turned his back and began to walk away. He sensed the agent had the voice of someone who believes in his own power. Someone used to getting his own way.

"And just where do you think you're going?" the grey-suited agent demanded. His luck had run out. He wasn't getting his way tonight. Not this time. That sentiment echoed in his voice.

"I'm going to see a movie, believe it or not," Mike shouted above the din of the crowd as he continued to walk away. "And I know enough about the law that you can't detain me. So piss off. I'm not in the mood for your games."

In a matter of minutes, Mike had calmed down. He walked a few seedy blocks filled with pimps and hookers, loners and dead-enders. And tourists as well. And now he was in front of The Egyptian. Even though he'd been there before, he reflected on how fitting the theater's name actually was. Not only were the building's motifs all ancient Egyptian themes, but the hieroglyphics were painted on the inside walls and there were small cat statues inside the main lobby.

Mike checked his watch. He saw that he could still make *Casablanca*. He felt elated.

"A ticket for one," Mike said. He handed over a crisp dollar bill to an attendant dressed in a white shirt and a crimson vest.

"Go on in," the attendant replied.

Mike walked into the single-screen theater. He took an aisle seat near the back.

In less than ten minutes, the theater went dark as night. The projectionist began running the film. And just like that, Mike was, for a brief moment, merely another anonymous patron in a movie theater. Another lost soul eager to leave the harsh world behind, anticipating a far more magical one up on the screen.

But Mike was somewhat less of a dreamer tonight than he was when Millie Johnson walked into his office. He knew all too well, that when the house lights came up two hours later, there'd still be plenty of grief and mayhem in the world. More runaways, unfaithful husbands, and criminal rackets. He had more than a gut feeling that the Nazis weren't done with him yet either. He had stirred up a hornet's nest; there would be no romantic Hollywood ending to his story. That old man in the pinstripe suit was out there somewhere. Along with who knew how many sympathizers, of all ages and nationalities.

And, of course, the cops and the Westchester DA's Office. For now, they seemed satisfied with Mike's story of how Wagenmann had died; how his enraged and drunken wife had executed him. Still, Mike knew from personal experience that things could easily change and that he could find himself the subject of a criminal investigation by a DA looking to add his list of convictions.

But that was another worry for another day. He deserved a break and some time off.

As the movie began, Mike settled his sore body into a surprisingly comfortable seat. Time to leave the horrors of the past behind and spend some quality time with Humphrey Bogart.

If only for one night.

The End